THE MIDSHIPMAN
PRINCE

THE MIDSHIPMAN PRINCE

by

Tom Grundner

Fireship Press
www.FireshipPress.com

ISBN-13: 978-1-934757-00-0
ISBN-10: 1-934757-00-4

BISAC Subject Heading:
    FIC014000   FICTION / Historical
    FIC032000   FICTION / War & Military

Address all correspondence to:
Fireship Press, LLC
P.O. Box 68412
Tucson, AZ 85737
Or visit our website at:
www.FireshipPress.com

2.0

To my brother, Ken, who would have enjoyed
Reading this book as much as I enjoyed
writing it.

CHAPTER ONE

LUCAS Walker did not want to open his eyes. He did not even want to continue living, but that was irrelevant. He knew he had to do both.

His world was pitching wildly. From his position, flat on his back in his cabin, it was as if he was motionless and the planet itself had gone insane. The timbers of the old merchantman, normally softly groaning, had been shrieking in agony for the past 12 hours. This had done nothing for Walker's head, which felt like it would explode any minute.

Below deck on a sailing ship was a fetid place even in the best of times. Beneath the main deck, beneath the orlop deck, beneath the cargo hold, lay the bilge. This was the nearly flat area where the ship's floor and the ribs met the keel. Because it was the lowest place on the ship, it was the place where all forms of liquid collected. Most of it was water that had slowly worked its way in between the ship's planks; but it contained other fluids as well—fluids that formed a soup consisting of seawater, urine, blood, decaying rats, spoiled vegetables and, more recently, vomit. It was the latter that proved too much for Walker and he knew he had to get on to the upper deck as soon as possible.

Walker exited his passenger cabin and, staggering with the roll of the ship, made it to the aft ladder leading to the upper deck.

Crashing through a storm hatch he immediately knew he had made a mistake. He had gone from purgatory to hell.

At first, he couldn't see a thing. The howling wind was blowing the rain nearly horizontally and it was attacking every inch of exposed skin with needle sharp stings. Turning downwind he was able to open his eyes enough to locate the rail, stumble over to it, and dry-heave for the third time that night. Turning back amidships, he slid down to the deck and sat there in abject misery.

He was a 22-year-old failure; there was no other way to put it. He had drunk his way through three teaching positions and was now on his way to Charleston, South Carolina to try again. "Try again?" He thought. "Try again and do what? Fail again? When you go from Harvard, to getting run out of Mrs. Harrison's Academy for Discriminating Young Ladies, you know there isn't much left." But still, he knew he had to try.

His despondent reverie ended in a curious way, however, when he suddenly became aware of a concert that was going on around him. The captain had taken down all sails except for a small storm jib that hung precariously between the foremast and the bowsprit. This scrap of canvas was intended to keep the bow of the ship pointed downwind so the ship, in theory, could run before the storm. But, the rest of the lines were barren—barren and singing.

Set into motion by the violent wind, the various ropes were vibrating, each creating their own unique sound. At the low end were the big preventer stays that ran from the bow to the main mast. In the middle were the topmast and topgallant stays. And several octaves above these were the Martingales up forward and the buntlines up high. Walker forgot his depression and seasickness; and for a moment he was a child again. He was lost in the wonder of the world around him—the thing that caused him to become a natural philosopher, a scientist, in the first place.

It took him a while to stand-up again, partially because he was so sick and partially because of the violent motions of the ship. He could handle it when a ship pitched. He could handle it when it rolled. He could handle it when it yawed. But, when it pitched, rolled and yawed at the same time, Walker was out of his league.

He no sooner got to his feet when he looked aft just in time to sea a huge wave tower up over the stern and crash down upon it. A wall of water was sluicing down the main deck to engulf him as he clung to the rail. "My God. What was that," he thought as he spit out a gob of seawater, and for the first time that evening felt a stab of genuine fear.

His fear was justified. Walker couldn't have known it, but his fate had already been sealed by an unusually warm summer off the coast of Africa and a careless workman in Portsmouth, New Hampshire.

That summer had been the hottest and driest in anyone's memory on the Cape Verde Islands. They said a pan of water set in the sun would evaporate in the time it took you to turn around three times. The conditions were no different out on the ocean. Water—tons of it—was evaporating off the surface of the ocean and rising high in the atmosphere. There it would cool and evaporate, releasing energy. The air spewing out of this chimney would be driven by that energy back to earth, which would form powerful winds, which, in turn, would be sucked up by the newer rising, hot, moist air, and continue the cycle. At first it was just a very nasty thunderstorm. But the cycles continued; and it developed into a tropical depression, then a tropical storm. At this point the coriolis effect of the earth's rotation started the clouds spinning around a central core, and the cycles continued. Eventually the storm dropped into one of the West African disturbance lines and, pushed by a high-pressure area over North Africa, set forth into the Atlantic headed west by northwest.

This was the storm—the hurricane—that had Walker's ship in its grasp.

Walker fought his way aft, toward the quarterdeck. In between gusts of wind and water he could see the captain and first mate hanging on to the binnacle box in front of the wheel with safety ropes tied around their waists.

Moving closer he could see a look of deep concern on the captain's face, a look of despair on the face of the first mate, and a look of sheer terror on the faces of the four helmsman who were trying to maintain control of the large bucking wheel.

The ship was taking the seas on the stern, which is just where the captain wanted them. They would be all right as long as the ship maintained that position relative to the storm; but one slip of the wheel, a parting of a rudder cable, a rogue wave running counter to the sea state, anything that would cause them to rotate sideways to the main waves, and they would be finished. If just one of those enormous waves ever hit the ship in that position, it would roll it over like a turtle.

The carpenter's mate came on deck to report to the captain. Walker couldn't hear the conversation; he could only make out isolated words. "Water rising." "Pumps" "Keep-up" "If this continues, she'll..." After a moment the captain dismissed him and the mate began to stagger forward and down into the innards of the ship.

Walker looked aft. He couldn't see very far but what he saw literally took his breath away. Huge, green, angry waves were forming behind the stern. Waves that looked threatening at a distance became more and more frightening the closer they got. As they reached the stern, some of them towered 25 and 30 feet above the poop deck before roaring down. Yet each time, miraculously, the ship would lift her tail, point it up the wave's slope and ride it out.

Walker had never been this afraid. It went beyond the visceral fear reactions he had known previously. It was a fear that numbed him—that froze his limbs and locked his brain into psychological immobility.

"Still... Maybe..." he thought. "Maybe we can somehow come through this. If only... Dear God! What was that?"

And this brings us to the workman in Portsmouth.

In point of fact, he was a good workman. Well, usually he was, anyway. But this morning was different. He had had a real knock-down, drag out, fight with his woman. She was arguing about money, he was complaining about the kids, and neither was talking to the other—just yelling. By the time he got to the shipyard his mood was foul and he was prepared to take it out on anyone who got in his way. Unfortunately, no one did; so he wound up taking it out on his work.

His job that day was to nail the strakes in place that would form the starboard bow of the merchantman he was working on. Quite frankly, he didn't care how the nails went in as long as he could pound on something. Some went in properly, some went in crooked, some went in bent, some boards had three nails, some had the regulation two, and some had only one. He simply didn't care that day.

The people who later caulked the hull noticed his workmanship, but said nothing. Other workmen who were fastening the large protective copper hull sheets in place also noticed it, but they too said nothing. After all, why get a fellow workman in trouble?

Live and let live, right? And those nails stayed just the way they were for nearly eight years.

If the merchantman had not run into a hurricane, it still might have been all right. She might have sailed for many more years without mishap. But she *was* in a hurricane; and it was *not* all right.

Walker knew he needed to find some rope, something— anything—to tie himself down. He grabbed the rail again as the ship's stern lifted up the side of an especially large wave and started to slide down its face. But this time things were different.

One nail, on one board, which had been pounded in crooked and bent over, gave way. This popped out its neighbor, which took with it the next board that only had one nail in it to begin with. Because the boards had not been properly steam curved, they sprang outward opening up the leading edge of a copper sheet. This sheet opened up several more poorly nailed boards, which sprung open more copper sheeting. In a matter of seconds, a ten-foot section of the starboard bow had opened-up like a zipper. Boards and sheeting that were supposed to keep water out, had formed themselves into a huge scoop that was funneling tons of water into the ship.

The merchantman started her long slide down the face of the wave, and then abruptly shuddered to a stop like a child's sled hitting a snow bank. She paused for a few seconds, and slipped the rest of the way down cocked at a funny angle.

The captain spun around to the helmsmen. "What have you done, you fools!"

The quartermaster who had charge of the helm screamed back into the storm. "Nothing, sir. We did nothing. Everything was going fine until she suddenly... It wasn't us, sir!"

But the captain had more to worry about at the moment. The ship was now broadside to the waves and another monster was preparing to break over them. The green beast slammed into the ship like a giant sledgehammer, snapping both the main and the mizzenmasts with cracking sounds that sounded like small cannon blasts. When the wave cleared, Walker could see the masts bent over at crazy angles, still supported by a few shrouds and stays. Worse, Walker looked over at the helm and saw that it was gone. The helm, binnacle, helmsmen and captain were nowhere to be seen. The first mate was picking himself up and moving his lips and jaw as if shouting, but no sound was coming out.

The next wave came down harder than the previous one, only this time after heeling way over on her side; the ship did not completely right herself. She had taken on so much water from the hole in her bow that she could not swing back. She just stayed laid over on her side. That made the third wave a killer.

The third wave slapped the ship 20 feet sideways and finished tearing open the hull on a line running from the starboard hawsepipe to near the foremast. The lurch was so violent that it threw Walker into the water. When he surfaced he could see the ship rapidly going down by the bow. All he could think about was the crew and passengers who were trapped below. Every hatch except the storm hatch that he had gone through earlier had been firmly battened down to keep the ship watertight. That same watertightness was now locking nearly 75 people below decks on a ship that was sinking. Walker thought he could hear them pounding and clawing at the hatch covers to get out. He couldn't hear them of course—not in that storm—but it was something he would nevertheless have nightmares about for the rest of his life.

Walker was a reasonably good swimmer, but it was not long before the weight of his waterlogged clothing began wearing him down. Just as he was about to give up, he spotted a spar floating in the water not far away. It must have been one of the mainmast spares they kept stowed on deck and was a good 16 inches around at its thickest point. With his last remaining strength, he paddled over, swung himself up, and lay on it with an arm and a leg dangling on each side. In that position he passed the night. The storm seemed to accept the death of the merchantman as appropriate tribute and soon after began to die down.

Walker did not think about his fear. He did not think about the nasty bump he had on his head. He did not think about his incredibly bad luck. He thought about one thing and one thing only—how utterly and completely *alone* he was.

* * *

This day began like any other for the men of the HMS *Richmond*; all hands were at battle stations. It was like that on every underway ship in the navy. They had gone to full battle readiness just in case the light of dawn should find them staring into the gun ports of an enemy ship. It was better to greet the sunrise with loaded guns and an alert ship's company then be sorry. That the

Richmond had the previous night come through one of the worst storms of the year mattered not at all.

"On deck there. Foremast here. All clear!"

"On deck there. Mizzenmast here. All..."

"On deck!" The mainmast lookout cut in. "Man overboard! Man overboard!"

Captain Charles Hudson spun around and walked to the stern taffrail. The ship's Master, John Rooney, had already turned aft and was looking out over the water. Rooney yelled back to the mainmast lookout, "Where away?"

"Two points off the starboard bow, Sir." Then added, "And about 150 yards out."

"The starboard bow," Rooney muttered. "How could there be a man in the water off the bow?" They were miles from land and there were no other ships anywhere in the area.

The two hurried to the starboard rail of the quarterdeck. Rooney tried to shield his eyes from the glare with his hand while the captain popped open his telescope and adjusted it to the correct focal point for his eyes.

"There'd better be something out there or I'll have that lookout's balls for breakfast," Rooney growled.

"I'll be damned," said Hudson looking hard through his eyepiece.

"Helm come about directly into the wind," he called to the helmsman who was on the deck below them and immediately in front of the quarterdeck. What Hudson had ordered was the equivalent of slamming the brakes on the ship. They were cruising along on topsails, but by turning directly into the wind, the sails would be taken aback. Instead of pushing the ship along from behind, the wind would now be directly in front, pushing the sails back into the masts and stopping the ship like a giant invisible hand.

"Mr. Rooney, sway out a boat and have a detail go fetch that poor bastard in."

While Rooney was shouting orders to the Bosun of the Watch, Hudson picked up the megaphone that was hanging on the Quarterdeck rail.

"Fore and main. Away aloft! Trice up and layout," he called and the ratlines leading to the fore and main topmasts were suddenly teeming with men scrambling up them. He waited a minute as the men sidestepped out on the yardarms and took in the stun-sail booms to get them out of the way. He then lowered the mega-phone pointing it to the main deck.

"Loose the topsail sheets," he ordered and several groups of men grabbed lines that held the topsails taught and loosened them from the belaying pins to which they were tied.

Pointing the megaphone to the masts again, "Take-in topsails." And the men on the yardarms started to grab handfuls of canvas sailcloth, pulling the two sails up and securing them in a loose bunting.

The ship was now at a dead stop.

* * *

Walker awoke from an exhausted nap to feel sunlight scratch-ing at his eyes. His head ached; his shoulder felt as if a sledge-hammer had hit it; but, worst of all, he was hopelessly confused.

In a rush the events of the previous night came back to him and he sat up to take a look around. He expected to see the death warrant of an empty ocean. Instead, he saw the most beautiful thing he could imagine. A few hundred yards away was a fully rigged sailing ship lowering a boat. Unable to trust his eyes, he sat up on the spar, started waving his arms and yelling. He was sur-prised when his yell came out as a mere croak.

"HERE!! OVER HERE!" His voice cracked as he waved his arms while trying to stay up right on his perch. He kicked his feet to try to propel himself higher so that he would be more visible.

"HEY!! HERE!!" He knew that they had seen him, but he con-tinued to wave his hands anyway as if, by stopping, they might somehow go away.

Strong hands grabbed him and hauled him into the boat. After a minute of catching his breath he looked up to see a young man staring, concerned, into his face. He was a little younger than Walker and had on a British naval uniform.

"Are you all right?" The young man asked.

"Yes. Yes, I'm fine. But do you have... do you have some water."

The young officer nodded to a seaman who opened a small wa-ter butt that was carried in the boat. He gave Walker a cup, which he eagerly drank, coughing as he did so. Then another.

"Now, who the devil are you."

"I am Lucas Walker. I am... I was a passenger on the ship *Mary Louise*. We went down in the storm last night."

"You went down?" The officer's head shot up to look around and he could begin to pick out bits of debris floating in the vicinity but no other people. "But where are..."

"Everyone went down with the ship. It happened so fast they... they never had a chance. I think I am the only survivor."

The man just nodded slowly, looked around one more time and muttered, "I'll be damned."

By this time, they had arrived at the ship, and a rope boarding ladder was dropped. Walker pulled himself up and soon found himself on the main deck of this strange vessel, dripping wet, facing two men who were obviously in charge and a small crowd of seamen.

"I am Captain Charles Hudson of His Britannic Majesty's Frigate, *Richmond*. This is John Rooney, the ship's Master. Do you speak English?"

Walker looked up and saw a man in his mid-thirties in a blue jacket with gold-lace, two large gold tasseled epaulettes on his shoulders, faded light blue breeches, and a cocked hat placed sideways on his head. He was handsome in a boyish sort of way, except for his eyes. His eyes were a penetrating green and suggested there was some steel behind his youngish good looks. "Yes, more or less," Walker replied with a limp smile.

"Good. Then who the devil are you and what are you doing bobbing around the middle of the ocean?"

"As I explained to your... to him," nodding over at the young man who had now joined them, "I am Lucas Walker. I was a passenger on a merchantman called the *Mary Louise*. It went down last night with all hands... except me."

The captain said nothing but looked shocked, although he covered it up better than the young man had.

"What is your nationality, Mr. Walker, and where were you bound?"

That, Walker knew, was a loaded question. Healthy young Americans were, likely as not, to be pressed into the British navy if they were anywhere near shorthanded—and the ships were always shorthanded. Making matters worse, Walker was exhausted and not thinking clearly. If he had been, he would never have blurted out the first thing that came to mind.

9

"I am an American," he paused, and then went on quickly. "I am a military officer and claim protection as a prisoner under the Articles of War." Walker was smugly proud of himself. He had just foiled any attempt Hudson might make to press him.

"And what type of officer are you, sir? What branch of the military? What unit?"

For some reason Walker was not expecting to be pressed on the matter. He looked quickly around and blurted out, "I am a naval officer. I was on my way to join my ship at... Well, I am sorry sir, but I am not at liberty to give you my ship's location."

Walker was getting into this game. He was surprised at how clever his answers were, and he should have left it at that. Unfortunately, all too often that simple ability was not in his nature. He decided to press on with his bravado.

"So, you see sir, I demand that you turn this tub around and take me to the closest port where I may be exchanged."

Hudson's eyes widened. "You demand?" He sputtered. "This TUB?" Captain Hudson's face began to flush, and his hands clenched into fists. Behind him, two red-coated Marines started forward with fury in their eyes, and Walker knew he had gone too far. Fortunately, Rooney intervened to defuse the situation.

"Captain, if I might have a word with you." And quickly drew him aside. This also gave Walker a chance to assess his situation.

The most striking immediate thing was the hostility radiating from the crowd standing around him. Nobody said anything but that just made the intensity of their hostility even worse. He was a pretty good judge of men and there weren't many here that he would care to meet in a dark alley.

Hudson and Rooney finished their conversation, and the captain turned around. In an icy tone he said, "Mr. Smith, take this gentleman down to the sick-berth and have him looked over by the surgeon's mate. Then get him some dry clothes, something to eat if he's hungry and show him to the fourth officer's cabin. Mr. Rooney, please get the ship underway. There we have it."

Hudson started to walk to a door that was directly behind the helm. Rooney began bellowing orders:

"All right, the show's over. Look alive there. Main and fore, standby to loose top sails. Waisters, standby to sheet her home..."

With that the young man from the rescue boat came forward and said stiffly: "I am William Sidney Smith, First Lieutenant aboard this ship; and if you ever insult the captain or this ship like that again, I will personally break you in half. Now, follow me, please," and he turned and walked away without bothering to see whether Walker was following.

It was a dark world inside that ship. There were no portholes to let in light or shafts for ventilation. The light and air that did get in came from the hatches and ladders leading from one deck to the other. The men that he could see were, as a group, fairly small men but, even so, many of them had to walk slightly bent over because the overheads were so low.

They descended two decks into the orlop deck when Smith finally halted.

"Whitney! Got some fresh meat for you," Smith called.

To Walker's surprise, around the corner came a woman holding a curved knife in her hands.

"Yes, sir," she said acknowledging Smith and putting the knife into a case. "Ah, you must be the jack they fished out just now. All right, have a seat; let's have a look at you."

She was short, not much above five feet tall, not thin but not overweight either. She had the kind of pleasant body that Walker thought of as designed to comfort a man, not seduce him. Her wiry brown hair was pulled back and tied off in a bun with the inevitable errant strands casting loose in odd places. But, the most amazing thing about her was her smile. It seemed to light up what was, in fact, a dark and dreary room.

"What hurts," she continued.

"Look, I am fine. I bumped my head and my shoulder's a bit sore."

"We'll see about that. Take off that jacket."

She maneuvered his arm for a while with a gentleness that surprised Walker and finally grunted in satisfaction. "Arm's all right. Your head..."

"Is fine."

"...needs a little bit of St. Vincent's Balm." She reached into a nearby drawer and uncapped a jar of foul smelling unguent. Using a small damp cloth, she gently cleared away the blood, then smeared a bit of the ointment over the cut on Walker's forehead. It stung like hell for a few seconds then, amazingly, seemed to go numb.

"You'll have a bit of a scar there but that'll just make you more attractive to the ladies. Where's Mr. Smith?"

"Right here. And here are some dry clothes," he said while dropping them at Walker's feet rather than handing them to him. "Better change."

Walker, who was becoming more uncomfortable by the moment in his wet clothes eagerly agreed.

"Are you hungry?" Smith inquired as he led Walker up one deck and walked aft.

"No, not really," Walker replied.

"Good because we'd pay hell trying to rouse the cook to come up with some rations in-between meals."

"Lieutenant, I've got to ask. What's a woman doing on board?"

"There are women on board almost every ship in the fleet. Some are the wives of commissioned officers, some the wives of warrants, some tend to the Marines on board. We currently have three women on this ship. Susan Whitney, the person who just took care of you, was the wife of our ship's gunner, but he was killed in action about a year ago.

"And before you even think about it... keep your hands off. Those women perform important functions on this ship, and we don't need the disruption of jealousies and intrigue."

They finally arrived at the aft part of the gun deck and Walker was led to the fourth door on the starboard side.

"Here's your cabin."

Walker looked into what he could only describe as a large closet. On one side was a wooden frame hanging by chains from the overhead rafter. On the frame were a straw mattress and a rather stained feather pillow. In the corner was a chair and, other than some hooks on the wall and a chamber pot, that was it.

"Whitney says you've had a rather nasty blow to the head and you need to get some rest."

Walker was tired; he had to admit that. In fact, he could hardly remember ever being this fatigued both physically and mentally.

"Well, perhaps I could lie down for a while," he said. And "for a while" turned into the following morning.

* * *

Walker awoke to the sound of men yelling from the forward part of the deck he was on.

"All hands! Wakie! Wakie! Show a leg! Starboard watch, rouse out! Out or down! Out or down, you lubbers!" And, thus, the new day began.

It was 5:00 AM, still well before dawn. The men rolled out of their hammocks, most of them fully clothed, and started running along the deck and up the ladders to the main deck. Walker followed them.

Some men ran to their positions as members of the gun crews serving the ship's 32 guns. Others ran up the ratlines and out on the yardarms to handle sails. Red-coated Marines took up positions along the main deck rails and in the tops of the main and mizzenmasts with loaded muskets. The big guns were run in, loaded with powder and shot, and rolled out again, ready to be fired at a moment's notice. Men were walking along the deck squirting water from a kind of fire hose. Just behind them were other men throwing sand down on the deck like farmers sowing a field. And then, everything came to a halt. All was quiet, waiting for dawn in a time of war.

Dawn finally arrived, and the lookouts from the three masts reported "All Clear." Walker could see the ship's company visibly relax. They began securing the guns and came down from the masts and yards.

The rest of the morning followed a routine. By 7:00 AM the decks would have been scrubbed by men dragging a very large stone called a "Holy Stone" across the deck. A smaller version of the stone, used for getting into small spaces, was called a "Prayer Book." Other men could be seen using brick dust to polish anything metallic that could be polished.

At 7:30 the Bosun's Mate blew a particular call on his pipe and started yelling: "All Hands, up hammocks." The men disappeared below to fold their hammocks into tight rolls and bring them on deck to store them in netting along the sides of the ship. This not only aired out the hammocks a bit, but provided additional protection against musket fire and splinters should they see action that day. Several of the bosun's mates held metal hoops. If a man's rolled hammock could not fit through the hoop, he had to do it again.

By 8:00 AM, the ship's Bosun piped the men to breakfast. Walker took a seat at the inboard side of a narrow wooden table that was hinged into the wall, then swung down and suspended by two ropes. There were four men seated along one side and two, plus Walker, on the other.

Another man soon appeared with two pots. The first was a bread barge with the mess table's number stenciled on it. From it, he placed two biscuits on each man's plate. The second was a mess kid; a small tub-shaped barrel with a rope threaded through holes in the top. It too had the mess table's number on it and was used to carry hot food. From it, the man ladled out a kind of milk-less oatmeal porridge the men called "burgoo." The "wealthier" among the men had pewter plates and cups of their own. The less endowed used wooden cups and bowls issued by the ship. Everyone provided their own cutlery and Walker was given loaners.

The biscuits were hard and stale, but Walker was ravenously hungry so he started with those. After consuming the first one, he bit into the second and noticed an interesting habit the men around him had. Before biting into their biscuit, they would tap it several times on the table, put it down and wait a few seconds. At that point, Walker could see several weevils exiting each of their biscuits. It was only then that they took a bite. Walker examined his second biscuit—the one he had just bitten into—and could see where he had severed a weevil in two with his bite. God knows how many were in the first one he had devoured.

His appetite was now somewhat diminished.

The rest of the morning would find half the ship's company on watch and half off. The ones who were off duty would be given various repair and cleaning assignments by the petty officers, but when they ran out of those they mostly skylarked or napped until noon when it was their turn to go on watch.

Every day at noon, a ceremony of sorts would take place on the quarterdeck. The Ship's Master, Master's Mates and Midshipmen would assemble with their sextants to take a noon sighting of the sun. They then, independently, calculated the ship's position. The ship's Master, in this case Rooney, would go around and examine each midshipman's work—some earning praise, others a cuff on the head.

Near the mainmast, Susan Whitney had set up a table, a small chest of medicines and equipment and was holding sick call. Eight or ten men stood in line with a variety of complaints ranging from fever, to follow-up treatment for a broken arm, to treatment for syphilis.

At exactly 12:30, Walker followed Lt. Smith to the foremast to supervise the mixing of rum and water (one part rum to three parts water). Each man was poured a cup (called a "tot"), which was clearly one of the high points of the men's day. If there was no rum then a kind of small beer was used or, if they were in the Mediterranean, perhaps a cheap wine called "Blackstrap." Either way, the men *would* have their tot twice a day, noon and evening, and woe-betide the captain or purser that failed in the delivery of that treat. It was one of the few things over which the men could near mutiny, and not have anyone blame them.

After that, they again disbursed and went about their various duties.

* * *

About 3 o'clock, Walker was standing on the fo'c'sle looking out at the ocean, trying to make sense of his situation. The bosun's mates, circulating through the ship tweeting their whistles, had interrupted his thoughts: "All hands. All hands on deck to witness punishment. All hands."

"Witness punishment?" Walker murmured. "What now?"

The captain and ships officers were standing in a line on the raised quarterdeck. Below, on the main deck, a row of Marines in their red coats and white belts was lined up across the deck between the ship's company and the officers—muskets in hand, bayonets locked onto the muskets. A wooden grating, taken from a hatch, was leaning against the face of the quarterdeck.

On the main deck, in front of the captain, stood the Bosun's Mate carrying a red bag and a burly fellow who Walker later learned was the ship's master-at-arms. In between the two was a fellow who looked wretched.

"Captain," began the master-at-arms, "two nights ago Ordinary Seaman James Hix was assigned duty on the fo'c'sle as a lookout during the mid-watch. At four bells he was found by the bosun's mate of the watch, sitting on the deck, leaning against the starboard side long nine, dead asleep."

"Hix, what have you to say for yourself," the captain snapped.

Hix looked up at the captain with tears misting in his eyes. "Nuthin', sor, other than I never done anythin' like this afore and, I swear, I'll never do it again. It's just.., I don't know, Cap'n, I were just so tired that night."

Hudson pursed his lips and looked around. "Are there any officers or warrant officers who wish to speak for this man?"

At first there was silence, then a young man spoke up from the officers line.

"Sir. Hix is in my division. Basically, he's a good seaman, sir—making steady progress toward being rated able; and, it's true, he's never had any previous problems."

Hudson nodded to the officer, turned back to Hicks, unfolded a large piece of printed parchment paper and studied it for a few seconds.

"Seaman Hix, I read to you Article 26 of the Articles of War: 'No person in or belonging to the fleet shall sleep upon his watch, or negligently perform the duty imposed on him, or forsake his station, upon pain of death, or such other punishment as a court martial shall think fit to impose, and as the circumstances of the case shall require.'

"Were you aware of this Article?"

"Yes, sor."

"Do you know what it means?"

"Yes, sor."

"And did you fall asleep on watch?"

"Yes, sor."

"Hix, before I pronounce judgment I must ask you: do you understand that you have the right to a formal court martial?"

"Yes, sor."

"And do you waive your right to that court martial? Do you except whatever my verdict might be?"

The man swallowed hard but replied, "Yes, sor."

"Well then, there we have it. I have no choice but to find you guilty of willfully violating Article 26."

The captain paused for a bit as he thought things over.

"In view of your record and since this is your first violation, I am NOT going to sentence you to death."

Hix's knees buckled, but he caught himself. Tears of gratitude filled his eyes. Walker was spellbound by the drama going on before him.

The captain continued: "However, through your negligence you placed this ship and all who sail on her in mortal danger.

What you did simply cannot be countenanced. Not on this ship. Not on any ship. Accordingly, I hereby sentence you to 24 lashes.

"Bosun, seize him up and strip him."

Hix was led to the hatch cover grating. His shirt was taken off, and he was tied, standing spread-eagled, to the grate. While this was going on, Captain Hudson had a chance to assess the tenor of the men.

Seamen in the British Navy were not well educated, but they had a very highly developed sense of fair play. Sometimes after a flogging has been ordered, a captain will hear the men muttering. If he does, he knows he either has the wrong man, or the punishment was too severe. Hudson, to his satisfaction, heard nothing. The men had confirmed his sentence with their silence, and "It's fair. Hix has it coming" was their collective verdict.

"Seized up, sir."

"Bosun, do your duty," Hudson ordered.

The bosun reached into the red baize bag he was carrying, pulled out a wicked looking cat-of-nine tails and shook them out. Walker could see the extra knots that were tied to the end of each of the tails.

He stepped back a couple of paces, freed his arm, and swung the flail with all his might, stepping into the swing like a criquet player driving a ball.

"WHAP!"

"One," proclaimed the master-at-arms.

Walker stiffened, and his eyes grew wide. "What the hell," he murmured.

"WHAP!"

"Two."

"WHAP!" The bosun drove the flail again into Hix with all his might.

"Three."

By the sixth blow, deep livid welts had formed across Hix's back. "This is unbelievable," thought Walker, deeply shocked yet unable to take his eyes off the scene.

By the tenth blow the skin had broken, and blood was running freely down to the man's waist. By the sixteenth blow, blood was spattering in all directions with each strike of the flail. By the twentieth-fourth and final blow, Walker thought he could see part of a backbone sticking out of the man's shattered back. Walker was too stunned by what he'd seen to speak.

After completion of the flogging, the Bosun walked over to the side of the ship and threw both the cat-of-nine tails and the red bag overboard. No 'cat' was ever used twice.

The men began quietly disbursing and Walker felt as if he were wandering in a fog. He found himself by the helm as the captain walked by. He started to say something but, for once in his life, he thought better of it. Just as the captain was turning away, they both heard a commotion behind them near the mainmast. One of the older men was grasping his chest.

"I... Oh, God!" He fell to his knees and then toppled on his side.

Walker rushed down the gangway ladder and pushed his way through the men who were just standing around the fallen man.

"Why don't you *do* something," Walker demanded.

" Woss there ter do, sor? 'e's as good as dead," replied one of them.

"But he's not dead yet, is he?" exclaimed Walker.

Walker wasn't sure he knew what to do either; but fragments of a long-ago conversation—probably while half drunk in some tavern—started to surface. It was something about...

He fell to his knees and rolled the man over on his back, felt for a pulse in his neck then listened for breathing. "Damn," he exclaimed.

He shifted over a few feet and pounded the man's chest once, hard. Then, placing his hands on the old seaman's rib cage, he started compressing it.

That was it. It was something about... you could bring a man back from the dead if he had a heart attack by pressing hard on both sides of his rib cage. No one knew why.

Walker kept compressing and could feel himself getting very tired and dizzy when the man's hand suddenly grabbed Walker's arm. He rolled over on his side, coughed twice and took a huge breath. Within a few minutes, the man could stand up and was led below.

Walker started back toward the quarterdeck, but there was no need to push his way through the crowd this time. It opened before him; a pathway of hard-bitten seamen with their eyes wide and mouths hung open in wonder.

18

He glanced up at the captain as he walked past. What was that on his face? Curiosity? Amazement? Yes, both of those, Walker thought, and perhaps even a trace of fear.

* * *

The following day Walker was summoned aft to the captain's cabin, which was, by far, the most spacious on the ship. Captain Hudson was seated behind a large table. Standing to his right was John Rooney and to Rooney's right was First Lieutenant Smith.

"Have a seat, Mr. Walker," the captain said.

"You present a bit of a problem to me and I don't like that. I have enough problems running a 220-man frigate without having additional ones dropping in on me, it seems, out of the sky. Surely you can appreciate that."

"Yes, I can," Walker replied honestly.

Accordingly, to simplify my life, as of this moment you are now a member of His Majesty's Royal Navy. You have been pressed."

"Pressed?" Walker shot bolt upright in his chair. "You can't do that. I am a citizen of the United States of America and an officer in the United States Navy."

"Really? Let's examine those claims.

"You claim to be a citizen of the United States. But, Mr. Walker, there *is* no United States. What you call a 'country' consists of a ragtag Army that has had its butt kicked from one end of the colonies to the other, and a collection of deluded old men that have decided to call themselves a 'Congress.'

"There *is* no country, Mr. Walker, and there never will be. There are thirteen colonies—*British* colonies—and, if you are from one of them as you say, then you are a British subject and therefore may be pressed into service to your king.

"Then there's your claim to being a naval officer. For two days now I've watched you wander around this ship like a child attending his first circus. You barely know the bow from the stern."

"Sir, I am an officer in the..."

"Enough, Mr. Walker!" Hudson shouted as he banged his hand on the table.

Hudson paused for a moment. "Let's say you have command of a ship, Mr. Walker. Suppose you are on a lee shore, and had neither room to veer or stay, nor any anchoring ground, how would you put the ship's head round the other way? What would you do, sir?"

Walker was silent.

"Quickly, sir. You're about to go aground! What would you DO?"

Walker remained silent.

Without removing his eyes from Walker, Hudson said, "Mr. Smith. Answer the question."

Smith looked startled at being included in the discussion, but responded anyway. "Well, sir, first I would put my helm hard a-lee. When she comes head to wind, I'd raise the fore and main tacks directly, make a run with my weather braces and lay all aback at once. Then I'd haul forward my lee-tacks and bowlines as far as I can, so the ship could fall round on her heel. When the mainsail begins to shiver; I would haul it up, fill my headsails, and shift the helm hard a-weather. When the wind finally comes on the other quarter, I'd haul on board the main-tack, and bring her close to the wind."

"Mr. Walker that question, or one like it, is a standard one on our Lieutenant's Exam. There isn't an officer in the navy—in *our* navy, at least—that can't answer it. No, you're no officer, at least not a naval officer.

"On the other hand, you're obviously not without education. You're no gentleman as far as I am concerned; but you are not of the common rabble either."

Hudson paused again as if thinking over for the last time what he was about to say.

"Tell me, do you know anything of the sciences?"

"I've had some courses, yes."

"Do you have a working knowledge of trigonometry?"

"Yes. Why?"

"As captain of one of His Majesty's ships, operating independently with no superior officer nearby, I have a fair amount of latitude in terms of how I organize my personnel. Accordingly, I am hereby appointing you to the rank of Warrant Officer aboard this ship with specialty as Ship's Philosopher."

Walker was now totally confused. "Ship's Philosopher?"

"Yes, it's an old position, not used much any more, but it's still on the books. Maybe we should use the modern term instead. You will be the Ship's Scientist. You will report to Mr. Rooney and will be especially responsible for creating navigational charts of any landmasses we encounter, or improving upon our existing charts. You will pay special attention to the identification and plotting of rocks, shoals, and other navigational hazards on those charts. You will also make such other observations or measurements of wind, tide, ocean conditions and natural phenomena as may be of interest to the Navy Board."

Walker just sat there with total disbelief coursing through his body. It was only with considerable effort that he was able to return his attention to Captain Hudson.

"...as you will also be the Ship's Surgeon."

"What? Ship's Surgeon," Walker protested. I am not a physician."

"I never said you were," replied Hudson. "Indeed, if you recall, I never said you were a scientist either. But, after that stunt you pulled yesterday—and I have no idea how you did that—the men *think* you are a physician, and that's what's important. They think you can literally raise people from the dead, Mr. Walker. Imagine that.

"So, if I may continue... The Ship's Surgeon that was assigned to us was indisposed when we left Charleston."

"He had been dead drunk for 20 days," sniffed Rooney.

"Was indisposed," repeated the captain. "We need a Ship's Surgeon, and so, you're it. You will have a good surgeon's mate and two loblolly boys under you.

"You will be paid as a surgeon—5 pounds per month, plus 5 pounds for every 100 cases of venereal disease you treat. You will sleep in the Fourth Lieutenant's cabin and dine in the officers' mess. When we get into the next port that has a packet going to England, I will forward both appointments to the Sick and Wounded Board at the Admiralty for approval. They will, of course, reject them both out of hand; but, meanwhile..."

"And what if I refuse to perform these duties?" asked Walker.

The steel now came unsheathed in Hudson's gray-green eyes as they bored into Walker's. He leaned forward on the table: "Then I will place you in irons in the hold, among the ships rats, on bread and water for the duration of this cruise. When we reach port—which might be a month or more from now—I will transfer you to similar princely accommodations on a ship headed for England.

Once in England you will be placed aboard the prison brig in Portsmouth Harbor until your trial as an American spy is called and you are hung—unless, of course, someone carelessly forgets to give you a trial at all and simply hangs you. Am I making myself clear, Mr. Walker?"

"You are indeed, sir. Quite clear."

"One more thing. I am assigning Mr. Smith here as your 'Sea Daddy.' His job will be to bring you up to speed on this ship and her operations as quickly as possible. A cram course, if you will, in being... a REAL officer." The irony was dripping from Hudson's voice.

"There we have it. Are there any questions?"

"No," Walker replied.

"That's 'No SIR,' Mr. Walker," snapped Rooney.

"No, SIR... Sir."

CHAPTER TWO

ALL RIGHT. Let's go over it again. Tell me about shrouds."

"Shrouds are the lines that extend from each masthead to the starboard and larboard side of the ship. They support the mast.

"What supports the masts fore and aft?"

"The backstays and the forestays," he said smiling. "I knew you were going to ask that."

It was early afternoon on a glorious late summer day. The sky was such a bright blue that it almost hurt your eyes to look at it. Below was a darker blue extending as far as the eye could see, and way up high there were wisps of white clouds to provide little accent marks to the scene. The *Richmond* was cruising along at 5 or 6 knots under mere topsails, riding the southerly breezes and the recently named "Gulf Stream" current. She was making the sounds that all wooden ships make while underway—the sounds of wood rubbing against wood—ranging from low harmonics coming from deep within the hull, to the higher, shriller sounds of the upper masts and yardarms. It was not the sound of distress, Walker noted. It was almost as if the ship was humming to herself as she made her way across the ocean.

Walker and Smith were on the fo'c'sle. Smith was leaning against one of the two nine-pounders; Walker was sitting on a hatch combing. In the past few days, they found themselves forming something of a friendship. Smith's stiff, proper, British demeanor was in sharp contrast with Walker's loose, irreverent, American brashness. Yet, despite that, or perhaps because of it, they were finding in each other something that they sensed they perhaps lacked in themselves.

"All right, now, what are the names of the mast sails starting from the deck up," Smith quizzed.

"Mainsail, topsail, topgallant and royal."

"Right, and sometimes you'll see a fifth sail deployed above the royal called a 'skyscraper,' but it's mostly for showing off. It doesn't really add much to the speed of the ship.

"Now, let's cover the fore and aft sails..."

"Sidney, how old are you?" Walker suddenly asked.

"How old am I? Almost 18. Why?"

"How many years have you been in the navy?"

"Let's see... going on seven years, I guess."

It was a number Walker had not expected. "Seven? You mean to tell me you've been in the navy since you were 11 years old?"

"Yes. Oh, I know that was a little young. Most young gentlemen have to wait until they're at least 12 before they're admitted, but, because of my father, I got appointed as a captain's Servant at 11; and by 12, I was a midshipman aboard my first ship. Actually, if you count my home life as a child, in a sense, I've been in the military my whole life."

"Who's your father?"

"He's a drunk."

"I am guessing that drunks don't have the influence to get their sons into the navy at age 11."

"You don't want to know."

"Well, actually, I do; but if you don't want to tell me, that's all right too."

Smith looked at Walker hard and knew that he was at a crossroad of sorts. Walker represented something that Smith had wanted all his life but never had—a friend. He had had many acquaintances and several drinking buddies, but never—even when he was a child—did he have someone he could genuinely call his friend. "Maybe it was time for that to change," he thought, and decided to roll the dice.

"My father was a soldier, a captain in the Horse Guards, and was involved in the Battle of Minden back in '59. To make a long story short, he was aide-de-camp to General George Sackville. Right at the end of the battle, when one more blow would have finished the French off, Sackville was ordered to attack with his cavalry. He refused."

"Why"

"Because he didn't want his cavalry commander, Lord Granby, whom he detested, to get any glory from leading the attack."

"Oh, terrific."

"Yes, well, it gets worse.

"So, after the battle General Sackville gets sacked, no pun intended, and is hauled before a court martial. Not only does the court martial find him guilty but they declare him: '...unfit to serve his Majesty in any military capacity whatsoever.'"

"So, what's this got to do with your father?"

"Well, my father gets it into his head that this moron Sackville has been wronged and decided to deal a crippling blow to the British army, sell his commission and resign. The British army, as you might have noticed, somehow managed to survive that mortal blow."

"So how does that get you into the navy."

"I am getting to that. It all has to do with a wash tub and a girl."

"Oh, this ought'a be good. Pray continue."

"All right," Smith said while cracking a smile for the first time.

"It was during the summer just after I turned 11 years old. We were staying at a cottage on the grounds of Midgham Hall in Berkshire; and I decided one afternoon to entertain a neighbor girl who was about my age but with considerably more ah... 'experience,' shall we say?

"Anyway, I got this huge old washtub and launched it on the pond that was on the grounds there. I placed the girl; I don't even remember her name, in the tub and poled out into the middle of the pond to attempt to explore a meaningful relationship with her, if you get my drift. In so doing, however, I knocked the pole into the water and it quickly drifted out of reach.

"About that time, I heard several blasts on a horn coming from the cottage. That was the signal that my brothers and I were supposed to return immediately to the cottage for evening prayers. We were never allowed to miss that. I knew that they would wonder where I was at, and soon my father and some of the grounds workers were searching for me, thinking I was hurt.

"Naturally, they quickly found me with the girl, who by now was becoming hysterical, but no one had any idea how to get us in to shore. So, I finally told them to get the string off my kite, tie it to the collar of my dog and I would call him out to the raft.

"Sure enough, the dog paddled out, I got the string by which they could send me a rope and they pulled us in. But, you have to picture it... me standing with one foot on the rim of the tub trying to look as heroic as possible; a dog gleefully shaking himself, spraying water in all directions; and a girl at my feet who had come completely unhinged."

Walker was convulsing with laughter. "So, what happened when you got to shore?"

"Before my father could say anything, I stepped ashore and, calmly as you please, said: 'Now, father, we will go to prayers' to which he replied in some exasperation: 'Yes, we had better.'"

Walker was still laughing. "I still don't see how this got you into the navy."

"Well, my father had always been something of a rakehell; but after he got out of the military he became even worse—with heavy drinking thrown in to boot. He simply decided that two rakehells in the immediate vicinity was one too many. Besides, my brothers and I were consuming far too many of his 'resources' for his comfort. So, my oldest brother, Charles was sent off to become a page to Lord Harcourt, the Viceroy of Ireland. I was sent off into the navy and, as I understand it, my youngest brother, Spencer, will be placed upon the navy rolls later this year."

"But, why the navy and not the army, like your father?"

"My father could not afford a commission for me. Besides, I preferred the navy."

"What do you mean by that? You said your father 'sold' his commission, and just now you said you could not afford to 'buy' one."

"Well, in the army, that's how you become an officer; you buy your commission. Becoming a captain cost more than becoming a lieutenant, and becoming a colonel cost more than a major. If you decide to leave the service, you can sell your rank to the next person who wants to occupy your position. To become a coronet, the lowest officer rank, would have cost my father anywhere from

£450 for a line infantry unit, to £1200 for a commission in the Horse Guards. Hell, for £6,000 I could be a Lt. Colonel in the dragoons right now."

"That's crazy. You must have an awful lot of incompetent officers in the army."

"We do. But, we also have some brilliant ones. Don't ask me how that happens."

"How did a system like that get started? Bribery run amuck?"

"No, actually the system makes perfect sense. Remember that 130 years ago we had a civil war during which army officers in droves defected to Cromwell's side. This left the Royalist Army in desperate need of experienced leadership. When Charles II regained the throne he decreed that, henceforth, all officer commissions would be purchased—under the theory that if someone had a small fortune invested in his military commission, he would be much less likely to run off with the first honey-tongued traitor that shows up."

"The navy's not like that?"

"No. There is favoritism, to be sure, but you can't just buy your rank.

"If your family has any influence at all you start out as a midshipman, usually about age 12. You can get in earlier as a captain's servant—as early as age 9, if you want—but, either way, you have to persuade some captain to take you on. That's where the influence helps.

"Anyway, as a midshipman you're an officer in training and you're expected to learn seamanship, navigation, and the million details involved in running a ship, in addition to standard school subjects like mathematics, reading and writing. After a minimum of six years at sea, at least two as a midshipman, you can take the test for lieutenant, and it's a serious test. You stand before at least three officers who are captains or higher, and they fire questions at you—questions about all the things you learned, or were supposed to have learned, as a midshipman. Little or no favoritism is shown. You either know your stuff, or you don't. If you don't... well, I know of one midshipman who was 57 years old before he finally passed. There are plenty who are in their 20's and 30's."

"Did you pass the first time?"

"Yes, actually, I got to take the exam early. You're supposed to be at least 20 years old before you can make lieutenant, but that rule is often ignored if you can pass the test."

"So what happens then, after you pass?"

"You work your way up through the ranks with successive positions, starting as a fourth lieutenant somewhere, then as third, second, finally first lieutenant.

"If you're lucky; or have shown great merit; or have a lot of patronage; or all three, you will someday go from being a first lieutenant to having command of your own ship. You'll be a captain and will wear a captain's epaulette on your right shoulder. The most important thing in getting a command, however, is patronage."

"How do you mean?"

"Look at it this way. There are far, far, more lieutenants in the navy then there are ships. To get a command, you need to either have political pull in parliament, or get under the wing of an admiral. That admiral has to promote your name, or even directly appoint you, when it comes time for a ship command to be given out. The problem is that the system is a two edged sword. If you are the protégé of Admiral Barnacle and Admiral Barnacle retires or dies, you're in a bad way unless some other admiral wants to take you on.

"I once personally met a lieutenant by the name of Tom Moody. He was 67 years old and had been a lieutenant for 47 years."

"Why?"

"Because his admiral, Sir Charles Knowles, retired before he could secure him a command.

"You said a captain has an epaulette on the right shoulder. Why does Captain Hudson have two epaulettes?"

"He's a Post-Captain, someone who has been a captain for three years or more and who commands a rated ship. When you make 'post,' that's when you start your climb toward becoming an admiral."

"Which is accomplished by?"

"Out living everyone who's more senior to you. That's how you make admiral. As the more senior post-captains retire or die, your name moves up the list until... viola... one day you have your own flag. You might not have command of anything, in which case you are called a 'yellow admiral' and you're on the beach, but you *will* be an admiral."

"What about you, Sidney? You aim to become an admiral?"

"Lucas, all I want in this world is to be a post-captain in His Majesty's Royal Navy—a fighting captain. I want to command a frigate and go toe-to-toe with the French, or the Spanish, or even you Americans if the war lasts long enough. I want to know what it's like to have shot screaming around me and still remain calm and function. I want to know what it's like to capture another ship and lead her into port as a prize."

"I see. Sort of an unquenchable desire to bleed for your country, is that it? That's great." Walker was being sarcastic, but he had known young men that talked like Smith. Almost to a man, they had been killed, and he feared for his young friend.

"No," Smith said looking directly at Walker. "I have no desire to either bleed or die; but I will if that's the price."

Walker said nothing and just looked at him quizzically.

"You don't understand, Lucas." Smith's voice became very intense as he rushed on. "Some day I am going to do something great. I know it. I simply *know* it. I don't know where, or when, or how, or what it will be, but it will be magnificent. They will erect a statue of me in Greenwich. People will write novels about my exploits hundreds of years after I am dead." Smith abruptly stopped talking and looked at Walker as if he had said too much.

Walker wasn't sure what to say, or whether to say anything at all. In the few days they had been thrown together, Walker had come to like Sidney Smith a great deal and enjoy his company; but he doubted if Smith had ever seen combat before. Walker's father had served in the French and Indian War. He never talked about his experiences much, but when he did it was nothing like Smith's romantic view.

According to him, it was hours and hours of boredom followed by instant noise, confusion, and people yelling orders—usually contradictory ones—over the screams and sobs of people who had been hit. It was the smell of gunpowder so strong you could hardly see because your eyes were watering so badly. It was the urgent sensation of fear that jammed every organ in your body into overdrive followed, after it was over, by the shakes as the fear left.

It was fighting, but it was not for God, country or some political ideal. You fought, first and above all, for the people around you. You fought because you wanted their respect. You fought be-

cause, if you didn't, one of your friends might die. You fought because, if you didn't, YOU might die. And, you fought because there
was a piece of your soul that urgently needed the answer to a simple question: "When the enemy comes, will you run or will you
stand?" That was a question that Walker believed was seared into
the soul of every male who has ever lived—including himself.

"What's the likelihood you'll get your chance for 'glory' on this
trip?" Walker finally asked.

"What do you mean?"

"I mean, what the devil are we doing out here, anyway."

"Good question. I can tell you what I know, but it's not all that
much.

"As you might know, since the spring of last year our troops
have been rampaging around the southern colonies. We captured
Savannah. We captured Charleston; and, we pretty much laid
North and South Carolina to waste.

"Last March General Cornwallis decided to move into the Virginia Colony, which was probably a pretty good idea. Virginia's the
largest and richest of the colonies. Its tobacco output alone could
provide enough revenue to support the rebels for years. If Cornwallis can conquer Virginia, there are a lot of people, me included,
who think the rebellion will collapse.

"So, last May, Cornwallis' army entered Virginia. After tramp-
ing around half the state for several months, he started looking for
a suitable port from which he could receive supplies, additional
troops and, if need be, to serve as a means of escape.

"A few weeks ago, he settled on a place called Yorktown which
was a perfect choice. It's on the James River, has a large deep water anchorage that runs almost to the shore; it's easily accessible
from the sea and it's more-or-less defendable."

"And there was no American Army anywhere to challenge
him?" Walker asked.

"Right. They're all up around New York City somewhere hoping to retake the place, I suppose, or at least we thought.

"So there we were in Charlestown, happily eating, drinking and
whoring ourselves under the table, when we received two pieces of
very bad news.

"First, soon after Cornwallis had made himself nice and comfy
in Yorktown, American troops arrived from God knows where and
sealed him off on the Yorktown peninsula. Second, we got news

that the French were going to get involved in a big way. Some frog admiral named de Grasse arrived in the Caribbean with no less than 28 ships of the line, not to mention frigates, tenders, and whatever all else.

"On August 5th he left Cape Francis to head north with supplies and additional French troops to help the rebels at Yorktown. A few days later, when our Admiral Hood heard about it, he gathered up the British fleet in the Caribbean and took off after him.

"That's about all I know for sure—that, and the fact that we're carrying some dispatches. Our job is to find the British fleet, give the dispatches to Hood, and place ourselves at his disposal."

"So, where are we now?"

"Almost there. Come on, I'll show you."

Smith walked aft and Walker followed him. He stopped directly in front of the helm and put his hand on a shielded box held up by a stand, which was anchored firmly to the deck. "This is called the binnacle. It holds the ship's compass."

Walker could see the ornate object and that, on either side, was a special windproof lantern so the helmsman could see the compass at night.

"Under here," Smith continued, "is a drawer where we keep whatever chart is operational at the moment." Smith reached in, pulled out a large document, spread it across the light shield and pointed.

"There are three rivers that empty into the Atlantic hereabouts. To the south is the James River; in the middle is the York River, and north of that, the Potomac. Over here is Chesapeake Bay. To get to any of them you have to go through a narrows formed by two peninsulas. At the tip of the peninsula to the north is Cape Charles; to the south is Cape Henry.

"The thing is; you can't just sail straight in. Right in the middle is a horror of silt and sand known as the Middle Ground. If you want to get into or out of the Chesapeake, or any of the three rivers, you have to come in through here along Cape Henry."

"Why couldn't you go into the north of the Middle Ground over by Cape Charles?" Walker asked.

"It's too risky. Sometimes the currents will scour a channel five fathoms deep over there and the next day it will be one fathom. The hell of it is you never know which it is until you get into it, and then it's too late.

"No, the safe route is to hug the coast by Cape Henry but even then not too close 'cause there are shoals that come out from Henry as well."

* * *

A few hours later, the *Richmond* was about as ready as she could be for entering "The Capes." She had taken in all her canvas except the foretopsail and had slowed to a crawl. The ships two anchors, one forward and one placed aft, had their bucklers removed and the anchor lines were ready to run if they had to drop one of them and come to a screeching halt.

Rooney was on the quarterdeck with Captain Hudson. "Steady as she goes, helm," Rooney said. "Just keep the Cape Henry tip about two points to larboard and we'll be fine."

"Captain, once we make contact with Hood's fleet..."

Whatever Rooney was about to ask was interrupted by a shout from the mainmast lookout.

"On deck there! Sail, ho."

"Where away?" Came the automatic reply from Rooney.

"One point orf th' sta'board bow, sor. Several masts at th' entrance to th' Chesapeake wi' even more behind 'em."

"Very well. Give me a count."

Rooney then turned to Hudson. "Well, captain, it looks as if you've found your Admiral Hood."

"It does indeed."

The lookout was now calling: "Six... eight... twelve..."

"I'll be in my cabin if you need me, Mr. Rooney."

"...fifteen... sixteen... twenty..."

The captain stopped abruptly, frozen in place as he was reaching for the knob on his cabin door. Suddenly, he whirled around and raced back to the quarterdeck.

"...twenty two... twenty six... twenty eight..."

"All hands to the braces," Hudson was screaming. "Topmen away aloft. Come on! Come on! Get cracking. Do it NOW!"

Rooney was not far behind the captain, for he too had figured it out. He had picked up the megaphone from its storage slot. "Helm hard a'starboard," Rooney yelled. "Waisters stand by to wear ship. Top men, fore, main and mizzen... drop every stitch of canvas we've got. Let's go! Let's go! Let's get the hell out of here!"

Walker, hearing all the commotion, came on deck. Grabbing a seaman who was busy unlashing one of the 12-pound guns he asked, "What's going on?"

"Th' French fleet, sor. We was about ter sail in and drop us an anchor, pretty as yer please, in the middle of the 'oole chuffin' French fleet."

"How do you know?"

"Because Admiral 'ood only 'as 14 ships. The lookout were at 28 and still countin' wen the captain called quarters."

To most people, it would appear like a blur of random activity. In the past few days, however, Walker had learned enough to know that battle station activities were anything but random. Each man was rushing to a specifically assigned place, to do a specifically assigned task, in a specifically assigned way.

They scrambled up ratlines and sidestepped out on the yards, ready to take in or let out sail. They ran to precise locations on deck, standing by to haul on lines that would alter the direction or stiffness of the sails.

Below decks, the cook would be dousing the cooking fires; and men would be taking down room dividers and hauling below anything that was not directly needed for battle. The ship's boats would be quickly swayed over the side, and anything that could get in the way or serve as a source of wooden splinter shrapnel was stowed.

Susan Whitney would be laying out instruments and pushing several of the midshipman's trunks together to form a crude operating table. The gunner would be in the powder room hanging felt drapes all around and dousing them with water to suppress any sparks that might enter. He would have on felt slippers so he wouldn't cause any sparks that might, in turn, cause the "explosion you will never hear." Outside the room the ship's boys—powder monkeys they were called—would be lined up to get measured charges in flannel bags from the gunner, place them in wooden boxes and race to the guns they were assigned to serve, then race back to pickup the next charge.

But, above all, the men ran to their gun stations—26 12-pounders on the main deck, four 6-pounders on the quarterdeck and two long-nines on the fo'c'sle—heaving, sweating and cursing until each gun was loaded and each gun captain could stand next to his piece, fist raised in the air, signaling that his gun was ready to fire.

They had all done it before—hundreds of times, in daylight and at night, in fair weather and foul, when feeling sick and feeling well. No thought whatsoever was required; and that was exactly what the officers wanted. In a matter of minutes, the ship and the men had transformed themselves into a single, unified, flesh and oak machine.

"Mr. Smith, away with you to the maintop. Take a glass and tell me immediately if any of those ships are starting to get underway."

"Aye, Sir."

Sidney Smith flew to the larboard side mainmast ratline, and starting scrambling up like an outraged husband was chasing him. When he got to the main top platform he bypassed going through the lubbers hole, the easy entrance to the platform. Instead, he crawled out along the futtock shrouds, briefly hanging in an upside down position, and swung up on the platform.

"On deck there," he cried a few moments later.

"Deck, aye," came the reply from the quarterdeck.

"I confirm 28 ships of the line with possibly a few more farther up. Definitely French, Sir. They're in two groups. The smaller group's in Lynnhaven Bay and the other strung out up into the Chesapeake. I see three ships flying a broad pennant—three admirals. And... wait... yes... that one has to be the *Ville de Paris*—de Grasse's flagship."

"Do any of them seem to be getting underway to come meet us?"

"No, sir. The water's alive with small craft ferrying supplies and men to the shore. Looks like they're too busy to bother with the likes of us.

"Wait one," Smith continued. There was dead silence on deck as everyone, officer and seaman alike, strained to hear the report. The men knew that what they were hearing could spell either continued life or death by nightfall for many if not all of them.

"There's a sloop-of-war underway from Cape Henry and heading toward us. It's probably the picket boat that should have intercepted us before we ever got in this far. And behind her is a frigate—no, two frigates—preparing to get underway"

"Very, well. Mr. Smith stay up there and let me know if the situation changes in any way."

"Mr. Rooney, as soon as we clear the middle ground I want you to plot a course due east. Stay on it until we can no longer see land or, more important, they can no longer see us.

Rooney cut the corner of the middle ground as close as he dared—and closer than the captain thought possible—and shot out into the Atlantic. The sloop pursued as far as the place where the *Richmond* had first spotted the fleet and then turned back. The frigates never got underway at all.

Two hours later, the land had dropped below the horizon, and they were in the clear. Everyone on board breathed a lot more easily for they knew that if just one of those ships of the line had bestirred itself to get underway, the *Richmond* would now be a pile of floating match sticks. Any one of them would be faster than the *Richmond*, and their 32-pound guns could easily reach out and touch someone over a mile away with considerable accuracy. They would simply mutilate a small frigate like the *Richmond*.

"Where to now, sir?" Rooney asked.

"Good question," Captain Hudson replied. "But an even better one is: Where the devil is Hood?

"He couldn't have doubled back to the south or we would have seen at least some part of his fleet. Heading east makes no sense. No... I'll wager he headed north. He probably headed for New York to link with Admiral Graves' fleet and so, therefore, shall we.

"Let's fly, Rooney. I don't know whether he knows that the French have arrived in Yorktown; but, if not, he and Graves, and Governor Clinton, need to know right away. That fool Cornwallis has trapped himself on that peninsula."

With that Rooney sprung into action, bellowing orders. "All hands secure from quarters. Bosun set the Watch. "Helm, come around to..."

The officers and men of the *Richmond* were quite right in thinking the stakes were high. But, it would be some time before they would learn how high.

* * *

It would be at least another two days until the *Richmond* could get to New York. With good winds maybe they could cut it to a day and a half, bad winds maybe three or four, no wind... forever. That's the way it was on a sail-powered vessel.

The ship settled back into its routine, but now there was an edge to it that Walker had not seen before.

Outwardly, everything looked the same. At dawn, the men were at quarters, followed by scrubbing the decks, lashing up the hammocks, taking their tot of rum at noon, another at supper, down hammocks, lights out and sleep. It was what he saw in-between those events that had changed.

Fire drills, sail handling drills, practicing musket loading for speed and shooting for accuracy. The more skilled were holding cutlass classes for the less skilled; and the ships armorer had his wheel on deck and going all day long. Every cutlass, pike and dirk on the ship was receiving a new and sharper edge. Gun drills were different, too. Besides there being a seriousness of purpose that was not there before, each gun crew was now practicing firing the guns shorthanded. Seven man guns were being loaded and fired by five and four man teams in silent acknowledgment of the reality of battle where comrades could and would fall.

True, the men's off-hours were much the same. There would be socializing and "make and mend" during the dogwatches. And, as the day started to cool off, fiddles or penny whistles would come out and off-duty men would dance the occasional hornpipe be-cause... well, because they were young and they could.

But, there was another side that Walker also noticed. A lot more people were spending time by themselves reading through prayer books or dog-eared Bibles. Those men in the ship's com-pany who could write would setup impromptu tables in secluded areas where other men could quietly come and have letters, per-haps final letters, to loved ones back home written for them.

But, all this paled in comparison with the shock he received the second day out of the Chesapeake.

Susan Whitney had come on deck with a chest of knives and saws and proceeded to the armorer to have them sharpened. Nor-mally, Susan was welcome anywhere on the ship. Her lively per-sonality, radiant smile, sense of humor, and the fact that she genu-inely cared for the well being of each seaman, made her easily the most popular person on the ship. Woe be unto any man who mis-treated her because he would be facing the vengeance of 200 adopted "older brothers" within the hour. That's not a pretty thought on a ship with lots of out-of-the-way dark places.

This time, however, the men pretended to be suddenly busy with something else—anything else—when she came on deck. They knew what she was carrying, and they knew why the instruments needed to be sharpened. They just preferred not thinking about it, that's all.

When the armorer was done, she came over to Walker who was standing by the larboard rail. "Mr. Walker, may I have a word with you?" she said rather sternly.

"Of course, Susan. How are you doing?"

She ignored his question. "Do you know what's in this chest?"

"Yes, I saw the armorer sharpening them. They're surgical instruments... some rather nasty-looking saws and knives."

Susan nodded. "And do you know what they're for?"

Walker was getting a bit disturbed. "Why was she talking to me like I was a child," he thought. "Yes, I do. If we get into a battle men are going to be hurt, some very seriously. Some will have to be operated on, legs removed and such."

"Uh-huh. And precisely who do you think will be wielding these instruments if and when that comes to pass?"

It was at that point that the enormity of Hudson's words came back to him: "...and you will also be the Ship's Surgeon."

"Holy Mother of God," he muttered. "Susan, you're not suggesting that I... I mean, look, I have no training, no experience at all in... I couldn't possibly..." Walker was unable to get a coherent sentence out.

"Mr. Walker, like it or not, you *are* the Ship's Surgeon. Now, I've been doing the sick calls and all the other work ever since you were appointed. I don't mind that, but you're going to have to start pulling your weight."

"No, you don't understand, Susan. You see I am NOT a physician. All right, I know a little about anatomy, sure, but that doesn't qualify me to take care of the sick and wounded, and it certainly doesn't qualify me to perform operations."

Susan looked at Walker for a long moment, cocked her head and said: "Do I somehow look like I went to Oxford?"

"No, but..."

"But nothing. I was made assistant to a surgeon who hasn't had two back-to-back days of sobriety since I've known him. Men were suffering, and in some cases dying, because of his incompetence. So, do you know what I did?"

Walker shook his head dumbly.

"I learned, Mr. Walker. I *learned*." And, with that, she spun on her heels and proceeded below to the infirmary.

* * *

Walker's routine changed once again. When Smith was off-watch, Walker was with him learning at least something about both the practical and theoretical aspects of seamanship. When Smith was on-watch he was either with Susan Whitney learning the practical aspects of medical care, or he was reading the many medical textbooks his predecessor had shipped aboard. And, in his private time, what little of it there was, he thought about his predicament.

In many ways, the easiest thing to learn was the medical side. In 18th Century Britain, it was not required to have a college degree in order to practice medicine. Indeed, you could do so without any formal training whatsoever. Some of the universities, most notably Aberdeen, would award the M.D. degree upon payment of the appropriate fees—attending classes was completely optional.

So, Walker didn't have far to go to become at least as good as some of those who were, on land, considered full-fledged practicing physicians. Helping also was the fact that the field of medicine itself was not terribly complicated.

To the physician of the time, all disease was caused by one of three factors. The first possibility was that the patient was simply predisposed to the illness because of occupation or station in life. Everyone knew, for example, that Walker's seamen were predisposed to pneumonia, scurvy, diarrhea, and dysentery. Why? Because they were seamen.

The second possibility was that the patients symptoms were caused by "antecedent causes." either miasma's or contagions. "Miasma's" were invisible disease causing particles that were produced by rotting animal or vegetable matter; and "contagions" were similar particles emitted from other people who had the disease.

The third possibility was that there was a disturbance in one or more of the "six non-naturals." These were air, quality of food and drink, quantity of food and drink, sleep, exercise, and mental state.

While all disease was considered to be the result of one of those three factors, the classification was not of much help in knowing what to do about the problem. Diseases were not classified and treated according to their causes. At that time, the symptom *was* the illness and no further inquiry need be made.

Nevertheless, some standard procedures did evolve. For example, in the case of a fever, it was noticed that the patients almost always had a rapid pulse. So, obviously, the first thing a competent physician would do is to reduce the "irritability of the heart" by inducing vomiting. This helped to rid the body of whatever it was that had upset its "balances." Failing that, he might give the patient a tonic to strengthen the heart and arteries. This, in turn, would also speed the removal of whatever factors were causing the imbalance and thus the illness. In short, the chief task of the physician, Walker learned, was to restore the normal balances of the patients' humors, the tensions within his circulatory system, and/or the body's acid and base levels.

Fortunately, seamen were, in general, a healthy lot. Over 50% of the illnesses reported by the men were colds, flu or pneumonia. Another 25% was accounted for if you added diarrhea and dysentery. He knew that with most of those diseases people would recover no matter what he did—or if he did nothing at all. Add to that syphilis, gonorrhea and scurvy (about which neither he nor anyone else could do a thing) and these illnesses would account for about 80% of his "practice." It was the other 20% that worried him. While colds and flu might account for 80% or his patients, injuries accounted for 80% of the deaths and disabilities, and that scared the wits out of Walker.

Injuries were a fact of life aboard any sailing ship. You've got several hundred men, working in a very confined space, under conditions that would give a modern day OSHA inspector a case of the vapors; so, of course, you're going to have accidents—lots of them. Fortunately, here Susan Whitney and her wealth of practical experience came to the rescue.

She showed him how to apply olive oil to burns to keep the air away and to keep the skin soft while healing; how to manipulate a loop of intestine back into the abdominal cavity and how to design a truss that would keep the hernia closed; how to cut and drain boils and abscesses; set broken bones and even how to pull teeth—at which Walker eventually got to be quite good.

In return, he taught her everything he knew about anatomy, chemistry and biology. Together they were forming a close-knit team, and Walker found himself very much enjoying the time he spent with her. He couldn't quite explain it, but he found himself enjoying just being around her.

But, there was one area that neither one of them wanted to bring up—combat injuries. Susan didn't bring it up because she knew first hand what happens to small men on big wooden ships when shot starts to fly. Walker didn't want to bring the subject up because he didn't want even to think about the responsibility that would be in his hands when someone had to root around for a musket ball lodged in a person's chest, or when the first leg or arm had to come off. He honestly didn't know if he could do it and told Susan so.

"Don't worry," she replied. "No one knows if they can do anything until the time comes and there are simply no other options."

Walker could see that some hideous scenes were replaying in her mind; so, he decided to say nothing and just put his arm around her. She moved into him and said nothing. She just nuzzled her head on his chest for a moment while quiet tears formed in her eyes.

The peace and tranquility of that moment was transformed by a call from one of the lookouts.

"On deck, there!"

"Deck, aye," replied someone from the quarterdeck.

"Sails dead ahead!"

* * *

As the *Richmond* sailed toward the line of ships, a frigate broke station on the outside of the battle line and headed toward her.

"Message from the approaching ship, sir," called the signals midshipman who was stationed with a telescope at the maintop, a platform about halfway up the main mast.

"He's sending an identification challenge: the four-flag at the maintop and seven at the foretop."

Rooney went to the binnacle box and pulled out a small book entitled: "Private Signals: American Station." The first page held the "Table for Challenging and Distinguishing Friend from Enemy" which consisted of four vertical columns divided horizontally into 10 rows. In the top left box were the numbers 1, 11, 21, 31 and referred to those dates. The next box down held, 2, 12, 22; the next, 3, 13, 23, and so on until all ten boxes were filled and every date of the month was covered. At the top of the next column were the words: "The First Signal Made is—" and the column to the right of that was entitled: "Answered by a—." The next two columns were titled: "Main topmast head" and "Fore Topmast head" respectively and each box contained a number.

Rooney quickly found the correct date and ran his finger over to the correct reply.

"Send them our ship number followed by eight on the foretop and seven at the main," he called back with the challenge reply number for all British ships anywhere on the American Station that day. The midshipman got busy seeing that the proper signal flags were hoisted.

"She's replying with her ship number: 288."

Rooney leafed to the back of the book and said to the captain, "It's the *Santa Monica*, sir."

"The *Santa Monica*. That's one of Hood's frigates. "Mr. Rooney, steer for Admiral Graves' flagship and have the signalman run up: 'Enemy sighted' and 'Report to Follow.'"

Twenty minutes later, the *Richmond* was drawing close to the biggest wooden object Walker had ever seen. Admiral Grave's flagship was the H.M.S. *London*, a 98-gun ship of the line. She was 176 feet long, 46 feet wide and had three ominous looking gun decks that were operated by a ship's company of over 800 officers and men.

The *London* acknowledged the *Richmond's* signal, replied with "Send Report," and took in enough sail to allow the *Richmond's* Second Lieutenant to be rowed over to deliver Hudson's written report on what they had seen on the Chesapeake.

A half-hour later, he was back with a handwritten note from Graves that said:

Charles,

Well done.

You and your ship are hereby assigned to Adm. Hood's division. He has only one frigate and could use your help.

Regards.

Graves

And as Captain Hudson was wont to say: "There we have it." The *Richmond* took her place in the line of battle, heading to the Chesapeake and a winner take all fight with the French.

* * *

Walker had to admit, it was the most spectacular sight he had ever seen—twenty-seven men of war, under full sail, in calm seas, on an absolutely gorgeous day. It was nothing short of breathtaking.

The battle group was divided into three squadrons sailing in a single line, bow to stern. In the lead was the group under the command of Rear Admiral Samuel Hood. Six capital ships: the *Alfred* (74 guns), *Belliqueux* (64 guns), *Invincible* (74 guns), *Monarch* (74 guns), *Centaur* (74 guns), and Admiral Hood's flagship the *Barfleur* (90 guns). In the middle was Rear Admiral Thomas Graves' squadron consisting of: the *America* (64 guns), *Resolution* (74 guns), *Biddeford* (74 guns), *Royal Oak* (74 guns), *Montage* (74 guns), *Europe* (64 guns) and his flagship the *London* (98 guns). Bringing up the rear was the squadron lead by Rear Admiral Francis Drake with the: *Terrible* (74 guns), *Ajax* (74 guns), *Aldila* (74 guns), *Intrepid* (64 guns), *Shrewsbury* (74 guns) and the flagship *Princessa* (70 guns).

In addition, there were the frigates, dashing out to scout ahead of the convoy or serving to relay signals. Despite the frigate's speed and maneuverability, they really weren't all that much help in a major battle. The *Richmond*, for example, carried 32 guns all of which were 12 pounders or smaller—that is, the shot they fired weighed 12 pounds or less. The *London*, on the other hand carried 98 guns all of which were 12 pounds or *larger*—including 28 32-pounders. For a frigate to enter the fray against the likes of these ships would be like a boy entering the ring to get between two professional prizefighters. He wouldn't inflict much damage and could only get hurt. Still, despite all that, the frigates had their usefulness.

One of the biggest problems during battle was communications. All the major navies had developed a system of signal flags. Various colored and patterned flags stood for letters and numbers, which, in turn, stood for phrases that could be looked up in a codebook.

The problem with 18th Century naval communication was this. The ships normally went into battle in a long single file. If the admiral signaled a command with flags, the only ships that could clearly see them were the ones immediately in front or behind the flagship. The flag hoist would be blocked from other ships' view by the sails of the ships in front of them.

To solve this problem the fleets started placing frigates some distance away from the ships of the line but on a parallel course. From there, the frigates could see the flag hoists of all the ships in their squadron and repeat the signals so everyone else could see them. It was not a popular role for most frigate captains, but everyone knew it had to be done.

This was the role of the H.M.S. *Richmond*.

* * *

The evening watch had just been set when Walker retired to his quarters. Sleep, however, did not come easy for he had way too much on his mind—way too many things he had to sort out.

He was an American—a citizen of the United States, no matter what Captain Hudson thought of that claim—and there was no force on earth that could cause him to take-up arms against his country.

Yet, in the next few days, in all likelihood, he would be carried into battle aboard this ship against the French and possibly directly against the Americans. "Would I be taking up arms against my country if in the eyes of the world my country doesn't really exist yet," he thought. "Am I bound to a flag that has yet to be created, let alone recognized?"

"On the other hand, what if Sidney or Susan were injured or about to be killed? Could I possibly *not* do something to help them? What if it meant killing one of my own countrymen? What would I do if I had to defend my own life?

On the other, other hand...

Sleep was indeed hard to come by for Walker that night.

CHAPTER THREE

THE first indication that today would be "the day" came when the HMS *Solebay* came streaming back over the horizon, racing for the fleet. As a fast frigate, part of Admiral Graves' squadron, she was tasked with scouting ahead and she was now returning flying the signal flags for "Enemy Fleet in the Southwest." It was 9:30 in the morning of September 5th, 1781.

By 10:00 AM, the British ships were running southwest by west and Cape Henry was some six leagues (about 18 miles) west by south of them. At 10:30, Grave's flagship sent up the signal "Prepare for Action" followed at 11:00 by "Form line of battle ahead" and "two cables separation" (about a quarter mile).

"By God, we've got 'em," Captain Hudson murmured as he looked anxiously through his telescope. Then, much louder: "We've *got* them, Rooney. Have a look," and he handed the brass instrument over to his sailing master. Rooney quickly opened it out to the small mark indicating his particular focal length and snapped it up to his eye.

What he saw caused him to smile. The French fleet was clearly visible, still at anchor, and strung out across the entrance to the Chesapeake from Cape Henry to the middle ground. The wind was behind the British and the weather was fair. Even more importantly, the French were taken by surprise. Over 90 officers and 1800 men were either ashore or ferrying materials back and forth to the beach.

"We do indeed, sir," replied Rooney. "We've still got a ways to go, but they'll never get that herd of cattle underway in time to beat us to the Cape Henry choke point. The tides going in, the wind's against them... they'll have to tack like mad to get out and by then we'll be in position to pick-off each one as she emerges."

"Exactly! Summon the men to quarters. And place us in our communications relay position two cables off the beam of the *Bar-fleur*. And while you're at it, I'd admire if we took some speed off so we don't outrun our station. You can start by getting those stuns'ls off her."

"Aye, aye, sir." Rooney spun around, walked to the quarterdeck rail and began exercising his not inconsiderable lungpower. "All hands, general quarters. General quarters!" The bosun and his mates began trilling on the whistles they always wore around their necks, and took up the cry. It was because of those whistles and their shrill sound that the bosun's mates were called "Spithead Nightingales."

"Starboard watch, stand by to take in stuns'ls," Rooney cried next.

The maneuver was a simple one. They were going to take in the studdingsails, an extra set of sails that hung off long booms on both sides of the ship to give it extra speed. The orders came from Rooney like a Gregorian chant, only at five times the volume.

"Away aloft... Settle the halyards... Haul out the downhauls... Haul taut... Come on there, damn your eyes, I said haul TAUT on that line... That's the way... Lower away, men... Lower away... Haul down..." And with that sequence, the starboard sails were on deck, being subdued and folded by other seamen before the wind could get to them. The quartermaster quietly reminded the helmsmen to mind the rudder. With one stuns'l in and the other out, the ship was going to try to skew around.

The larboard sails quickly followed, which left the booms from which the studdingsails, had hung still sticking out on either side of the ship. They were the next to go.

"All right, starboard watch, stand by to rig in the booms.... Rig in... Aft lower boom... Top up... Now, ease away the fore guy and haul aft..."

The ritual continued until both the starboard and larboard stuns'ls were in and Rooney could finally bellow: "Starboard watch, carry on at general quarters."

It was a big ballet and Rooney was the chorus master calling out the steps. No one hurried. No one looked lost. Everyone knew exactly where and when he or she needed to be on the stage and exactly what they would do when they got there. They had done it all a hundred times before.

During the middle of all this activity, Captain Hudson waved Smith over to his side.

"Mr. Smith I want you to gather our three keenest lookouts. Give each a glass and assign each to watch a different squadron for signals. How well do you know the tactical signal book?"

"I believe I have it memorized, sir. At least I should by now."

"Well, keep it with you anyway."

Hudson reached into a canvas bag that was riddled with brass grommets holding holes open. In the bottom of the bag, a heavy lead weight was sewn in place. This was the bag that contained the ship's codebooks. If the *Richmond* were ever taken—if it even looked like the *Richmond* MIGHT be taken—that bag along with the code books were to be tossed over the side. Failure to do so was simply the end of your career and every captain in the Royal Navy knew it.

Hudson handed one copy of the codebook to Smith. "I am placing you in charge of the communications lookouts and the quartermasters who will be operating the signal flags. You will repeat to the other ships every signal you see, and I want you personally to keep me informed of every signal that comes in. Understood?"

"Aye, aye, sir."

Walker heard the commotion and came up on deck. Looking around, he knew immediately what was happening and that he would probably be ordered below if he made himself conspicuous. The action was all taking place to starboard so Hudson and Rooney were on the starboard side of the quarterdeck one level above him. Walker quietly slid along the larboard side of the main deck and positioned himself along the rail where he could see and hear almost everything, but not be easily seen himself.

The ship was a study in casual nervousness. The men were at their stations, the guns had been rolled back from the gun ports and all the rammers, swabs and other paraphernalia were out of their storage lockers and in the hands of seamen. Shot was lined up in racks along the side of the ship, tubs of water were at hand for swabbing out the guns after each firing, slow matches were lit and smoldering over the water tubs for use in firing the great beasts, and the powder monkeys were standing by amidships with their first charge of powder in boxes between their feet. The decks all had a layer of sand and water spread on them—to provide the men's feet with extra traction, said some—to stop any spilled powder from igniting, said others—to soak up the blood, said still others. The truth was that all three reasons were correct.

"It's funny," Walker thought. "The only people who don't seem nervous were the powder monkeys." These were boys of 10-12 years old who simply had no idea what was coming. "Everyone else however..."

Walker looked around to see men studiously inspecting the roundness of shot, others testing the sharpness over and over of the cutlasses they were issued, others were lounging in various positions trying to make jokes with their shipmates, and still others were sitting on hatch combings or standing by the rails, quiet, lost in thought, just staring out to sea.

Across from him on the upper deck catwalk was Smith looking like a hen who knows the fox is somewhere, but is not quite sure where. He would pace forward, then aft, look up at the *Richmond*'s signal hoists, then look through his telescope to the flagships, then look in his signal book, pace some more, look at the signal hoists and so on. He was already a wreck and the battle hadn't even started.

Up on the quarterdeck Captain Hudson was the picture of casual indifference, standing on the starboard quarterdeck rail with his hands behind his back. He looked like he was out for a pleasure boat ride on the Thames. But then, he *had* to look that way. Nothing would cause the men to come undone quicker than a captain who shows worry or, God forbid, panic.

Amidships on the quarterdeck was Rooney who reflected the same casual indifference as the captain. Fortunately, as it was nearing noon, he had something to do in organizing the midshipmen and master's mates to take the day's noon position. Walker sensed that none of them had ever been happier to be looking through a sextant rather than looking out at the American, or worse, the French fleet.

By noon, the British fleet had sorted itself into the proper order and the frigates had all come back in and positioned themselves to serve their signal relay duties. The British battle line was divided into three divisions. The leading division, called the van, was commanded by Admiral Hood and consisted of six ships, plus the frigates *Richmond* and *Santa Monica*. Next in line was the center division commanded by Admiral Graves, who also had overall command, and his seven ships, including the massive 98-gun flagship, the *London*. Bringing up the rear was Admiral Drake's division with his six ships.

At 1:00 Smith sang out, "Signals from flag, sir. The signal for 'Line ahead' has been taken down. They've just run up..." Smith quickly consulted his codebook. "'To all ships,' 'Form an east-west line,' 'Heading West by South,' and 'One cable separation.'" Graves had ordered the line to turn and head toward Cape Henry where he knew the French would have to come out.

"What do you think, Mr. Rooney? Will the weather hold?"

Rooney looked skyward and gave his usual noncommittal sniff when adjudging the weather. "It'll get a bit squally, sir, but nothing that'll affect us." He held up the eyepiece to his telescope again. "What I am more worried about is the fact the tide is ebbing and the French are finally getting underway."

Within five seconds, every officer with a telescope had it to his eye to confirm Rooney's observation. Within one minute, word of the French getting underway had transferred itself from the quarterdeck to the fo'c'sle at the other end of the ship. And, within five minutes, every person aboard the ship from the mainmast lookout, to the man checking the water level in the bilge knew of it.

"It looks like we'll have the honor today," Hudson said to Rooney. "Obviously Graves wants to pin each French ship between us and the land as they come out. They'll have to run a gauntlet of our ships as they exit the Cape Henry gap and they'll bloody-well run into our division first. It will be glorious, Mr. Rooney. Glorious!"

The tension on the ship rose yet again as everyone who could steal a glance over the bulwark at the French, did. On the opposite side of the bay, the French were making a mess of it. Twenty-four major ships were trying to get underway at the same time. About a third were trying to rendezvous with their squadron leaders, another third were trying to force their way out any way they could, and the final third simply looked lost. The *Pluton* was about to run her jib booms into the *Marseillais* who had just cut off the *St. Esprit*, who shouldn't have been anywhere near either of them. It was like that all over the bay.

By 2:00, the French had sorted themselves out and they came pouring through the Cape Henry Gap.

"Signals from flag, sir. 'To all ships:' 'Execute on my command,' 'Wear ships on larboard tack.' 'Form line ahead,' 'Heading east.'"

This time Captain Hudson, watching the signal flags himself, had decoded the message before Smith. "No, it can't be."

Rooney was more practical. "All hands man the braces. Standby to wear ship. Helm standby to come four points to larboard." Rooney was responsible for the navigation of the ship and didn't have time to question the order. He had to make sure that the *Richmond* could make the turn and still keep perfect station on the *Barfleur*.

Admiral Graves had made what many historians would later call the mistake that cost Britain the war. Actually, it was one of three major mistakes he would make that day but this one was perhaps the most serious.

Upon his command, all British ships were to make a simultaneous 180 degree left turn and, yet again, form into a single file line, only this time heading due east. This would place the British line parallel to the French line and headed in the same direction. He then, amazingly, ordered his entire fleet to back their sails and come to a stop. In short, Graves was letting the French come out of Cape Henry without challenge.

It only took a few minutes for word of this maneuver to reach all hands aboard the *Richmond*. The response was predictable with expressions of disgust emanating in four known and one unidentifiable language. The British could not now challenge the French when and where the French were the weakest. They had to wait until the French had emerged and formed themselves up and *then* fight them.

Worse, from the standpoint of Captain Hudson, his division was no longer in the lead. When it did its "about face" the British line had reversed itself so that now Admiral Drake's division was in the van, Admiral Graves' division still in the center, and Admiral Hood's division, along with the *Richmond*, in the rear.

For the next two hours the British and French fleets ran parallel to each other with the British fleet having the weather gage. In other words, the British ships were up-wind of the French, which gave the British a major advantage. By having the weather gage, the British could attack at the time of their choosing and have the wind at their back. If the French wanted to attack first, they would have to sail against the wind to do so. The ball was clearly in the British court.

At 2:30 Graves had decided the British line was stable in its new formation and ordered the *Shrewsbury*, the lead ship in the formation, to "Lead the formation more to starboard." He repeated the command at 3:17 and again at 3:34. The problem was that the wind that was blowing from off the British larboard beam was also pushing the French ships away from them.

Finally, Graves had had enough. It was after 4:00 and they would be running out of daylight soon. He had to attack now or postpone the attack until tomorrow—and who knew if they would even be in contact with the French in the morning.

The same alternatives had occurred to the men of the *Richmond* but the betting heavily favored the notion that no fight would be happening this day. That was not necessarily a good thing from a morale standpoint. The men were willing and, more importantly, ready to fight. They had resigned themselves to the fact and were mentally prepared for what was to come—at least as prepared as one could be. To have to stand-down from that readiness would make it that much harder to achieve again the following day. Besides, the men also knew that the two fleets would lose visual contact with each other when night came. In the dark of night, either fleet could lose the other just by sailing off in a slightly different direction.

"Two signals from the flag, sir. To all ships. 'Maintain line ahead,' and 'Bear down and engage.'"

Hudson screamed: "Smith, damn your eyes, pay attention to what you're doing sir or, I swear by God Almighty, I'll have you busted to midshipman before the day is out."

Hudson face was red with fury while the blood seemed to have drained completely from Smith's.

"Those are two completely contradictory orders, damn you," Hudson continued. "'Line ahead' means the ships must remain in single file, bow to stern; and 'Bear down and engage' means the ships are to break ranks and engage their opposite in battle. You can't have both at the same time 'midshipman' Smith."

Smith's hands were shaking but he retained enough presence of mind to snap the telescope up to his eyes and look again.

"I am sorry, sir; but those *are* the flags that are flying."

"By God, he's right, sir," chimed in Rooney looking through his telescope. "Both flags are flying at the same time."

"Then it's a signal mistake. Does it look like they're about to correct it?"

"No, sir. I can see the flag hoist," Rooney replied. "I can even see two officers standing in the vicinity; but no one's moving to change anything."

"Then what's he doing?" Hudson muttered. "What in God's name is he DOING?"

This began the second of Graves' three mistakes on the day. Indeed, flying those contradictory signal flags would be hotly debated for decades to come in the hallways of the admiralty. What was supposed to happen was this:

In the British rules of engagement, it was called a "Lashing Approach." Drake would lead the line to starboard, approach the French from an oblique angle to form a "V" with the converging lines, and make first contact. This was to be followed shortly afterwards by the center division (Graves) who would open fire on the French center division, followed shortly thereafter by the rear division (Hood) who would arrive and do the same to the French rear division.

The problem was that the maneuver was designed for two lines of ships that were running in perfect lockstep order. The British had such a line but the French did not. Whether by a fluke of wind and sea, brilliant tactical planning or bad seamanship, the French line was staggered. The van was the closest to the British, the center was offset about a half mile farther away, and the French rear division was a half-mile beyond that. In order for the British center, and especially the rear division, to reach the French more or less together, they would have to really crack on some sail. *That* was what Graves was trying to convey with those two flags. He was saying: "Let's keep our line ahead formation, but center and rear... you're going to have to aggressively close with the enemy because your counterparts are each so much farther away." But there was no signal in the British codebook to communicate that intent. So, he ran up *both* "Maintain line ahead," and "(Aggressively) Engage the enemy" in hopes the squadrons would figure it out.

They did not.

When everyone saw the contradictory signals, the British line broke into chaos. Admiral Drake, in the lead division interpreted the flags as: he should close with the French and begin the battle.

Admiral Hood, in the rear division, knew that according to British rules of engagement the "Line ahead" signal superseded all others, so his division remained doggedly in line, in the rear, and never fired a serious shot. The center division was split. The lead ships, the *Europe* and the *Montagu* headed off after Drake's ships to join in the fight. The middle two ships, the powerful *Royal Oak* and the *London*, decided to bombard the French from while slowly closing. And the rear ships in the division, the *Bedford*, *Resolution* and *America* fired a few long-range shots but stayed in line ahead.

Walker could contain himself no longer. He worked his way over to the main mast ratlines and climbed part way up so he could have a clear view of what was happening. What he saw took his breath away. The six ships in Drake's van had closed to within 40 or 50 yards of the French—point blank range for both sides—and simply started slamming shot into each other.

The British approach to naval warfare was to fire solid shot into the other ship's hull. When the balls penetrated, they would shower the French personnel on the other side with wooden splinters, very much like the shrapnel that would be used in future wars. The theory was that you couldn't fight if you had no men to fight with. The French approach was different. The lower gun decks were tasked with firing round shot at point blank range, like the British and for the same reasons. In addition, the upper gun decks would fire bar-shot at the rigging and masts of the British ships. Bar-shot consisted of two half cannonballs joined by an iron bar. When it came out of the barrel centrifugal force would cause the bar-shot to spin. This whirling object would then rip through the British rigging, sails and masts, tearing them apart. The theory? You can't fight if you have no masts or sails with which to control the ship.

Two different philosophies of warfare were being brought to the ultimate test before Walker's eyes. 517 guns were blasting away at "pistol shot" range—225 on the starboard sides of the six British ships and 292 on the larboard sides of the eight French. By way of comparison, while this battle was occurring General Cornwallis was facing a *total* of 100 American guns spread across the whole Yorktown peninsula—and this was virtually every cannon the American military owned! 517 naval guns were in action and the center and rear divisions of both fleets had yet to commit themselves!

Within minutes, the hulls of the ships on both sides were obscured from Walker's view by gun smoke. All that could be seen were mastheads sticking out above the smoke clouds and flashes coming from within them. It was the flashes that Walker would forever remember. Terrible flashes. Two here. One there. Then three in a ragged volley. They followed each other in rapid succession like random lightning flashes in a deranged storm cloud, followed a few seconds later by the driving "boom" of their report.

Making it worse, Walker could imagine what those flashes and bangs meant. With this flash, a British seaman would fall to the deck with a 12-inch splinter sticking out of his left eye. With that boom, a French seaman would have his right arm torn off by a round shot. With another flash, a British man would never see his children. Boom again and two French brothers would die.

FLASH-BOOM! FLASH-BOOM! FLASH... BOOM! Walker could not stand to watch it, nor could he take his eyes off it. It was like watching gods hurling lightning bolts at each other.

The two ships that had broken off from Grave's center division had now arrived on the scene and the intensity of the battle increased in fury and volume as the other French ships also joined in. To those who were in the middle of it, it was an unending stream of horror

It continued like that for over an hour before Graves finally lowered the "line ahead" signal leaving just the "Bear down and engage." Unfortunately, it was too little too late.

The *Shrewsbury* reeled out of the battle in shreds. Her main topmast was tilted at a crazy angle. She had so much rigging blown away that what was left of her sails looked like so much laundry being hung out to dry. Her starboard side, the side facing the French, was punctured by so many shot holes that it was hard to make out which holes were gun ports and which were gaps caused by the French gun fire.

The next ship in line, the *Intrepid*, wasn't in much better shape. Her rigging too was in ruin; in addition, her rudder was torn to pieces. In short, the *Intrepid* was out of control and being blown by the prevailing breeze toward the French fleet where she would almost certainly be taken captive.

The bow sprit on the *Montagu* had been shot away, which caused her main topmast to snap and hang over the side acting like a sea anchor, spinning her around so she was facing in the wrong direction. The *Princessa* was about to lose her main topmast; and the *Ajax* and *Terrible* were listing at crazy angles, a sure sign that they were taking on water rather badly.

"Another signal from the flag, sir. It's our number and says, "Assist..." Smith paused while he leafed through the back of the signal book where it showed every ship in the British Navy and their identification numbers. "Assist *Shrewsbury*, it says."

"Very well," Captain Hudson replied. "Mr. Smith acknowledge the signal. Mr. Rooney, get us there." Rooney started barking orders to the sail handlers and the *Richmond* leaped off station like a greyhound being taken off a leash.

"Mr. Smith, make signal to the *Shrewsbury*. " Can we assist?"

Almost immediately, the *Shrewsbury* sent back: "Need medical help."

Captain Hudson passed the word for Walker and Susan Whitney and was surprised to see Walker already on the main deck watching him. He and Susan arrived on the quarterdeck just as Rooney pulled the ship up next to the *Shrewsbury*, backed sails and stopped her exactly where he wanted her to be. It was an amazing feat of seamanship that would have drawn openmouthed admiration from anyone who saw it, were not those same people fighting to keep their ship, and by extension themselves, alive.

"Walker, the *Shrewsbury* needs medical help. You and Miss Whitney, gather together whatever you need and off you go."

"Captain, I am *not* a physician."

"I am well aware of that, sir; indeed, you've made that fact abundantly clear on several occasions. But that ship over there needs our help and you, God help us, are the best we have to send. Now, get your buttocks into that boat they are putting over the side, or I will..."

"Yes, sir. Sorry sir," Susan chimed in while literally pulling Walker away from the captain and down the ladder to the main deck.

"Walker, would you please just shut-up for once. The captain has no choice but to send us. *No choice*, do you understand?"

"But..."

"I said, just shut-up. The *Shrewsbury* is a 74-gun ship with over 600 people on board. They are going to have a surgeon on board, possibly two of them—real ones—plus a host of surgeon's mates. They need help. All right, fine. We go over, give them a hand here and there, and come back in a couple of hours. All right? Now, just relax."

* * *

He and Whitney arrived on the *Shrewsbury* to a scene of total carnage. On the main deck, just before the fo'c'sle, bodies were piled up like firewood, presumably to get them out of the way. Some were missing arms or legs, some had huge wood splinters sticking out of them at odd angles and others did not seem to have anything wrong with them at all. They were just dead.

Walker turned to see a number of starboard guns that had been blown off their carriages by direct hits, their gun crews lying on deck as if still hoping to service the gun in death as in life. He had special trouble taking his eyes off one man who had been crushed when an exploding gun landed on top of him. It was obvious that the gun had been red hot from firing and the man had not died immediately. He felt gorge forming in his throat and looked away.

Numerous holes had been blown in the *Shrewsbury*'s side— holes of random size and placement, and so many that it reminded Walker of a large slab of Swiss cheese. When he looked up, he could see the main topmast had broken off and was about to fall either on deck or overboard depending on how far over the ship was listing when it finally let go. Every sail on the ship was in tatters with ball and grapeshot holes in them. Lines and shrouds of all kinds were parted and flapping in the breeze so that Walker had no idea what was still holding the fore and main masts up. Beneath his feet was the sand and water mixture they always put down on deck before battle and Walker wondered where on earth the *Shrewsbury* had gotten all that red sand to mix in with the standard brown. He then realized it was not red sand.

Walker had seen blood and bodies before, but nothing like this—nothing even remotely of this size or savagery. He thought he was numb by the time he and Susan had been led down to the orlop deck to the cockpit where the surgeons had set up what passed for a hospital.

Arriving in the cockpit was like experiencing a scene from Dante's Inferno. His eyes had not adjusted to the dark of the lower deck so initially the only senses that were truly working were his senses of smell and hearing. His nose revealed the odor of rum mixed with the coppery smell of blood. His hearing, however, revealed a series of low moaning sounds as if he were in a darkened pen with a small herd of cattle.

"Make a hole, there. Come on, damn you. Get out of the way. Your turn'll come." Walker looked up and saw a young seaman crossing the room, his front covered in blood and carrying an arm that had just been detached from some hapless soul.

In the center of the room, several large trunks had been pushed together to form an operating table. Hunched over it a surgeon was busy sewing up the former owner of the limb he had just seen being carried away. Bodies were strewn all over the place, some quiet, some moaning softly, and some vigorously calling for help.

Closest to Walker was a man whose right thigh had been torn off close to the pelvis by a round shot and his right arm was shot to pieces. The stump of the thigh presented Walker with a large slab of mangled flesh to view. Most amazing of all was that the man was very much alive, awake and coherent. He was waving his shredded arm in the air and calling out to anyone and everyone to help him. No one would, of course. The man was as good as dead as there was nothing that could be done for injuries that severe. The surgeon's mates were needed to help those who had at least the possibility of living.

As soon as the stricken men saw Walker entering the room he was assaulted on all sides by fresh melancholy cries for assistance by the wounded and dying, coupled with pitiful moans and wailing from men convulsed with fear, pain and despair. Hands, sometimes only stumps, reached out to him. He felt himself start to panic, turned toward the cockpit hatchway, took a step, tripped over a body and fell to his knees. He looked down to see a man who had been near a powder charge that had gone off prematurely. His clothes were in tatters and his face looked like a steak that had been left too long on the grill. It was more—WAY more—than Walker could bear and to his horror he threw-up all over the man. Curiously, the man didn't say a word. He just briefly looked at him as if to say: "That's all right, mate, nothing can happen to me now that's worse than what's already been done" and continued to stare off into the distance calmly awaiting death.

Walker rushed for the orlop deck ladder and ran up the stairs as if the furies of hell were chasing him. He got to the gun deck paused for a second to find the gangway ladder, ran up those stairs and finally lurched out on deck. Finding an unoccupied area, he rushed to the side of the ship and leaned over and screamed. He finally slid down the bulwark until he was seated on the deck Indian style, his head in his hands. His breathing was labored and his eyes, filling with tears, were seeing nothing.

He didn't know how long he had been in that position when he felt someone sitting down beside him and putting an arm on his shoulder. It was Susan Whitney. She had on an apron that already had spots of blood on it. She, of course, had dived right in as soon as they arrived on the orlop deck. After a while, when she could not find Walker anywhere below deck, she surmised what had happened and followed him up.

"Susan, I am sorry. I just can't do this," Walker choked out.

"I know. It's not easy, especially your first time."

"No, you don't understand. I can't do THIS anymore," he said waiving his hand around him. "Any of it. None of it. I don't fit. I don't understand any of it. I don't know what to do; I don't know what not to do; and I don't know how to get back to my normal life. I want out Susan, and I don't know how to get out. I only know I can't do it any more." Walker's eyes began to mist over.

Susan Whitney said nothing for a while.

"I don't know what to tell you, Lucas; but, whether you belong here or not seems pretty irrelevant to me."

"What do you mean?"

She hesitated for a moment. "I am not an educated person like you or Mr. Smith; so I can only speak plainly. I was always taught that all of life's problems are one of two kinds—those you can do something about, and those you can't. You ignore the things you can't change, and work like the devil on the things you can.

"Look, you were aboard a ship that was wrecked in a storm, right?"

"Right."

"So, if there's nothing you can do about that. It goes on the 'I can do nothing about it' pile.

"You are a member of the ships company of the HMS *Richmond*, right?

"Correct."

"Can you do anything about that?"

"No, apparently not."

"So that follows the previous problem onto the 'I can do nothing about it' pile.

"You are the ship's surgeon on the *Richmond*, right?"

"Yes... against my will."

"No matter. You *are* the ship's surgeon. Can you do anything about that?"

"No."

"And there's where you're wrong, because you can *choose*. You might not have had control of Captain Hudson's appointment, but you can choose whether you want to be a good surgeon or a bad one."

"But..."

"But, nothing. Look, Lucas, I think basically you're a good person; but, right now, you're the most useless piece of dung I've ever seen.

"You were given a responsibility and you've run from it. You whine about what's happened to you, but don't give a damn about the people you're harming."

"Who am I harming?"

"Me, for one, because I have to do all the damn work you should be doing. But, more importantly, you're hurting the men aboard the *Richmond*. They need to believe in you, Lucas. They need to believe that you'll be there for them if they're sick or injured. And what about those men below decks just now. Do you think *they* don't need you?

"You're a smart fellow. I saw the way you absorbed those medical books. You have skills. You could be of help. Instead, you'd rather wallow in self-pity. 'Woe is me. I've been pressed. I therefore beg leave to be an utterly useless prick.'

"Yet, I don't get the sense that you're, by nature, that way. That's what I don't understand. You have "leader" written all over you. I can see it in your eyes. Yet you've chosen to be worthless. You've chosen to put your life on the 'I can do nothing about it' pile. And that, I am sorry, disgusts me."

And with that, Susan got up and disappeared down the forward gangway ladder.

Walker sat alone on the deck for nearly 20 minutes. No one knows what he thought about as, later on, he never talked about it. What we do know is this. He arrived on deck that day a 22 year old who was going on 18 years of age. When he finally stood up and followed Susan below, he was 22 going on 40.

* * *

Walker had no idea how long he had been asleep but, however long it was, it wasn't enough.

"Meester Walker, Sir. Meester Walker. Time to geet up. De Captain wants to see you and Meester Smith." Angelo, the wardroom steward, a native of the Windward Islands, was vigorously shaking him awake.

"Tell him I've died," Walker replied and rolled over.

"No, I tol' him dat last time and got in trooble." Angelo got Walker to sit up and swung him around placing a cup of coffee in his hands. Walker never ceased to be amazed at Angelo's ability to come up with real coffee beans for his coffee, as opposed to the burnt breadcrumbs and hot water that was otherwise called "coffee" on this ship.

With Angelo's help, he managed to splash some water on his face and shave. As he dressed in the clothes Angelo laid out, he realized that he no longer felt like he was putting on a costume when he got dressed. The clothes of an 18th Century gentleman felt good, even if they were castoffs and loaners from the other ship's officers. He drew the line at wearing what he called "culottes," however. He had never liked them. Trousers had recently been introduced and they were the rage in London. That gave him all the excuse he needed to wear them.

The sunlight caused his eyes to water as he walked out on the main deck and looked out to sea. The French were still there. It had been two days since the Battle of the Capes and not much more had happened. The two fleets had continued east, warily eyeing each other but no one wanted to make the first move to renew the fighting. The *Shrewsbury*, *Intrepid*, *Montagu* and *Princessa* were off station tagging along after the fleet as they underwent repairs. Admiral Drake, a descendent of the great Sir Francis Drake, shifted his flag from the *Princessa* to the *Alcide* and it was reported that Captain Robinson of the *Shrewsbury* had had his leg amputated below the knee. Captain Colpoys of the *Orpheus* took over for him. The *Terrible* was taking on so much water that Graves had ordered her burned and the *Ajax* was leaking badly. A pall of disappointment and despair hung over the ship's company.

Walker proceeded to the captain's cabin and found Smith already standing before the captain's long table. Walker joined him.

"Ah, there you are, Mr. Walker," the captain said jovially. It was the first time he had ever talked to him in a friendly voice and it startled Walker.

"First of all, I've received a report from the First Lieutenant of the *Shrewsbury* stating that you had worked tirelessly during your time onboard and may be credited with saving the lives of any number of their men—including that of their captain. For that, he sends his respects and gratitude and, to which, I add mine. You reflected very well on this ship."

Walker didn't know what to say. He remembered the time only as a blur—endless hours of cutting, and sewing, and removing musket balls, and wood fragments. He did not sleep and only took two breaks for water and a few ship's biscuits. He was still working off the sleep deficit.

"Thank you, sir."

I also received a message from Admiral Hood, although, I must admit, I am not quite sure what to make of it. It seems the *Richmond* has been selected for what the admiral describes as a 'very important mission,' which will require two dependable officers. I selected Smith and he selected you. Don't ask me to provide the logic behind that choice, but there we have it."

Walker looked over at Smith who smiled and gave a small, almost imperceptible, shrug.

"In any event, the admiral wishes to see the three of us this afternoon at four bells. Be on deck and ready to go 20 minutes before that.

* * *

The *Barfleur* was the largest wooden object Walker had ever seen up-close. She was 177 feet long and 50 feet wide. She mounted 90 guns on three decks, weighed almost 2000 tons and drew 21 feet. Everything about her was big—including the access ladder—which allowed the three of them to scramble up the side with little effort.

Admiral Hood's stateroom followed the pattern of size. The *Richmond*'s captain's cabin, wardroom and officer sleeping area would have fit in Hood's meeting room alone. The room was tastefully appointed with fine furniture, hangings and lamps from the best London shops. Given that, Walker was startled when he looked down at a floor that was covered in plain canvas and painted in a black and white checkerboard pattern. It provided almost a comic contrast from the high quality furnishings.

Contrary to his reputation as a dour man of few words, Hood seemed positively gregarious.

"Captain Hudson! Good to see you again."

"Good to see you too, admiral. May I present my First Lieutenant, William Sidney Smith; and our ship's surgeon, Mr. Walker."

"Good afternoon, gentleman. Please, be seated. I have a rather exceptional Madeira here if you would care for some." Hood didn't wait for an answer but walked over to a sideboard and poured four glasses. This gave Walker a chance to study him over.

Hood was not a large man but, nevertheless, seemed to exude authority. He had a small almost frail build with a head that seemed too large for his body. Indeed, his head was his most striking feature.

At first Walker thought he was wearing a powdered wig but it turned out he was wrong. Hood had a full head of pure white hair that hung down in carefully coffered ringlets. His face bore a striking resemblance to the pictures he had seen of George Washington, except Hood's nose was bigger and he had two shaggy, almost unruly, eyebrows.

Hood, returning with the wine glasses, broke Walker's reverie.

"Gentlemen," Hood began, "I'll not detain you long; but there is an urgent matter that I must discuss with you. Before doing so, however, I must warn you that what I am about to tell you, and the mission you are about to perform, is of the utmost secrecy. Is that clear?"

Hood paused for a moment to look at each of them. His eyes were dead serious.

"As I am sure you know, Our Sovereign, George III, has nine sons. The third oldest of these is Prince William Henry. You might also know that, for the past several years, the prince has been enrolled as a midshipman in His Majesty's Navy; and, truth be known, he has actually developed into quite a good one.

"What you might not know is that several months ago Prince William was sent to New York on a mission to raise the morale of the troops, not to mention the morale of the Tory population of the city who are sympathetic to us. Nothing quite like having a real-live prince at your gala ball to boost the spirits, what?

"Anyway, shortly after his arrival Washington moved his army from New Jersey to the outskirts of New York in an obvious move to lay siege to it. He knew the prince was there and at least one attempt was made to capture him, but it failed.

"It was therefore felt prudent to send the prince off to go build morale somewhere else, so he was sent to visit his 'Uncle Cornwallis' in Yorktown. What could go wrong there, right? Cornwallis had about a third of the British Army with him, and he had been rampaging through the southern colonies, almost unopposed, for months."

Walker looked around. Smith seemed shocked, but Captain Hudson had visibly gone pale.

"But that means... I mean, sir, are you saying..." Hudson stuttered.

"Yes," the admiral answered. "The prince is currently in Yorktown. Cornwallis is cut off on the landward end of the peninsula by some 22,000 rebel troops—6000 under Lafayette, 4000 French troops brought by De Grasse, 4000 more frogs from Rhode Island, and 8000 rebels that Washington moved down from New York. They have over 100 heavy guns dug in and pointed down Cornwallis' throat. To combat this, Cornwallis has 6000 or 7000 exhausted troops and a handful of 6-pound cannon that I wouldn't use for ceremonial purposes, let alone to fight. His only hope was that our fleet—that we—would control the seaward side so he could remain supplied and, if necessary, evacuate his troops. And, we failed."

"But, sir," Hudson began. "With all due respect to you and Admiral Graves, I am not sure we *have* failed. Certainly, we seemed to have lost the fight a few days ago, but that was only a skirmish. Even now, we could engage and still win."

"Yesterday afternoon there was a meeting of Admiral Graves, Admiral Drake and myself—a rather heated one, I might add. Admiral Graves has determined that we suffered too many losses on that first day to engage the enemy again."

"Then why don't we pivot around and race the French back to the Chesapeake? I am sure our ships are faster than theirs. His fleet has been at sea a long time in the Caribbean. Their hulls must be completely covered with moss and barnacles, which would slow them down considerably. Let's get back there first, form up at the mouth of the Chesapeake and dare them to take the place away from us. No French fleet has ever sailed into a bay or harbor occupied by one of our fleets to fight us. Not once. They won't do it."

"You know, you might make a good admiral yet, Charles. Of course, you're right; but Admiral Graves doesn't see it that way. He believes De Grasse's real objective is New York—never mind that Washington and most of his army is now here at Yorktown. He thinks as soon as we head to the Chesapeake, De Grasse will head north, land troops, and take the city. So we tag along and tag along, not retreating but not fighting either, until we see what he's up to."

Hood gave a tired sigh as if he couldn't believe the stupidity of his senior officer, then added: "Meanwhile, you have a job to do.

"Here are your official orders." Hood slid a sealed envelope across the table to Hudson. "You and the Frigate *Iris* are to detach yourself and make best possible speed back to the Yorktown peninsula. Upon arrival, the *Iris* is to go into the bay and destroy the French anchorage. It seems that in their haste to depart most of the French ships did not haul in their anchors. They put buoys on their anchor cables and just let the cables run out to be retrieved and reattached later. The *Iris* is going to destroy the buoys, which should cause a great deal of confusion on board the French ships when and if they come back. That confusion might come in handy at some point.

"While the *Iris* is busy in the Chesapeake, you are to proceed to Yorktown. You will land, I presume, these two gentlemen, get Prince William Henry and take him, again with best possible speed, to New York and deliver him to Governor Clinton for immediate transport back to England."

Hood slid another sealed envelope across the table. "In case you run into any objections anywhere along the line—including from the prince—this is a letter from Governor Clinton authorizing and requiring the full cooperation of any authorities you should meet. He makes it quite clear, however, that these orders are not coming from him but directly from His Majesty.

"Are there any questions?"

Smith and Walker shook their heads, Captain Hudson said "No, sir," and Admiral Hood stood up to see them off.

"Oh yes, Charles. One more thing..."

"Yes, sir?"

"Don't even think about failing."

CHAPTER FOUR

CAPTAIN Hudson had made his gig available to transport the two men ashore. There were six seamen on board, three on a side, rowing at a steady, measured, pace. In the bow sat a young midshipman trying to look as dignified as possible having just been evicted from his usual place in the stern by Smith and Walker. A ship's bosun's mate manned the tiller. All of the men were in their regular work-a-day clothes, although that would certainly change if this same group came back to pick up the prince. Walker was looking glum.

"Come on, Lucas. I've done you a good turn. We'll spend a night ashore, eat some decent food for a change, gather up His Nibs and be gone. Besides, there are other possible delights."

"Such as?"

"The Town of York was not evacuated prior to the arrival of the !@#$% Jonathan's. Which means there are, I am sure, any number of young ladies up ahead who will be delighted to make our acquaintance."

"Oh, yeah. Seven thousand males running around loose and the ladies are just waiting for a penniless lieutenant and a half-crazy surgeon to show up."

"Have a little faith, will you?"

"Right."

The *Richmond* was anchored at the mouth of the York River while the *Iris* was a few miles away doing its mischief at the French anchorage in front of the Chesapeake. The boat ride was a short one, no more than a half hour from the ship to the Yorktown wharf.

Smith stepped out of the gig and on to the Yorktown pier. "Let me say it one more time, you men are to meet us tomorrow, at precisely noon, at the mouth of Wormley Creek about three miles down river from here. Is that clear?" Smith looked around at the nodding heads. "Very well, then. Off you go."

And with that, the boat was dismissed. Smith and Walker glanced around briefly, strode down the long wooden walkway and found themselves at the corner of Water and Read Street.

"Do you have any idea where you're headed?" Walker asked. They were walking up Read Street, a long winding incline, which reminded Walker how far out of shape he had gotten. It also re-introduced him to the concept of humidity. By the time he had reached the top of the hill, both he and Smith were drenched in sweat.

"More or less," Smith replied. "I know that this way is the main part of town. Someone there's bound to know where Cornwallis has... There! There's Cornwallis' headquarters, right there." Smith was pointing off to the left at a large two-story brick building.

"How do you know?"

"Look at the garden behind it, and the steps to the front door. Ever seen so many officers without a damn thing to do in one place? That's got to be headquarters."

The building they entered was easily the most imposing in town. It was a two-story mansion built with expensive glazed Flemish bond brickwork. The house was on a small hill. Behind it and one tier down was an expanse of lawn; and behind that and another tier down was a classic English garden. It was formerly the home of Thomas Nelson, Jr. He was a signer of the Declaration of Independence, a former Governor of Virginia and currently, as commander of the Virginia Militia, was several miles away planning to blow the hell out of his own house if that was what was needed to defeat Cornwallis. Being a naval officer, Smith's entry into the wide foyer of the mansion created a bit of a stir.

"Lieutenant? I am Captain Wilcox, General Cornwallis' Aide-de-Camp. May I help you?"

"Yes, I am Lieutenant Smith and this is Mr. Walker. We've come from Admiral Hood. Is the General available?"

"I'll see, but I am sure he'll want to see you right away. Please be seated." Wilcox slipped out of the room and returned in a few minutes. "The General will see you now."

They were led into what must have once been a lovely parlor. It was now Cornwallis' office with a desk at one end and a meeting table at the other that was currently covered with maps. Cornwallis was standing at a window looking out at the garden when the two entered. He turned and got immediately to business.

"Lieutenant, Mr. Walker, please be seated. Welcome to Yorktown." Smith and Walker settled into two overstuffed chairs before the General's desk and tried to ignore the sweat that had soaked their shirts. Cornwallis continued to stand at the window where the sunlight streaming in seemed to emphasize his size. "At one time," Walker thought, "he must have been a very powerfully built man." And in all likelihood, he still was, but he had that portly look almost all large men develop in their latter years. The most striking thing about him, besides his receding hairline, was his eyes. They seemed to Walker to look so tired—like they had seen everything they wanted to see and more.

"My aide tells me you bring news from Admiral Graves."

"No, sir. We come from Admiral Hood. It's about Prince William Henry."

"Prince William Henry? What's he got to do with anything? What about the fleet? Where's the fleet?"

"When we left, the two fleets were about 60 miles off shore continuing to parallel each other. As you know we had an action a few days ago, but it was... ah... inconclusive."

Smith was trying to be charitable. Walker was thinking, "We got our tails kicked, as far as I am concerned."

"Did Hood say when Graves would be returning?"

"No, sir."

"Then what the hell's going on? Graves has got to get back here and secure the mouth of the Chesapeake. Even if he can't hold the French off forever, he can at least hold them long enough for me to get my troops across the York or the James River and off this God forsaken peninsula. We can't stay here any longer."

Cornwallis seemed to catch himself and after a moment said: "I am sorry, lieutenant. That's not your problem, of course.

"You say you're here concerning something about Prince William?"

"Yes, sir." Smith stood up and handed over the letter from Governor Clinton and Cornwallis read it immediately, his face darkening with each paragraph.

"I see. I know Admiral Hood quite well. Did you know that my younger brother William is a naval officer? He's captain of the *Lion*, off with Admiral Rodney somewhere or another. Through him, I know Sam Hood and I know he wouldn't have sent you if he didn't think it was necessary—very necessary."

Cornwallis turned back to the window and seemed to drift off for a few moments. "All right," he said coming back to the present. "How do you plan to get the prince back to your ship?"

Our ship, the HMS *Richmond*, is currently at the mouth of the York River. I've arranged to have us picked up tomorrow at noon where Wormley Creek enters the York. We selected an out-of-the-way pickup point because I want the prince's departure to be as quiet as possible—at least until the *Richmond* is safely away."

"Good thinking," Cornwallis said as he drew Smith and Walker over to the table with all the maps.

"Just here is a house that was once owned by a loyalist planter by the name of James Moore. You gather up the prince and explain what's going on. I'll have his things packed, shipped over to Moore House and I'll authorize horses for the three of you. You can go to Moore House, spend the night there, pick up his things, take them to Wormley Creek and... well... God speed."

"Thank you, sir. By chance do you know where the prince might be right now?" Smith asked.

"Where he always is. You'll find him a bit further down Main Street at the Swan Tavern. He only comes by here to sleep.

"I think that will be all, gentlemen. If you need anything else, please let me know. If not, good luck with your mission."

Cornwallis shook hands with both men and the two quickly found themselves out on the street headed for The Swan.

* * *

The Swan Tavern was actually a complex of several buildings at the corner of Main and Ballard Streets. The main structure was a one-story white frame building with a large white swan hanging off of a post out front. It was a tavern but it also doubled as a small hotel. As you walked in there was a hallway and stairs directly before you. As opposed to most open taverns, the main floor of the swan was divided into four rooms; each about 20 by 30 feet and each with a small fireplace built diagonally in a corner; and each contained several tables for eating or drinking.

The hallway led to a set of stairs in back, which led down to a door, which opened to the back yard. Along one side was a stairway leading to rooms upstairs in what Walker would have called an attic. One room was for the innkeeper and his wife, the others were for travelers; with often as many as eight or ten people stuffed into each. Behind the tavern were four other buildings: a kitchen, a smokehouse, a stable and a privy, plus a well.

Walker and Smith entered through the front door and stepped to one side as their eyes got used to the relative darkness of the tavern's interior. Only two of the tavern's eight tables were occupied. In the room to the left, by the door, two men were drinking and talking with each other. Walker would not have found that remarkable except for two things. First, one of the men had a shock of the most outrageously red hair he had ever seen; and, second, the man with the red hair seemed genuinely startled to see Smith walk in. A raucous card game was in progress in the room to the right. One of the players, a lad of about 16, dressed in a naval midshipman's uniform and quite obviously drunk, suddenly stood up almost tipping his chair over.

"Trump! Trump! Trump! Trump! He yelled, slamming a card down with each exclamation. "That'll be a Guinea each, gentleman," he said sitting back down with evident satisfaction and reaching for a tankard. "And, thank you for your contribution to a poor midshipman's sustenance."

"I think we've found our man," Walker said as he and Smith walked over to the table and caught the prince's eye.

"Ah, and now the fleet's in," cried the prince. "That calls for another round to salute my brothers of the waves," he said signaling a bar maid over.

She stood before the prince's chair smiling as he fondled her buttocks. "A round for my two friends here, my dear.

"You two," he gestured at two of the army officers who had been playing cards with him. "Get lost." Then he gestured to Walker and Smith. "Gentlemen, please, take seats. What news have you?"

Walker was looking at the prince like he had crawled out from under a rock, while Smith just sat and sputtered. Under normal circumstances, Smith was one of the most confident people Walker had ever known. Be that as it may, he was still a commoner and had a commoner's tendency to come unglued in the presence of royalty.

"Sir... I mean, your Highness... Ah... We've just come from Admiral Hood and... ah..." Smith was tripping over words like an adolescent boy trying to ask a girl to his first dance.

"Hood? Sammy Hood? I thought Graves was in charge?" The bar maid had returned with a tray of wooden tankards which she was distributing. The prince had his hand underneath her dress this time.

"Will that be all, my Lord?"

"For the moment, yes; but who knows about later on." She blushed, smiled, and moved to another room.

Turning back to Smith and Walker: "Well, gentlemen, do we not drink a toast to our great fleet's victory? I'll bet Graves has those Frogs running, or should I say hopping, halfway back to Brest by now."

"Well, sir, not exactly. You see, we've been tasked with..."

"Barney, you old snake!" The prince was waiving at a senior officer who had just walked in." Walker wished he understood British army insignia better. He had no idea if the new officer was a general or a coronet. "Good to see you!"

"Your highness, if I may continue. You see..."

It was at that moment that the prince somehow managed to both burp and fart at the same time. At a college student party, Walker might have expected it; but coming from this overbearing charter member of the Lucky Birth Club... it was too much.

Walker's voice was low and conspiratorial. "Your Highness, what my friend here is trying to say is that there are some matters we need to discuss that are... state secrets, for your ears only, you understand," he said as he furtively looked around him. "If we could perhaps adjourn to a more discreet area."

"Oh yes, I see. Quite. Quite."

"Perhaps out back, Your Highness."

Walker and Smith half supported the prince as they made their way down the brief stairs and out the back door.

"So, what is..." the prince started to say.

"Not here. Perhaps over there." Walker led the prince to the back right corner of the yard where there was a slightly dilapidated livery stable with a large, very full, watering trough in front. When they got to the trough Walker turned the prince around so he was facing him. He then slipped his right leg behind the prince and flipped him over his hip into the trough.

"Walker!!" Smith let out a horrified yell, but Walker was already on the prince. Despite Smith's best efforts to drag him off, Walker grabbed the prince by his shirt collar, plunged his head under water, and then brought him up.

"Now listen up, gumdrop! We've got some important business here so..." The prince's head went under again, then back up. "So it's time for you to sober-up." Back under and up. "Is that reasonably clear to you?" The prince was coughing which mattered not a bit to Walker. Under and up again. "Are you starting to get the picture here?" He started to put him under again but the prince was shaking his head and grabbing Walker's arm.

"No. Please, that's enough."

Walker threw him back in the water and stood up. Smith was wide-eyed and utterly paralyzed. And the prince? The prince started laughing.

"Oh my," he said as he got up out of the fetid trough. In between peals of laughter he said: "Oh my, you have no idea how bad that water tastes."

Climbing out of the trough the prince immediately grew serious and said: "All right, now what's going on."

The prince was a slightly built lad with light brown hair, thin lips and a pale almost feminine complexion. His blue eyes were set off by a natural rosy coloration in his cheeks and he had an underlying air of confidence, almost cockiness, about him. All in all, he was a very handsome young man.

"Perhaps we should start this again from the beginning. I am Lucas Walker, ship's surgeon from the *Richmond*. This is her First Lieutenant William Sidney Smith. We've just come from the fleet." And Walker explained the situation and the very real danger that existed for the prince.

"I see," said the prince. "And you're convinced that the Frogs will again secure control of the Chesapeake?"

"Yes, I am, and so is Admiral Hood. That's why he sent us to get you the hell out of here. You can understand the international implications of your being captured or, worse, killed."

"So, what are we to do?"

"From here we go to someplace called Moore House and spend the night. General Cornwallis will have your things packed and sent there. Tomorrow at noon, we'll rendezvous with a boat and go out to the ship. From there, we head to New York to give you over to Governor Clinton. And from there, I don't know; I suspect you'll probably be shipped back to England." The prince looked saddened by the news, especially the prospect of being sent back to England.

"All right," the prince sighed. "It's getting late so we'd better get some horses." The three men turned and started walking back to the tavern, the prince still sopping wet.

"Oh yes, Walker, one more thing."

"Yes?"

The prince turned and caught Walker on the side of his chin with a roundhouse right that sent him staggering back several paces and almost knocked him down.

"That's for dunking me in the tank."

It was Walker's turn to laugh. "Maybe this guy isn't so bad after all," he thought.

* * *

Horses were waiting for the three when they got back to Nelson House and they began their journey along the road headed southeast out of town. As they were getting on their horses, however, Walker looked back and saw the man with the red hair and his companion walking down Main Street. Walker got Smith's attention.

"Sidney, don't do it obviously, but look behind me at those two men walking by the Custom's House across the street," he said. "Notice anything strange about them?"

Smith glanced over Walker's shoulder and studied the two over.

"They're sailors, aren't they?"

"Yes, but how did you conclude that?"

"Look at the way they walk or, I should say, waddle, with their feet wide apart as if expecting the ground to start rolling and pitching under them at any moment."

Walker was impressed with Smith's power of deduction.

The prince quickly assumed the role of the affable host pointing out the uniforms of the various regiments as they headed out of town—the 17th Foot, 33rd Foot, the Royal Artillery and the two units composed of American loyalists: the British Legion and the green-coated Queen's Rangers. He saved special pride, however, for the Brigade of Guards and the Jagers.

The Brigade of Guards was composed of men from three units that ordinarily served as bodyguards to the king—the Grenadier Guards, the Coldstream Guards, and the Scots Guards. The brigade that was presently at Yorktown consisted of 15 men chosen from each of the three companies. They were the elite of the elite, knew it, carried themselves that way, and backed it up with a reputation as utterly fearless fighters.

Equal in reputation to the Brigade were the Jagers. Very early in the revolution, King George III realized he didn't have enough troops to defeat the rebels and meet all his other military obligations around the world. However, in addition to being the King of England, he was also the King of the German Principality of Hanover; so, he drew troops from there and from neighboring kingdoms and sent them to America. In all, some 30,000 troops were raised in that way.

The Jagers were from Hesse-Kassel and were recruited from among the gamekeepers and foresters of the area. These were men who had lived their lives in the woods and, coupled with being crack shots, this made them extremely useful as light infantry and reconnaissance units.

"Look, over there," the prince pointed out. "See those men with the green coats and brown pants. Those are the Jagers.

"Want to know their ranks? There are two officers, one sergeant and seven enlisted."

"How can you know that from this distance, Your Highness?" They all looked the same to Smith.

"Simple. Look at the feathers in their hats. If the feather is all white, the person is an officer. If it is white with a red tip, he's a sergeant; and if the feather is green, the person is an enlisted man.

"Terrific fighters, those men. It's said they can knock the eye out of a squirrel at 300 paces with those new rifles they're carrying. They cost us a fortune, make no mistake; but the Jagers and their rifles have paid for themselves a dozen times over."

They passed through the close-in town defenses and crossed the second defensive line at Redoubt #9 with a friendly wave toward the soldiers stationed there. The redoubt itself was nothing more than a large circular trench with the earth piled on a mound on the inside. Sticking out of the mound and hanging over the ditch was a series of sharpened logs. To take the redoubt the opposing force would have to lose valuable time overcoming those sharpened logs in the teeth of an enemy firing down on them. Redoubts #9 and #10 were designed to anchor the British left flank and Walker could see no easy way of taking them.

About a mile later, the three turned off the main road and up a long drive to a neat white frame, two-story, building. It was nearly dusk but the house staff saw them coming and were lined up outside to greet them in typical English manor fashion. A black groom led the horses away and the housekeeper showed them into the parlor and poured them each a glass of a spectacularly good Cabernet Sauvignon and left several bottles.

Walker, the ex-alcoholic, looked very uncomfortable and slightly agitated. He demanded that the servant remove his wine glass and produce a pitcher of lemon-drink, which was quickly done.

The three sat around the parlor table looking down at the green felt in awkward silence.

Smith finally spoke first. "Your Highness, would you like..."

Walker rolled his eyes. The prince caught it.

"Right, Walker. I quite agree."

"Look, Smith, I am a midshipman in His Majesty's Navy. As such, I do not use my title. You are a lieutenant and you are senior to me, so how about we dispense with the 'Your Highness' and 'Your Lordship.'"

"Certainly, Your..." Smith began, and then corrected himself.

Silence.

"All right then," the prince broke the lengthy pause. "If you two are going to be my rescuers, perhaps I should know a bit more about you, what?

"Lieutenant, could we begin with you?"

Smith started as the prince topped off his and Smith's glass with some more wine and Walker's with some more lemon-drink. He provided an abbreviated version of the story he told Walker several days earlier, omitting the parts about his father's character but mentioning his resignation as a result of the Sackville Scandal. The prince asked several pertinent but not unkind questions about the affair and let it go.

Next up was Walker, and the prince started pouring another round of drinks.

"Well," he began. "I am an officer in the United States Navy." The prince shot upright, looked at Smith who, in turned, looked like he wanted to crawl under the table. After a few seconds, however, the prince smiled.

"Oh, very good, Mr. Walker," he said laughing. "That's a good one."

Walker was not smiling. Smith looked stricken.

"All right. Maybe I am not an officer, but I *am* an American—no matter what *some* people might think of the legitimacy of that claim."

Walker then launched into his story of his shipwreck, rescue by the *Richmond* and of his being pressed into British service.

"Your Lordship," Smith interjected. "I must point out that, despite his protestations, in the recent engagement Mr. Walker was singled out with distinction for his medical efforts on behalf of our men and officers."

"I see." Prince William mused. "But tell me, Mr. Walker... Lucas... If you feel so strongly about your nationality, if you have such patriotism and devotion to the rebel cause, why are you not out there with General Washington fighting for that cause?"

Walker again looked uncomfortable and it took him some time to reply. "As of a few years ago, I was the youngest Professor of Natural Philosophy in the history of Harvard College... and I was a good one." Walker looked up sharply as if to emphasize the latter point. "And then, I don't know, but it all went wrong.

"Part of it, I think, was my disillusion with higher education... the phoniness of it all, the rampant intellectual dishonesty. And then... something else happened. Anyway, to shorten my story, I had long had a problem with drinking; but now I started drinking with a vengeance. Within a year I was bounced out of Harvard after a rather embarrassing incident, then kicked out of the College of New Jersey, then... well, let's just say things went downhill from there.

"I knew I had to stop drinking or it would be the end of me. So, I did."

Walker paused for a long moment and breathed a mirthless laugh. "'So, I did.' My God, that phrase makes it sound like it was so easy—like snuffing out a candle. It wasn't. It was as close to hell as I expect to encounter prior to my arrival there. But, I did it. By God in heaven, I *did* it.

"Shortly after that, I heard that a new college had been formed called the College of Charleston, so I was on my way to South Carolina when that double-damned storm hit.

"And, believe it or not, at one point I *did* try to volunteer for the army. I showed up, dead drunk, and generously offered my services. Needless to say, they were politely declined." Walker smiled briefly; "More specifically, some burley Sergeant physically threw me out of the tent."

Walker sat back in his chair. "So, as you can see... I don't belong in Washington's army, and I don't belong in King George's. In point of fact, I don't belong anywhere, at any time, for any purpose. But, however poor an example I might be, I am an American." And Walker took a big sip from his lemon drink.

He watched the prince's expression go from alarm, to perplexity, to amazement.

No, Walker decided. He wouldn't advertise it, but if he were ever pressed about his background again he would stick with the story as it happened and let the chips fall where they may. With luck, maybe people would simply view him as a harmless old drunk and let him be. "Ah, there was Smith," he thought, "right on cue."

"I am sure that story sounds a good-deal more extreme than is warranted. I must point out that when we picked him up he had a severe gash that might cause him to exaggerate..."

"It was just a scratch," corrected Walker.

"...a *severe* gash," Smith repeated glaring daggers at Walker, "over his left eye. You can still see the scar there. But, I can assure you, my friend here is a most capable individual."

"Yes," the prince replied. "I am sure. And I hope for the speediest of recoveries from your... ah... injuries, Mr. Walker."

"Oh, I am quite recovered," Walker said smugly. "But thank you anyway."

Another silence while the prince poured another round.

"What about you?" Walker finally asked. "Tell us about yourself. I don't even know your name. William Henry something."

The prince laughed. "'William Henry Something' is about as good as anything. You see, technically, I don't have a last name. Officially, I am The Prince William Henry, Duke of Clarence and St. Andrew's, Defender of the Faith, etc. etc. But when I joined the navy, they needed a last name to put on the rolls. My father is of the German House of Hanover, so that became my official navy name: William Henry Hanover."

"Why the navy?"

"I am the third son and you know how it goes. The first son inherits, the second goes into the military, and the third goes into the clergy. Well, the clergy certainly wasn't going to happen in my case, so I moved up a rung to the military instead. I vastly preferred the navy to the army; and, for once, someone actually listened to what I wanted, so I was enrolled as a midshipman."

Hanover was starting to feel the effects of the wine and of a very long day. "I love it, gentleman, I truly do."

"Love what?" Smith asked.

"The navy."

"This is because you have a penchant for bad food, perhaps?" Walker asked.

"No, I am perfectly serious." Hanover paused to think about what he was going to say next and whether he should say it. The wine he had consumed decided the matter for him. "Do you understand that the sea does not give a tinker's-damn that I am the son of His August Majesty King George III? It simply could care less.

"When I am on watch the wind and rain is just as cold for me as it is for everyone else. The sea tosses me about, just like it does everyone else. The wind blows when, where and how IT wants, not the way I want. And, if the ship sank, my drowning would be just the same as that of the lowest cabin boy."

"Am I missing something here? I am still looking for the benefits of going to sea."

"I just stated them. You need to have grown up a royal to know what I am talking about, Walker. Everything, and I mean every-

thing, in your life is planned to the last detail. Where you go, when you go there, whom you'll see, and what you'll say has all been choreographed weeks in advance.

"You'll not credit the extent to which the sea gives me a sense of freedom. Whether I rise or fall is up to me—and only me. I can be a man, or at least find out if I am a man, on my own merits. Hell, back in London, there are people who would sell their soul for the 'honor' of wiping my ass once a day so I wouldn't have to do it myself. "Yes, indeed, Madam. I am the Lord High Keeper of the Royal Toilet Paper. My job is to make sure the prince need never make an ass of himself again.'"

Hanover erupted into a contagious laughter at his own joke that even had Walker going.

"No, thanks. I am a midshipman. I am still learning. In a few years, I'll be eligible to take the lieutenant's exam and if I pass or not, I'll have no one to blame but myself. I like that, gentlemen. I truly do."

"But what about... I mean, aren't you in line for the throne or something?"

"Oh, no! My father was thoughtful enough to provide an heir and a spare ahead of me. My brother George is Prince of Wales; he will inherit. Next is my brother Frederick, the Duke of York and the spare. Then, there is me. As the spare, Fred's job is to sit around and make sure George still has a pulse each morning. I am the one who actually gets to have a life.

"How about you two? Any brothers or sisters?"

Smith nodded and told him about his two brothers Charles and John Spencer. Walker replied "Two older brothers, Lawrence and Kenneth; and a sister with the fancy name, Victoria Alexandrina. We used to tease her unmercifully about that."

"Really? Her name is Victoria Alexandrina?" asked Hanover. "My younger brother Edward swears that if he ever has a girl-child he is going to name her Alexandrina Victoria. What a coincidence!"

Walker was leaning on the back two legs of his chair, feeling warm and good. He was idly mulling over Hanover's last remark about "Victoria Alexandrina" versus "Alexandrina Victoria" when an idle thought appeared in the back of his head.

"I wonder." Walker mused out loud. "If Edward's future daughter ever became Queen, would she be Queen Alexandrina, or Queen Victoria?

Hanover laughed. "Let's hope that never happens. In order for that to occur I would have to be both dead and childless. Let's see, I would be King William... the fourth, I believe. Yes, King William IV."

With that, William raised his glass. "Gentlemen, a toast: Here's to King William IV and Queen Victoria... May England never come to such a sorry state of affairs."

After the toast, all three men lapsed into a dreamy silence, lost in their own thoughts. Smith was contemplating how he would tell his father that he had been in the presence of royalty. William was thinking with distaste about his probable return to England. And Walker was thinking about William.

"William IV?" he thought. "Who knows? That half-snockered kid across the table from me might someday be the damn King of England—that is *if* we can get him to safety. And what happens if we don't? Let's see... no William IV and God knows what he will do or not do during his reign... and if there was no William IV would there ever be a Queen Victoria? I wonder," he thought to himself, "if we really *are* playing with history here."

"Lucas?" Smith inquired. Walker looked up to see both men watching him carefully. "Are you all right?"

"Yes. Yes, I am just fine.

"I think we should be getting to bed soon, gentlemen. We've got a long day ahead of us tomorrow."

And with varying mumbled assents, the three men headed upstairs to their rooms.

* * *

Perhaps it was the effect of the wine but all three wound-up sleeping-in on a perfectly gorgeous Virginia morning. The prince's trunks had arrived late the previous night and were still in the wagon. After a leisurely breakfast, the three mounted up and, with the wagon trailing, began a journey of less than a mile to the rendezvous point where Wormley Creek emptied into the York River.

As they got close to the headland overlooking the juncture, Smith trotted on ahead. When Hanover and Walker caught up to him, they saw him kneeling next to his horse, sitting back on his legs, staring out to sea.

Walker and Hanover joined him at the cliff edge and looked out at the magnificent blue of the Chesapeake to their left, and the blueish-green of the mighty Atlantic to their right. In the foreground was the HMS *Richmond* riding tall and proud at anchor. To her left was HMS *Iris* looking equally splendid. And between them and the ocean was... the entire French fleet. They had beaten the British back to the Chesapeake.

The three men stood by helplessly as the events of the afternoon unfolded. Within a half-hour a frigate detached itself from the French line, positioned itself about 300 yards in front of the *Richmond* and fired a single gun on the starboard side. It was a challenge to come out and fight. "Fight who?" Smith thought. "The whole damn fleet?"

Within the hour, they could see movement aboard the *Richmond* as two of the largest boats were lowered over the side. The boats were loaded with the ships' women and children and were rowed by the most elderly seamen. These were the people who would be least likely to survive what could be years in a French prison.

After the boats were well away and could no longer be considered part of the *Richmond*, Captain Hudson walked to the base of the mizzenmast and personally lowered the colors. There were tears in Smith's eyes and, truth be told, even a little misting in Walker's, as she surrendered.

They stayed to watch French officers come on board both the *Richmond* and the *Iris* and accept the swords of both captains.

They stayed to watch the French boarding parties come over to herd the men below deck under guard, and substitute officers and men of their own to run the ship.

They stayed to watch the two refugee boats from the *Richmond* and one from the *Iris* draw near and then pass by Wormley Creek, on their way to the Yorktown docks.

And then they could watch no more.

* * *

No one said much as they ate an evening meal that the Moore House staff had hastily assembled. It was dark out and the only sounds that could be heard were the chirping of the night insects outside and the muted clink of cutlery inside.

The staff cleared away the dishes and brought out a large bottle of sherry and another pitcher of Walker's lemon-drink. Glasses were poured but still nothing was said.

Walker felt rather than heard someone sit down in the chair next to him. He looked up from contemplating his glass to see Susan Whitney sitting there, her hands folded in front of her as if she had been at the table the whole time.

"Susan?" Walker could hardly believe his eyes. "What the hell are..."

"Lieutenant Smith, are you going to hog that sherry all night or are you going to offer a lady a drink?"

Smith scrambled to get another glass from the credenza. "What are you doing here?"

"The same thing you are. I assume you know the *Richmond* was taken today. Before surrendering, Captain Hudson put the women and powder monkeys into some boats and we made for the Yorktown docks. After I got ashore and got everyone more or less settled. I asked around Cornwallis' headquarters to see were you were. A clerk said he thought you were at Moore House, so I walked out here and... here I am.

"So, what's the plan?" She cheerfully concluded.

"The plan is to get you back to town the first thing in the morning. You can't stay with us," Walker insisted.

"Oh, and why might that be?"

Walker was stumped until inspiration struck him. "We're going to make a break out of here. It will be a rather desperate gamble—far too dangerous for you."

Whitney said nothing for a long moment, and then replied, "Have you ever thought about what my options are at the moment, Walker? No? Well, let me review them for you.

"First, when Cornwallis surrenders, and he will, I could be treated as a straight prisoner of war. After all, I was a surgeon's mate aboard one of His Majesty's ships and, therefore, a combatant. I would then be carted off to whatever prisoner of war camp they have in mind for the duration. Have you ever thought about what being a female in a prisoner of war camp might be like?

"Or, perhaps, they will have mercy on me and simply put me out on the street. What then? How exactly do you think I will survive? If I am lucky maybe I could get some officer to take me in—to clean his house, do his laundry and be his bedmate. If less lucky, maybe some enlisted man might have me. If less lucky still, maybe a squad might give me food in exchange for passing me around the tents each night.

"You see some other options, Walker? Because I don't."

"She's right you know," said Smith quietly.

"Oh, damn it. I know she's right," Walker fumed. "All right, you're in. But, I am not going to be responsible if you get hurt or killed."

"Oh, that's refreshing. Do remind me to put that in my diary tonight."

"I am afraid these gentlemen have the advantage of me, madam. Of course, if they were real gentlemen they would have introduced us a long time ago."

"Oh, I am sorry Your... Damn, I am sorry... William. We were just so surprised to see Susan show up." Smith then completed the introduction to Hanover and filled him in on Susan's role aboard ship.

Susan was horrified. "I am sorry I did not give you a curtsy like a proper lady when I came in, Your Highness. And, I am afraid I am not dressed for..." Susan started self-consciously clutching the threadbare gingham dress she was wearing.

"First, if you're going to be a part of this group you need to for-get all that. I am Midshipman William Hanover. Period. You can call me Bill, if you like. In fact... 'Bill' – I rather like that. Sort of a rough and ready colonist name, what? Anyway, Susan, if we're all going to be in this together, so forget the royalty nonsense, all right."

"Yes, sir... er... Bill."

"And the dress is fine," he said in passing. "You fill it better than 99% of the countesses in England."

Susan blushed to the soles of her feet, but was also more pleased with that remark than she could ever express. "My God." she thought. "I've just been complimented by a prince. What would mother think about *that*?"

"Now, Walker, you have something to report, I believe."

"I do?"

"Indeed. Did you not just tell this lady about the desperate break out plan we had in mind. Well... out with it, man."

"Actually," Walker began, "I've been thinking about it since the *Richmond* surrendered this afternoon. Let me see if I can get a map around here." Walker found a servant who showed up in the parlor a few minutes later with a map of Yorktown and one of the Chesapeake area, which was all the house had. Walker unrolled the map of Yorktown first.

"Gather 'round.

"Now, the one thing we know is that we can't stay where we are," Walker began. "It's only a matter of time before Cornwallis has to fold his hand. So, we have to get out of here and somehow get behind the American and French lines. But how and in which direction do we go?

"We can't go east, west or south of Yorktown. The Americans are dug in to the east and south; the French are dug in to the west. Moreover, they will be at full alert at all times because they half-expect Cornwallis to try a forced breakout at any moment.

"But look over here to the north, across the York River, there is a little peninsula called "Gloucester Point." There's already a small British garrison over there. They're cut off from advancing any farther by American troops, but they are there. It's also easy to get there as there are small boats going back and forth all the time."

"So, why would it be any easier to get through the American lines there than somewhere else?" Smith asked.

"The reason is because Gloucester Point consists of several small units that have effectively been eliminated from the fighting—and they know it. They are the backwater of this battle and the American troops will not be at nearly the same level of alertness as their brethren on the other shore.

"So, tomorrow I suggest we take one of the supply boats over to Gloucester Point."

"All right but once we get there, how do we get through the American lines?" asked Smith.

"I don't know."

"Assuming we get through the American lines, what do we do next?" asked Hanover.

"I don't know," replied Walker again.

"Well, that certainly sounds like a plan to me," quipped Susan.

CHAPTER FIVE

THE worst of it was the mosquitoes. It was as if each plant was home to hundreds of them and, in the absence of any kind of breeze, they were a plague.

Walker, Smith, Hanover and Whitney had made it across the York River on the noon supply barge. After a brief survey of the British lines, they made their way to Redoubt #4 which anchored the British right flank. Since then, they had been sitting in the redoubt staring at the terrain in front of them.

The eastern edge of the Gloucester peninsula was nothing but marshes and sandy beaches punctuated by lazy creeks coming from inland and coves cutting in from the ocean. About 100 yards directly ahead was Sarah Creek that extended about a quarter mile inland. The water was brown and murky and they had no idea of its depth. About a hundred yards beyond the creek was the left flank of the American lines. They had no idea how many men were over there. Farther to the left, in the distance, was a small hill, also occupied by the Americans. To their right, on the other side of the creek, was a low lying beach about 30 yards wide that ended abruptly in a steep rise on the landside. The beach and the rise went off into the foreseeable distance.

"Ideas?" Smith asked the group. They had been staring at the ground ahead of them for some time and it was getting dark.

"Yes. I have an idea that this whole thing is hopeless," said Hanover. "There they are. Here we are. We're as trapped as Cornwallis, only on a smaller scale."

Walker wasn't quite as sure. There was an idea percolating through his brain. He could feel it periodically rising to the surface of his consciousness only to submerge itself again at the last minute, just as he was about to get a hold of it. Finally, it emerged and stayed put.

"Yeah, actually I *do* have an idea." He had the undivided attention of the other three.

"Look over there at their sentry. Watch his movements. He starts his patrol at the rise overlooking the beach. Then he walks about 150 paces along the American line, turns, comes 150 paces back, and repeats."

"So?" Hanover asked.

"He does it exactly the same way, each and every time. My guess is that his replacement this evening will also do it the same way.

"Then, I repeat... so?"

"We wait until dark, cross over to the other side of the creek and position ourselves on the beach under the lip of the rise. Once the sentry starts back in the other direction on his patrol, we sprint down the beach. He'll be walking away from us at that point. If we can get past the guard post and far enough down the beach before he gets back, he won't see us and we'll be home free."

"How do you propose getting across the creek?" Smith asked.

"If it's not very deep, we wade across. If it's too deep to wade, then we swim."

Silence.

"Come on, it's a good plan."

Silence.

"You all *can* swim, can't you?"

Embarrassed silence.

"Oh, for Pete's sake," Walker exclaimed. "All three of you are in the Royal Navy. How can you be in the navy and not know how to swim?"

"Lucas, I don't even know anyone that can swim," said Smith. "If your ship goes down, where are you going to swim *to*? Knowing how to swim only prolongs the drowning, so why bother to learn?"

It was a logic that Walker was not able to assail at the moment.

"Well, unless someone has a better idea, we go tonight. We'll wade across the creek. If it gets too deep to continue wading, we'll come back ashore and get some logs for the non-swimmers to float on. But, we're going tonight."

* * *

The water was warmer than he expected and the muck on the bottom was thicker—much thicker—than he thought possible, slowing their progress to a snail's pace. It was like walking through knee-deep cement, each step causing hydrogen sulfide and methane bubbles to come up from the murky bottom creating an unbelievable stench.

As they waded across the creek, the water grew deeper. First to their waists, then to their stomachs, then chests; finally, Susan called out in a throaty whisper, "Lucas?"

He turned around to see Susan Whitney with the water up to her neck. "All right, move over here, put your arms around my neck and climb on my back," he whispered.

They continued, the water rising ever higher until it was up to their necks when Smith stopped.

"Lucas, I wasn't kidding earlier. I really can't swim. If we keep going..."

"I can't either," Hanover added. "Oh God!"

"What is it?" Walker asked.

"It's a rat. There's a rat in the water with us!"

"Don't worry about it; he won't bother you. Besides, it's probably just a muskrat. They don't eat much."

"That's not funny, Walker. It's a *rat*. I am sure it is. I hate them. I..."

Walker remembered an old saying that no plan ever survives the first five minutes of battle. This plan was apparently no exception for, as soon as they were about half way across the creek, the American sentry felt the need to take a leak. Where was the most convenient location to do that? The beach, of course.

As the sentry scrambled down the bank, Walker harshly whispered, "FREEZE. Everyone freeze. Don't make a sound, don't move a muscle, until he leaves."

Nothing could be heard but a light breeze through the neighboring trees and the curses of the sentry as he scrambled down the bank. The water stank and was starting to generate small waves in reaction to a breeze that had developed, each successive ripple lapping a little higher up on their necks.

In the background was a clear, star-filled, sky with a surprisingly bright moon casting its beams across the water. Near the waterline was the sentry unhurriedly opening his fly, and in the foreground... well... in the foreground, as if he were casually riding one of those moonbeams across the water, was the biggest water rat Walker had ever seen—paddling away, headed straight for them.

The sentry had placed his musket over his shoulder on its sling. Apparently he had one of the old style trousers, 13 buttons holding a flap up, which he was unbuttoning. He seemed in no particular hurry.

The rat drew closer.

The sentry found the object of his needs and began urinating into the water. The rat, hearing the sound, angled away from it and moved even closer to the group.

Now, rats are not the brightest creatures on the planet but they do have an inbred curiosity that is matched by few other animals. Seeing three new kinds of logs in the water, he departed from his intended course to check them out.

The sentry's stream seem to last forever.

Smith was the first "log" the rat came to and he did a half-circle around it, stopping briefly to investigate Smith's ear. He then headed for Hanover.

"Steady, Bill." Walker whispered.

"Jesus, God," Hanover whispered back in agony. "Tell me when it's gone."

"That damn sentry must have consumed the water ration for a regiment," Walker thought.

The rat did a 360-degree loop around Hanover, seemingly fascinated by the fact that a log should have hair.

The sentry finally finished and was slowly re-buttoning his pants.

The rat gave Walker and Whitney a cursory once over and continued on his way, convinced the logs represented nothing to eat and nowhere decent to live.

And the sentry started his climb back up the rise to his post.

"Now slowly, quietly, let's just all keep walking, Walker said.

They made it to the other side and hurried to drop down in the sand under the rise. Walker crawled a bit further down the beach to peer over the lip of the berm.

"All right." He waved them over. "He's about 50 yards down and moving away from us. It's now or never. I'll keep an eye on him while you guys' start running. And for God's sake be quiet when you run. Just keep on going until you're well out of sight down the beach. I'll join you in a minute."

"What are you going to do?" Susan asked.

"I am going to watch the sentry to make sure he doesn't see you."

"And if he does?"

"You don't worry about that. You just keep running no matter what. Are you all ready? All right..." Walker popped his head up over the berm for one last look at the sentry. "GO!!"

The three started running in a crouch. After 30 or 40 yards, it became a sprint, desperately fighting the soft sand with each step but determined to get as far away from this awful place as possible. Once they were a hundred yards or so down the beach, Walker checked the sentry once more. He still had not made the turn at the other end of his rounds, so Walker took off after the others.

About a half mile later, he caught up to them, exhausted, lying in a heap in the sand. Walker too was dying—his lungs felt like they were about to explode, his legs were rubbery, and he had a pain in his side that felt like a knife wound. Running... no, sprinting on sand is no fun.

He collapsed next to them to recover.

After a few minutes he looked up when he heard Smith starting to chuckle. He was pointing at Hanover and Whitney both of whom were covered with sand and disgusting muck. The chuckle turned into a laugh. Hanover and Whitney looked at each other and at Walker and started to laugh as well; and the laughter quickly escalated from gentile to hysterical.

Suddenly the enormity of the danger they had just faced, the muck, the sentry, the rat... especially the bloody rat... it all hit them at once and the tension was transformed into howling laughter.

After a minute, Walker picked up Whitney and carried her, screaming and kicking, over to the ocean, waded in with her and dumped her into waist deep water. The other two joined them and a general water-fight began—two against two, one against three, every man for himself—like kids. Eventually the four, exhausted but clean, waded ashore.

"All right Walker, what now?" Susan asked. "You've been doing a pretty good job so far."

"Let's keep walking up the beach a bit farther and we can talk about it."

Walker outlined his thoughts. The objective was to get Prince William into British hands as quickly and safely as possible. The problem was that every British military unit of any strength south of New York was with Cornwallis and trapped on the peninsula. Baltimore was no good, no British troops there anymore. Philadelphia was pretty much a rebel stronghold; which left New York. But, how do you get to New York?

Walker came to the conclusion that trying to get to New York by land was too risky—especially when there is no way of knowing which people along the way were Tories and which were Patriots, who was friend and who was foe. No, he reasoned, they needed a ship or a boat of some kind so they could sail to New York. The problem was that neither he, nor any of the others, had a clue as to how or where they might get one.

"Well, I do know this. We aren't going to get help by walking along this desolate beach forever. Let's cut in here. If I recall that map we saw at Moore House, if we head west, sooner or later, we're going to come across the Gloucester Road. We can take that to the Town of Gloucester. It's big enough so we can blend in, but small enough so we might be able to get more information."

* * *

The sandy shoreline quickly gave way to the rich brown dirt of the Virginia countryside. The moon gave just enough light to keep them from bumping into things but not enough for them to stand out. Before long, they ran across the dual-rutted tracks of a farm-to-market road heading west and they took it.

Roads in colonial Chesapeake were not as highly developed as in other parts of the colonies; they didn't need to be. Most towns were located on creeks, rivers, or on the bay itself and it was a lot easier, cheaper and faster to move goods and people by water than by land. The exceptions were a handful of roads that linked the marine towns to larger cities in the interior. In good weather, these were navigable by almost any kind of conveyance. Feeding in to these main arteries were the farm-to-market roads that linked the individual farmers to the major highways and frequently involved opening and closing gates as the traveler passed from one property to another.

Travel by horse was fairly uncommon. The reasons for this were twofold. First, horses were expensive to buy and maintain; and second, the average person could usually travel farther and faster on foot then he could on a horse. A human on foot could cover 25 to 30 miles in ten hours of walking and do that day after day. A horse could go faster, but after 15 miles or so would need to be rested until the next day. Far better—and cheaper—to just walk.

Be that as it may, Walker was very much wishing for a horse as the evening developed. Contrary to his name, walking was not something he did much of and he could see the same was true of the others.

Susan was walking up ahead with Hanover and Sidney had dropped back to talk with Walker.

"So, what do you think, Lucas?" Smith began.

"About what?"

"About all this. Our chances of pulling this off."

Walker was silent for a minute. "I don't know. I really don't. It's like one minute I am sure we can do it and get out of this mess. The next... I think we don't have a prayer.

"How about you?"

Smith shrugged. "I think it doesn't matter."

"What do you mean?"

"Look at it this way, Lucas. Think of it as a giant circle—a wheel, if you will, that's turning. The purpose of a wheel is to turn. That's all it knows; that's all it does. But in order for that wheel to make one revolution, in order for it to complete itself, that which was high must become low, and that which was low must become high."

Walker was trying to make out Smith's face in the moonlight. "What the hell are you talking about? You sound like some kind of mystic or something."

"No, not at all; at least I am not trying to be. All I am saying is that we are strapped to that wheel. Its purpose IS to turn and there isn't a damn thing we can do about it. Today you can be as high as you can be, tomorrow as low as you can go. Tonight we succeed and we blow past a bored sentry without being seen. Tomorrow we might be watching our entrails spill out on the ground, complements of a rebel bayonet.

"There is nothing we can do about it either way, Lucas. Nothing at all."

"Jesus, you're sounding so pessimistic."

"Pessimistic?? Oh, good God, no. It's glorious, Lucas, absolutely glorious. While I admit, we're just along for the ride—what an incredible ride it is. Didn't you feel it tonight?

"When we were in the water and the sentry was taking a leak, and we had that damn rat swimming past us, and we had to remain motionless... didn't you feel it?"

"Feel what? Stop talking in riddles."

"Christ, Lucas, have you ever—and I mean *ever*—felt more alive than at that moment. Are you telling me your eyesight was not keener, your hearing more acute, your sense of smell and touch and taste—all as sharp as a knife's edge? You didn't sense that?"

"Well, yeah, I guess I did."

"And was it not glorious?"

Walker bit back a smart remark. Besides, Smith was trying to make a larger point here and he wanted to understand it. "You make it sound like a game."

"No, it's not a game. That sentry really would have killed one or more of us if he had caught us. On the other hand, it *is* a game. A wild, wonderful, one.

"And if it's a game... All I know is that I want to be a part of it. I want to play it until I can play no longer. Can you think of any possible way of spending your life that would be better than that?"

Walker continued walking and was silent. He listened to the night sounds as they passed through woods and fields. He listened to the crunch of his footsteps on the earth and stone of the roadbed. He smelled the unseen plants and trees. He marveled at the unbelievable canvas of stars above him. And, he thought about what Smith had said. He thought hard.

* * *

Sometime just before dawn they came across the Gloucester Road and turned north. With the morning sun came welcome relief to bodies that had been chilled too long by the autumn night. They slipped into a stand of trees and bedded down as best they could. Smith had the first watch but it wasn't more than two hours before he was shaking the others awake.

"Up! Everyone up. Someone's coming," Smith whispered. The four moved to a nearby group of shrubs and peered through.

"Down the road, about a half mile. By that rise."

It was more visible by the plume of dust than anything else but, sure enough, something was there. In a few minutes, they could make out a horse drawn cart.

"It's a blagger," Smith hissed.

"A what?" asked Walker.

"A blagger. Profiteer. Total scum. These are people who provide the soldiers with all the things the army is supposed to provide them, but doesn't."

"That doesn't sound so bad to me."

"You don't understand. The reason the men don't have those things is because the blaggers have siphoned them off with everything from bribery to outright theft. You see, it's not the big items they go after. They don't steal muskets, they steal the cleaning kits and spare parts the men need to keep the muskets working. They don't steal food but if you want a kettle to cook it in—see the blagger. Want shoes? Want a new blanket? A sewing kit? Want paper and ink to write home? See the blagger and he'll sell it to you... at ten to twenty times the actual cost. They're bastards."

While the group was watching the road Walker heard a rustle and saw Susan pull Sidney Smith aside. They were having an animated conversation but Susan seemed to have the last word. They returned to the lookout spot.

"You two stay here. And I mean *stay here*, no matter what you see—or think you see," Susan said. And, with no further explanation, Susan and Sidney stood up, walked to the road and started walking down it. Sidney was walking ahead as if he could care less whether Susan followed or not; Susan followed with a dejected shuffle.

The blagger soon pulled alongside and after some initial conversation began a dialog with Smith. After a few moments, Smith pulled Susan over by the wrist and said something to her. She seemed to cringe. Smith then batted her on the back of the head—hard—snapping her head forward. Both Walker and Hanover tensed but stayed where they were. Slowly Susan lifted her skirt displaying two very pale but rather shapely legs.

The blagger got down from the wagon. He seemed to be all smiles but it was hard to tell at that distance through the multiple chins on his puffy face. Hitching up his pants around his belly, he handed something to Smith, and then grabbed Susan to kiss her. She coquettishly pushed him off and indicated a stand of trees a hundred yards or so on the other side of the road. Smith leaned against the wagon casually examining his fingernails as they went off.

Within five minutes, Susan had returned alone and Smith was wildly gesturing to Walker and Hanover to come down.

"Get in," Smith yelled as he took the reins and spurred the horse into action. The horse took off at a shambling trot which, given the horse's condition, was probably full speed for him.

"What the hell's going on?" Hanover demanded.

"I just sold Susan and we now have a horse and wagon."

"You did WHAT," Walker demanded, his eyes open wide.

"Well, I didn't really sell her; I sort of... rented her out. Got a nice price, too."

Susan quickly jumped in. "Relax, Lucas. The gentleman and I just went for a little walk."

"A little walk," Walker sputtered, not knowing what else to say.

"Well, it seems he had some amorous intentions as well."

"And what happened to this amorous gentlemen?"

"I am not sure exactly. I think a tree limb must have fallen on his head somehow," she said innocently. "I have such terrible luck with men, you know."

Walker was stunned. "Of all the stupid, idiotic, things to..."

"Wait a minute." Hanover placed his hand on Walker's arm. "What's keeping this man from coming after us right now, or rather when he wakes up."

Susan didn't say a word. She just dropped a bundle on Hanover's lap containing the man's pants and shoes.

"Just how much *did* you get, Sidney?" Susan asked.

* * *

The four ambled along in the cart for the remainder of the day alternately sleeping and eating from the profiteer's extensive provisions. Susan was up in the buckboard and Hanover was driving, each alone with their thoughts until Hanover finally spoke up.

"Where're you from, Susan?"

"Where am I from? Portsmouth. Actually, from Portsmouth Common up on the north side of town."

"Family?"

"Father's dead, mother's still in Portsmouth last I heard; but it's been quite some time. Had a brother before me but he died while still an infant."

"What did your father do?"

"Ah, we were a seagoing family, we were. My grandfather was a master carpenter at the shipyards. My father was an able seaman aboard the *Swiftsure* under Sir Thomas Stanhope. He died at the Battle of Quiberon just before I was born. Don't know how. They never told us."

"I am sorry to hear that. That must have been hard on your mother and you."

"Oh, yes. My mother was in her late 20's at the time—so she was far too old to attract another man. With no money coming in, we had a rough time all right. And, you know the worst of it?"

Hanover shook his head.

"As I said, my dad served with Sir Thomas on the *Swiftsure* which had one of the best prize records in the Mediterranean. With all that prize money he was, by our standards, a wealthy man. When he died, though, all that money was forfeit to the Crown. 'How can we pay a dead man?' they told us." Susan was getting exercised now.

"Well, the man might be dead, but he died in the king's service and he still has a family. Instead, the bastards just take the money for themselves. You'd think the king has enough money without grabbing a few pounds from widows who..."

Susan suddenly realized to whom she was talking. The king was Hanover's father and the "bastards" in question were his relatives.

"Oh my God. I am sorry, sir. I didn't mean to... that is, I guess I just started thinking of you as 'Bill' and I forgot..."

"Relax, Susan. I am Bill, and don't you forget *that* or it's liable to get us all killed. Besides," he said with a smile, "I'd give a hundred pounds for some people I can think of to hear what you just said." He then got a far away look in his eyes. "In fact, if I ever get back to England... they damn well will.

"Anyway, do go on. What happened then?"

"Well, she eventually got work with some other women making slow-match in the ordinance shed at the shipyard—I think someone there remembered my grandfather and got her the job. Anyway, she's worked there my whole life—21 years. I am afraid she's doing poorly now, though. All those years of breathing those chemicals."

"So, you were destined to go to sea, somehow, yourself?"

Susan laughed and showed her wonderful smile. "Oh, Lordy no. That's the last thing my mother wanted. She wanted me to be a lady."

"A lady?"

"Yes. Oh, not in the sense of highborn folks like the ladies you know, but a lady nonetheless. When I was a little girl she used to save every penny she could so on Sunday I could wear a dress with silk ribbons sewn on it. I mean, *real* silk, Bill. I don't know how she afforded that. Anyway, she'd spend all Saturday night combing my hair, humming to herself, and then dress me up on Sunday morning to go to church. And, she'd tell me, 'Act like a lady, Susan. Always act like a lady, because someday you're going to *be* a Lady. A beautiful lady. As good as any of them.' And, you know what?

Hanover shook his head.

Susan laughed, "I almost became one.

"I don't know if you know this, but Portsmouth has a school. It's called the Portsmouth Grammar School—it's over on Penny Street—and they allow the children of Portsmouth—both boys and girls—to attend for free. My mother made sure I attended. That's where I learned to read, write, and do math... In fact, I'll bet I can discuss the classics and the great works of literature as well as almost anyone you know. Anyway, I was well on my way to marrying the son of some rich merchant and becoming the lady my mother wanted me to be."

"So what happened?"

Susan laughed again. "I met a gunners mate.

"Oh, he was a rogue, all right. Flashing black eyes. Childlike smile. So handsome, he was; and I was so in love. My mother was crushed, of course, but I didn't care. She eventually forgave me, but I was so stupid.

"Anyway, I ran off with him. We never did get properly married. That's why I reverted back to my maiden name, Whitney, after he died."

"What happened to him?

"We got into a dustup with a French frigate off Charleston. The Frenchie had surrendered but apparently someone on the lower deck hadn't gotten the word. Out of the blue, a gun went off back aft. The ball came crashing through our bulwark and caught my husband square in the back. Killed him instantly.

"I was terrified that Captain Hudson would put me off the ship as soon as we got back to England, so I tried to make myself as useful as possible. Unfortunately—or fortunately—our ship's surgeon was a drunk and I was able to become useful as a surgeon's mate.

"That's where I was when the *Richmond* was captured and we were put ashore."

It was a sobering story for Hanover to hear and put him deep in thought for the next few hours.

The cart rambled on. It seemed like each turn in the road brought some fresh new experience. They were in a wild country, that's for sure; and neither Whitney, Smith or Hanover were quite prepared for it.

The Brits were used to the ordered farms and fields of England. They were used to seeing crops planted in almost every clearing with stonewalls or hedges bordering them. What they found here were random clearings over run with weeds, yet containing some of the richest soil they had ever seen—soil that had never, ever, felt a plow.

By early afternoon they entered a huge virgin forest, something again none of them had ever seen, and again they were in awe. Yellow pine, white oak, walnut and chestnut trees grew together so thickly in places that sunlight never reached the ground. They saw trees over 90 feet tall with branches spreading almost as wide. They saw tree trunks 16 feet in diameter with limbs thick as a mans' waist, branches that did not begin to reach out until they were 20 feet or more in the air.

Even the calls of the birds were different, placing mystery, upon wonder, upon majesty. But the biggest surprise came just before getting to Gloucestertown.

Susan was still sitting next to Hanover and Walker and Smith were in the back. The forest eventually ended and, while cresting a rise, Walker felt the wagon stop and heard Susan gasp, "My God."

Walker rolled to one side and peered over the wagon edge and saw... daffodils. Not just dozens or even hundreds, but daffodils stretching as far as the eye could see. The land was covered in a sea of yellow flowers that waved and rippled like the ocean in obedience to the wind.

By mid-afternoon they had reached the Town of Gloucester. By the standards of Richmond, Baltimore or even Yorktown, Gloucestertown wasn't much, but it was different. Instead of having a square grid of streets running off of a town square, the Gloucester town "square" was an oval with a three foot high brick wall running around it's perimeter.

To the north and outside of the circle was the Gloucester Courthouse. Inside the oval were several houses and a debtor's prison. To the south and across the street there was, of course, a tavern. They headed to the latter.

The tavern had only been built about eleven years earlier where it was originally known as John New's Ordinary. Later it was renamed the Botetourt Building, after an early governor of Virginia; but the locals just called it the "Courthouse Tavern." It was a large two-story brick building with a roofed porch that ran the entire length of the building front—some 100 feet. Unlike most wooden colonial porch floors, this one was made of brick laid in a parquet pattern that Walker found fascinating and it boasted eight wooden pillars that held up a stately porch roof.

Inside was the usual eating and drinking area and hearth, and upstairs were 12 rooms that were let out to travelers. But the thing that really made the Courthouse Tavern unique was a back room complete with an honest-to-God, made in London, imported at who knows what expense, billiard table. Hanover and Smith were beside themselves at the prospect of playing a few gentlemanly games.

They checked in with the three men in one room and Susan having one whole luxurious room to herself; and met downstairs after they had gotten settled and the horse and cart put away. A pitcher of ale sat in the middle of the table with four mugs sitting in front of four dour faces.

"Well, you're probably wondering why I gathered you here." Walker quipped.

"Huh... What?"

"Never mind. I guess we'd better figure out what we're going to do next, you think?"

"Quite," Hanover agreed.

Smith took the lead. "Well, so far I think we've done quite well. At least we're no longer in danger of being swept up in Cornwallis' defeat.

"All right, let's review it again. We know we want to get to New York. We can do that either by land or by sea; but I agree, we should rule out trying to get there overland. The tide of the war has clearly turned, so finding American Tory supporters along the way to help us might be difficult at best.

Everyone seemed to agree. At least, no one objected to Smith's premise.

"So," Smith continued, "that leaves the sea. All we need to do is to beg, borrow or steal a ship, evade several dozen French Men-o-War at the Chesapeake entrance, traverse a few shoals, and head up the coast to New York without being detected by any other ships be they French, American, or privateer.

"Nothing to it, what?"

"Hear, him! Hear him!" They chanted while lifting their mugs. So much had already happened to them, in such a short period of time, that all new problems began to look slightly ludicrous.

When they had settled down again, Walker finally spoke for all of them. "How *are* we going to do that anyway?"

* * *

Two days went by with little progress. A few miles from Gloucester, the Ware River ran into Mobjack Bay, an arm of the Chesapeake. At the southerly entrance to the bay was Drum point; and on Drum Point was a small fishing village called Bailey's Wharf. Smith managed to obtain some nautical charts on a quick trip there. The other three found out nothing more than if they wanted a ship or a boat, their best bet was to cross over to the eastern shore. There were a lot more ship building towns over there and maybe something could be arranged.

Gloucester was not untypical of most colonial cities or towns. The first thing you notice about the place is the aroma—primarily that of rotting garbage. Because formal garbage collection was unknown, everything from rotten food to feces was simply tossed out into the streets or strewn about individual yards. Along with the garbage came clouds of flies and armies of rats. To make matters worse, pigs ran wild through the streets feeding on the garbage and leaving droppings that mixed with the horse manure to produce yet another category of offensive odor.

Walker was a Boston "city boy" so he thought he knew what city noise was all about. It was nothing compared to this. From dawn to dusk, squealing animals, clattering horses, squeaking wagons, blacksmith hammers, screaming children and besotted drunks assailed him from all directions.

It was the afternoon of their third day in town when something happened that was to unravel all their plans; and, the strange thing was that only Susan saw it occur and she didn't say anything.

They were sitting at their usual table when a short, bowlegged, ex-seaman by the name of Nathan Taft came in to the tavern and took a seat by the door. He ordered a pint of what was billed as "Genuine German Lager." Before his order could even arrive, he spotted the foursome, gulped a few times like a fish freshly pulled from a pond, and shot out the door. Susan briefly saw him and thought she recognized him, but it all happened so quickly she wasn't sure. A half-hour later the Gloucester Sheriff and two deputies arrived and walked over to the table which held the four travelers.

"Good evening gentlemen," he tipped his hat to Susan, "and Lady. I am Jonathan Chase the Sheriff of Gloucester County. These are my deputies, he said pointing to the two somewhat bedraggled but well armed men. And you are?

Smith answered. "I am Sidney Smith and this is my cousin Bill," he said, nodding at Hanover who smiled politely at the Sheriff. Across the table is a good friend of ours, Lucas Walker and his... ah... wife, Susan."

"I don't believe I've seen you here in Gloucestertown before."

"That's right. We're just passing through."

"May I see your letters, please?"

Hanover and Whitney had no idea what he was talking about. Smith and Walker, however, knew exactly what he meant. Smith continued to speak for the group.

"I am sorry Sheriff, but we're just in town for a few days and we have no letters of introduction from anyone here."

"You've been in town more than three days, haven't you?"

"Yes."

"Then I'll need to see your letters. Anyone staying in Gloucester for more then three days must have a letter of introduction from either a local resident or from someone known to us outside of the town. If you don't have them, then you're in violation of the law."

"Oh come, Sheriff," Smith began. "I know a lot of communities had that law in the old days, but no one enforces it anymore."

"I'll be the judge of what gets enforced and what doesn't around here," the sheriff snapped. "Besides, we've had a lot of trouble with strollers lately and I understand you folks have been asking a lot of strange questions.

"Now, all of you, raise your right hands."

Everyone complied as if they were taking an oath, while the Sheriff looked closely at each palm.

"All right. You gentlemen are going to have to come with me." And, with that, the sheriff's deputies moved their hands closer to the pistols they carried in their belts and fanned out behind the foursome. "I am afraid we don't have accommodations for the lady so you can stay here. I don't suppose you'll go far with your husband in 'the house,' though."

The town jail wasn't really a jail in any true sense of the word. It was a small, single story, brick building that consisted of a single square room, 20 feet on a side with a barred window in front and one in back providing the only light. The interior walls and ceiling were 1 ¼ inch thick planks laid horizontally and whitewashed. The studs were intentionally placed very close together and laid flush against the bare brick wall. The point of this arrangement was to keep the prisoners from picking away at the wood and mortar, removing bricks and, thus making an escape.

The room had a small fireplace, two straw mats along the far wall, a table with two chairs, a chamber pot in the corner; and the only door was made of thick oak. It was designed as a debtor's prison but rarely used because, unlike in England, the courts in

America figured a person who was out of jail was far more likely to pay off his debts than one who was in.

Hanover, Smith and Walker were unceremoniously thrust through the door, which was quickly slammed behind them and locked.

Smith protested the whole way. "Sheriff, this is an outrage. We've done nothing wrong. When can we see a judge?"

From the other side of the door the Sheriff replied. "The judge is out riding the circuit."

"When will he be back?"

"Whenever I bother to send for him," he laughed, while walking away.

The three were silent for a few moments as they took in their new home. Finally, Hanover spoke up. "Does someone want to explain to me what just happened?"

"I don't know. Something's going on here," Smith replied. "This just isn't right.

"We're in here because we don't have a letter of introduction from anyone in this town. Fifty years ago, to travel anywhere you needed such a letter so the town law officers knew you were a legitimate visitor and not some criminal on the run.

"But that's what's so strange. No one enforces that law anymore. He claimed we might be 'strollers,' itinerant con men, but he could see we were not that."

"What was all that 'raise your right hand' business?" Hanover asked.

"He was checking to see if any of us had a criminal record. They use a system here in the colonies where, if you're convicted of a crime, they place a small brand on the base of your right thumb. He was checking to see if any of us had a brand."

For the first time Hanover understood the origin of "raising your right hand" when being sworn in during a court proceeding.

"So, what now?"

"Don't know. Unless Susan can work some miracle, we'll just have to wait until the judge gets back... whenever *that* might be."

* * *

"It's a miracle," Susan thought as she watched a small boat come in to the dock.

It was the afternoon of the day following the arrests and Susan had taken the horse and wagon over to the fishing village Smith had discovered a few days before. She probably would not have been able to articulate why she went there; but she was tired, depressed, more than a little scared, and there was something comforting about seeing a body of water again.

Bailey's Wharf consisted of six small houses clustered around a waterfront that was dominated by a large brick building. A wooden pier jutted 50 yards or so out into the Ware River. At the base of the pier was a combination warehouse, general store, tavern and chandler's shop, which was easily the most substantial building in town.

It was made of sturdy brick and primarily stored hogsheads of fragrant tobacco awaiting shipment to Elizabeth Town where it would be sold to buyers from England and Europe. It was also used as a tavern and dining hall. As you walked in the door you were immediately struck by the large chimney and huge fireplace across the top of which were strings of seasoning red peppers, pickled oysters, ears of red and white corn and freshly picked onions.

Susan sat down near the fireplace where some children, both white and black, were sitting on the floor listening to an old black man spin tales "Fo' de war, when y'all warn' born." She felt like ordering a large tankard of ale but she knew that would invite stares and possibly questions. Instead, she ordered a demure pot of tea so she would look more like the wife of a fishing boat captain in town to do some shopping.

After several hours Susan left the tavern and wandered out on the pier, just looking at the water, trying to pull herself together. She enjoyed looking at the water. In a strange way, it calmed her; always had, even when she was a girl. The dark blue of the water, the powder blue of the sky, the white clouds high overhead, the shrill cries of the gulls, the smell of salt air—all conspired to remind her of home and of simpler, safer and saner times. Would she ever see Portsmouth again?

It was late afternoon and the fishing boats were starting to come in. As ships go, they weren't much—mostly ketches, doggers, and a peculiar craft she had no name for that was apparently used by the local clam fishermen. A bit further out two sloops sat at anchor all afternoon with a third one just now coming in. The newcomer was much smaller than the others, only a single mast, but was handled beautifully. After dropping anchor, she could see the crew putting a boat over the side and the boat being rowed to the town dock.

A man got out of the boat to tie it up and was followed by another person who was obviously the primary passenger. Susan couldn't believe her eyes.

"Hugh? Hugh Hayes? Is that you?"

"Susan? By God, what are you doing here?" He then seemed to catch himself. Looking around suspiciously, he asked, "Is the *Richmond* in port somewhere hereabouts?"

"Nope, don't worry. She's probably halfway to France right now. She was captured a few... days ago." Susan caught herself. My God, it *was* only a few days ago.

Hugh Hayes was one of the biggest, most powerfully built men Susan had ever known. From a distance, you would think he was short. It wasn't until you got close-up that you realized he was over six feet tall and was simply a massive person.

He had thick legs, a barrel chest, and arms like tree limbs, little in the way of a perceptible neck, and a roundish face that was always slightly red and usually smiling. One of the most popular seamen on the *Richmond*, he had been rated "Able" in record time and was the ship's Master-at-Arms—the ship's policeman, if you will—until he went ashore one day on ship's business and simply never returned.

"Hugh, it's so good to see you. I haven't seen you since... ah, that is..."

Hayes laughed. "It's all right Susan. I ran from the *Richmond*. You don't have to be polite about it."

"So, are you working on that ship?" she asked, quickly changing the topic.

"Yup, I am her captain."

"Captain?" Susan clapped her hands with delight. How'd you become captain of a ship?"

"Well, after the *Richmond* pulled out, I made my way to Balmore by shipping out on a merchantman. I was sitting in a tavern and I overheard two people—investors they were—talking about a ship they were going to buy and how hard it was to find a capable man to captain her. I sidled over and said I used to be a master's mate in the navy and I might be able to help them out.

"All right, so it was a bit of an exaggeration. I was never a master's mate, but the ship ain't nothin' but a little, single masted, fore-and-aft rigged river sloop and I figured I could sail her well enough.

"They were desperate; I was desperate, so they offered me the job and I took it. Been running small cargos around the Chesapeake ever since.

"What about you?"

As soon as he asked the question, Hayes saw a reaction in Susan he thought he'd never see. She looked like she was about to cry as she summoned her thoughts and, except when her husband died, he had never—but never—seen her cry.

She told him everything, as if she were unburdening her soul, starting with Walker's peculiar appearance on the scene, the Battle of the Capes, the surrender of the *Richmond*, the rescue of the prince and their escape. Hayes stopped her a few times for clarification but otherwise just leaned against a bollard and let her talk.

"And where are these gentlemen now?"

She completed the story with the strange arrests in Gloucestertown.

Hayes sat in thought, not saying a thing. After a few minutes he simply said: "All right."

"All right, what?" Susan asked.

"All right. You and I are going to go into that tavern over there and have us the best roast beef dinner they can provide. I haven't forgotten how you took care of me when I got sick that time in the Med."

"And then."

"And then we go bust your friends out of jail."

CHAPTER SIX

IT was nearing midnight as the wagon entered Gloucester. Susan was convinced they were making enough noise to awaken half the county. Hayes had the horse at a slow walk and had shifted their track off the well-worn ruts to lessen the number of potholes they would encounter. Susan's fears notwithstanding, they were being about as quiet as could be expected while driving a broken down wagon and an even more broken down horse.

"Do you know where the jail is?" asked Susan.

"Oh yes," Hayes replied with confidence, but did not elaborate on the reason for that assurance.

He was right. He pulled off the town circle and alongside the Debtor's Jail at just the right spot. Susan scrambled off the buckboard and went to the jail's rear window.

"Walker? Smith? You in there," Susan whispered.

A few seconds later Smith's voice replied, "Susan? Is that you?"

"Yes, I am here with a friend. We're going to get you out."

"How?"

Susan suddenly realized she had forgotten to ask Hayes how he was going to do it. She turned to him, "How?"

Hugh stepped to the window. "I've got the wagon here. I am going to pass you men a rope, tie it around the bars. When you're ready, let me know and I'll start this nag slowly pulling on it. I don't want to tear down the whole damn wall; it'd make too much noise. I just want to free up the bars from that cheap cement they used so you can slide through the window."

"Who are you, and how do you know the cement will give way?"

"It was a government project. We'll make introductions later."

Within a few minutes, Smith and Walker had crawled out of the building through the now destroyed window; but Susan kept looking back. "Where's Hanover?"

"Gone," Walker replied.

"Gone? What do you mean, gone? You mean as in: We've misplaced an heir to the throne of England? That kind of 'gone'?"

Hayes stepped in. "Look, we can discuss this later. Right now we need to get the hell out of here as quietly as possible." With that they all boarded the wagon and Hayes continued his slow, quiet, procession out of town.

* * *

"This is an outrage. I am a midshipman in His Majesty's Navy and you have no right to keep me here." Hanover had summoned up all of his well-schooled imperial indignation, but it was falling on deaf ears.

As of that afternoon, he had been semi-happily ensconced in the town jail with his two friends. Suddenly the door swung open and the sheriff walked in with his deputies and a new person. He was of medium height and rail thin; but the most distinguishing thing about him was his pale complexion and flaming red hair.

"This the one you want?" the sheriff asked.

"Yes, that's him," the man replied. And, without further comment, Hanover was taken from the cell, blindfolded, his hands tied behind him, helped on to a horse and led away. An hour later, he was deposited at a farmhouse, but that was about all Hanover knew of his location.

The house was small but reasonably well appointed. It had several rooms: a living/dining area and a separate kitchen and bedroom—quite unusual for those parts. It was located in a clearing with a well, a small stable, and an outhouse in back along the fence line.

"I don't know what you think you're going to get for kidnapping me. Midshipmen don't fetch much with the rebel military, you know."

The red haired man waved the guards out of the room, sat down at the table and poured himself and Hanover a glass of wine.

"My name is Finch," he began "and you are not 'Midshipman Bill Hanover.' You are Prince William Henry and, more importantly, you are now mine."

Hanover looked straight at the man, despite his worst fears having been realized.

"And what is it you think you're going to do now that you have me?" Hanover tried to remain defiant.

Finch began laughing. "You know what? I honestly don't know... but it's not because I lack options. You tell me, your 'highness,' whom do you think will pay more?

"There are the American's, of course. They would love to have King George's third son as an additional bargaining chip with which to end the war. Then there are the French, who would love to have you simply because they hate the English. And the Spaniards would want you for no other reason than to frost off both the Americans and the French. Finally, of course, there is your daddy and his government. What would they pay to *keep* you from falling into the hands of the Americans, the French or the Spanish?

"I really don't know what I am going to do with you; but, whatever it is, it's going to make me a very, very rich man."

"You're wasting your time. The war's almost over, if it's not over already. When that happens, you'll have lost your bargaining power." It was a weak argument but Hanover thought it was pretty good for a spur of the moment thing.

"I'll take that chance," Finch replied. "It's a good business risk and I am a good businessman. Besides, the hardest part, finding you, is already over. I've been on your trail for months. Thought I had you in Yorktown until those two friends of yours showed up."

"Business risk? You're nothing but a cheap kidnapper."

"I'll beg your pardon for that remark, good sir. I am not a kidnapper; I am a privateer. I am *Captain* Finch, thank you, owner and commander of the *Cardinal*—rather appropriate name for my ship don't you think."

Hanover said nothing.

"A privateer, Your Lordship, is a pirate with papers. Surely, you're familiar with the concept? You Brits invented it. Ever hear of Francis Drake? Oh, excuse me. He was so successful as a legalized pirate he became *Sir* Francis Drake. Well, I am the same kind of businessman as Drake; only the other side signed my authorizing papers. Would you like to see them?"

"I have no need to see them, but please tell me where you keep them. I want to be able to get hold of them to read to the crowd when they hang you."

"Not likely, Sir. Your navy has already given its best effort in that regard. Ever hear of Washington's Wolfpack?"

Hanover, of course, had. Every British seaman on the American Station had heard of them. In 1775, Washington's forces out numbered the British troops that were holding New York City. Unfortunately, this advantage was doing him little good. Britain controlled the sea and, because the U.S. had no navy at that point, there was nothing he could do to stop the supply ships from going in and out of the harbor at will. So, he formed the Wolfpack—a collection of American merchant schooners hastily fitted with guns—to harass and, hopefully, capture British supply ships.

"Yes, I've heard of them. What of it?"

"Well, I was one of the original members of the pack. In fact my Letter of Marque, authorizing me to be a privateer, is countersigned signed by Ol' George himself."

"So what?"

Finch became deadly serious. "So this, Your Highness," he said sarcastically. "With nothing more than schooners we out-sailed, out-smarted, and when necessary, out-fought some of the best frigate captains in your whole damn navy. Oh, its true New York was re-supplied anyway; but have you thought about what's going to happen if this nation ever starts building warships? I mean REAL warships, and starts giving command to people like me.

"I repeat. So what? The war is probably over by now and we don't even know it."

"And you think this will be the last war ever—the war to end all wars? Not hardly. Indeed, I will happily wager whatever sum you wish that the U.S. and England will be back at each other's throats in my lifetime. And when that happens, there *will* be a U.S. Navy, and there *will* be warships worthy of the name, and I *will* have command of one of those ships, and we *will* kick your ass up one ocean and down the other."

"You're a madman. We have more warships sitting in our repair docks right now than the U.S. could possibly build in your lifetime."

Finch said nothing for a long moment, and then said quietly, "Mark my words. The day will come when the U.S. Navy will be able defeat not just any navy in the world, but all the navies of the world, combined."

Hanover said nothing. He knew Finch was insane; but he also had a feeling in his gut that what he was saying was true. For the first time, he looked at Finch and felt a touch of genuine fear.

* * *

The next three days were fun for no one. Hanover was the "guest" of Captain Finch and under heavy guard at all times. Walker, Smith and Whitney were holed-up in the forest just northwest of Gloucester in an abandoned hunting lodge. The only person free to travel was Hayes, and he made the best of it.

He knew that sooner or later whoever had Prince William would have to move him. If they were to move him by water, they would probably go through the fishing village. If by land, maybe someone in Gloucestertown might have wind of it. So, he kept moving between the two locations spending part of each day in town and part in the village. About all he had learned was that the sheriff was available to the highest bidder, but he had pretty much figured that out on his own.

It was early evening on the third day when Hayes caught a break. He was sitting in the Courthouse Tavern when he overhead a man, who obviously had had a pint too many, loudly complaining to the tavern keeper.

"I'll be damned if I know why I always get the lousy jobs. Always me! Now that red headed bastard wants me to come to town to buy food for eleven men. Eleven men! Do I look like a damn purser? And you know whatever I buy won't be the right things. And who will they blame? ME! That's who. Why for a tuppence I'd skip out on that bastard and return to sea where I belong."

Hayes listened carefully for several minutes, gaining information with every word. Why would he be buying food for 11 men? Not for a ships crew, or he'd be buying less perishable things at the chandler's shop. It can't be for one of the local plantations. They grow their own food. Besides, they don't have "men," they have slaves. He decided it was time to "renew an old acquaintance" and he wandered over to the man's table.

"Why you old dog, you!" Hayes slapped the man on the back almost dislodging his shoulder blade. "I ain't seen you since we was on the old *Pittsfield* together." How the devil are you?"

"I am sorry but I don't think we..."

"Tavern master, bring me and my old shipmate here a pint, and make it the good stuff, not that bilge water you usually serve."

At the prospect of a free drink, perhaps even more than one, Nathan Taft knew when to be quiet.

"Why you old son of a bitch. How long's it been? Five, six years, I'll be bound. God, where does the time go? Last time I seen you we had put into Bal-more and the *Pittsfield* paid off."

It went on like that for some time. Taft made up a recent history for himself on the spot and agreed with Hayes's recollections of former shipmates, who were equally made up on the spot. But the important thing was that the liquor continued to flow and so did the information.

Hayes found out about Captain Finch – Taft alternately condemning the man as the worst captain he'd ever served under and then, paradoxically, claiming Finch was going to make him first mate any day now. He found out Finch was holding someone important, but Taft didn't know who he was. He found out there were nine men assigned to guard the prisoner; and, most importantly, he found out where the prisoner was being held. The last item was a close race between Taft divulging the information and passing out.

Hayes left Taft snoring in a corner of the tavern and returned to the hunting lodge where everyone gathered around the lodge's only table to hear Hayes' report.

"All right, so let's go get him," Susan chimed in.

"We'll do no such thing," replied Hayes. "Go get him how? If Taft is right, there are nine armed men patrolling the property, plus Finch. We're supposed to attack that? With what? We've got three men, a woman, and not a weapon between us.

"No, tomorrow morning I am going over to scout the place out. You keep doing what you're now doing until I get back."

"But we aren't doing anything," Susan protested.

"Exactly," replied Hayes.

* * *

Taft might be a fool, but he was no liar—at least not while drunk. The farmstead was located exactly as he described and Hayes was able to spot at least six different guards.

Hayes was a patient man, and methodical. In a later age, he would have made a good detective. He settled down with his supply of food and water in the bushes on the hillside over-looking the farmstead. He settled down to just watch and wait.

By mid afternoon the following day he finally had a plan. He went to get the others and returned with them to the hillside. Reaching into the back of the blagger's wagon he pulled out a small saber saw, and disappeared down the hill. About 20 minutes later, he returned and sat with the others.

"What exactly are we waiting for?" asked Smith.

"Look down at that farmstead. You see a weakness?"

Everyone looked and saw the farmhouse, a stable where the guards stayed, a well, and an outhouse on the back edge of the property abutting a thicket that ran to the top of the hillside. There were three guards, all armed, standing in the shade by the side of the farmhouse.

"No, frankly, I don't."

"I do. Those are sailors down there. You can tell just by the way they walk. And if sailors cherish anything, it's routine. Be they officer, midshipmen or seamen they love to have an order to their day. I am betting that yesterday's routine will be duplicated to the minute today."

"What happened yesterday that caught your eye?" asked Walker.

"Any moment now, they'll be taking the prince out for a half hour of exercise. It's during that period that they let him...

"Wait. Quiet. Here they come. I want all of you to stay here. I'll be back in a few minutes." And, with that, he disappeared down the hill.

Following the thickets, he arrived at the back of the outhouse, where he was still hidden by bushes behind it. Two guards brought the prince out of the farmhouse and one accompanied him to the outhouse door before walking over to the well for a drink.

Hayes very carefully and quietly pulled out a section of the back of the outhouse that he had cut free on his earlier trip. The prince was seated in the customary fashion when Hayes reached in, slipped a hand over his mouth and yanked him out through the back of the outhouse. Hanover started struggling but Hayes had him on the ground and there was little Hanover could do.

"Be quiet," Hayes hissed, "I am a friend. I am going to get you out of here."

Hanover stopped struggling and Hayes released him.

"Who..."

"Be quiet, I said!"

Hayes then very carefully placed the wooden section back on the outhouse and wedged it in place with several twigs. "Follow me."

It was with nothing less than complete astonishment that the group greeted Hayes' return with Hanover in tow.

"Let's go. I figure it will be at least 10 minutes before they wonder what the prince is doing, 15 before they start banging on the door, and another 10 before they figure out what happened. So we've got maybe 25 minutes to get clear of here."

They piled into the wagon and spurred the bedraggled horse into action, only this time in earnest. It wasn't all that far from the farm house to the fishing village—maybe five miles. But if you were a horse that actually looked forward to going to the glue factory, it's a long way indeed—especially when your insane human owners wanted you to *run* all the way.

Several miles down the road, Susan could contain herself no longer. "Bill, how on earth did you make your escape?"

He paused for a moment gathering his thoughts. "Like several of my ancestors, I was forcibly removed from my throne." He then started laughing wildly and said no more.

Arriving in the fishing village, they sandwiched into Hayes' gig that was still waiting for him at the pier. They rowed directly for the *Trojan*, Hayes' ship.

Scrambling aboard, Hayes told the second mate to get underway immediately. He protested that half the crew, along with the first mate, was still ashore. Hayes replied that he didn't care. "Man the windless!" he snapped.

The *Trojan* was what some people called a "river sloop." It was about 100 feet long with a single tall mast located far forward, near the fo'c'sle. Off that mast were three fore-and-aft sails. The largest was the main sail that ran from the mast to the aft end of the ship. It was anchored at the bottom by a long boom and at the top by a smaller arm called a gaff. The gaff could be hauled up and down the mast thus raising and lowering the main sail which, in turn, gave the ship most of its motive power. Providing much of its directional stability was the jib, a sail that ran forward from the mast to the very end of the bowsprit, a pole that stuck out from the bow of the ship like a swordfish's beak. At the very top of the mast was a small triangular topsail whose peak was tied to the mast-head and whose base was tied to the gaff. The ship was not con-trolled by a wheel and rudder; instead, it had a large tiller in the stern.

Mounted on a stand in the bow was an antique swivel gun. There's no way it could ever fire, it had a crack down the side of the barrel, but the owners bought it cheap and they thought just the sight of it might discourage some of the small-time pirates that operated in the bay.

Behind the swivel gun was the windless with a length of thick rope wrapped around it leading to the anchor. Continuing aft was the hatch leading down to the cargo hold, the mast, the main cabin and finally the quarterdeck, with the ships tiller. The small yawl boat was hoisted up and secured to the stern.

"Man the windless," the second mate repeated and the abbre-viated crew swung into motion. A fo'c's'lemen disappeared down the forward hatch to coil the anchor rope as it came in; two others worked the windless that hauled in the anchor. The ship's bosun, watching the anchor line, called back: "At short stay," meaning the anchor cable was taut and stretched on a straight line to the sea-bed.

The heavy main sail was still lashed to the boom with the gaff tied securely on top of that. It was time to get the main sail cleared and ready to run up.

"After-guard and idlers lay aft." And a group of men appeared next to Hayes near the tiller.

"You men," he said pointing to several in the group, "ease away the downhauls and tack the tricing lines. You others, off main sail gaskets." The first group began slacking certain ropes while the others slid along the boom untying the small strips of canvas that held the gaff and mainsail to the boom.

A call came from the fo'c'sle: "Up and down, sir!" Meaning that the anchor cable was now vertical. And a moment later, the Bosun added: "Anchor's aweigh!" The ship was now free of any direct connection with land.

By this time, Hayes had found a megaphone. "Man the topping lift. Haul taught and belay. You there, overhaul that mainsheet then man the throat and peak halyards." Some men grabbed the ropes that would haul the sail upwards and others prepared the sail for unfolding.

When they were ready, Hayes called out: "Haul taut and hoist away. Come on. Come on lads, look alive! We got 'ter get outta here."

The huge main sail started crawling up the mast and began to fill. "Overhaul that main sheet, damn it. Right, now tally aft."

He turned to the quartermaster who was at the tiller. "Are you getting a bite yet?"

"Yes sir, just starting..." And a few seconds later, "The helm is answering, sir." And, with ponderous grace, the *Trojan* started to move.

Just as they turned into the wind to make their way out of the bay, Walker turned around and saw a large group of men on horseback thundering into the fishing village. At the head was a very thin man with flaming red hair.

At about the same time, they passed the first of the larger schooners that were anchored in the bay. Walker looked at its stern plate to see its name.

It was called the *Cardinal*.

* * *

You have to give credit where credit is due; the *Cardinal* was a beautiful ship. She was a topsail schooner and, at 97 feet length and 17 feet beam, she was slightly shorter, thinner and much faster than the *Trojan*. On that hull, she crowded two masts to the *Trojan*'s one, and over 2000 square feet of sail.

Both masts held fore and aft mainsails that, like the *Trojan*, were tied down to a boom and gaff arrangement. Instead of a single jib, it had both a jib and a forestaysail. But the most distinguishing features were the topsails. Instead of fore-and-aft, they were square. In effect, it gave the *Cardinal* the best of both worlds.

Heading into the wind, she could use the highly efficient fore-and-aft sails, and running before the wind, she could use the square topsails. Into the wind, she was not as fast as a pure fore-and-aft ship like the *Trojan*, and before the wind not as fast as true square-rigger; but, as a compromise, she was superb.

The *Cardinal* had one other characteristic that the *Trojan* lacked. She had guns—six 12-pounders, three on a side, and one 6 pounder in the bow and one in the stern as chasers. She would never strike fear into the heart of a genuine man-o-war; but the 12-pounder was not a trivial weapon. Nine feet long, it could throw a 12-pound iron ball over two miles; and with a 4-pound powder charge, it could penetrate a foot thick piece of solid oak at 1000 yards. In short, the *Cardinal* was more than enough to overcome or even sink an unarmed Chesapeake merchantman, and that's what the *Trojan* was.

"She's getting underway," Smith muttered to no one in particular as he watched the *Cardinal* through his telescope. The *Trojan* was now well into Mobjack Bay and had every stitch of canvas set.

"Quartermaster, come to east-southeast and hold her steady."

Standing next to Hayes, Smith asked: "What are your plans?"

"I plan to do the only sensible thing *to* do in this situation."

"Which is?"

"Run like hell."

After a minute or so of silence, he could sense the concern of the four refugees gathered around him, and decided to share his thoughts. "All right, here's the way I figure it," he began. "The *Cardinal* is faster than we are at all sailing points except into the wind. She might even be faster there too, but I think we can at least hold our own.

"The wind is out of the east, as it usually is this time of year, so if we were to try to make a run north—to Bal-more, she'd catch us by night fall. The same thing is true if we try to head south and leave the Chesapeake by the Cape Henry passage. She'd catch us before we ever got to open ocean.

"No, the only direction we can go is easterly, and sail as close to the wind as we can."

"Wait a minute," Smith interjected. "We certainly can't leave the Chesapeake over the top of the middle ground. So, sooner or later, we'll have to turn south to make for the Cape Henry passage. Either way, if we go to Baltimore or Cape Henry, he'll get us."

"I know. That's why I plan to leave via the Cape Charles passage," Hayes said quietly.

"What?" Smith and Hanover asked simultaneously. Not sure if they had heard him right.

"Cape Charles."

"But with Cape Charles you can never tell if the channel is open. Sometimes the current will shift the sand one way and you can take a first rate through. Other times you can't get a rowboat through without grounding. How do you know which way the passage will be?"

"I don't; and if he follows us in, neither does he. How lucky do you feel today?"

The *Trojan* plunged on, running as close to the easterly wind as she could. Fortunately, that tack also took her on a direct line from Mobjack Bay to the tip of Cape Charles.

Walker and Smith had gone below to see if there was anything in the hold that could be used as weapons. Susan Whitney went below, with some trepidation, to inspect the galley. Hanover stayed on deck with Hayes as they executed the long reach to Cape Charles.

Had they not been running for their lives, it would have been a glorious day for a sail. The sky was crystal blue with high white fleecy clouds. Gulls swooped and sailed on the freshening breeze and the water was just beginning to white cap. The *Trojan* was handling the full set of sails well and the sound of wood working on wood could be heard throughout the ship—not harsh or strained but measured and even, like the breathing of a horse that has hit his stride.

There was nothing for the two men to do but watch the direction of the wind, the set of the sails and watch the ship behind them that was pulling every nautical trick in the book to catch up.

Finally Hanover asked, "Why are you doing it, Hugh?"

"Doing what? Heading for Cape Charles?"

"No, all of this. Risking your ship, even your life, to get us away. As you say, you're not a British subject anymore. Indeed, the navy would hang you if they could find you. So, why do it?"

Hayes thought for a moment. "There's two reasons, I guess. The first is Susan Whitney. I don't know how well you know her, but she's a very special lady. There isn't a man on the *Richmond* that wouldn't give up his right arm if she needed it. Take me, for example.

"Two years ago we was in the Mediterranean, up along the coast of North Africa. We put into some port—don't even remember which one it was. Anyway, we put in to replenish our supply of water and firewood and I was in charge of the shore party.

"I was helping to load the firewood and reached down to grab some logs when something bit me or stung me—never even saw what it was. But the pain wasn't much, so I didn't think anything of it.

"Later that night my hand started to swell up and the pain started. After a few hours, it got worse and the swelling started to move up my arm. The ship's doctor was drunk, as usual, so I went to Susan who tried to treat it. She soaked my arm, put compresses on it, did everything she could. Then the fever started. I would go from sweating to chills and back again in the span of a few minutes.

"For two days and nights she never left my side. Putting wet compresses on my head, keep me covered when I'd toss off my blankets, spoon-feeding me burgoo, and mostly just talking to me. That's what I remember the most. Even when I was half crazy from the fever, she would just talk to me so I would know that someone was there. I might have been delirious, but I *did* know. I knew that someone cared and that made me less afraid. She saved my life as far as I am concerned.

"I am telling you, Bill. If that woman were to ask me to walk through hell for her, I would hesitate only long enough to ask her where the entrance was located. And, it wasn't just me. I seen her do the same kind of thing, time and again, for other members of the crew."

Hayes went silent, lost in recollection.

"You said there were two reasons," Hanover reminded him.

"Yeah, but the second one is harder to explain." It was clear Hayes was not comfortable talking about this next item.

"Look, I was born and bred an Englishman. I remember once, as a child, my dad took me to see the king make his annual progress to Canterbury. He put me on his shoulder, he did, just so I could catch a glimpse of him and have something to tell my grandchildren. There was no one that believed in 'God, king and country' more than I did.

"Then, I got pressed into the navy. Just picked up off the street and hauled away like I was a criminal. And even then, that wouldn't have been so bad, but once you're on a ship, you're almost never let off—at least not in an English port. They never let common seamen go ashore for fear they'll run away, and I didn't step foot on land for years. Hell, it was over a year before I could get a message to my family and let them know what happened to me. They thought I was dead.

"So, we were in Charleston harbor. By this time, I was the ship's Master-at-Arms and they trusted me, so I was allowed to go ashore to help the ship's purser pick up some supplies. I was on American soil. I knew freedom and a new life lay within reach; so, I took it. I ran and I became... well, I became both an American and an Englishman."

"How can you be both?"

"Ah... yes, well, that's the thing that's so hard to explain. It's also the thing that's so hard to explain about this damn war we're fighting. I would still be as loyal a subject as ever walked the earth, if they had just left me alone that day in Chelsea. That's all. That's all I ever asked, was to be left alone.

"That's all these people are asking for. They don't want to fight a revolution. They don't want to rebel against their king. They would be as loyal and devoted as any subject if the government had only let them be. That's what all this yammer about 'freedom' and 'liberty' is all about. We just want to be left alone. Is that too much to ask?

Hanover had no reply.

"Anyway, I ran across Susan and she told me about you. I decided I couldn't let Susan down and, in a funny kind of way, that I couldn't let my king down either—even though he's not my king any more. Does that make any sense to you?"

"I am not sure."

"I am not sure either, but that's the way I feel. Hell, it's the way I think most Americans feel."

* * *

"Ouch! Damn it," Walker swore. "That's the third time I've hit my head on a beam."

"Then be more careful," Smith replied. "Rest assured those beams are not jumping out to hit you. You are hitting them."

"Feels the same either way."

Walker and Smith were going through the hold to see if there was anything that could be used as weapons if the *Cardinal* should close and try to board her. There was not much to choose from.

Most of the cargo consisted of bails of tobacco. In front of the tobacco were several trunks, probably containing some southern merchant's personal effects. Next to that were a couple kegs of long hull nails, a keg of gunpowder and some crates, all bound for a general store somewhere. Walker levered open the first two crates and found spools of cloth destined eventually to become ball gowns for some lucky Baltimore debutantes. The third contained a dozen silver candleholders; each placed in a protective wooden tube and covered with straw.

"Well, maybe we can throw the candleholders at 'em," Walker remarked.

"That's a wonderful idea," replied Smith sarcastically. "Fetch a man along side the head with a candleholder and, I am telling you, it's a fearsome thing."

"Three fathom, this line!" The two heard the call coming from on deck.

"What's that?" asked Walker.

"They're taking soundings; we must be getting close to Cape Charles. You about done?"

"Yeah, let's get back on deck."

The two men emerged on to the main deck in time to hear the second call from the fo'c'sle. "Two fathoms plus a half, this line."

The ship had reduced sail for their transit of the dangerous Cape Charles passage. Walker looked aft and saw the *Cardinal* had gained on them alarmingly.

"Three fathoms."

"What's the plan, captain?" Smith asked.

"That's Cape Charles up there on the left. We know there's a shallow off to starboard and in-between is the passage. What we don't know is how deep the passage is; it changes literally every day."

"What's your draft?"

"We draw about eight feet; the *Cardinal* draws nine or ten."

Hayes had placed his second mate in the fo'c'sle where he could watch the water ahead. His job was to look for lighter colored water indicating a shallow area, or even for actual sandbars peaking above the waves. By using hand signals, he could direct Hayes to avoid the hazards.

With this combination of hand signals from the second mate, soundings coming from the leadsman and pure luck, Hayes was able to thread his way through the Cape Charles passage. The thing was the *Cardinal* also had a man in his fo'c'sle sending signals and a man swinging a weight. What they didn't have was luck.

"Sir, the *Cardinal*... She's grounded!"

All hands looked aft and, sure enough, a sandbar that had just tickled the keel of the *Trojan* had caught the slightly deeper drafted *Cardinal*. "It's like watching a bad carriage accident in slow motion," thought Walker.

The *Cardinal* was driving along at about eight knots when it hit the submerged sand. The prow struck first and climbed the bank followed by the rest of the bow, which displaced a huge quantity of sand as it plowed in. The effect on the ship's occupants was dramatic. Everyone shot forward and, unless they happened to be holding on to something, were knocked off their feet.

The burden of the damage, however, was borne by the masts. When the hull came to a sudden stop, the masts continued to move forward. Add to that the fact that the masts grow thinner as they move higher and that they had their topsails run out; and the *Cardinal* was lucky that only one of her masts whipped forward and snapped.

Walker looked back and saw the *Cardinal*'s bow much higher out of the water than it should be and the foremast topsail slowly toppling over at a crazy angle, like a badly broken arm.

"We got'em," Walker exclaimed, pumping his fist.

"Maybe, maybe not," replied Hayes. "The main thing is we've gotta get out of here as quick as we can."

"What you do mean, 'maybe not'? They're high and dry?"

"I'd feel a lot better if they were hung up on rock or clay instead of sand. Rock usually breaks open the hull. Clay usually creates a suction that keeps the hull stuck fast. But sand? Let's just hope their skipper doesn't know what he's doing."

Unfortunately, while Captain Finch might have his failings, incompetence at sea was not one of them.

* * *

"Damnation and hell fire," swore Finch as he picked himself up off the deck. He knew exactly what had happened and his main immediate worry was whether he still had any masts left. He looked up relieved to see that only the foretopmast had gone by the boards. Everything else seemed to be holding. He quickly ordered his men to release the lines holding up the mainsails and jibs. By dropping those sails, all forward motion was taken off the ship to keep his situation from getting worse.

He knew there were only two ways to get off the sand bar, by using the sails to push her off, or by using the anchor. Doing the latter, called kedging, would involve placing the anchor in a small boat, rowing out 30 or 40 yards, dropping the anchor, securing the free end of the anchor line to the windless, and using human power to haul in on the anchor rope, pulling the ship off the bar.

The fastest way to do it was with the sails and, with the *Trojan* free of the shallows and about to round Cape Charles, speed was of the essence.

He decided to try it, first, by using his remaining topsail. It would not give him much thrust but if it worked, it would make it less likely that he would back into yet another sandbar, perhaps destroying his rudder. On the other hand, he had hit the sandbar under full sail so he knew he had driven on pretty hard. The only thing he could do was try. The *Trojan* had almost disappeared around the cape and with it went his dreams of wealth and fame.

He snapped an order to his afterguard and the square-rigged main topsail started to swivel around the mast so that it's face pointed directly into the wind. This mashed the sail directly against the mast, which was the opposite of its usual configuration of pushing the sail from behind. The wind was coming in off the port quarter, an oblique angle, to the ship so Finch could not hope that it would push the ship straight back. But maybe... just maybe... it would exert enough side pressure to break the bow loose.

By now the *Trojan* had disappeared around the corner of the cape, which made Finch even more frantic. Two minutes, three minutes, five minutes went by and the *Cardinal* was still hard aground. He could only stare at the men who were cutting away the useless fore topsail and wish he could bring it into play.

Another set of commands and the boom for the fore mainsail was swung to port and the sail hoisted so that it's face, too, was facing the wind. Three minutes, five minutes, no luck. But Finch had one more trick to play with the sails.

He gave a series of commands that ran up the mainsail and swung the main mast boom out to the starboard side. By cajoling his crew to pull ever harder, he got the boom past 90 degrees so that it too was catching some of the eastern wind.

Nothing happened. Three minutes, five minutes, 10 minutes, still nothing.

"Bosun, prepare one of the small boats to take the anchor. We're going to have to kedge this damn thing off. I want you to also…"

"Sir, she's coming off," came a cry from the fo'c'sle.

Finch ran to the bow. About half way, he almost tripped as the ship slipped back another foot or two. Just after arriving on the fo'c'sle the ship gave an abrupt lurch, then another, and then he could feel it sliding clear. He looked over the side and saw swirling brown water as further evidence he was off.

"Furl all sails except the fore topsail," he yelled. Then turning to the bosun, "I want two men up here with sounding leads. We're going to tiptoe out of here and if we go on to another sandbar, we're going to kedge off using your body as the anchor. Is that clear?"

* * *

Activity on the *Trojan* was no less frantic.

"We're clear," exclaimed Susan who was standing at the taffrail watching the *Cardinal* disappear behind Cape Charles. "He's still on the sandbar. We're free. Let's make a run for it."

"He won't be on that sandbar forever. We are not free. And we ARE making a run for it," replied Hayes. "This is as fast as this tub will go. The problem is that he'll eventually catch us; he's that much faster then we are. No matter how much of a lead we have, somewhere between here and New York, he'll get us."

"So, what do we do?"

Hayes was now addressing the group. "He saw us round the cape with Fisherman's Island to larboard, so he thinks we're headed for open ocean. But see that spit of land over there off our port bow? That's the southern tip of Smith Island. We're going to take the inside passage which will eventually put us in Hog Island Bay. If we can get that far by nightfall without him seeing us, we can hole-up until morning. I am hoping he'll come screaming around the cape, assume we headed north to New York, further assume we're just on the other side of the horizon and come after us."

"What if he doesn't?" asked Walker. "It seems to me he has two choices: either we are somewhere on the inside passage or we are hull down on the other side of the horizon."

"Then, he has a 50/50 chance of being right."

"And what happens of he guesses right?"

"Then we are well and truly screwed."

With that, Hayes altered course a few degrees, ducked in behind Smith Island and slowed to a crawl. The islands provided a nice visual barrier to hide behind as they made their way north, but the track was a torturous one. Hayes did not have a chart of those islands, after all, he was a Chesapeake sailor, and so he had no idea of the water depth. He would have to go slow, sling the lead, and be patient.

They picked their way inside Smith Island, Myrtle Island, Ship Shoal, Wreak Island, and Cobb Island. Just as night was falling, they entered Hog Island Bay, dropped their anchor, furled their sails, took a deep breath, looked up—and there was the *Cardinal*, guns run out, anchored inside the mouth of the Great Machipongo Inlet, the only way out of the Bay.

Finch had guessed right.

* * *

The Council of War was finally called at midnight and it would be hard to find a more dejected group. They gathered on the quarterdeck, Walker and Smith were leaning against the taffrail, Hayes and Hanover were sitting on empty kegs, and Susan was sitting Indian-style on the deck. Everyone was silent.

Hayes finally opened the proceedings. "All right, folks, here's the situation." he said.

"Hogs Island Bay has only one way out of it and that's through the Machipongo Inlet. I know, you can see some other exits to the north, but they're too shallow—little more than creeks, really.

"Finch is anchored at the mouth of the bay. He's laying out there just waiting for dawn to take us; and, unless someone has some other ideas, I think we're about done."

"Why can't we fight past him?" Smith asked.

"With what? He's got six guns; we've got none."

"What about that swivel gun forward?" Susan asked.

"Doesn't work. Never has. We got a keg o' gunpowder below but we're just shippin' it. I'd certainly never try using it in that old swivel."

Walker was silent, thinking hard.

"Look, I don't want to make this sound like a bad novel, but I am the one Finch wants," Hanover said. "I really appreciate everything you all have done for me. Really, I do. But, the game is over. If I give up, he'll let you go. I am sure of it."

"I am sorry, Your Highness, but you don't have a vote," Smith said.

Hanover snapped back. "First of all, it's 'Bill' not 'Your Highness.' I thought we had that settled. And second, what the hell do you mean I have no vote?"

"Not anymore. As you said, the game is up. We are not discussing the fate of Midshipman Bill Hanover here; we're discussing the fate of Prince William Henry. God only knows the implications to the crown, the empire and even the world if you were to be captured. You would become the world's greatest bargaining chip and there's no way of knowing where that might lead."

"No, we have to get you out. That's all there is to it."

"Hugh, if you had a few guns, could you get us out then?" Smith asked.

"I can't guarantee anything but, yeah, it would increase our odds considerable. I could use our speed in sailing against the wind to try to blow past him. A couple of guns, even small ones, might keep him at bay long enough to do that. After that, assuming neither ship is badly damaged in the exchange of gunfire, it would be a foot race and I would make sure it's a foot race to windward. It's not much of a chance, but it *would* be a chance."

"But we don't have any guns," Susan pointed out.

"Precisely," Hayes added.

"I don't care. There must be a way to fight them. We can't just give up the prince," Smith said, and as far as he was concerned, that was that. "There must be a way."

The wind could be heard slapping various lines and cables against the mast. The water could be heard lapping up against the side of the hull. A heron could be heard registering a complaint from across the water; but no human voice was answering Smith's challenge.

After a painfully long pause, Walker finally muttered, "There's a way."

And Walker immediately put everyone to work.

* * *

He started by taking a three-inch diameter auxiliary spar and cutting off pieces like he was slicing bologna. He cut 12 that were about two inches and 12 that were about 1 inch thick and set Smith to work drilling small holes through the center of each. When he was done, Smith was to take the two-inch slices, fill the holes with carpenter's glue and slide a hull nail through each so that a six-inch spike stood out from the end.

Susan was tasked with cutting 12 poles each about 6 feet long from some railing materials that were in the hold, and then drill two holes about six inches apart at one end. Turning to Hanover, Walker put him to work as well.

"Bill, I want you to find a hammer and pound some charcoal."

"Pardon?"

"I said, find a hammer somewhere. Then go down to the galley and get that sack of charcoal the cook uses to supplement his wood supply. Pound the charcoal until it's as fine as you can make it."

Hanover looked at him like he was crazy, but started work anyway. Seeing everyone busy with his or her tasks, Walker mysteriously disappeared below.

About an hour later, the various tasks were done. Walker reappeared and, with the help of several crewmen, was carrying the crate of silver candleholders, a keg of gunpowder, some light line and some fuses. Without a word to anyone he opened the crate, took out each of the 12 wooden tubes and began throwing the candleholders over the side, putting the wooden tube lovingly back into it's pigeon hole.

Hayes went nuts! "Are you crazy? Those candle holders are almost pure silver!"

"Oh, sorry." And he shifted his aim, throwing the candleholders into the scuppers as if they were trash and treating the foot and a half long protective wooden tubes like they were gold.

"All right, folks. It's time for you to begin assembling these things."

"Sidney and Bill grab a tube and a spike-plug. I want you to put some carpenter's glue around the side of the wooden plug then slide it into one end of your tube with the spike sticking out. When we have all 12, let them dry for a bit and give them to Susan and me."

About an hour later, Susan and Walker began attaching the poles by sliding nails through the holes Susan had made and pressing them through the soft wood of the tubes. Thus anchored, Hayes and one of his crewmen began tightly tying the poles to the tubes to give them extra support. They then put the tubes, spike down and pole up, into their pigeonholes in the crate.

"All right, we're almost there. Now, Bill and Sidney, I want you to take this measure and pour exactly two scoops of gunpowder into each of the tubes. Place a length of fuse through the hole so there are a couple inches running out each side. Then, put some more carpenter's glue around the edges of the plug and shove it down on top of the gunpowder.

"Oh, yeah, one more thing. Do your best to not blow us up."

When they had finished there were twelve devices sitting, face down, in the packing crate. Each had a steel spike glued into a wooden plug, gunpowder in the middle and another plug, with a fuse, behind the gunpowder. There was still several inches of space, however, between the gunpowder plug and the end of the tube.

"Here's where we put in the final touch," Walker announced.

He put a measure of gunpowder into a bowl, added a quarter measure of the charcoal powder Hanover had produced and thoroughly mixed them together. As a last step, he dampened the compound with a small amount of water, kneaded it into a kind of damp putty and packed the result, along with a short fuse, into the back end of the first tube. He repeated the procedure with each of the remaining tubes.

"That's it. We're done."

"Wonderful," Smith announced. "Now, would you care to tell us what it is we are done with?"

"It's simple," Walker explained. "Tomorrow morning when the *Cardinal* moves in for the kill, we'll have a little surprise for them." And he picked up a device to illustrate, pointing as he went.

"It's called a rocket. A friend of mine back in my Harvard days was experimenting with them. We light the fuse in the back end. The gunpowder/charcoal mixture will do a controlled burn—not explode because of the extra carbon I mixed in—and go off. We'll launch each one at the *Cardinal* and, when it gets there, it will stick in the side of the ship via the spike. At that point the 'engine' powder will have burned to the bottom and ignited the fuse coming out of the gunpowder compartment, which ignites the gunpowder and... BOOM!"

The group was quiet for a moment, lost in embarrassed silence, not knowing how to break the news to Walker. Finally, Smith piped up.

"Lucas, people in the British Navy have been talking about rockets for years. The Fire Master at the Royal Laboratory in Woolwich, General Desaguliers, has actually experimented with them and William Congreve—the son, not the father—will talk your ear off about them. But I've seen them tested, Lucas; and they don't work. They're a bust; everyone knows that.

"Sure, in theory, they sound great, but they're uncontrollable. They fly all over the place and no one, but *no* one knows where they're going to land. I've personally seen rockets actually double back and attack the people that fired them. What's going to keep your rockets from doing the same thing?" Smith finally asked.

"Nothing," Walker replied to the now silent group. After a pause he continued. "My friend thought that the mistake was that the stabilizing poles were not long enough. He calculated that they needed to be at least four times the length of the rocket body. Well, that's what I"ve done. I made the poles four times the length of the body."

"Did he ever try out his calculations?" Susan asked.

"No. Not that I know of; but come on... what else have we got?"

The group fell silent again, until Susan again spoke up. "All right then, what the 'ell. Let's give it a go."

Sidney, entering into the spirit of things agreed. "Absolutely. We'll show them what a little ingenuity can do, what? But, Lucas... ah... how do you fire the bloody things?

Walker held on to his sample rocket. "Step over here, my friends, and all shall be made known."

He took the group to the ancient swivel gun that was mounted on the fo'c'sle. Tied to the top of it were the results of Walker's activities below decks while the others were building the rockets. It was an extremely simple mechanism consisting a sheet of copper hull plating about six inches wide and curved along its length into a "U" shape. It looked like a long pipe that had been cut in half along its long axis.

"We'll have three people manning this launcher. One person places the rocket into this copper tray, like so. You have to make sure that the tray is supporting only the rocket body and the pole is on top and not obstructed. That person then steps back to get another rocket.

"The second person points the swivel gun just as if he were going to fire a ball at the other ship. When he..."

"Or she," Susan chimed in.

"Or she," Walker continued without missing a beat, "is happy with the aim he... or she... will lock the gun's barrel by putting this shim in the swivel, and get out of the way. The third man will quickly light the short engine fuse with a slow match.

"Any questions?"

The group was silent for a moment, and then Hanover spoke up.

"Will it work?"

Sir Sidney Smith
1764 - 1840

Two 32-gun Royal Navy frigates, similar to the
HMS Richmond

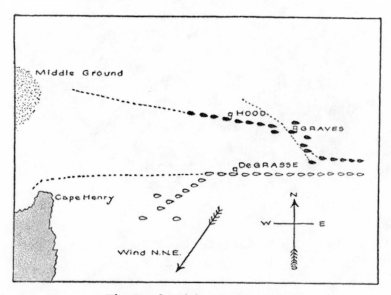

The Battle of the Capes - UK
(Battle of the Chesapeake - US)

Swan Taven - Where Smith and Walker first met
Prince William

Moore House - Where the team of Smith, Walker
and Whitney first formed

Admiral Thomas Graves

Admiral Samuel Hood

Count François de Grasse

Captain James Saumarez

Admiral George Rodney

Captain Sir Charles Douglas

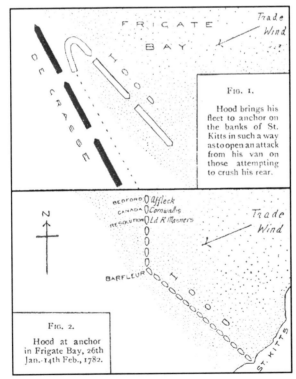

The Battle of Frigate Bay

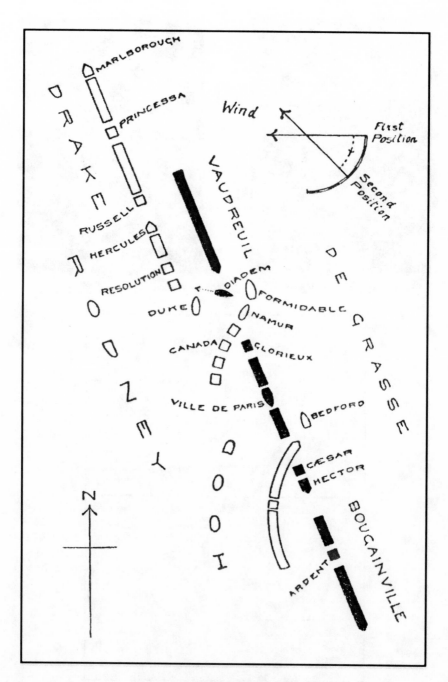

The Battle of the Saintes

CHAPTER SEVEN

THE sun came up over Hog Island in a most unusual way. Because it was low in the sky, it was, of course, a large, brilliant, orange ball; but off in the distance some high thin clouds bisected the sun making it look like it had rings, like Saturn.

Hayes used the traditional nautical definition of "dawn"; namely, it's dawn when you can "tell a gray goose from a white goose at a distance of a mile." By that definition, or any other, it was now dawn and orders were being given to get the *Trojan* underway.

Hayes set the topsail and jib, started the ship slowly running toward the *Cardinal*, and called the four refugees together.

"All right, here's what we're going to do," Hayes began. "We have one card I want to play before we resort to those... whatever they are... things you made. We're gonna approach the *Cardinal* slowly, like we're giving up. Then, at the last minute, I am going to drop the Mainsail and sheer off on a starboard tack. The wind is easterly again so I am hoping I can get by him and into the wind before he can react. By the time he comes around to chase us, we'll have a lead—one that I hope I can significantly increase."

All right, granted, it wasn't much of a plan, but it was a plan, so everyone nodded agreement.

The *Trojan* closed to 200 yards. Then 150... 100... "Stand-by to raise mainsail," Hayes ordered. At 75 yards, Hayes was going to sheer off, but he never got a chance to do it. Without warning, three red lights blinked along the starboard side of the *Cardinal*. Before a warning could escape anyone's lips, a hole appeared in the *Trojan's* mainsail, a chunk disappeared from the mast about 10 feet up, and a corner of the captain's cabin exploded in a shower of splinters. A split second later the retort of three 12-pound guns could be heard, followed by confused voices simultaneously saying things like: "He's opened fire!" "Get down!" "Jesus Christ!" "That son of a bitch" and other observations that need not appear in this record.

"Up mainsail," Hayes screamed as he shoved the tiller over. The sail filled with a loud bang and the *Trojan* surged off on a tangent away from her tormentor. The *Cardinal*, however, was expecting the move and raised her canvas as well.

The two ships fell into a race to see which would reach the mouth of the Great Machipongo Inlet first. If the *Cardinal* could get there, the *Trojan* would be trapped in the bay where they could force the surrender of the prince and then pick the *Trojan* apart at her leisure.

Both ships put on all the canvas they could, given the tack they were on and the *Trojan* indeed proved to be faster to windward; but, the *Cardinal* had two advantages on the *Trojan*. First, she had the angle on any race to the inlet mouth; and, second...

The back quarter of the captain's cabin came apart with a crash, another hole appeared in the mainsail this time closer to the mast and the first hole appeared in the jib.

"He's got one gun trying to take out our tiller and two trying to bring down our mast. But he knows he's got to shoot carefully because he doesn't want to hurt or kill the prince. Now's the time, folks. If those things you cooked up actually work, now's the time to use 'em," yelled Hayes above the sounds of the ship.

* * *

Hayes assigned sail handling tasks to his crew while Hanover picked up the case of rockets and, with strength no one knew he had, carried them forward to the swivel gun. Susan raced ahead of him and threw the cover off the gun revealing the rocket tray, and Smith followed with a lit slow match.

Hanover pulled the first rocket out and placed it in the tray. Susan, who had sandwiched herself between the swivel gun and the jib, now made last second sight adjustments and slid a wooden wedge into the gun's swivel thus locking the barrel in position. She stepped back and Smith touched off the fuse.

Walker looked on in horror as the fuse sputtered to a stop without igniting the rocket motor.

"Damn," Walker exclaimed, and ran forward to throw the rocket over the side just as the next volley came in from the *Cardinal*. Two more holes appeared close to the mast and one more ball whizzed by Hayes' head back at the tiller.

"Any time now, folks, would be just fine," yelled Hayes while getting up off the deck.

"Bill, give me another one."

Susan checked the sighting on the swivel gun. "Sidney! Now!"

The fuse was lit and the rocket took off with an amazingly satisfying WHOOSH. It fishtailed toward the *Cardinal*, passing over her deck and landing in the ocean beyond.

When Walker turned around, Hanover had already placed another rocket in the tray and Susan, unleashing a string of oaths that would have done a bosun proud, was re-sighting the swivel gun. Smith stepped forward and... WHOOSH...

The third rocket hit and stuck in the hull near the bow. A few seconds later, a huge B-O-O-M echoed across the bay and Walker did his best to keep from dancing.

Hayes broke up the celebration, yelling from the stern: "Could you people act like maybe you've done this before and send another one?"

The *Cardinal* and the *Trojan* then settled into a slugfest while racing for the corner of the inlet. Both ships were suffering. The *Cardinal* had huge gouges taken out of her hull and superstructure. The *Trojan*'s aft hull was not in much better shape. In addition, the top 10 feet of her mast, along with the topsail, was hanging down and the jib was in tatters.

The climax of the battle, when it finally occurred, happened by accident.

The *Trojan* was heeled over when a round shot hit low on her hull on a spot that normally would be underwater. When she righted herself, water started pouring in. As all this was happening, the *Cardinal* tacked exposing a similar stretch of vulnerable hull and was nailed by one of Susan's rockets. Nether gunner planned the hit. Neither was aiming at that particular spot; yet, both ships were now seriously damaged.

As water poured into each ship, they both slowed down and further heeled over, exposing even more areas for target practice. The difference in the battle finally turned on the *Trojan*'s ability to fire her weapons so much faster than the *Cardinal*.

With only three rockets remaining, Susan stuck two into the *Cardinal*'s exposed hull before the *Cardinal* could get off another volley, and it was all over. The *Cardinal* was sinking and had put boats over to take the crew to nearby Hog Island. However, the *Trojan* wasn't in much better shape. The *Cardinal* had blown a hole in her side, which might have been managed, but it also opened up seams all over her ancient hull. The *Trojan* was sinking too, it's just that she was sinking slower than the *Cardinal* and could sail on—at least for a while.

At first, the four weren't sure what to do; they just looked at each other. Susan was standing next to the gun, her hair disheveled with strands sticking out in all directions, sweat was pouring down her face making rivulet lines through the soot from the rocket exhaust, dress seams were torn in several places from unaccustomed exertions and, peeking through it all was her smile. Walker thought he had never seen a woman look more beautiful.

Hanover finally broke the silence: "Way to go gunner!" And they fell into a group embrace, hugging, backslapping, and attempting (without much success) what in a later age would be called a "high-five."

The *Trojan* exited the inlet and swung north. Some of the ship's crew were working the pumps while others were bailing with buckets, but there was no hope. The *Trojan* was a river sloop, great for rivers and sheltered bays like the Chesapeake; but not designed for open ocean travel with holes in her hull. Several hours later Hayes called them together.

"Well, the one thing I can guarantee you is that we're not going to make it to New York. We're a couple miles off Chincoteague Island and I am pretty sure I can get us there. We can ground the ship and everyone will be perfectly safe; but you'll be stuck on Chincoteague. There are no towns or villages there, at least none that I know of, and there may or may not be water.

"Or, we can try to make the Delaware River and put into Lewes. I have some friends there that, I think, will help us out. The problem is that I don't know if we'll make it. If those seams get worse and we take in more water, or if the wind shifts to the north or northwest, we're dead.

"Name your poison, folks."

The group was quiet for a long moment. Finally, Susan spoke up. "Hugh, if we ground the ship on Chincoteague you'll loose it. If we make it to Lewes will you be able to save it?"

"Probably. There's a good shipyard there and I can charge the repairs to the owners. However, if we don't make it and sink, we'll not only loose the ship but we'll also quite probably drown in the bargain."

Susan looked around at the others and the decision was made without a word being spoken. "Set a course for the Delaware, Hugh."

The *Trojan* lasted for another five hours, which was about three hours longer than Walker thought it would. The shot hole had been plugged but seams were sprung below the waterline on both sides of the hull and the crude pump was fighting a loosing battle. To make matters worse, the wind had backed as Hayes had feared and the *Trojan* was now fighting it's way through it rather then being pushed from behind or from the side. The working of the ship's timbers while trying to sail close hauled made the seam problem even worse.

Nothing was being said. Nothing needed to be said. Silence had descended over the group. "After all we've gone through," thought Walker, "to have it end like this. It's absurd, really. Simply absurd."

Fifteen minutes later, the bow lookout called back. Actually, it was more of a question than anything else. "A sail? Sir, I think I see a sail."

"Where away?" Hayes automatically replied.

"One point off starboard, sir." Hayes adjusted his course to head for it while Smith jumped up on what was left of Hayes' cabin with a telescope.

"I think it's one of ours. A frigate," Smith said.

"How do you know it's one of ours?"

"I don't. The hull has French lines to her but those sails... those sails are English cut. I am sure of it."

An hour later, they heard a voice coming from across the water, faintly, but in perfect English. "Ahoy, the ship. Do you require assistance?"

As the group was celebrating, Susan noticed that Hayes was silent.

"Why are you so quiet, Hugh?

"I am not going aboard. I am going to stay here with the ship."

"Stay with the ship? The ship is sinking!"

"Yes, I know. But I'd much rather drown than be hanged."

"What are you talking about?"

"Susan, have you forgotten? I ran from a king's ship. They hang deserters."

The celebration immediately ended, as what Hayes said was true. The silence lasted a full minute, then another, before Susan quietly said, "No, you didn't."

"What?"

"No, you didn't. You didn't run. You were one of the men who rowed the women and children to safety at Yorktown, just before the *Richmond* was captured."

"Yes, of course." Smith instantly saw what Susan was suggesting and its implications.

"It's no good Susan," Hayes replied. "I am on the ship's books as a deserter."

"And where, exactly, are the ship's books? At this moment they're probably sitting in the corner of a clerk's office at the Admiralty in Paris, and will probably be used to start fires this winter."

"But the officers and men..."

"Are in a French prisoner-of-war camp, and probably will be until the war's over. After that, who'll care?"

"You rowed us ashore at Yorktown, Hugh. I saw it!"

"As did I," said Smith.

"As did I," said Walker.

"As did I," said Hanover. "And I dare even the First Lord of the Admiralty to call *me* a liar, even if he is my cousin."

***

By anyone's definition, the *Tisiphone* was a beautiful, well-run 36-gun frigate. Smith was right, she had French lines to her because she had been captured a few years earlier, patched-up, refitted and given over to Captain James Saumarez who now commanded her. They were met at the entry port by the ship's first lieutenant. After ascertaining they needed no immediate medical help, they were taken directly to the captain's cabin.

Sweaty, covered with soot, bleeding from several minor nicks and cuts, the four sat in straight-backed chairs in front of Captain Saumarez's desk. Saumarez was in his late 20's, a short, bantam-rooster of a man, who was the nephew of the great Admiral George Anson, the first Englishman to circumnavigate the world. His career, however, did not depend on his pedigree. He was a superb seaman and had a reputation as a ferocious fighter.

"Gentlemen, may I offer you some brandy or a tonic to fortify you after your ordeal?" Saumarez began. They all agreed except Walker. "Might I have a glass of lemon juice, if that is possible?"

"Certainly. Certainly." Saumarez signaled to his servant.

"Perhaps we should begin at the beginning. I am James Saumarez, captain of His Majesty's ship, the *Tisiphone*. And you are?"

Sidney spoke for all of them. "I am Lieutenant William Sidney Smith, formerly the first officer of the frigate *Richmond*. This is Mr. Lucas Walker, surgeon, and Miss Susan Whitney, surgeon's mate, also of the *Richmond*. At the end is Midshipman William Hanover who was stationed at Yorktown when we met."

Saumarez's eyes shot over to Bill. "Midshipman William Hanover? You are Prince William Henry?"

"I am," William replied, "although the title is not used when I am aboard ship. In the navy I am Midshipman Hanover, sir."

Saumarez fell back in his chair blowing out his breath in a deep sigh. "Yes, quite.

"You realize, of course, that no one knows where you are. Half of New York thinks you've been captured and the other half thinks you've escaped. God only knows what they think in London."

Shifting his gaze back to Smith, "Lieutenant, perhaps you could explain what you were doing bobbing around the ocean in a shot-up sloop with His Magis... with Midshipman Hanover in tow?"

Smith started with the meeting with Admiral Hood and proceeded from there. He didn't leave anything major out and embellished only enough to place Hayes on one of the Richmond's refugee boats at Yorktown. As he spoke, he realized the scope and enormity of the things that had happened to them—something that didn't occur to him while they were doing it.

When he concluded, Saumarez just sat there for a long moment. "Lieutenant, if I hadn't picked you up and seen your sloop myself; if I hadn't just met Midshipman Hanover; I would have you before the surgeon in a trice for a mental evaluation."

Walker smiled: "And he hasn't even heard *my* story yet," he thought.

"But, alas, I have," Saumarez continued.

"All right, you need to know we cannot turn back to drop off Midshipman Hanover. We are on our way to the West Indies to deliver important news to Admiral Hood. There's been a battle in the Bay of Biscay off France. We finally won one and it will have direct impact on Hood's operation. I'll take you to Admiral Hood and he can decide what to do with you.

"Meanwhile, Lieutenant Smith, you are tasked with writing a report on this little adventure of yours. I am sure the admiral, the Admiralty, and the king himself will be most interested in reading it. Mr. Walker and Miss Whitney, I will introduce you to our ship's surgeon. I am sure he'll be glad of the additional help. Mr. Hanover, my first lieutenant will escort you to your quarters.

"Which I hope will be in the midshipman's berth where I can resume my duties as a Midshipman in His Majesty's service."

That wasn't where Saumarez was about to send him, but he covered it well. "Yes, quite."

Before Saumarez could stand-up to end the meeting, Smith spoke. "Sir, we've been out of contact for many weeks. Could you apprise us on what's happened since we left, and what happened in the Biscay?"

"Yes, I suppose you have been a bit out of touch.

"You probably know that Cornwallis surrendered. After that debacle at the Capes, Graves took the fleet back to New York and De Grasse re-assumed his position at the mouth of the Chesapeake. There was nothing Cornwallis could do—his 5000 troops against 22,000 Americans and French—with no escape possible. In early October, Washington started to push his lines in; and on October 19th, Cornwallis surrendered.

"It must have been quite a sight. They say that, as the troops were marching out to give up their arms, the regimental band was playing the song: 'The World Turned Upside Down.' I am not quite

sure how that could be because I understand that Cornwallis had
no band at Yorktown; but it makes a good story because the song
fits so perfectly. Do you know the song, lieutenant?"

"No, sir."

"Well, the lyrics start out:

If buttercups buzz'd after the bee,

If boats were on land, churches on sea,

If ponies rode men and if grass ate the cows,

And cats should be chased into holes by the mouse,

If the mamas sold their babies

To the gypsies for half a crown;

If summer were spring and the other way round,

Then all the world would be upside down.

"The irony of it was that on that very day, October 19th, Hood
had left New York with a relief fleet for Cornwallis, more ships,
more guns, and 5000 more troops. If Cornwallis had only held out
four more days, the fleet would have been there with blood in their
eyes, to avenge their earlier defeat."

"Why did it take so long for the fleet to come back?"

"The usual dithering. Some people thought we should stage a
diversionary attack on Philadelphia to draw De Grasse out. Others
wanted to wait for more ships to be prepared. And there are some
who would say that there simply was no one around with the nerve
to sail back to the Chesapeake, fight their way through the French
fleet, land troops and supplies, and fight their way back out again."
With his voice Saumarez made it clear he was of the latter opinion,
without actually saying so.

"You see Washington figured out that no land force can act de-
cisively unless they also control the sea. Unfortunately, that has
not yet dawned on our generals. So, Washington, being no fool,
did his best to get De Grasse and his fleet to stay around and help
him attack Charleston or even tiny Wilmington. No dice. He said
he was committed to the Spanish to get back to the Caribbean to
help take Jamaica. But despite that, as a sop to Washington, De
Grasse headed to Yorktown. Yorktown was settled and it turns out
it all depended on having a fleet. Cornwallis was promised one;
Washington had one. And that was that."

"How did they take the loss at home?" Smith asked.

"Not well. When the Prime Minister, Lord North, heard about it, they say it was like he had been shot. He grabbed his chest, said 'Oh, God! It's all over!' and collapsed in his chair. For some reason, though, the people didn't blame Graves for losing America. They just said that if Rodney had been there it would never have happened. The French, of course, called for a national holiday."

"Excuse me, sir, but why is everyone talking about losing America? Cornwallis' surrender is a very serious matter indeed, but his forces only represent about a quarter of the British troops in America. We still vastly outnumber the rebels."

"But America is not the only thing going on. You might not have heard that the Spanish have recaptured Western Florida from us, Tobago was taken by the French and Jamaica is about to fall if De Grasse has his way. Minorca in the Mediterranean has been under siege for the past seven months, Gibraltar is about to surrender; and, to top it off, a combined French-Spanish fleet is currently cruising around the entrance to the English Channel like they owned it.

"No, I suspect America will soon be put on the back kettle. But that's all right, we'll be back."

"Why do you say that?"

"This American 'independence' is nonsense—just a stupid quarrel that's gotten out of hand. Once the Americans taste what it means to be a truly independent nation—the complexity, the problems—they'll come running back to us like lost children. They're lead by a collection of wild-eyed madmen who can rant and rave all right, but can they govern? Never!

"Besides, we can always send some more troops over at any time and take it back if we need to."

Walker had to bite his tongue to keep from saying anything.

"What happened at the Bay of Biscay, sir?" Smith prodded.

Saumarez paused, then looked off into the distance, "Oh my, what a day *that* was.

"You see, in the West Indies the frogs are running short of everything but yellow fever; and the arrival of De Grasse's fleet hasn't made that supply situation any better. In addition, they need more men if they want to take Jamaica from us. So, they put together a huge relief fleet that was being protected by nineteen ships of the line and I don't know how many frigates and support ships. We set out to meet them, under Admiral Kempenfelt, with twelve ships of the line and only two frigates, ours being one of them.

"On December 12th we ran into light fog so the admiral sent us to scout ahead and see if we could locate the French. I am proud to say we did exactly that. As the fog got thicker, however, did 'Old Kempy' tell us to reduce sail? No, indeed. Instead, he re-positioned us in the fog, and how we kept from colliding with each other I'll never know.

"Anyway, late morning the fog lifted and downwind from us was the French merchant fleet and *downwind from them* were the French warships. Kempenfelt had seen through the fog better than De Guichen, the French admiral, had seen in broad daylight. We could scarcely believe our eyes. We wore into a line abreast and went into... I don't know how else to describe it... but we went into what amounted to a cavalry charge.

"It was unbelievable. I don't think I'll ever see anything like it again—fourteen ships of the line with every inch of canvas laid on and studdingsails lashed to the yards. I swear if we thought it would have given us an extra half-knot, we would have hung out the men's laundry.

"We plowed pell-mell into that helpless merchant fleet like the Horse Guards on a drunken terror. Broadsides going off in all directions, ships surrendering all over the place, and the French warships, downwind, helpless to beat upwind in time to do anything about it. We captured twenty ships that day, lieutenant. Imagine! Fourteen British ships captured twenty merchant vessels—each loaded to the gunnels with supplies that Britain badly needed and which we did *not* want to see in the West Indies.

"In any event, I was then dispatched to bring the news to Admiral Hood. It wasn't until I got to New York that I learned that in December he had already sailed for the Caribbean."

"And here we are," said Smith.

"And here we are," replied Saumarez.

* * *

The four quickly fell into the routine of the *Tisiphone's* day. This wasn't hard because every British warship everywhere in the world shared that same routine and they were used to it.

Smith spent most of his time at his desk working on the report—a report that had to be just right because it would be the first notice of his name among the powers that be. Hayes and his crew blended into the ship's company where, as experienced seamen, they were readily accepted.

Lucas Walker and Susan got to know the *Tisiphone's* surgeon, Hiram Boult. Boult was a tall handsome man in his early 40's with a ready smile and easy-going nature. He was an exception in the British Naval Medical Corps in that he was a fully qualified physician, sober most of the time, and genuinely cared about the health and well being of the seamen. What made him especially unusual was that he cared about more than just the men's immediate aches and pains. He wanted to know about their health in the context of their life in the navy and in the context of the wives, loved ones and families they left behind. More than once Walker saw him writing letters home for seamen who were illiterate and who wanted to get word to their families. This made him a maverick with his peers; but it also helped to make him a ship favorite and immediately drew Susan and Lucas to him.

Boult had a growing scurvy problem on his hands and Walker tried to help as much as he could. Both Whitney and Boult—not to mention Lucas himself—were astonished when out of kindness he gave some of the stricken men a bit of his precious personal lemon drink supply to ease their thirst and, within days they, and only they, got better. There couldn't be a connection. It had to be just chance. But it was certainly a curious affair and Boult decided he would investigate it further.

Other than that their duties under Dr. Boult were light, which gave the two a chance to genuinely relax for the first time in months. They spent hours on deck just appreciating the things around them; and the farther south the *Tisiphone* went, the more wonders there were to appreciate.

Walker had never seen flying fish before, yet there they were—schools of them leaping out of the water, fleeing from some threat. Occasionally a school would leave the water only to realize, too late, that a ship was occupying their intended landing zone. Occasionally a fish would land on deck through an open gun port to be picked-up by an eager seamen where, later, he would try to coax or bribe the cook into preparing it. They looked and tasted like herring, and having one land at your feet was considered a certain sign of good luck.

Overhead, were the huge white birds the men referred to as "Mother Carey's chickens"; Walker never did find out their proper name.

They were pure white, stately, and among the most graceful birds Walker had ever seen. They always seemed to be on some important errand, however. You could see them heading out to sea in the morning, flying on a direct line due east, and come back in the evening flying due west. What they did during the day no one could image because there was simply nothing out there in the direction they were going.

Then there were the occasional whales. Mammoth creatures, they would suddenly surface near the ship, blow water into the air and parallel the ships course for a while. They seemed to have no fear of the ship. If anything they seemed to be attracted by the ship's size as if it were some long lost, but strangely silent, cousin.

But everyone's favorites, from ships boys to grizzled old seamen, were the dolphins that danced around the ship. They cavorted like children, seeming to play a game of who could cut across the bow of the ship the closest without touching. But what truly astonished everyone was their speed. The *Tisiphone* had to be making at least eight knots, yet the dolphins were dashing around her like she was at anchor in a sheltered cove.

Then, just as you found yourself entranced by the beauty and benevolence of the sea, you would be jerked back by the sight of a shark's fin cutting the water; and the reality of life in and on the sea would be brought home. The sea was beautiful, no question of that. But, benevolent? No.

Those flying fish learned to fly because, without it, they would be eaten alive. Indeed, every living thing in the ocean was, in reality, potential dinner for something else—from plankton to whales. And, of all the creatures that do not belong there, the chief one is man.

Ask any sailor who has fallen overboard or had his ship shot out from under him. Ask anyone who, for any reason, has found themselves thrashing around alone in the ocean. Man has no natural business at sea. Ships are merely devices designed temporarily to keep a man from drowning.

* * *

The sun had dropped suddenly as it seems to do in the southern climates and a cooling early evening breeze was sweeping the deck. Walker and Susan were standing by the starboard rail marveling at the almost painfully beautiful colors of sunset.

"Lucas, tell me about your life before... you know, before you came here."

Walker laughed. "There isn't much to say, and certainly nothing worth hearing."

"Tell me anyway."

Lucas gave that request some thought. He had no particular inclination to tell anyone much about his past, but there was something different at work here. He could feel the bonds that had formed between himself and Susan and Sidney. It was almost as if they had become like brother and sister to him—in some ways not quite that, in other ways a whole lot more. All right, maybe Susan had a right to know.

"As I say, not much to tell. I was born in Boston. Well, actually, it was in a place called Noddle Island, just across the bay from Boston. My mother was a Williams and her family had a large estate out there, so that's where she went when she was pregnant with me. But I grew up in Boston.

"My father was an apothecary and he had a very successful shop on Hanover Street, right on the corner of Hanover and Union. We lived in a huge old house a few blocks away on Queen Street. That's about it."

"Come, come, Lucas. Tell me about your brothers and sister."

"Two older brothers. The eldest started a firm that makes carriages; at least that's what he did initially. The other is an itinerant salesman. My mother died when I was 12. My younger sister got married when she was 16 and now lives in a little New Hampshire settlement called Franklin. I was the one that was supposed to follow in my dad's footsteps."

"I am sorry to hear about your mother. Truly I am. My father also died and I still miss him... more than I can say." The conversation paused for a moment.

"What was your childhood like?" Susan eventually continued.

"Oh, it was wonderful! One block to the west of us was a large park called Beacon Hill. Two blocks north was the Mill Pond over by Barton's Point, and three blocks to the east were the main docks for the city." Walker smiled as he went on, "My brothers and I would play army in the morning on Beacon Hill, go watch the ships unload at the docks, and play navy on the Mill Pond in the afternoon. I make an especially good pirate, by the way."

It was Susan's turn to smile.

"But the thing I remember the most was my dad's apothecary shop. Just the exotic odors alone that came out of that place... I can smell them even now. The pungent odor of leopard's bane and mimosa tree bark, mixing with the fragrance of Virginia spiderwort and scorpion grass, all clashing with the sharp tang of hartshorn and the spirits of wine which he used to distill them. You could walk in at any time and touch a root that came from far-off China, or a dried berry that came from South America. The place was magic. Simply magic."

"So, why didn't you become an apothecary?"

"My brother inherited the business."

"Your brother? I thought you said you were supposed to follow your dad?"

"Not when your child is a sot."

Susan said nothing for a moment. "You want to tell me?"

"You sure you want to hear?"

"Yes." Susan said it in a flat unemotional voice—a simple statement of fact.

"I guess it started about the time my mother died. Cholera took her and it was... well, it was bad.

"Anyway, my middle brother and I started to sneak drinks from my dad's supply. At first it was just a couple of kids trying to act like adults. But, for some reason, the alcohol seemed to affect me a lot more than my brother. My brother just got sick and stopped doing it. Oh, I got sick too, but not before experiencing... I don't know, I'll call it a feeling of peace—however brief—that I hadn't known since before ma died.

"So, the drinking continued on into my teens and became a growing problem; not that I recognized it as such, you understand. To me everything was normal. But now it was taking a lot more alcohol to get me drunk than before, and some of my friends started getting on me about it. So, I changed friends. I turned in the old set for a new group that was just as drunk as I was most of the time. Big improvement, huh?"

"But you graduated from college. You can't graduate from college and be a drunk at the same time."

"Yes, you can." Walker replied. "Oh, yes you can.

"What I found out is that, if you are bright enough, you can do next to nothing and scrape by; and I was bright enough. I doubt if I actually went to a third of the classes I was supposed to attend.

"So I graduated and got a job teaching at Harvard College. Actually, things were going fairly well until one evening at a formal dinner I got into my cups and somehow decided that the dean's young wife had a bosom that absolutely cried out for exploration, right then and there, at the dinner table.

"A month or so later I got my next job over at the College of New Jersey. The drinking had gotten worse. After all, an unemployed gentleman had a right to get drunk, didn't he? I lasted about a month before it was pointed out to me that to teach you actually had to show-up in a classroom now and then.

"My last stop was Mrs. Harrison's Academy for Discriminating Young Ladies. This was a 'finishing school' for young women where they primarily learned how to catch a husband—preferably at some point before their eggs dried up. The less said about that institution the better."

Walker stopped talking, seemingly lost in thought.

"And then?" Susan prodded.

Walker awoke. "Then I got mad."

"At who? It was your own fault."

"I know. And that's who I got mad at.

"I took a room at a run down inn and plunked a healthy purse in front of the innkeeper. He was to place two meals a day before my door and a pitcher of lemon juice three times during the day and once in the evening. Under no circumstances was he to open the door or to react to anything he heard going on behind it. He looked more than a bit dubious, but the purse was a hefty one so he agreed."

"Why lemon juice?"

"I thought maybe I could get rid of the alcoholism simply by flooding my blood stream with lemon juice. Besides, I like lemon juice."

"So what happened?"

"Oh, it was bad, Susan. *Really* bad. There was nothing simple about it. At first I got the shakes, then hot and cold flashes, vomiting, nightmares, hallucinations, and the cycle would start all over again. I thought it would never end, that I was simply going to die. In fact, I wanted nothing more in this world than *to* die. It went on for five days and then it started to taper off. Not go away, mind you, but taper off. After about eight days I was able to hold down both meals, and on the tenth day I ordered the innkeeper to make up a bath for me."

"And that ended it."

"No, it did not. To this day... if I could take a drink right now, I would, but I can't. Upon my life I can't and I won't. I will drink water, and I will drink my lemon juice; but that's it. I will *never* go through that again."

"And now?"

"And now, I have no idea. I am stuck on these ships, a half-baked, self-taught, surgeon. If I ever get off... I don't know. I hear there are a lot of colleges being built in the south and maybe they'll be far enough away from the dean's wife so even I can get a job at one."

"I am so sorry, Lucas," she said as she took his arm. She wasn't sure she completely understood everything he said, but he had taken her into his confidence, and she was moved.

* * *

"If I wasn't a gunner I wouldn't be here. Number two gun, FIRE!

"Away from my home and my family so dear. Number three gun, FIRE!

"If I wasn't a gunner I wouldn't be here. Number four gun, FIRE!"

The *Tisiphone* had rounded the point leading into English Harbor and was firing its salute to the governor. It was an old tradition, designed originally to show that an incoming vessel's guns were now unloaded and it meant no harm, but later used simply as a sign of respect. To reduce the waste of gunpowder the admiralty limited the maximum salute to 21 guns—and that only for royalty. Because the Governor of Antigua was the equivalent of a senior Rear Admiral, the *Tisiphone* was firing 13 guns at five-second intervals. To achieve that exact interval the gunner's mate was using the time-honored chant: "If I wasn't a gunner I wouldn't be here." Fort Berkeley, which they were now passing on their larboard side, replied with seven-guns. Technically Saumarez, as a mere captain, didn't rate a salute at all, but seven was given as a courtesy.

In 1782, the Caribbean was still being carved up by the major powers. Spain had taken control of the four major islands Cuba,

Hispaniola (now Haiti and the Dominican Republic), Jamaica, and Puerto Rico, and disdained the lesser islands. France and England, however, knew that these "lesser" islands controlled the southern and eastern sea routes to the Caribbean and a mad scramble was on for what was called the Lesser Antilles.

The Lesser Antilles runs in a long crescent from the Virgin Islands, off the coast of Puerto Rico in the north, to Trinidad and Tobago off the coast of South America. It consists of over 25 significant islands and no one knew how many smaller ones. The French started things off by conning the indigenous people, called Caribs, out of Martinique and Guadeloupe, the largest islands in the chain. The British then simply took Barbados, St. Kitts, Nevis, Antigua and Montserrat.

The French quickly established their main base of operations in Martinique and built a very large facility at Port Royal. The British, however, were less lucky. Originally, they wanted Barbados to be their Caribbean base but there was no bay suitable for their large ships of the line; so, their second choice was Antigua.

Geographically Antigua was further north and further leeward than they wanted but it had the advantage of English Harbor, a lovely natural bay. It was here that in 1725 the British built the English Bay Dockyard. A deep drafted ship could easily come in, be careened (laid on it's side), and worked on. Smaller ships could be repaired either there or in Frigate Bay on St. Kitts.

The main thing was that all these islands, French and British alike, were windward of the Spanish possessions. The Antilles is subject to a ferocious continual wind from the east, the kind of thing that causes trees to grow bent over to leeward. It was said that the downwind trip from Antigua to Jamaica would take seven days; and the upwind trip back could easily take three weeks or more. Any Spanish ship coming out of the Caribbean had to tack against those winds; the British and French ships did not. They would have the wind at their backs.

The *Tisiphone* sailed past Fort Berkeley and dropped anchor across from the dockyard where the harbormaster came out to greet them. The Governor, Sir Thomas Shirley, was across the bay supervising the building of additional fortifications for the harbor and they would have to trek up a small mountain to meet with him. Captain Saumarez took Smith and Walker with him in case the governor had any questions concerning the presence of the prince.

"Have either of you ever met Governor Shirley?" Saumarez asked when they were almost there. Both replied in the negative.

"Then you're in for a real experience," Saumarez said cryptically.

"Ah, my good friend Captain Saumarez!"

They found the governor sitting underneath a canopy wiping his brow with a cold cloth and sipping some kind of fruit beverage. He was a thin, nervous man, the kind who always seemed to be in a hurry while, at the same time, not actually doing much of anything.

"I saw the *Tisiphone* come in and remembered you from your last visit. Please, sit down, all of you. Sit down." He waved with irritation at a black steward who immediately produced three more chairs.

"Thank you, sir. I'd like to introduce Lieutenant..."

"So, have you been assigned to us," Shirley inquired?

"Well, no sir, you see..."

"Quite. Quite. But we could certainly use a good man such as you. I tell you; these are dangerous times, Saumarez. Dangerous times. As soon as I heard of our defeat at Yorktown, I started work on this fort up here. Oh, Fort Berkeley is all right; but we need more than that. More, Saumarez! What with America lost, the damn frogs are going to go into a feeding frenzy down here. De Grasse already is around here somewhere loaded to the gunnels with troops and supplies to take Jamaica, I'll wager. I am thinking of calling it Fort Shirley, Saumarez. What do you think? Has a nice ring, what?"

"Yes sir, it certainly seems to..."

"And what do you think they give me to stop them? I have five officers and 300 slaves. Five officers! Can you imagine? And look at those blacks out there, each one works slower than the one next to him."

Thankfully, Walker was not a part of the conversation and had the time to look around. They were on the heights overlooking English Harbor and the view was breathtaking. The lush green vegetation of the hilly island ran all the way down to the sparkling blue of the ocean on all sides of him. Far below, he could see the *Tisiphone* at anchor and not far away a hillside that had been blasted away to create the careening area, with warehouses and storage areas behind and to the right.

He looked to his left and could see a small army of black figures toiling away, cutting and placing the rocks that would eventually make up the fort's walls. To his right and behind him, however, was the real reason for the importance of this and every other island in the chain. There were sugar cane fields as far as he could see. White gold.

Antigua's development was fairly typical of that of the other islands in the Lesser Antilles. It was founded in 1632 by a group of English colonists from St. Kitts. Their intention was to start some plantations to grow tobacco, ginger, indigo and sugar; but, of these crops, only sugar did well.

The problem was that sugar was a very labor-intensive crop. At first, they used native Indians and even whites as slaves, but the Indians tended to succumb to disease too easily and the whites could not take either the diseases or the climate. That left African blacks as their only source of cheap labor. Both the blacks and the sugar cane seemed to thrive.

Smith re-focused his attention when he heard Saumarez speaking again.

"Yes, sir. That is a most difficult situation. But my main reason for being here is that I am looking for Admiral Hood."

"Hood? Hood, you say? Hood is a great sailor, no doubt; but he can't do it alone. He was in here a few days ago. You just missed him. His ships are a mess, I tell you. He took on water and victuals, but we didn't have much in the way of bread to give him so we had to give him breadfruit and yams.

"I tell you, Saumarez, these are hard times. Hood's ships look like something the cat wouldn't have. The men are tired, most of his ships are rickety, and he's short just about everything you can think of—food, water, rope, sail-cloth, spars—you name it.

"Hard times, Saumarez. Hard times and dangerous ones too."

"Sir, do you know where the admiral might be right now?"

"Last I heard he's around St. Kitts, although what the devil he's doing there I have no idea. Can you come tonight for dinner, Saumarez? You and your young gentlemen?"

The very last thing Saumarez wanted to do was to spend dinner with this bureaucratic boob, but he couldn't think of a way to avoid it.

"Yes, sir, we'd be delighted," he said with a smile.

"Jolly good. I'll see you about 8:00 then. My residence."

* * *

It was a long walk back down the hill. They followed what was once probably a goat track that had been expanded into a crude dirt road in order to build the fort.

"Captain, can I ask you a question about what I just saw?" Smith asked.

"Certainly."

"Those slaves. It's the first time I've seen any."

"Well, if you get posted to the West Indies, it won't be your last."

"I know, sir, but... well... Sir Shirley was complaining because he had only five officers to handle over 300 slaves. 300 to 5? Why don't the slaves just revolt and take over the place?"

Saumarez gave a quick laugh. "They do. There have been dozens of slave revolts in these islands. They always loose."

"Why?"

"Mostly lack of leadership. And when a genuine leader does arise, he's quickly dealt with.

"Take here in Antigua, for example. They had a revolt back in '36 lead by a black named 'Prince Klaas.' They caught him, broke him on the wheel, hung six others and burned 77 of his followers alive."

"Broke him on the wheel?"

"Yes, and if you can avoid seeing that happen I'd recommend you do so.

"Basically the person is tied, spread eagled, on the ground with pieces of wood placed under his wrists, elbows, ankles, knees and hips. The executioner then slams a large hammer or iron bar down on the wood blocks smashing each limb in several places and all the major joints—including the shoulders and hips.

"At this point the victim has been transformed into a howling puppet with four tentacles instead of arms and legs. He is then lifted up, his arms and legs are threaded through the spokes of the wheel and the wheel is lifted to the top of a pole where he is left both to the crows and to his maker.

"Now, after seeing that, how eager would YOU be to become the next black leader?"

Walker could contain himself no longer. "I am sorry, sir, but that's simply revolting. I cannot understand how someone could do that, or even countenance it, and still call himself civilized. I can't even understand how anyone can tolerate slavery. I mean stealing human beings—kidnapping them. Forcing them aboard ships where half of them die in transit. And then selling them, for God's sake."

"Are you a tea drinker, Mr. Walker?"

Walker was puzzled by the question. "Yes, sir. I prefer coffee but I do have tea."

"Do you take sugar in it?"

"Yes, but I fail to see how..." And suddenly Walker understood the relevance of the question and, more than that, his personal tie to slavery.

"Believe me, I understand and, personally, I sympathize with your feelings, but I am afraid you are lacking some understanding. For example: Where do you think those slaves come from, Mr. Walker?"

"Where do they come from? Why, they're captured in Africa by the whites and forced into slavery."

Saumarez started laughing. "No, sir. Not in a thousand years. A white man would not last an hour in those jungles. If you didn't die from the bite of some hideous snake or insect; if you didn't contract some deadly disease from the miasma; then the blacks would have a poison tipped arrow in your back faster than you can say: Jack Sprat.

"Those slaves are sold to the whites by other blacks. What do you think those people were they before they were sold?"

"Slaves," Smith interjected almost miserably.

"Right you are, Mr. Smith. Mostly they are prisoners of war or political enemies of a chief who, instead of torturing them to death for amusement, sold them to the white men.

"I personally once saw two chieftains arrive at the same time at Whydah with strings of slaves in tow. They had just finished two months of warring with each other and each had many of the other chief's warriors and women on his string. What do you think they did? Exchange prisoners so they could have tearful reunions with their families? Hell no. The two chiefs slapped each other on the back, threw a big feast, and sold every last one of them to the white men.

"Even if that were the case, captain, it still doesn't justify the inhuman conditions aboard those slave ships."

"I quite agree. Those ships are awful. They're designed to transport as much human cargo as they will hold; and they certainly are not designed to maximize the comfort of that cargo. They need speed and they need carrying capacity. That's all."

"Yes, sir. That's what I am saying. How can anyone justify those death ships?"

"Death ships? Let me ask you: Do you suppose the owners of those ships know, on any given trip, how many slaves were purchased in Africa?"

"Certainly. There would have to be an accounting of the money spent."

"And do you suppose they know how many were gotten to the West Indies and America and sold?"

"Yes sir, they'd have to. Again, there would have to be an accounting."

"Exactly. Every slave represents money that a slaver has invested in his or her purchase. Every slave that does not make it to market represents a loss of forty to sixty pounds just as sure as if you threw the money overboard. Given that, what do you think would happen to the captain who looses large numbers of slaves in transit?"

Walker said nothing.

"Exactly. Not only would the captain himself have a lesser share of the profits but he would probably find himself on the beach and unable to ever get another ship. Do you think that doesn't cross their minds?"

Smith finally decided to re-enter the discussion. "But, sir. Those people are still slaves. They've lost their freedom."

"Indeed. So let's say you are commanding a ship some day, lieutenant, and you capture a slaver. What do you do with those slaves?"

"I believe the policy is to drop them off at the nearest point of habitable land."

"That's correct. And, do you ever wonder what happens to them after that?"

"No, sir. I've never thought about it."

"I have.

"When I was a young third lieutenant on the *Topaz*... about your age, as a matter of fact... we captured a slaver off the Bight of Biafra. We put them ashore in Sierra Leone and told them to go till a plot of land and have a good life.

"Now keep in mind, these were all slaves from the interior. They spoke different languages, had different dietary needs, carried old tribal hatreds for each other, and had no idea how to till a plot of land. They didn't even know what we were talking about.

"When we came back a month later every one of them was either dead—killed by each other's hand—or run off into the jungle where they probably died.

"Did we do them a favor, lieutenant?"

Smith said nothing.

"Mr. Walker, you have slavery in the American south do you not?"

"Yes sir, we do"

"All right, let's take two men. One is transported to the southern United States or England as a slave, the other remains in Africa. Now, you know and I know that slavery can't last forever. So run the clock out, let's say, 200 years or so. Which person's ancestors will be most likely to be living well?"

Walker was silent for a moment. He had never thought about the matter in quite this way. He finally replied: "But, Mr. Smith is still right, sir. If they were returned to Africa, at least they would be free," said Walker.

"Free? Free like whom, Mr. Walker? Free like the white man?

"Let's clarify what we're talking about here. I once saw a ship in which upwards of 600 men and women were confined below decks in heavy shackles, most of them double ironed. They lived in miserable filth, Mr. Walker, with vermin their constant companion; and no amount of moaning or pleading would help them one bit. They eagerly ate food that would make you or me sick just looking at it. Their keepers were of the lowest class of human beings, devoid of all feelings, ignorant, inherently brutal, and made tyrannical by the power they had. Is that what we are talking about?"

"Yes, sir. The slave ship."

"No, Mr. Walker. What I just described was a prison hulk—there are about a dozen of them operating in England right now. It's where we throw our *own* people, not just for weeks, but for years—even decades—at a time and for as little as stealing a handkerchief.

"I invite you to take a walk around London someday and look at the beggars in the street—people who have no idea where their next meal is coming from. Are they free? What about the man who works at some odious job from dawn to dusk, six days a week, for his entire brief, miserable, life. Or, how about the country girl who is driven by starvation to the city; where she becomes the maid and sexual plaything of the master of some house? My word, sir, look at the men aboard our very own ship that have been pressed into duty as seamen. Some of them have not set foot ashore or seen their families for years. Are they free?

"No, sir. Slavery exists in every country in the world; it's just you can't always see the fetters."

"I am not sure I understand, sir. Does that mean you support slavery or that you would not stop and board a slaver?"

"No, Mr. Smith. It means: I am an officer in His Majesty's Royal Navy; and I would do my duty no matter what. My opinion is of absolutely no consequence."

Unfortunately, it was Saumarez's concept of "duty" that was about to get them all killed.

CHAPTER EIGHT

THE *Tisiphone* would be laid up in English Harbor for several days. There was no choice in the matter and none of Captain Saumarez's pacing and swearing could change it.

The ship needed to replenish its supply of food, water, gunpowder and wood for the cooking stoves, plus several minor but important repairs needed to be made. The only thing that kept Saumarez from getting underway without attending to those things was the wise counsel of his First Lieutenant. He asked the captain whether he would rather attend to these matters now, or join Hood's fleet then have to leave, perhaps on the eve of a battle, because we were out of water; or break off during an engagement and flee from the enemy because we were out of powder.

That settled it. He didn't like it, but Saumarez would rather die than report for duty with a ship that was unfit to accomplish its duties.

So, for the next few days the bay was filled with small craft going back and forth between the *Tisiphone* and shore. Tons of supplies were shipped aboard—kegs of water, fresh fruits and vegetables, meat, casks of small beer, bags of breadfruit (English Harbor really was out of bread), and cords of wood. In addition, there were the thousand little things that made life bearable, and sometimes possible, when you crammed 200 men in a wooden container 124 feet long and 33 feet wide. Chief among these smaller items was mail.

Very few things aboard ship had the importance of mail call. To begin with, it only rarely happened and mail could take anywhere from six months to several years to catch up to you. To send a letter a family member or friend would, first, send it to the Fleet Mail Service at Falmouth. The mail service employees would place it in a bag depending on which fleet the ship was with (i.e. Mediterranean, American, Channel, West Indies, and so forth). Several times a week small, light, fast ships called packets would leave Falmouth to deliver the bags to their assigned chief of station—wherever he might be.

The mail packet had arrived in English Harbor about a day after the *Tisiphone*, and immediately the tenor and tone of day-to-day life changed. Suddenly, the most popular men aboard ship were those who could read and write. The smartest of them knew how to convert that skill into extra tots of rum, if not cold hard cash, by reading and then writing replies for their shipmates.

The bag was brought aboard the *Tisiphone* and opened by the first lieutenant. Official dispatches, of course, were removed first along with mail intended for the warrant and commissioned officers. The remaining mail was placed in piles according to the specialty of the recipient and given over to the officer or midshipman in charge of that division. That afternoon, before the first dog-watch, the mail would be distributed to the men.

This was both among the happiest and the sadist times aboard ship. News of births, marriages, good health and good fortune, arrived alongside letters concerning news of deaths, sicknesses and disaster. Messages of eternal devotion tumbled out of the bag along with letters beginning "Dear John." Seamen would be happy or sad, but none would be indifferent to the arrival of the mail packet.

Captain Saumarez called Sidney Smith to the quarterdeck and introduced him to Lieutenant James Cornwallis, Master and Commander of His Majesty's armed brig *Badger*. Saumarez came right to the point.

"Smith, we're going to be stuck here for I don't know how long getting re-supplied and refitted; but Admiral Hood needs to get my dispatch as soon as possible. Lieutenant Cornwallis here is on his way to Hood. I want you to deliver this message pouch to him personally. You can rejoin us when we catch up in a few days."

"Yes, sir. Can I bring..."

"Yes, Walker can go with you. You'd think you two were brothers or something."

"In a way, you know, maybe we are," Smith thought as he went below to gather his few possessions and say good-bye to Susan Whitney and Bill Hanover and promising to see them again in a few days.

* * *

The armed brig *Badger* actually began life as the USS *Pitt*. She was captured from the Americans in 1776 and was quickly purchased into the Royal Navy to serve the West Indies station. She was 68 feet long, 21 wide, carried about 90 men and had numbered among her captains such men as Horatio Nelson and Cuthbert Collingwood.

The *Badger* had two masts, the foremast was square rigged and the main was fore-and-aft. This gave the *Badger* its two primary virtues: it was fast and maneuverable. With the square rig, it would run before the wind like a man of war. With the fore and aft sails, it could sail into the wind like a Barbary pirate.

The "armed" part of its designator was more psychological than anything. She had 12 "long fours" (four-pound carriage guns) on her main deck and two half-pound swivel guns. While that might sound impressive, it was not. Ignoring the swivel guns, it meant she could only throw a broadside of 24 pounds. While that might give pause to a lightly armed privateer, it was laughable to any serious warship.

No, the *Badger* was built for speed and speed was what she was showing as she left the island of Antigua in her wake.

The ship proceeded down the leeward side of the Leeward Islands looking for the British fleet. Lieutenant Cornwallis (no relation to the general) was slightly older than Sidney Smith and was probably senior to him as a lieutenant. That was a moot point, however. As soon as they stepped foot aboard the *Badger*, Cornwallis shed his erstwhile rank of lieutenant and became the Master and Commander of a ship of the Royal Navy. Aboard that ship, he had all the rights, privileges, authority and responsibilities of the captain of a 100-gun first rate. There were things even the king himself could not order him to do—at least not while on board his own ship.

Cornwallis bore the responsibility lightly. He was no tyrant or tyrant in the making. He was maybe 20 years old and drove the ship like a teenager with a fast new horse. He knew when to rein his impulses in, but there were other times when he had the *Badger* nearly leaping out of the water in obedience to his commands. He could not imagine anything on God's green earth being better than having command of a fast packet.

Walker was standing in the bow of the ship enjoying the feeling of the warm Caribbean air cascading through his hair as the *Badger* plowed through some low rolling waves. His solitude, however, was broken by a call from the main mast lookout.

"On deck, there. Two sail, two points off the larboard bow."

Cornwallis quickly replied, "Very well. Keep a sharp lookout and tell me when you can identify them." He handed one of the precious telescopes—one of only two on board—to a midshipman and told him to take it up to the lookout.

Walker started walking back toward the quarterdeck as he saw Smith emerging from the hatch to the officer's cabin. They met at the ships tiller where Cornwallis was standing.

"Who do you think they are, captain?" Smith used the honorific because it was both technically correct and he knew that no lieutenant ever tired of being called "captain."

"It's hard to say. Probably ours but I am going to head over there to find out."

Fifteen minutes later, the lookout called again. "On deck! I make out three, no, make that four, sail now. They look like they're maneuvering for a fight."

And no sooner had the lookout said those words than a series of red flashes could be seen on one of the ships followed a few seconds later by the unmistakable sound of a broadside being fired.

"Helm, come up a point or two. We are duty bound to go over there to help with the injured, and anyone that's in the water, but I do not intend to get this little barky in the middle of *that* dog fight."

And "that" was referring to one of the countless skirmishes that occur in any war—unrecorded by history and unremembered by anyone who was not there. In this instance, two British ships of the line from Hood's fleet, the *Torbay* (74) and the *London* (98), came across the *Scipion* (74) and the *Sibylle* (32) of De Grasse's, and all concerned were immediately cleared for action.

As with most naval battles, large and small, most of the time was spent jockeying for position. When the battle was joined, however, it developed into a running fight that lasted from 3:00 in the afternoon into the night. The climax came when the *London* managed to close to within pistol shot range of the *Scipion*. A furious exchange of gunfire then occurred in which the *London*, though it had more guns, amazingly, got the worst of it. Having sustained serious damage and with her steering almost completely shot away, the *London* broke off the fight, sheered away, and almost ran into the *Torbay* in the process.

The French knew there was no way they were going to be able to board and capture either ship. The British were heavily damaged, but they were not defeated, and the French were keenly aware of the difference. So, they simply sailed away leaving the British to lick their wounds. Unfortunately, the French ships broke in the direction of the *Badger*.

This began the process of everyone on board the *Badger* willing themselves and their ship to become invisible. During the battle, there probably weren't a dozen men on either side who were aware that the *Badger* was even there. Now her survival depended on her being such small fry that the French would ignore her and just sail on past.

She was not to be so lucky.

The *Scipion* moved first. She was following the *Sibylle* and swung out so that the two ships, bracketed the *Badger*, the *Scipion* to larboard, the *Sibylle* to starboard. When they came up to the *Badger* the *Sibylle* hauled her wind and dropped open her gun ports. That was the end game. Cornwallis knew that if the *Sibylle* fired even a half-broadside, the *Badger* would come apart like a child's toy.

With a pale face and shaking hands, he walked over to the main mast, drew his sword, sliced a halyard and watched the British flag flutter down to the deck.

* * *

Hanover swung around the corner of the sick bay and found Susan cleaning up some instruments after the *Tisiphone*'s afternoon sick call.

"Susan, do you know who is on board this ship?"

"Yes, almost 600 men, 87 of whom seem to have one version or another of the clap at the moment."

"No, silly. Sir Charles Douglas is on board. He's being transported to take command of the *Formidable*."

"How wonderful for him," she said without enthusiasm as she continued putting a series of bottles back into a cabinet.

"No, Susan, seriously. Sir Charles is probably the world's leading expert on gunnery. Why the changes he's made in gunnery, his inventions... He's a living legend."

Susan closed the door on the pharmaceutical cabinet, grabbed a rag and paused to look at Hanover before starting to scrub down the foldout counter.

"And you're telling me this because...?"

"While we were in English Harbor, we got 12 of the new firing mechanisms that Sir Charles invented."

"Please, Bill, I am very tired. Could you get to the point?"

"We've got the mechanisms and Sir Charles himself is going to give us training on how to use them in a few minutes. All officers, midshipmen, gunners and gunners mates must be there."

"You've noticed, I assume, that I am a surgeon's mate?"

"Yes, well..." and suddenly Hanover was less sure of himself. "I just thought that you having been married once to a gunner... and you always seem interested in anything having to do with the ship... that..."

"That I might want to attend?"

"Yes."

Actually she didn't. Her husband's death and the way it happened were not that far in the past. She still thought of him, missed him in some ways, though their brief marriage was not exactly the best one in the world. Still, Bill was right; she was interested in anything having to do with the navy. It was one of the things the men really liked about her.

"All right. I can finish this later. Lead on."

The relevant cast of characters had assembled on the gun deck where the twelve 24-pound guns had been stationed, six on a side. Most of the gunners, gunner's mates and officers were there along with all the midshipmen. The captain and Sir Charles had yet to make their appearance.

The ship's gunner was fluttering around the guns making sure everything was in perfect order. That, by itself, wasn't unusual. He normally arose at 5 AM each day to make sure the guns were properly washed, cleaned and dried. After that, he would inspect each gun to make sure it was well secured and ready for service, that their vents were clear, tompions in, and no shot was loose in the barrel. He would continue his inspection routine several times during the day, and any discrepancies would be noted and corrected immediately.

Technically, he was an officer, although he held that position through a warrant issued by the Board of Ordnance. It was his responsibility to keep the gun crews trained and, to do that; he would exercise at least two guns each day, except on Thursday and Sunday.

Normally a taciturn man, he seemed to have come unglued at the thought of having Sir Charles on board and about to, in effect, inspect him, his guns and his men.

The naval gun at that time was not much more than a muzzle loaded pipe bomb. It was thicker at the breech to resist the force of the explosion, but tapered toward the mouth. About a third of the way up from the breech two sturdy metal arms, called "trunnions," stuck out from the sides. These rested in a wooden frame on wheels called a carriage that bore the weight of the gun and allowed it to be moved around and pointed. At the back of the barrel, a knob stood out called a "cascable." A stout three-inch rope ran from a deadeye and pulley imbedded in the hull on one side of the gun, around the cascable, and back to a deadeye and pulley imbedded on the other side. This rope was to limit how far back the gun would recoil when it was fired. The pulleys allowed the gun to be run out again.

Gun sizes were rated by the weight of the ball it fired. These were generally either 6, 9, 12, 18, 24 or 32 pounds each, although some of the seamen still used the old fashioned terms: Cannon royal, Cannon, Demi cannon, Culverin, Demi-Culverin, Falcon, Falconer, Minion, Saker, and so forth. The 24-pounders, like the ones Susan and Hanover were looking at, could shoot about 3,000 yards with accuracy and up to 1.75 miles accompanied by a prayer. Even a little 18-pounder could send a ball through 2 ½ feet of sold oak at 400 yards.

Captain Saumarez and Captain Douglas soon emerged from the captain's cabin and made the short walk down the gun deck to where the group was waiting. Douglas was a beefy man, about six inches taller than Saumarez with a large square jaw and bushy eyebrows. He had to duck at each overhead beam as he walked to the waiting group. His size, however, was offset by a soft voice that spoke with a highland burr.

"All right then, which of you is the gunner," Douglas began.

"That'd be me, sir. Lawrence Woolsey." Woolsey stepped forward and knuckled a salute. Instead of returning the salute, Douglas held out his hand. "Good to meet you, Mr. Woolsey." Woolsey shook hands with him and took on the look of a man who had just kissed the ring of the Pope.

"If you'd be so kind, please assemble a crew for this gun, release the breeching and run it out as if you are about to fire it."

When Woolsey had done that the group moved in closer to hear what Douglas had to say.

"I am sure you are all familiar with the standard 24 pound naval gun. The one before you is that same gun with certain modifications I have made which I hope you will view as improvements.

"Now, let's say this gun has just been fired. At this moment, what is the biggest danger? You sir?"

One of the ships many lieutenants spoke up: "The gun will recoil backwards where, until the breeching rope stops it, it could run over a seaman. There is also the possibility that the rope could break sending the gun across the deck and possibly crash through the opposite side."

"Very good, lieutenant. Quite correct. This brings us to improvement number one. Mr. Woolsey if you would have your crew slide that ramp over here about eight feet behind the gun.

"This simple ramp will now be placed about this distance behind the gun. When the gun fires, it will recoil back until the rear wheels of the carriage slide up this ramp, thus breaking its travel. When the recoil energy is spent, it will roll the gun back down the ramp where it can be serviced for the next shot. You'll notice also that the front of the carriage is attached to a rope, which is attached to a heavy spring, which is attached to another rope, which is attached to the hull. This too will help in controlling the recoil.

"This does three things. First, it helps keep men from being run over by the carriage because it's not rolling back so far. Second, it eliminates the possibility of the breeching rope breaking because the gun never goes back far enough to put a serious strain on it. And third, it returns the gun to a position much closer to the gun port, which means it won't take as long for the crew to roll it back into firing position. In short, you can thus fire it faster.

"You there, the midshipman on the end. What would happen next in our firing sequence?"

A young man, about 17, stepped forward—an older midshipman who was about ready to take his lieutenant's exam.

"Next, sir, the gun would be cleaned out with the worm," he reached over and grabbed a pole with a metal corkscrew on the end, "followed by a swabbing with the sponge on the other end, wetted down of course. That gets rid of any sparks left over from the previous blast that might set off the new charge. Then you..."

"All right, stop there," Douglas interrupted. "None of those things are now necessary." Douglas paused while his statement sank in and the astonished murmuring ran its course.

"First, we will now be using pre-cut wetted pads." He reached into a tub of water sitting near the gun and pulled one out. By using these pads, there will be no shower of sparks from the wadding when the gun is fired. Second... son, if you'll hand me that..." a small boy timidly approached and handed over a wooden box. Douglas opened it and held up a new kind of powder charge.

"Second, you'll notice the charges are now different. They are contained in flannel bags—not silk like the old charges. Silk causes sparks; flannel simply disintegrates with no sparks. By using wetted pads and flannel powder bags, there will be no burning residue in the chamber, thus no worming, thus no sponging, thus again, a faster rate of fire.

"All right, midshipman, you're doing a fine job. What happens next?"

The midshipman beamed. "Well, sir, next a powder charge is placed in the muzzle of the barrel and rammed home, followed by a wad, followed by the ball, followed by another wad, and the gun is run out."

"Excellent. Now, young man, who fires it?"

"Each gun has a Gun Captain. On my old ship, they called 'em 'Quarter-gunners;' here they call them 'Gun Captains.' He's supposed to aim and fire the gun."

"Fine. Do we have a quarter-gunner here?"

"Aye, sir. McGinty, sir."

"Tell me, McGinty, how do you fire the gun?"

"Aye, sir. I takes a thin rod, like that one over there, push it down the vent hole and swish it around a bit. That breaks the powder bag that's in the chamber. Then I pour a little bit of special fine grain powder down the hole."

"All right, stop there. You won't be doing that any more."

"Sir?" McGinty was astonished along with everyone else. No one could imagine any other way of doing it.

Douglas reached over, pulled out a small box, opened it and from among several dozen in the box, pulled out what looked like a short writing quill without the feathers.

"Another little invention of mine, gentlemen. These quills are hollow and filled with a special mixture of gunpowder kneaded in spirits of wine. You just push it down into the vent hole. The quill breaks the bag, and you don't have to pour any powder down the vent. It's already inside the hollow quill.

"All right, McGinty, what happens next?"

McGinty peeled his eyes, now grown somewhat larger, off the box of quills. "Then I takes the slow match from the fire tub, blow on it a few times to get the tip hot and touch it to the powder that I just put into the touch hole."

"Is the slow match always lit when you pick it up?"

"Oh no, sir. Sometimes the spray from the ocean has put it out, sometimes it's fallen into the water in the fire tub, and sometimes it's just plain gone out and I don't know why."

"That's all right. The slow match is gone too, McGinty."

"But, sir, how do I..."

"Ask this marine here," he said pointing to one of several marines that were observing from outside the circle of seamen.

"Sir?" said the surprised marine suddenly straightening into a posture resembling attention.

"How does your weapon fire, private."

The marine held up his flintlock musket. "It's easy, sir. I just pull back on the hammer. When I am ready to shoot, I pull the trigger; the hammer drops forward, opens the pan and strikes this piece of flint against the striker. That causes a spark, which ignites the powder in the pan, which travels into the chamber and ignites the charge, which blows out the ball."

When the marine ceased talking, all hands turned back to Sir Charles who was, miraculously, holding an oversized flintlock firing mechanism in his hand.

"And what I have here is a much larger version of the one that's on that marine's musket, only this one is going to fire this gun," Douglas said while screwing the flintlock mechanism into a special hole the ship's armorer had earlier cut into the side of the gun.

"McGinty, you will now fire your gun the same way that marine fires his musket. After you insert the quill, you place a small amount of powder into the pan, just here. Then you pull back the hammer, take up this string and, when you are ready, pull it."

"Oh lord, sir. Can there be anything else?" McGinty spoke without thinking and was immediately embarrassed. The group, along with Douglas laughed, however.

"Actually, yes. One more thing.

"How do you know *when* to shoot it, McGinty?"

"Sir?"

"I mean, you are on a ship that's constantly rolling back and forth. If you fire too early on the roll, the ball will fly over the enemy. If you fire too late, you'll just be shooting the ocean. How do you know when to fire?"

"Well, I look out the gun port and try to judge it."

"Does that always work?"

"No, sir. Most of the time the smoke from all the gun fire is so thick I can't even see the water, let alone the enemy."

Douglas walked around the carriage to the gun port. Next to it a small metal device hung out from the hull, and hanging from it was a pendulum.

"Then you'll be glad to see the addition of this device. It's nothing but a simple pendulum but, if you watch its motion, it will tell you when the ship is dead level. That is the moment to fire. No more guessing.

"As you can see, gentlemen, there have been a number of changes which, I dare say, are improvements in what we have been doing. With them, you should be nearly able to double the French rate of fire, *and* be more accurate in the bargain.

"Do you have any questions?"

No one moved. No one said a thing. Douglas' presentation had been such a revelation that most of it was still sinking in.

Captain Saumarez then spoke for the first time. "Thank you Captain Douglas. That was most enlightening.

"Woolsey, I want you to organize this group into a training party, and exercise them on the new Douglas System. That's everyone," he said looking around, "including the officers. Then, I want you to expand your training to every day, morning and afternoon except Sunday, until every man jack on this ship is proficient in handling the guns under this new approach. Is that clear?"

"Aye, aye, sir."

As the two captains retired to the cooler breezes found under the awning over the quarterdeck, Woolsey began shouting orders to form the group into gunnery teams. "A bit of a competition between some of the young officers and the men might be an interesting diversion," he thought.

Susan slipped out of the crowd and looked back at the eager expressions on the men's faces. "What IS it about men and things that go bang?" She thought. "They are drawn to it like a moth to a flame. Yet, we women... we women and our children are the ones who have to live with the consequences for the rest of our lives when they fly too close."

* * *

The French officer spoke more than passable English and was more than passably efficient, for a Frenchman.

"You are the captain?" He said to Cornwallis.

"I am."

"And you surrender this ship?"

Cornwallis paused for a moment, looking up at the mammoth ship riding not 50 yards away with at least 30 workable guns pointed right at him. Nevertheless, these would be the hardest words he would ever have to say, but he got them out. "I do." And he handed his sword over to the Frenchman, who accepted it.

"Very good. Now I wish you to order all your officers up here to the quarterdeck and all your men to the fo'c'sle." Cornwallis passed the order on to his bosun to handle.

"This is a mail packet, is it not?"

There was no sense in denying it. "Yes, it is."

"Then you will lead me to where your mail bags and dispatch pouches are located."

Twenty minutes later, the men were arranged on the fo'c'sle as instructed. Walker and Smith stood next to each other along the larboard rail with the other officers near the quarterdeck. The mail pouches were piled amidships near the mainmast. Both groups and the mail sacks were under close guard by the French marines.

French seamen were below deck removing anything that could even remotely be used as a weapon prior to locking the *Badger's* men up. Everyone else was watching several small boats get underway from the *Sibylle* to come and pick up the *Badger's* officers. Walker spoke quietly.

"Sidney, look on top of that pile. There's the dispatch pouch we were supposed to deliver to Admiral Hood."

Smith looked at the mail pile, then at the marines guarding it. "Yes, I know. So what?"

"We need to make a break for it."

"What are you talking about?"

"Look, you work your way over to the ship's wheel and stand in front of it. Go slowly so no one pays any attention to you."

"And then?"

"Then, I'll shoot between those guards, grab Hood's pouch and toss it over to you. I'll then continue to the starboard rail, you throw it back to me, and I'll toss it overboard."

"You're mad."

"Yes, we've already established that. But, this'll work. Trust me."

"Trust me," he says. "Trust me, when he was the one who..." Smith continued grumbling to himself as he causally worked himself over to the wheel.

Walker saw his opportunity when one soldier moved out of the way to talk to his sergeant. He shot between two very startled guards, grabbed the pouch and backhanded it to Smith. Smith caught it and raised it above his head.

As Walker expected, the guards all followed the progress of the pouch and moved toward Smith. He then ducked between two more guards, banged his shin against a hatch cover, recovered, and arrived at the starboard rail. Smith then arced the pouch over everyone's head to Walker with a two-handed toss. Walker caught it and, in one continuous motion, flipped it into the water. He had a chance to see it bob to the surface once and then slowly sink again before the rifle butt caught him on the back of the head.

* * *

When the *Sybille* was moving up on the *Badger* scant attention was paid to her condition. Now that Smith, Walker and Cornwallis were on board, they could see the pounding she had taken. Several guns had been overturned; and gaping holes appeared where orderly gun ports once stood. The mizzenmast was tottering at a strange angle because of stays and shrouds that had been cut away. Chunks of wood and splinters were everywhere and men, some still bleeding from minor wounds, were furiously trying to repair the damage.

A few days later the *Sybille* fell in with the *Diadem*. The three were transferred on board just before the *Sybille* headed for Martinique to lick her wounds. On board the *Diadem* they were simply left standing around on deck while the officers and men went about their business. Twenty minutes after that, a somewhat older lieutenant led them down to what proved to be the captain's cabin.

"Gentlemen," he said upon arrival, "may I introduce to you Capitaine De Vaisseau Jacque De Monteclerc."

Captain De Monteclerc was not what any of them had expected. He and the *Diadem* had gained quite a reputation in the West Indies as a serious foe, yet he looked like anything but a warrior. Thin and effete, he looked more like an unsuccessful tailor than anything else. It wasn't until you noticed that the slight sneer he wore on his face was a permanent fixture that you realized there might be some nasty steel under his dandified appearance.

"Gentleman," he said in broken English, "welcome to the *Diadem*. As you know, you will be our guests here for a while.

"Which of you is Captain Cornwallis?"

"I am, sir."

"I see. And your ship is... was... the mail packet *Badger*?"

"It was."

"Cornwallis, eh. Are you related to the general?"

"No sir, although he does have a brother who is serving with Admiral Hood. We are not related, at least not that I know of."

"But you were on your way to Admiral Hood, is that not correct?"

"It is."

"Where were you supposed to meet him?"

"I wasn't. My task was to try and find him."

"You're telling me, you have no idea where he is but your task was to deliver dispatches to him?"

"Yes, sir. We heard he was in these waters but had no idea where."

De Monteclerc's voice suddenly grew stern. "Lieutenant, do you think for a minute that I actually believe you?"

"Believe me or not, sir; it's true."

"Yes, I am sure.

"You then must be..." He looked down at a sheet of paper. "You must be Lieutenant Smith and the other is Dr. Walker."

"I am," said Smith.

"Well, actually I am not really a doctor, you see. I am..."

Walker shut up when Smith's elbow cracked into his ribs.

"And, I suppose you both have the same amnesia with regard to Hood's whereabouts?

Neither man said a word. De Monteclerc eyes bored in on Smith, who was placidly gazing at a spot on the wall just above Monteclerc's head.

"That was quite a stunt you pulled with that dispatch pouch aboard the *Badger*. Would you care to explain to me what was in it?"

"I have no idea, sir. I just assumed, whatever it was, His Majesty would prefer that you not have it. Because I was entrusted with it, it was a matter of honor that I get rid of it."

This was an argument De Monteclerc could understand. The British and the French had been bitter enemies for generations; but there was a code of honor among and between officers that both sides understood and respected.

"I see.

"Well, I have to do something with you three. Dr. Walker, I will expect you to report to our surgeons to help tend our wounded. You other two are confined to your quarters until further notice."

"No, sir." Cornwallis said.

"Pardon me?"

"I said: No, sir. That's not acceptable. If you wish our surgeon to help your surgeon, then all of us must be given freedom of the ship."

De Monteclerc thought about it a moment. He had just returned from the cockpit and had seen first hand how overwhelmed his surgeon and his mates were.

"Dr. Walker?"

Walker wasn't quite sure what was going on but decided to play along anyway. "Yes, sir. I will not serve unless all of us are given freedom of the ship." Whatever that means, he thought. "Plus, Lieutenant Smith here must be assigned as my assistant."

"What?" Smith wheeled around in surprise.

"Be quiet. It'll do you good." Walker hissed.

"Then I assume I have parole from each of you?" De Monteclerc asked. By giving their parole, each was agreeing on his honor that he would not try to escape nor do the ship or its men any harm.

"You do, sir, unless and until this ship comes into armed conflict with one of our own." Cornwallis replied.

"Done. But if that is the case, Captain Cornwallis, then I am assigning you back to your ship. I expect you to serve as a resource to our officers in case any question should arise concerning the peculiarities of handling your vessel."

"I agree, but I remind you again I will not fight against our own."

"Agreed. I would not expect you to. Now, if you'll excuse me, I have work to do."

"Captain, one more question, if you will," Cornwallis ventured. "Where exactly are we going?"

"I don't suppose it will harm anything if you know. We're going to meet Admiral De Grasse at Frigate Bay on the Island of St. Kitts."

* * *

"Where?" Susan asked.

"Frigate Bay on the Island of St. Kitts," Hanover repeated.

"Why are we going there?"

"I don't know; I am just a midshipman, remember? But, for some reason, that's where Admiral Hood thinks De Grasse is."

The *Tisiphone* had been underway for two days before it finally found Hood's fleet just off the island of Barbados. Captain Saumarez went over to deliver his good news about the Battle of Biscay Bay and returned with some bad news. No one had seen anything of the *Badger*.

Susan and Bill consoled themselves with the fact that this was not at all unusual. It was a big ocean and ships, even whole fleets of them, were easy to miss. The *Badger* was still probably stumbling around the islands somewhere looking for them.

They still hadn't adjusted, however, to the appalling condition of Hood's fleet. It was torn, tired and hungry; short of just about everything you could think of: food, gunpowder, sailcloth, rope, and spars—you name it. On the other hand, there was something they didn't find—namely, despair and despondency.

De Grasse, at the Battle of the Capes, had humiliated this fleet. They not only had taken a serious physical pounding but worse, they had been outwitted. They knew General Cornwallis had surrendered and wondered if they were being blamed for it back home. They could be forgiven if some depression had set in; but, that's not what Bill and Susan saw.

Admiral Hood was known throughout the Navy as one who did not suffer fools gladly. When the Royal Navy was shamed, Hood spoke with scathing satire in condemnation of all and sundry responsible. He held back nothing. But all this changed when he found himself in command of the very fleet that had suffered this recent loss. Suddenly, as if by magic, his sarcasm was replaced by kindness and geniality. His cheerfulness pervaded the whole fleet to the point where the men were now ready to go anywhere and do anything for their new commander.

Their chance for revenge would not be long in coming.

* * *

St. Kitts lies about halfway between St. Eustatius and Nevis. It is said that Christopher Columbus named it thus because it looked like his patron saint. If so, then the real St. Kitt must have been a peculiar person because most people describe the island as shaped like a bowling pin lying on its side, with the tip pointed slightly down and to the right.

Frigate Bay was on the western or leeward side of the island and should probably have quotation marks placed around the second word of its name. As a "bay," it wasn't much more than a slight indentation along an otherwise featureless shore. But, still, it had a long wide sandy beach that was currently being filled with men and supplies from De Grasse's ships. The British had a small outpost on St. Kitts, and the French meant to take it.

"All right. I'll admit it," said Sidney Smith.

It was late afternoon and the two were on deck taking a break from their duties in the sick bay. Both had on white smocks that were stained with blood. Both had the far-away looks of people who had gone beyond being tired.

"What's that?" Walker asked.

"You were right. Working down there... I had no idea..."

"Sidney, someday you're going to command one of these ships. I never will, but you will. I think you're going to be a good captain; but you'll be even better if you don't forget what you've just seen."

"Yes," Sidney replied and turned to look out over Frigate Bay.

"So, how's your French coming along?" Walker finally asked. "Are you remembering any of it?"

"Actually, I am surprised how much I remember although I sure as hell wish I had learned more. Plus, there's a surgeon's mate who wants to practice his English, so we get along just fine. Between him and the patients I talk to, I am learning quite a bit."

"Such as?"

"Such as, since the Battle of the Capes, De Grasse has been down here picking off our possessions like he was gathering flowers for May Day. So far, we've lost Nevis, St. Eustatius and St Lucia and, as you can see across the way, we're about to lose St. Kitts. Next, he's going to go after Barbados and from there he can roll up the entire British Leeward Isles. Just in case that's not enough, apparently he and the Spaniards are planning to join forces to take Jamaica from us soon."

"Jesus, we could lose the whole of the West Indies in the next month. Have you heard anything about Hood, or Graves?"

"Not really, although one seaman I was helping said he had a friend who heard that Hood has taken over from Graves and that Graves had been sent home in disgrace for that fiasco off of Cape Henry."

"A bit late for that."

Just then, they heard a shout and a report from one of the lookouts.

"What's he saying, Sidney?"

"He's reporting sails coming around the tip of Nevis Island over there."

No false alarm. Over the next hour, more and more sails began to appear. Ships. British ships. But instead of appearing like a proper war fleet, they were in a haphazard formation like a group of lax merchantmen.

Smith and Walker naturally gravitated toward the quarterdeck. If there was any information to be had, this was where they'd find it.

Captain De Monteclerc, telescope in hand, saw them coming.

"Look at that mess, lieutenant. Do you call that a fleet? It's more like a collection of tubs manned by washer women."

"I don't know," chimed in Walker, "they look pretty good to me."

De Monteclerc shot him a quelling glance but said nothing and looked back at Smith. "Why are they here? Tell me that. We've already beaten them once. Are they really so foolish as to think they can stop us from landing our troops? Or, maybe they're just stupid. Maybe they didn't even know we were here—that Admiral De Grasse himself was here—with his fleet."

De Monteclerc paused for a minute then said quietly. "Yes, that's it. Look at them."

The British fleet had rounded the southern end of Nevis in a rag-tag fashion. Suddenly there were frantic signals being flashed from the flagship as if they had just seen the Frenchmen. Ships that had been cruising along on foresails and topsails now dropped all the canvas they had and came about.

"The fools," De Monteclerc continued. "The absolute, blundering, fools. They've fallen into a trap and they think they can run. They're too late for that, my friends. Way too late.

"Look there. The admiral is posting a signal: All ships to weigh anchor and pursue. We've got them, lieutenant. We've got them."

And so, as evening fell, Hood and his ships fled. De Grasse hauled in his anchors, shook out his sheets, and hauled off to the south in pursuit.

* * *

It was not a normal morning watch.

Normally, the midwatch and the morning watch in these waters was a thing of beauty. Both the sky and the sea were pitch black, and the only sound was of water playing along the sides of the ship and working the wooden planking. The trade winds were constant out of the southeast and tended to swirl around your body like they were caressing you. Overhead were more stars than the human mind could comprehend—some of them old friends from home, some of them strangers that had recently appeared over the horizon.

It was a time for quiet reflection. A time when you could both stand your duty and think about the things that were closest to your soul. Except that was not to be. For Midshipman Hanover, Susan Whitney and the rest of the men, it was a time of tension.

Captain Saumarez was on deck, pacing back and forth, alternately looking at his watch and at the tiny red stern light on the ship ahead of him. That light, like the one he had hung on the stern of the *Tisiphone*, was nothing more than a weather lantern with red glass placed in it. To the ship behind, it gave off a pinpoint of light—just enough so you knew where the other ship was located.

The thing about lights at sea at night is that they can be seen for huge distances, even small lights. The French could see those stern lights and the English knew it. The English wanted them to... at least for the next 10 minutes or so.

"Helm, standby."

Saumarez was still pacing, looking at his watch, looking out in the direction of the frigate posted several cables off his larboard beam, looking at the ship ahead of him, and then looking at his watch again. At precisely 60 minutes before dawn, two white lanterns were raised to the top of the mainmast of the *Barfleur*, Admiral Hood's flagship. Immediately, every frigate in the fleet repeated the signal. Immediately every red stern light on every English ship winked out. And, immediately, the entire line of ships began a slow, ominous, 180-degree turn.

CHAPTER NINE

DAWN seems to rise more quickly in tropical waters. One moment you're surrounded by the gray half-light that precedes the sun's fiery entrance. The next, there is a huge orange ball perched on the horizon; and a moment after that it seems the sun is already at full strength and boring into you.

The French do not follow the British tradition of standing their ships to general quarters to greet the dawn. For that reason Smith and Walker found themselves awakened by what sounded like chaos coming from above them. Emerging on deck, they found the French seamen were rushing to their battle stations but, even here, they differed from their British counterparts.

To the untrained eye, any call to general quarters, in any navy, looks like an overturned anthill. To the experience mariner, however, it is more like a ballet. People will be rushing about, no question; but each was going to a preplanned place, to carry out well-practiced duties. If you looked closely, you'd see that there was really a minimum of fuss and a maximum of efficiency in their motions. The French quarters, however, did not leave Smith and Walker with that impression. There was far too much shouting; far too many orders being given, and way, way, too much confusion.

Captain De Monteclerc was already on the quarterdeck getting a report as Walker and Smith hovered in the background.

"I don't know what happened, captain," said a visibly shaken young officer. "I was watching their red stern lights, just as I had been doing all night, when suddenly they winked out. I thought they were just getting ready for dawn a bit early. Then, when the light got better..." He pointed off the larboard bow, and there was the British fleet, in an orderly single file, coming directly back at them.

"So, they've decided to fight, have they?" De Monteclerc muttered as he examined the enemy through his telescope. "We'll soon see if..." He shifted the telescope to the *Ville de Paris*, De Grasse's flagship. "Yes, there, a signal from the flag: Form line of battle."

Snapping the telescope shut he ordered: "Helm, take station behind the *Glorieux*." And, after firing off a series of sail orders, he turned to Walker and Smith; "We'll soon see what happens when your Admiral Hood tempts fate twice."

The French fleet was headed south and struggling to get into some kind of battle order. The British fleet was on an opposite course, to windward, running with foresails and topsails and angling in on the French. It would be a classic larboard to larboard, single file, ship-of-the-line versus ship-of-the-line, battle. Or, so the French thought.

Suddenly the *Barfleur* ran down the "Close with the enemy" signal hoist and ran up another series of flags; flags that every ship in the column had been waiting for. The entire fleet, as one, dropped every bit of sail they had, including studding sails and steering sails, sheered off from the French, and started racing north toward Frigate Bay. It was the very maneuver that Admiral Hood had urged on Admiral Graves at the Battle of the Capes, which Graves had rejected.

For a moment, the French were confused, and then it dawned on them that they had been duped. By pretending flight, Hood had drawn them out of their anchorage; by pretending fight, he had frozen them in position long enough to blow past them. And with that sea room advantage, Hood might well beat them back to Frigate Bay and seize the anchorage for himself.

De Grasse instantly realized what Hood had done and was furious with himself for being taken in. That fury, however, quickly transformed itself into action; and the French fleet swung around in a long laborious curve and gave chase.

Walker and Smith had to stifle themselves and each other to keep from cheering. They were concerned, and rightly so, that they would be sent below, perhaps under armed guard, if they offered up so much as a peep. Instead, they did their best to remain invisible by positioning themselves well out of eyeshot and earshot of Captain De Monteclerc.

Smith was leaning against the bulwark just aft of the fo'c'sle. He had picked up a telescope that some officer or lookout had carelessly left adrift and was looking through it.

"The French van has almost caught up with the British rear and they're about ready to open fire. I can see St. Kitts not too far in the distance."

"Let me see," said Walker.

"Correction, the French *have* opened up. I can see muzzle flashes." Walker closed the telescope and turned around to see Smith with a huge smile on his face.

"Is there something about this that you find amusing?"

Smith could contain himself no longer and the smile turned into laughter. "Yes, Hood, that old fox. He simply thinks of everything."

"What are you talking about?"

"Hood hid a stinger in the tail. Look at the British rear. See those last three ships?"

"Yes. So what?"

"They are the *Bedford*, the *Resolution*, and the *Canada*. The *Bedford* is captained by Edmund Affleck, the *Resolution* by Lord Robert Manners, and the *Canada* by good old 'Billy-go-tight' otherwise known as William Cornwallis, brother of the general. If there were ever three captains you DON'T want to mess with, it's those three."

The leading ships of the French van were expecting to exchange a desultory broadside or two with the British rear while they flew past them and moved up the line. What they did not expect was to run into a buzz saw.

Three captains of the same mind had so superbly drilled their men that it was if they were one huge enormously deadly three-part ship. Suddenly chain shot was flying at French masts, 42, 32 and 24 pound balls were gouging holes in the ships sides, and the rate of fire was unbelievable. They were easily producing three rounds for every two coming from the French side; and, it didn't let up.

Round after round, volley after volley, was poured into the astonished French ships. As guns became dismounted and masts began to tip at odd angles, the French were forced to slow down. That was all Hood needed.

While De Grasse was trying to figure out what the devil was going on with the British rear, Hood had spun his center and van around in a tight 180-degree turn that stretched across the mouth of Frigate Bay. But, instead of having them turn back to engage the French line that was coming up, he sprung his second surprise. He ordered all ships to immediately back their sails, drop anchors and come to a halt.

The net effect was a wooden wall that stretched across Frigate Bay—a wall that bristled with more armament than was held by any castle. It was, for all practical purposes, impregnable. The French could not go around its left flank because the shoreline was there. It could not attack the middle without facing a hornet's nest of gunfire from anchored, stable, platforms. They could not go around the right flank because, again, the Frigate Bay shoreline was there. And, besides, the wind was coming from the wrong direction to do any of that.

The *Bedford, Resolution* and *Canada* finally took their places on the wooden wall and anchored. To his credit, however, De Grasse did not quit.

The French twice sailed up the line of British war ships firing away, but it was to no avail. The British, freed from the labor of having to handle sails, could give all their attention to firing guns. Eventually the gunfire stopped and the two fleets just looked at each other in silence.

"Astonishing," Walker said. "Simply astonishing."

"Quiet," Smith hissed. "Listen."

Walker strained his ears and heard the sound but couldn't quite identify what it was. He listened some more.

"What is it?" He finally asked.

"Laughter," replied Smith.

To this day scholars are in doubt as to where it started; but, sure enough, arising from deck to deck of first one ship then spreading to another, and another, was laughter. Joyous, sidesplitting, back-pounding, laughter. The men whose pride had been stung at the Capes and, before that, Grenada and Martinique, had now humiliated that same foe in return. Old seamen felt young again and, that night, many a yarn was told about the old days when Anson would capture a whole fleet or Hawke would descend out of nowhere like his namesake bird.

Hood, who had been called a madman and worse for advocating this very same strategy at the Battle of the Capes, had his vindication. Whatever was to happen in the West Indies, it was now perfectly clear that England might not have lost America if Graves had only heeded his advice.

On the French ship, however, Walker wasn't thinking about that. He turned to the quarterdeck where he saw Captain De Monteclerc standing next to the wheel. His face was a deep red and his fingers were white from clutching his telescope. He too could hear the laughter.

During the next few days, things were a standoff at sea, but were not going so well ashore. Hood had picked up some 1400 troops in Antigua and he landed them to help the beleaguered British garrison on Brimstone Hill. Unfortunately, it was not enough. De Grasse had previously landed over 8000 troops and the sheer weight of numbers eventually took its toll. On February 13th the garrison, half starved and nearly out of powder, surrendered, and control of St. Kitts turned over to the French.

This was a serious development. Once the garrison fell the French could now bring its land-based cannons to bear on the British fleet. They would be trapped between De Grasse on one side and the French shore batteries on the other.

It was time for Hood's third surprise.

* * *

"Ahoy the boat," came the challenge.

"Aye, aye," came the reply. And with that brief exchange, an important question had been asked and answered. "We see you coming alongside. Is there anyone important on your boat that we should know about, like another captain?" "No, there isn't," the boat replied. "Just routine business."

The gig pulled up to the side of the *Tisiphone* and a midshipman in the bow grabbed on to a side chain with a hook to temporarily hold the boat to the ship. A lieutenant, standing in the sternsheets, called up. "May I speak to your captain, please?" he asked.

A moment later, the captain appeared over the side. "I am Captain Saumarez."

"Good day, sir. Admiral Hood sends his compliments and requests you send over a lieutenant or senior midshipman from your
ship. He should arrive no later than six bells on the dog watch; and
he should bring with him a good pocket watch."

Saumarez was taken aback. This was the strangest request he
had ever heard. "Certainly, but may I ask the reason?"

"I don't know, sir. Another and I are tasked with passing this
message to each ship in the fleet."

"Very well. Carry on."

The midshipman released his hook and the mysterious boat
began stroking to the next ship in line.

* * *

The *Barfleur's* bell was struck six times in pairs of two. It was
six bells into the second dogwatch, but everyone had arrived at
least fifteen minutes before that. Gathered on the main deck of the
Barfleur were 22 officers, about a third of which were senior midshipmen like Hanover, all nervously standing around wondering
what on earth was going on.

As the ringing faded away Admiral Hood appeared with his
flag captain John Inglefield.

"All right then gentlemen, let me have your attention," Captain
Inglefield called out. "The Admiral would like a word with you."

"Thank you, John. I won't detain you long, gentlemen.

"You sir, could you tell me the exact time." He pointed to a
senior lieutenant who was obviously startled.

Pulling out his watch, "I have five minutes past seven o'clock,
sir."

"And you, sir, what do you have?" he asked, pointing to another.

"Sir, I have two minutes before the hour."

"As I thought," the Admiral said. "All right, I will ask each of
you to regulate your watch according to mine. On my mark, it will
be three minutes past the hour.

"Ready... MARK!"

"All right then, I have one other thing. I have sealed orders for
each of you to take back to your captain. My clerk will distribute
them," and he toddled off leaving a completely mystified group in

his wake. Before too much speculation could begin, the Admiral's clerk started calling off ships names and handing out packets.

"*Alfred... Belliqueux... Invincible... Monarch... Centaur...*"

* * *

"I don't know what else to tell you sir," Hanover reported. "He asked us to synchronize our watches with his and to take that packet back to you. The meeting was shorter than the row over."

"Very well, Mr. Hanover. That will be all." Captain Saumarez broke the seal on the packet just as Hanover was leaving his cabin.

Three minutes later a marine came running up to Hanover, saluted, and said: "Sir, the captain would like to see you immediately."

"Immediately?"

"Yes, sir. I am supposed to escort you."

Hanover arrived in Captain Saumarez's cabin and saw that he was still seated at his desk, Hood's letter open in front of him.

"Mr. Hanover, I'll trouble you for your pocket watch, if you please."

"My watch, sir?" He asked as he fumbled in his waistcoat.

"Yes, your watch. Right now it is the most valuable single object we have on this ship."

* * *

It was a repeat of the night before, "Dupe's Day" the men called it, when they fooled the French fleet into giving up Frigate Bay. Captain Saumarez was again pacing back and forth on the quarterdeck; only this time he had eyes only for Hanover's watch. Even more puzzling, his behavior had become as strange as the Admiral's.

First, he had taken possession of Hanover's pocket watch; then, not an hour ago, he sent a boat crew out to hang a lantern on the ship's anchor buoy; then he ordered the ship to a silent general quarters—which Hanover had never seen before—then he stationed two men with axes near the hawse-hole where the anchor cable left the ship.

He finally walked over to the starboard side of the quarterdeck, looked once more at Hanover's pocket watch, dropped his arm and hissed: "Now, Mr. Calvin, but be quiet about it."

Hanover could hear the muffled sound of axes cutting through thick hemp rope, followed by the word being passed from up forward: "Anchor's away, sir."

Saumarez then hissed a series of commands to get the foretopsail dropped and sheeted home.

The *Tisiphone* and every other ship in the British fleet simultaneously began to move, slowly at first, gradually picking up speed until they were soon well clear of St. Kitts.

De Grasse arose the following morning before first light and came on deck. He looked first at the set of his ship's sails, then to the sky to see if he could get any hint of the weather for the day, then he peered into the darkness for the trapped British ships.

As the light eventually increased, he realized the anchorage was empty.

* * *

The *Formidable* and her squadron arrived in Barbados on February 19th. On board was Admiral George Brydges Rodney, considered the best fighting admiral in the Royal Navy.

Rodney came from an ancient family. Sir Richard Rodeney fought with Richard the Lion-Heart and distinguished himself at the Battle of Acre. For five hundred years, the family estates at Stoke Rodeney in Somersetshire had been handed down in unbroken succession. His godfather was none other than King George I.

This kind of family background can breed men of dissipation as easily as it can breed men of steel; and, to look at Rodney, you would think the former had occurred. He was a tall slim almost frail looking man with the thin nose, sharp chin and piercing eyes of the aristocrat. He moved with graceful ease in the highest social circles; and, in the days of fancy lace for men, Rodney was among the most elegant. He was always perfectly dressed, totally fastidious, and loved the courtly comment and courteous phrase. In short, by all superficial accounts, he was a "dandy."

If you truly believed that of him, however, you did so at your peril. When the time came for sunlight to flash on cold steel, the supercilious dandy disappeared. Underneath was a tough, highly skilled warrior that would have done his ancestor, Sir Richard, proud.

At the time of the Battle of the Capes, Admiral Rodney was 62 years old and in comfortable retirement. England had been rocked by news of Cornwallis' defeat at Yorktown. That it had, in effect, been caused by a British defeat at sea made it even worse. People might not have known exactly why the battle was lost, but they did know that it wouldn't have happened if Rodney had been there.

De Grasse was loose in the West Indies; and, with no one to stop him; England could lose every one of its possessions there. Finally, at the direct request of the king, the old warhorse dug out his sword, dusted off his uniform, and went off in search of De Grasse.

After a lightning quick transit of the Atlantic (a mere five weeks), Rodney looked for Hood at Barbados. Failing there, he set off for St. Kitts and eventually found him in Antigua. One look at Hood's ships, however, and Rodney knew they would not be taking on De Grasse any time soon. So, he took his fleet, now numbering 36 ships, off to the careenage at St. Lucia for repairs.

Rodney knew how to squeeze the last drop of work out of a dockyard but, even so, his fleet was laid up from February through March in patching and mending. Some ships needed repairs. Some ships needed complete restoration. And some ships, had they been back in England, would have simply been sold to a wreaking company. Rodney did not have that luxury, however, so all ships were run through the yard.

* * *

Captain Saumarez was dressed in his finest uniform. He was standing on the deck of the *Formidable* waiting to meet with the Admiral. He had no idea why he was being summoned; he couldn't think of anything he had done wrong; but he was nervous nonetheless.

Eventually a young lieutenant came along to escort him to Rodney's quarters. They were the most spacious he had ever seen, but then again the *Formidable* was the largest ship he had ever been on. Rodney was looking out the stern windows of his cabin when Saumarez arrived.

"Ah, there you are, captain," Rodney began. He shook hands and invited him to sit down. Saumarez took a seat in front of the admiral's huge oak desk.

"A glass of port, perhaps, captain? It's an exceptionally good year."

"No, sir, thank you. I am fine."

"I won't keep you long but I wanted to give you these two packets. The first is routine business for your ship including, by the way, a list of prisoners held. We just exchanged lists with the frogs this morning.

"The second is more important. It's a package of dispatches." He shoved a sealed leather pouch across the table toward him. "They need to get back to the Admiralty as soon as possible. I am afraid I am going to have to dispatch you and the *Tisiphone* to get them there.

As the implications of his statement sank home, Saumarez looked at the package as if the Admiral had just offered him a rat that had died of the plague. He was only twenty-five years old. He was a good captain, a fighting captain; and now, with the fleet about to fight for its very life, he was not going to be allowed to stay. His heart sank.

"Sir?" His face had gone pale and he was fighting to keep a tremor out of his voice. "Sir, is there not some other ship that could possibly do this?"

"I am afraid there isn't, captain. We had no idea your ship would be joining us until you arrived. All the other ships have been assigned places and duties in the line of battle. Yours is the only one we can cut loose without changing all that around."

Rodney saw the disappointment in his eyes. "I am sorry, Saumarez. I know you're a good captain and I'd love to have you around during the coming fight. In a lot of ways you remind me of me when I was your age. But, I can't. These dispatches really must go through.

"If it's any consolation, you should know that I am not the only admiral who knows of your talents. Your day will come, son. Trust me. Your day will come."

Saumarez was disconsolate as he reached the gangway to go back to his ship. He couldn't leave right away, however, because another gig was pulling up to the *Formidable*.

"Ahoy the boat," went the challenge.

"*Russell*," came the reply. It meant that the captain of the *Russell* was arriving and proper honors should be observed.

Saumarez had known the *Russell's* captain, Tom MacArthur, since they were midshipmen together aboard the old *Seahorse*. He was strong as an ox, smart as a whip and had a wicked sense of humor that bordered on the perverse. As he climbed onboard ship, however, he could see that MacArthur looked as bad as Saumarez felt.

"Jim," MacArthur exclaimed, pumping his hand with an over-sized paw. "I knew the *Tisiphone* had joined us, but what are you doing here? Cultivating the admiral?"

"Well, I *was* here. I am being sent back to England with some damn dispatches."

"Really? That's terrific!"

"I am glad you find it entertaining. I do not."

"No, I am serious." Mac's voice lowered to avoid anyone else from hearing what he was about to say.

"Look, Jim, I've been having some... I don't know what you'd call it... some 'spells' lately. The quack surgeon on board my ship thinks it's my heart; and, well, I think he might be right. He says the only thing I can do is get back to London and see some specialists. That's why I am here. I am going to ask Rodney for leave to go back."

"My Lord, Tom, I am really sorry to hear that."

"Yes, well, I am sure they'll have me fixed up in no time. But, meanwhile, don't go back to your ship just yet, all right?"

It was the longest 15 minutes in Saumarez's memory. Finally, that same young lieutenant came by to escort him again to see the Admiral.

"Saumarez, I understand you've heard about Captain MacArthur's medical condition?"

"Yes, sir."

"Well enough. If you would be so kind as to give over the dispatch case to Captain MacArthur, I will have my clerk cut some new orders. I am placing you as captain of the *Russell* and MacArthur as captain of the *Tisiphone*."

Rodney gave a short smile. "I assume that will meet with your approval?"

Saumarez was at a loss for words. In the span of seconds, he had gone from commanding a frigate to commanding a 74-gun ship of the line. "Yes, sir. I... I don't know what to..."

"Just fight your ship well, Saumarez. That's all the thanks I need."

"Now, both of you get out of here. I've got work to do."

* * *

Captain Saumarez was still dressed in his finest uniform and waiting near the gangway when he summoned Susan Whitney and Midshipman Hanover on deck.

"Ah, there you are. I suppose you've both heard the news about my getting command of the *Russell*. I have to go over there now for a preliminary visit but, before I go, I wanted to speak to you." As he said this, he was pulling them aside and out of hearing range of the other men standing about.

"I am afraid I have some good news and some bad. In this morning's dispatch, I received a list of the British officers and men who are being held by the French. The two sides exchanged lists just this morning. I know you're worried about your friends Lieutenant Smith and Mr. Walker. I wanted to tell you that they are both still alive and well, but they are being held aboard the *Diadem*. The *Badger* was captured 10 days ago."

Hanover looked at Saumarez with relief. Susan looked stricken.

"Thank you, sir," Hanover finally replied. "It's good of you to inform us."

"Yes, well, I must be going."

"Sir, may I ask what is happening. Do you know when we might be getting underway?" It was actually an inappropriate question coming from a midshipman. But, midshipman or not, Hanover was still "Prince William" under that humble uniform and that bought him some occasional leeway, whether he wanted it or not.

"I don't know myself," Saumarez replied. "I do know that the Admiral is concerned about De Grasse's strength but no one can figure out a way to get into his anchorage to find out." Saumarez paused for a second. "Actually, getting in to the anchorage is no problem, we've just never figured a way to get anyone out again.

"Well, I must go. It won't do to keep my new command waiting, you know." And, he started to walk back to the gangway.

Susan's mind was working in overdrive. "Captain," she said, grabbing him by the arm and leading him out of earshot. "What if I had a plan to get the intelligence the admiral needs? Would you present it to the admiral?"

"I might. It depends on the plan."

Susan then launched into her idea. It took a minute or two to explain it, punctuated by occasional comments like "That's mad!" from Saumarez. At the end, Susan turned on her combination "little-girl/sultry women" smile and Saumarez was a goner. He agreed to present the plan.

* * *

Susan listened to the rhythmic beat of the paddles as the rowboat set forth across the anchorage. The boat was a beat-up old piece of junk that had been rowed in the previous night from the British frigate just off shore. The frail-looking old man in civilian clothes who was rowing was, in fact, a leather-tough able seaman from that same ship. Susan was dressed in a reasonably nice gown, complete with parasol, which she had borrowed from one of the other women on board the *Tisiphone*.

A woman, being rowed by an old man, in a beat-up boat was the last thing that was going to attract the attention of the French harbor patrol boats. They went completely unchallenged.

Pulling up to the *Diadem*, she demonstrated that the lessons learned at the Portsmouth Grammar School had indeed taken hold. She really could speak several languages—including French. It was not perfect, but she could make herself understood well enough.

"Excuse, me there," she said to the midshipman standing duty by the gangway. "But, I must speak to the captain."

"I am sorry madam, but he's not available."

"Please. Please, you must contact him."

"I said he is unavailable. Now go about your business." And he dismissed her as if she were a harbor whore, which he thought she probably was.

"You don't understand. The captain's the only one who can help me." And she started to cry... loudly.

Captain De Monteclerc, who was standing near the quarter-deck, could hear the exchange. "Yes, madam. I am the captain. Now, what is it?"

"You're holding my husband prisoner. Please, sir. I beg you. Release him to me and let us go on our way."

"And who might your husband be?"

"Lucas Walker," she said, dabbing her eyes.

"Ah yes, from that packet boat we picked up. Well, I am sorry madam, but that's not possible. You may take comfort in the fact that he is unharmed; and I am sure he'll be exchanged in due course for a French officer of similar rank and station. Until then, you'll just have to be patient."

"Sir, please. My husband is a surgeon, a man of healing. He's never fired a gun in anger in his whole life. I'll even wager he has voluntarily treated your own men. You say he's unharmed. Can I not at least come aboard and see him—to see for myself?"

De Monteclerc was about to dismiss her again but then thought about it. Walker *had* treated his own men and, by all accounts, did an excellent job. Even that other person... what was his name? Smith. Even Smith, although untrained, was a willing worker. That settled it.

"All right, Madam. You may come aboard and visit with your spouse; but only for a short period."

Susan moved forward to where a series of steps were built into the tumblehome of the ship. On each side of the steps were hand ropes. Timing her next move to perfection, as the rowboat rose in a swell, she transferred her weight to a step, simultaneously grabbed a hand rope and started up the ship's side. She was boarding like a pro, when it suddenly dawned on her that that was precisely the way she should *not* be boarding. To compensate, she managed to fake a suitable series of difficulties the rest of the way up. She landed on deck flashing a calculated amount of leg and gathered herself together.

About this time, Walker came up through the after hatch with Smith trailing behind.

"Susan? What the hell are..."

Susan ran to him, threw herself in his arms, and started covering his face with kisses. "Oh, darling. You're all right. I thought I'd never see you again."

Walker had no idea what was going on but he knew a good thing when he saw it. He started to return the kisses with equal passion—which, truth be known, Susan didn't mind at all.

Finally, Susan broke the embrace and turned to De Monteclerc. "Captain, might my husband and I be alone for a while?"

"I am afraid not, madam. After all, your husband is a prisoner. But, perhaps if you two were to walk back to the stern rail, I am sure the guard could watch you from here."

"Thank you, good sir." She took Walker's arm and escorted him aft. When they got to the stern rail, she gave him a quick kiss and hugged him tightly, swaying back and forth, with her head on his chest looking out over the starboard railing a few yards away.

"That's it, Lucas. Oh yes, that's wonderful. That's perfect."

Lucas Walker had never been a great ladies' man but, he had to admit, he *had* learned a trick or two in his time. Maybe he wasn't a swashbuckler, but he never knew a girl to complain. He smiled to himself. It was good to know that he hadn't lost the old Walker touch.

"Lucas, keep holding me but turn us around so I am looking out over the stern."

"Certainly darling, but whatever for?" He asked while kissing her hair.

"Because I am trying to count ships, you jerk. What do you think I am doing here?"

* * *

"Miss Whitney, this is spot on," Saumarez exclaimed as he read her report. "It's exactly what the Admiral needs. You've got ship types, number of guns, secondary ships, even the number of lighters they're using for transport. I can't believe it all worked out so well."

"Never underestimate the power of a devious woman, captain."

"Yes, I can see that," he replied. "And how are your two friends?"

"They seem to be doing just fine, especially Walker," she said with an enigmatic smile. "We only had a chance to speak briefly, though.

"Walker is assisting the French surgeon and Smith has been assigned to the sickbay as... well... basically as a loblolly boy." Susan was referring to the ships boys who were assigned to do most of the scut work in the sickbay. Because the porridge they served to the sick each morning was called "loblolly," these helpers became known as "loblolly boys."

"Did you see any possibility of escape for them?"

"No, sir. None at all. At least none that I could see right now."

"Well, this information is wonderful. If there is ever anything I can do for you..."

"Actually, captain, there is." She paused for a moment as if gathering her thoughts. "Would you be so kind as to authorize a transfer of Midshipman Hanover and myself over to your ship?"

Of the many things Saumarez might have expected for favor requests, this was not among them. Still, a new captain was traditionally allowed to bring over a limited number of people from his old command; and, what she had done really was quite daring.

"Miss Whitney, are you sure you want to do that? The *Tisiphone* is headed back to England, you know."

"Yes, sir. I am quite sure, and so is Mister Hanover."

"Mister Hanover, I am afraid, is a another matter. We must get him to safety as soon as possible."

"That might not be so easy, sir. I am afraid you will find him quite insistent. To the best of my knowledge, he has never 'pulled rank' in all the time he's been in the service, but I believe he's prepared to do so now."

Saumarez thought about that, and thought about the career ramifications of having an enemy two heartbeats away from the throne. "The devil take it," he thought. "Let Hood or Rodney make this decision."

Saumarez shrugged his shoulders. "Let it be so, then. Move your things over as soon as possible. I have no idea when we or the *Tisiphone* might be pulling out of here."

* * *

The sounds of a British ship of the line getting underway were unmistakable.

The bosun and his mates were scattering around the ship trilling on the silver pipes they continually wore around their necks like a badge of office. The pounding of several hundred feet, most without shoes, set up a patter like heavy rain falling on a wooden roof. On the main deck, one of the ship's boys was hammering a frantic beat on a drum, a captured French drum at that. Open gun ports were being slammed shut and the calls of officers could be heard encouraging speed as men ran up the ratlines and out onto the yardarms to handle the sails.

After the initial flurry of activity, the squeal of a fiddle could be heard from the vicinity of the foremast. A team of large and very strong men had inserted thick bars over ten feet long in the sockets of the capstan and were taking position behind them. A taut line was inserted through eye-hooks connecting the tips of the capstan bars welding them into a single unit. Locking their feet in the ribs built into the deck for greater traction, the men leaned their chests into the bars and wrapped their arms around them from underneath.

The fiddler then jumped on top of the capstan and began scratching out a perky tune. The men started walking in a circle, straining against the pull of the anchor cable, trying to get the anchor to break its hold on the bottom; while other men stood by to coil the thick rope into the rope locker, and ship's boys attached and released the cable from the messenger line that hauled it in. All that could be heard was the fiddler, the click of the capstan pawls and the calls of the bosun.

"That's it, lads! Heave around! Put your backs into it! Now you have it. Stomp and heave, boys! Stomp and heave!"

The bosun, looking over the side, called out to the quarterdeck. "Anchor's up and down, sir." And a few seconds later, "Anchor's Away!"

This began another series of quite different sounds. Orders were called up from the quarterdeck to the men dangling on the yardarms, held in place only by a thin rope at their feet. "One hand for yourself, one for the ship" was their rule. Sails started dropping as men undid the gaskets that held them to the yards. Men on deck manned ropes that controlled the downward movement of each sail, while other men were tasked with ropes that tightened the sails once they were fully released. With a loud POP, each sail opened and filled.

A fleet of ships, men of war, were underway and looking for a fight.

* * *

There is no such thing as a ship—any ship, in any time—getting underway without seamen's pulses quickening somewhat. This was doubly true for Walker. He stood on the deck of the *Diadem* not understanding a word that was being said around him, yet understanding everything that was going on.

He was standing on the equivalent of an 18-story wooden building placed on its side and moving through the ocean faster than he could run on land. The only sound was that of water rippling along the sides of a ship being propelled by wind—wind that had been blowing across these same waters for million of years.

And a second fleet of ships was underway looking for that same fight.

* * *

Admiral De Grasse sat alone at his desk in his spacious stateroom. Before him was a pile of orders, directives, correspondence and other miscellaneous paperwork that fell on his shoulders. The stern windows were wide open and a merciful breeze was drifting in, causing the lace curtains to billow and flap. But his mind was on neither the refreshing breeze nor the paperwork.

He pushed the papers away, unrolled a chart of the Caribbean and studied it for perhaps the hundredth time. He was not really looking at the lines on the chart; he had those memorized. In his mind's eye, he saw instead a way to humiliate and defeat the British.

He had linked up with the Spanish ships, 12 of them, bringing his total force to 45 ships of the line. More importantly, he had gotten to sea before the British and had at least several hours head start. He would go north following a chain of islands, all of which were owned by themselves or their allies, the Spanish. If need be there were any number of friendly ports along the way that he could duck in to. The Caribbean was no English Channel. As far as he was concerned, it was now a French lake.

He looked more intently at the chart. They would sail past Dominica, Desirade, Marie Galante, and a curious set of islands known as The Saints. He would fly past Guadeloupe, Montserrat, Nevis and St. Kitts. He would beat the British to Jamaica and offload his 15,000 troops.

To be sure, in time the British would come up, huffing and puffing, and lash out blindly like they always do. But, by then, it would be too late. The troops would be on shore and Jamaica would be doomed to fall. He could then turn his attention to giving the British a thrashing such as they have never received. And *then* what would the English do? Would they go back to St. Lucia to lick their wounds? Would they try to beat back against the trade winds with our ships following along, savaging them the whole way?

He stood up, walked to the stern windows, and looked out at what ships he could see. That glance filled him with even more confidence. De Bougainville, commanding his van was one of the most accomplished men of his age as an author, circumnavigator, scientist and soldier. De Vaudreuil, commanding the rear, was a magnificent sailor and came from an ancient Breton family known for their fighting skills. To be sure, Hood had wiggled off the hook at Frigate Bay; and he gave credit where credit was due, it was a clever move. But to what end? St. Kitts had nevertheless fallen along with its sister island, Nevis, and on his way back to Martinique, De Grasse had snapped up Montserrat. Where were the British when Dominica, St. Vincent, Grenada and Tobago fell?

Now the great island of Jamaica lay in front of him. Spain wanted it; it was the price of their alliance. Whether they would get it after the French took it, however, was another matter. One thing was certain. It too would fall, just as had all the others; and with any luck, he would destroy the British fleet in the bargain.

He rocked back and forth on his heels, his arms behind his back. "I will see to it," he muttered to an empty room. "I will see to it and there is nothing those British fools can do to stop me."

CHAPTER TEN

IT was early in the morning of April 8th when the sentinel frigates flashed the news back to Rodney. The French fleet was out of Fort Royal and headed north. He got the news at eight in the morning and within two hours the British fleet was underway in chase.

The wisdom of Rodney's decision to careen and repair his ships now became evident. In addition to much needed repairs, each ship had received at least a cursory cleaning of its bottom. Scales, barnacles and seaweed were roughly scraped off. It wasn't as thorough a cleaning at they might have received in England, but it was enough to add several knots of speed to each ship; and that speed advantage was to prove critical.

The wind was blowing out of the east as it always does in that part of the Caribbean. All day the French sailed north. All day the British chased them. Day turned to night and the chase continued. There were times when sharp-eyed lookouts swore they could see sails ahead. Their veracity, however, wasn't proven until the morning. At daybreak, French sails were visible from on deck; you didn't need to go up to the masthead to see them.

If the British could see the French, the French could see the British and De Grasse was stunned. He, in no way, anticipated that the British would catch-up that fast. "So be it," he thought. "Then let's make our stand here."

The "here" De Grasse was referring to was the Saints' Passage, a waterway to the north of Dominica. Dividing the channel, about 13 miles from Dominica and ten from Guadeloupe, was a cluster of islands that Columbus had discovered on All Saints' Day and named them accordingly.

De Grasse's first task was to divest himself of some 150 small merchant ships he had in a convoy. He ordered these into Guadeloupe. They would not be missed as far as he was concerned, as they carried no military supplies or troops, only merchant goods. Still, he had to detach two frigates to shield the convoy into port and this left him with 33 ships to fight the British 36.

* * *

"Blast and damnation!" Rodney's voice carried across the deck as he pounded the quarterdeck rail. Turning to his flag captain, Sir Charles Douglas, he exclaimed. "Sir Charles, would you be so good as to explain to me how comes it that the French have all the luck and we have none!"

The British van under Hood had reached the French fleet just as it was entering the Saints Passage. True to form, Hood immediately attacked. Rodney was delighted until he looked around and saw, to his horror, that the rest of his fleet was dead in the water, becalmed in the lee of Dominica. His vastly outnumbered van would surely be chewed up and spit out by the French.

"Sir Charles, get those damn ships out of that lee before Hood loses his whole squadron. Send them a signal to put over small boats and tow themselves free if necessary."

At this point, De Grasse made his first mistake. Instead of taking advantage of the situation by closing and demolishing the British van, he opened up at extreme range hoping to cripple his enemies aloft and thus stop the pursuit. In fact, he thought he had done so.

By late afternoon, the rest of the British fleet had caught enough wind to get out of the lee and join up with the van. Hood's ships had been hit all right, but it wasn't as bad as it looked. Rodney decided to heave to as if his fleet could go no farther and let De Grasse believe what he wanted to believe. Rodney was right. De Grasse thought the British were finally off his tail while Rodney lay in wait neither tired nor seriously hurt, but shamming.

The French lost one ship, the *Cato*, and that reduced De Grasse's fleet to 32. Nevertheless, they continued on their way and, a half hour later, the British quietly followed.

* * *

The two fleets chased each other all that night and into the following day. On the night of the 10th, however, luck finally began to smile on the British.

In every navy, there are incompetent officers. Some never make it past midshipman. Some never make it past lieutenant. But, some make it all the way to captain of their own ship of the line. This was the case with Capitaine du Vaisseau De Gras-Preville, captain of the *Zele*. How he received his commission, let alone his own ship is unclear, but he was probably among the worst seamen in either navy—or very possibly any navy.

In the British system, such incompetence is often masked by the presence of "masters" on board. Every British ship has a captain, of course, but they also have a master who is a highly skilled and experienced seaman and is in charge of actually navigating and sailing the ship. It's a holdover from the days before the British had a formal navy. The king would appropriate merchant ships, place guns on them and send them off to war. The merchant captains demanded in return that they at least go along to sail the ship and they became the first masters. The captain tells the master where the ship will go and what it will do, and the master makes it happen. The French had no such system.

The *Zele* had already collided twice before with other ships. Collisions three and, if you can believe it, four were to spell the end of French influence in the Caribbean.

The French fleet was traveling along under all plain sail staying well ahead of the British. At one point, the fleet was ordered to tack to accommodate a shift in the wind. The *Zele*, sailing behind the *Jason*, completely mishandled her sails and ran into the *Jason's* stern, seriously damaging her rudder. The Jason was able to make temporary repairs, but she was out of any fight.

De Grasse was down another ship.

When dawn broke the British were delighted to see that the *Zele* was straggling. No one could see the reason for it, but she was clearly vulnerable and Rodney made plans to take her.

This incident then became the turning point in French influence in the West Indies. What would De Grasse do? If he continued to sail on, there was every reason to believe that he could still reach Jamaica before the British. Once there, his fleet, combined with Jamaican shore batteries, would be invulnerable.

But to do that he would have to sacrifice the *Zele*. As incompetent as she was, the *Zele* was still a French ship, and De Grasse was a man of honor. As evening fell, he backed a topsail on his flagship, the *Ville de Paris*, and went to her aid.

* * *

Rodney had hardly slept a wink since leaving St. Lucia to pursue the French. He subsisted on will power and by drinking endless pitchers of lemon squash, his favorite beverage. Throughout the night, he kept his eye on the French stern lanterns and slowly maneuvered his ships to be in the best possible position when dawn broke. When the sun finally rose, however, Rodney could not believe what he saw.

The last Rodney had seen of the *Ville de Paris* she was preparing to take the *Zele* in tow. Somehow, in some way quite unimaginable to Rodney, during the night the *Zele* had managed to collide with her rescuer the *Ville de Paris*. De Grasse's flagship was relatively unhurt, but the *Zele* was a wreck. Her bowsprit was completely gone and with it the stays that held up the foremast. As a result, the foremast had come crashing down on her fo'c'sle. For all practical intents, the *Zele* was helpless and presented De Grasse with a dilemma.

Had he abandoned the *Zele* yesterday when she was lagging far behind, no one would have blamed him. After all, they were racing for Jamaica and possession of an entire major island was at stake. But now? Could he abandon her now that he had already circled back to her aid and the British were at hand?

No, he could not.

He signaled a frigate to tow the hapless *Zele* out of the way, hoisted signals for battle array to the remaining ships, and turned his fleet south to meet the British head on.

* * *

The British were ready for this fight. More than ready, in fact. The previous three years had been frustrating ones. Defeat after defeat in the West Indies, capped off by the humiliation at the Chesapeake, had been a bitter pill for a proud navy to swallow. But, as frustrating as those years were, they were also years of preparation for this one crowning moment. The men were confident. The ships were in order. And, for the first time in anyone's memory, the British actually had a numerical advantage.

The Battle of the Saints started out with what Walker would have called a "horse race." The wind, as always was out of the east, the French were in a single line approaching from northwest, the British were approaching from the southwest. Each commander wanted to get to get upwind from the other. In naval tactical parlance, it was called "getting the weather gage."

The advantage of having the weather gage, in the age of fighting sail, cannot be overestimated. We forget this in a time in which 10,000 horsepower ships make the wind almost completely irrelevant. We forget that sea battles once could be determined as much by a change in the wind direction as the skill of the combatants.

To have the weather gage, in simplistic terms "having the wind behind you," gave you the precious advantage of maneuverability. You could decide when the battle would start and at what distance it would take place. You could descend on the enemy with great speed, while the enemy would have to beat upwind to reach you. When gunfire started, the smoke would clear away from your ship while theirs was still engulfed not only in their own smoke but, shortly, yours as well. This gave you the vital ability to see what was going on sooner than your opponent; and, in fleet actions, also to see the signal flags of your flagship sooner and more clearly.

Every captain, in every ship, in both fleets, knew these advantages and was racing toward a hypothetical point in the ocean that would allow them to get to the windward side of their opponents.

On this day, the French won.

Rodney reluctantly turned his line of ships to the northwest setting up a classic set-piece naval battle. Two lines of ships would be traveling in opposite directions, passing starboard to starboard, at close range, with gun ports open, blazing away. When the lead ship of the British van, the *Marlborough*, reached about the sixth or seventh French ship in their line, Rodney ordered all ships to "Fire as you bear." In other words, as soon as the enemy comes into your sights, go ahead and open fire.

De Grasse, at this point, was quite pleased with himself. He had obtained the weather gage and Rodney had been forced into a standard line-of-battle fight. He believed this would be a short-lived scrap—a few hours at the most. He was wrong. In fact, the first broadside was fired at 7:40 AM and the last at sunset. The Battle of the Saints would rage for eleven bloody hours.

* * *

The *Russell* was the last ship in the van, with the *Marlborough* at the point and Admiral Drake's *Princessa* in the middle. She had yet to fire a gun but all was in readiness. The lower decks had been swept clear and anything that could be moved was moved to the hold. Partitions between rooms had been removed to create open spaces. Even the captain's cabin had been turned into a gunroom. On deck, hammocks had been rolled into sausage-like shapes and stowed in nets along the sides of the ship. Every small boat had been put over the side and was currently being towed behind the ship. The fewer boats that were on deck, the less the chance of a ball hitting one and creating a storm of deadly splinters.

The men had been at battle stations for hours. Some sat in small groups to quietly talk with their mates, some stared vacantly out to sea, some were sharpening cutlasses, some were examining round shot; but all knew what was coming and all knew that not all of them would live to see tomorrow's sunrise.

Hanover insisted on being a part of the fight and, as a midshipman, had been assigned to supervise a battery of three guns on the starboard side near the fo'c'sle. He, too, was lost in thought as Susan Whitney came up.

"Bill, could I talk to you for a minute?"

"Certainly, Susan. What is it?"

"Do you remember when I told you I didn't think Lucas and Sidney had a chance of escape?"

"Yes."

"Well, that was then, this is now."

Hanover looked puzzled. "What's that supposed to mean?"

"It means, while I was with them we discussed an escape plan."

"Are you serious? What is it?"

"I need your help to get one of the small boats we are towing hauled up close to the ship."

"And then?"

"Then I am going to get in it and you're going to let the line out again. When we pass the *Diadem*, I am going to use the boat's tiller to swing it out into the lane between the two ships. Walker and Smith are going to jump in the water and I am going to haul them out."

Hanover looked at her and said nothing for a long moment as if he wasn't quite registering what Susan had just said.

"Do you have any idea how crazy that sounds? What happens if you miss them on the pick-up? These ships are not going to turn around for anyone."

"It's not crazy, Bill. It's desperate, yes, but not crazy. Will you help me?"

"Walker and Smith agreed to this?"

"Yes, they did. It was either that or spend the next God knows how may years in a French prison camp or, worse, a prison ship."

"Honest to God, Susan. I don't know which of you three should be the first through the door at Bedlam.

"Yes, of course, I'll help. What do you need done?"

"I need you to get one of those boats we're towing back there alongside us."

Hanover spun around, "Olson! Trexler! With me."

The big Swede and the tough Cornishman had the small boat alongside in no time. Whitney climbed down into it carrying several lengths of rope and two small buoys. She gave Hanover a wave and the guy rope was cast loose. In a few seconds, the boat was back trailing behind the *Russell* with the others.

* * *

The initial broadsides between the British and French vans caused a great deal of smoke and noise but little damage. That was to be expected. The guns on both sides would still be warming up and both sides would still be getting the range of the other. It did not take long, however, for the deadly nature of this kind of warfare to assert itself. The French as usual were mostly aiming high, trying to bring down the masts and sails of the British ships with bar shot. The British, as was their normal tactic, were aiming low, trying to penetrate the French hulls with round shot.

Marines on both sides were up in the platforms and on the rat-lines with their muskets sending down sniper fire trying, espe-cially, to pick off officers. Other seamen were manning small swivel guns, sending over clouds of grapeshot to sweep the oppo-nents deck clear of men.

The flash of gunfire, large and small, was everywhere. The sound had grown so loud that it could not actually be heard any-more—only viscerally felt in your gut. And the smoke, the burning acrid smoke was everywhere, tearing at your throat, burning your eyes making it impossible to make any visual sense of anything that was happening more than 10 yards away from you.

Each man was on autopilot. There was no time to think. There was no time to reason. You did whatever it was you had spent countless hours being trained to do. Swab out the barrel. Load the shot. Fire the musket, reload and fire again. Race down to the powder room; get another charge and race back to your gun. If the man next to you was killed, it didn't matter; in fact, it barely regis-tered. If you slipped in a pool of someone's blood, you cursed, got up and continued on your way. The sound of men screaming and the sight of body parts that were never meant to be viewed became commonplace. If it had nothing to do with loading your particular gun, or firing your particular musket, or getting the next powder charge, it simply didn't register.

The British van, under Lord Hood, had passed the French van and was now coming up on the French middle. At the same time, the British middle, Rodney's division, was starting to engage the French van; and the first of the battle's many characters had emerged.

The lead ship in the British middle was the *Hercules*, Com-manded by Captain George Savage. Captain Savage was as brave as they come, but suffered terribly from the gout. It was so bad that he had to have a chair placed on the quarterdeck so he could sit down at frequent intervals. Gout or not, he was also a great be-liever that the British possessed a brand of courage that was uniquely theirs.

His approach to battle was to greet each enemy ship as it came along side with a broadside and a torrent of verbal abuse screamed through a megaphone. It is said he could stand by the rail, shake his fist and scream obscenities for a full five minutes, in three lan-guages, without ever once repeating himself. Bosun's mates throughout the navy held him in awe.

Badly wounded by musket fire, he was taken below but was soon back on deck where he ordered his chair moved over to the rail and had himself tied to the chair. From this position, he continued to abuse each enemy ship, by name, as it came by. Then, for good measure, when the *Hercules* had passed the last ship in the French line, he suddenly swung around the enemy's stern and contemptuously raked her from behind, just as she thought she was rid of him.

It was 9:00 AM and the battle was well and truly underway.

* * *

Susan was astonished at how fast she was moving. When you are on the deck of a ship fifteen feet above the water, its movement doesn't seem to be that rapid. When you're being towed behind that same ship in a small boat and you are only three feet above the water, it becomes a breath-taking sleigh ride.

She couldn't think about that right now, however. She had work to do.

She took the two 50 foot lines and separated them. One line was tied to the bow of the boat, the other to the stern. At the opposite end of each line, she attached a small buoy. This gave the end some weight—something she could sling around and around in a circle before letting fly; and it would hold the end of each line on the surface of the water once it landed. Both ropes were then carefully coiled so they wouldn't snag when she threw them.

"Well, they'll have two chances to catch on to a rope," she thought. "And God help them if they miss them both."

She then turned to the tiller and tested it out. Yes, the boat was making more than enough steerageway. She could turn the rudder with the tiller and the boat would swing out to the left or right as she wished.

"There. That's all I can do for now," she thought. "That's all I can do, except wait."

* * *

Behind Captain Savage in the *Hercules* came the *Resolution* under Lord Robert Manners. He was one of the "stingers" Hood had put in the tail of his fleet at the Battle of Frigate Bay. Next came the *Duke* under Alan Gardner with its gorgeous figurehead of William, Duke of Cumberland, and victor at the Battle of Culloden Moor, at its bow. In the middle was the *Formidable*, Rodney's flagship, and behind her was the *Namur* under Captain Fanshaw, who almost single-handedly saved a British convoy from the French at Grenada.

The *Duke*, the *Formidable* and the *Namur* were all "first-rates" and carried over 100 guns each. Just those three ships alone could lay a combined 150 guns on a single broadside target; and there were very few ships in anyone's navy that could withstand that kind of attack.

The two fleets slowly sailed past each other like warriors on a parade ground. It was a glorious sight perversely made even more glorious by the death and destruction represented by each gun flash and each thunderous boom that echoed across the water.

About 9:30 AM, Rodney's *Formidable* pulled alongside De Grasse's flagship the *Ville de Paris* and the two started hammering away. The two ships were evenly matched, both with 100 guns, both with the finest ship's companies in their respective fleets.

In the midst of the carnage, a French ball somehow managed to strike a hen-coop that had been left on the spar-deck of the *Formidable*. When the dust finally settled, a small head peeked out from the wreckage; and shortly a bantam-cock emerged determined to find out who was responsible for this outrage.

He fluttered to the quarterdeck rail, saw the *Ville De Paris* and instantly decided she was the source of his unhappiness. For the rest of the battle, every time the *Formidable* unleashed a broadside, he would leap about, flap his wings and, with his shrill cries, cheer on the British seamen.

Admiral Rodney was so charmed by the bird that he gave orders that, if anything should happen to him, the bird would be cared for and pampered for the rest of his life.

Thus, with the French being simultaneously abused by British guns, half-crazy captains who could swear in three languages, and an irate chicken—the battle moved into the late morning.

* * *

"Sidney, it's almost time," Walker whispered.

"All right, you go on deck. I'll be right behind you."

Smith climbed up to the gun deck and was about to climb the stairway to the main deck through the aft hatch when something caught his eye.

It was an elaborate collection of thick ropes running from the wheel on the main deck to what amounted to nothing more than an oversize tiller. The whole device, blocks, ropes and braces, had only one purpose—to move the rudder and thereby steer the ship. As he climbed the stairway Smith glanced at the apparatus, but its implications didn't immediately register.

Smith went to the rail where Walker was trying to look over the side and at the same time keep his head down in case a British sharpshooter should think it a tempting target.

"Ah, there you are," Walker said. I can't see Susan; but, then again, we aren't quite up to the *Russell* yet, either."

Walker turned to Smith, "Are you ready to..." His sentence died as he saw Smith's eyes grow wide, then saw him turn and race down the hatch he had just come through.

A minute later, he came back.

"Lucas, did you see that collection of ropes in the stern one deck below us?"

"Yes. I assumed it was the cable run for the rudder."

"That's exactly what it is. And what would happen if that cable was cut?"

Understanding now dawned in Walker's eyes. "It would be a catastrophe. They would loose control of the ship. The ship would swing into the wind and stop, and, unless they acted very quickly, the ships behind would pile into us."

"Precisely. We've got to cut that cable."

"Sidney, if we do that we'll miss our pick-up."

"I know, Lucas. I know." Smith was quiet for a moment while Walker looked over the side in the general direction of Susan's arrival.

"I am not going to ask you to do this, but I am going to stay and try to cut that rudder cable. When Susan comes up, I want you to get over the side and grab that line. I am going below."

"And I am supposed to leave you here? Just like that?"

Smith smiled at his friend and said, "Look, Lucas, you don't belong here—not really. This is my world. I joined it of my own free will, and I am quite prepared to die in it and for it."

Walker continued to look over the side and said quietly, almost wistfully, "There she is, Sidney. There's Susan, just like she planned it, coming up between the lines of ships."

Walker paused for a moment, and then a cold resolution flooded him. It was the kind of decision that does not come from your brain, it comes from your heart and your soul.

"If you're staying, I am staying. You get below and start work. I'll wave Susan off then join you."

"Lucas, if we ever get out of this, I going to... I am going to..."

"You're going to do what?"

"I am going to send your ass to medical school."

* * *

"What was it Smith had said?" Susan thought. "No battle plan ever survives the first contact with the enemy."

She had forgotten about the smoke—the horrible, acrid, blinding, smoke.

She saw the *Diadem* coming up, eased the tiller over, and swung her boat into the lane between the two lines of ships. Then the ship ahead of the *Diadem*, the *Glorieux*, let loose with a ragged volley of fire, followed by the *Russell* opening up and the *Diadem* launching their own broadside. The lane was now choked with a thick gray, swirling cloud of gun smoke which caused her to gasp and cough and her eyes to water.

She looked up again and a puff of wind had cleared a gap in the smoke. There was the *Diadem* coming up.

She tied off the tiller, moved to the bow of the boat, picked up the line and buoy and was about to swing it; when she looked up and saw Lucas Walker at the rail of the *Diadem* waving her off.

He was yelling something. She couldn't make out what it was but the intent was clear. He was calling off the rescue.

"Why?" she thought. "It had worked. She was here. The lines were ready to be tossed. All they had to do was..."

And she stopped. All "they" had to do? There was no "they." There was only Walker standing at the rail. Smith wasn't there.

She could only conclude the obvious. Smith was seriously hurt or dead. Her eyes began to water. "This damn smoke," she said to herself. "It's killing my eyes."

* * *

Smith was convinced that he had found the dullest ax in the history of the French Navy. He whacked away, again and again, at the rudder cable, making some progress, but not nearly fast enough.

Walker came bounding down the stairwell and found Smith at his labor.

"What can I do to help?" he asked.

"Unless you've got another ax—nothing. Just stand guard. Someone is bound to come down here sooner or later and find us. And we've got to get this thing cut no matter what."

"That's crazy. What am I supposed to do if someone does come? Here give me that ax."

Smith turned over the questionable blade, carefully slid his sword out and looked nervously around.

No sooner had Walker started work when three French seamen came running down the stairs. The first two swung around a stanchion and headed forward. The third caught Smith and Walker out of the corner of his eye.

At first, he could make no sense out of what he was seeing. Then it finally dawned on him and, with a scream, he rushed at the two with a seven-foot boarding pike in his hands.

He thrust the razor sharp head at Walker's exposed back. Smith's sword flashed down quick as a cobra strike cutting the pike in half just as the head was only inches away from ramming home.

The man looked at Smith, then looked at the shattered remains of his pike, and ran.

Walker kept hacking away and the first of three cables separated. He began on the next.

By this time, the other two seamen had doubled back. They were both armed with cutlasses.

The first man eyed Smith warily as he hefted his sword. Smith circled and suddenly flicked out his sword in a point. The Frenchman clumsily parried it. Again, the sword flashed, again it was parried. Smith circled some more and tried another point, this time cutting the man badly on his left arm.

This enraged him. He swore and mounted a furious attack, hacking away at Smith like a wild man, complete with spittle coming out of his mouth. Smith coolly dodged or parried each attack.

Circling again, Smith tried another point. The man parried with an inside guard which he then awkwardly tried to shift into a point. It was a bad idea. Smith anticipated his move, stepped quickly to one side and brought his sword down on the man's head.

There was a sound like a ripe watermelon being split as Smith's Sea Service cutlass tore through skin, bone and brain tissue. The man dropped to his knees, and then wordlessly fell over on his side. Smith extracted his sword from the man's skull with a yank and readied himself for the next fight.

This would be much more of a contest, for the third man was clearly a swordsman.

Walker kept hacking away and the second of three cables separated. He began on the third.

Smith had his hands full. They were no wild rushes from this opponent. He was content to thrust and parry, always watching Smith with cold steady eyes.

This was a fight to the death and both men knew it. Their sword play covered the whole aft end of the deck, each man attacking, then retreating, then attacking again. Neither wanted to quit, yet each man was growing painfully tired. It was the Frenchman who suddenly broke.

He knew that if he didn't finished off the Anglais soon he would be too tired to continue, and that could be fatal. The man decided to mount a frenzied attack.

In a burst of activity, he made a sudden lunge forward. Smith, with a beautiful half hanger, deflected the blade. But the man had put too much energy into it and he found himself off balance. Smith stepped to one side like a matador, changed his guard to a point and ran his sword through the Frenchman's throat.

The third and final cable parted and Walker dropped to his knees, exhausted.

* * *

It was 10:00 in the morning. The evening chill was gone, the sun was hot, the sky clear and the sea a profound blue.

The *Formidable* had finally passed the *Ville de Paris* and was now alongside the next ship in line, the *Glorieux*. To say the *Glorieux* was in bad shape was an understatement. She had already been quite battered and torn by both the *Hercules* and the *Resolution* when she came upon the *Duke*. Captain Gardner, who had a reputation for viciousness in battle, simply tore her apart. By the time the *Formidable* got to her, she looked like a broken child's toy. Every upright stick on her was in ruin. Her bowsprit was gone along with all three masts: fore, main and mizzen. Even the ensign-staff, which flew the French flag, was broken in half and dangling off the stern.

She might have looked like a total wreck, but she still had some fight in her. As the *Formidable* came up, carpenters could be seen frantically trying to nail a French flag to the broken stump of a mast. While they were at work, another man held the flag up on a long pole. Sharpshooters on the *Formidable* shot the man that was holding the pole through the hand; whereupon he simply shifted the pole to his other hand and kept on waving.

The response of the *Formidable* to this act of heroism was to pour a full 50-gun broadside into the *Glorieux*. The combined weight of that much iron slamming into her at one time literally moved the *Glorieux* sideways through the water. If your opponent was injured, you moved in for the kill. Always. Always. Always. For that is the way of war whether it is between armies, between ships, or between individuals.

There was a pause as the next ship in the French line, the *Diadem*, came up. The *Formidable* made ready to give her a taste of what they had just given the *Glorieux*. There was time, however. There was no rush. There was just simple brutal efficiency. On both sides of the battle men re-loaded their guns, while others tried to make temporary repairs, and still others began throwing bodies over the side, mostly dead but sometimes, by mistake, even those that were seriously wounded but still alive.

Admiral Rodney was pacing the quarterdeck with his flag captain, the gunnery expert, Sir Charles Douglas. Both were extremely pleased with how well Douglas' gunnery reforms had worked out—especially with the performance of a new gun he had installed called the "carronade." By the end of the day, the British seamen had christened it the "Smasher," and the French the "Devil Gun."

"Dashwood? Dashwood? Where the devil is that bloody midshipman," Rodney groused. "I told him to go to my cabin and mix-up a lemon-squash for me and you'd think he went back to Barbados for it."

Just then, Dashwood appeared on deck nervously stirring the Admiral's drink with his midshipman's dagger.

"Oh, for God's sake Dashwood," Rodney said with disgust. "That kind of thing is all very well for the midshipmen's mess but... look here, drink that yourself and just go get me a lemon to suck on."

Rodney cringed thinking about all the places that knife has probably been as Dashwood fled from the quarterdeck. "Sir Douglas, I swear, the midshipmen we are producing today are..."

"Sir, what's that? What the devil is she DOING?" Douglas was pointing at the *Diadem* with his mouth literally hanging open.

For no apparent reason, the *Diadem* had gone out of control. She slewed first one way, than another, then went into a severe roll as her helm went over all the way to the stops and jammed there. This placed her into a turn to windward that should never have been made at that speed. With her bow now suddenly pointing into the wind, the sails slammed back against their respective masts and brought the ship to an immediate and unplanned halt.

The effect was predictable. The ships behind the *Diadem* scrambled to take emergency evasive action. Some were able to do it, and others were not. But, the main effect was that a gaping hole now appeared in the French line as the *Glorieux* continued on her course and away from the *Diadem*. Douglas was the first to spot it and realize its implications. He turned to the Admiral.

" Sir George, I give you joy of the victory!"

"Posh," Rodney replied. "The day is not half won yet."

"Sir, we have them. All we need to do is to take our ships through that gap and break their line! If we can cross over to the other side, we will then have them under fire from two directions."

"No," said the admiral, "I will not break up *my* line to do that."

Douglas could not believe what he was hearing. It was all so obvious to him. "Sir, I beg you, break the line!"

"I said no, captain."

Douglas was beside himself. He looked at the French line, looked at Rodney, and then looked at the French line again.

"Sir, as captain of this vessel, I must protest. My duty is to fight her as effectively as I can and that duty tells me we MUST cut through their line.

"Helm, hard a'starboard!"

The helmsman started to comply when the Admiral shouted. "Helmsman, place your helm amidship." And he complied.

"No, sir," Douglas countered. "Helm to starboard."

"Helm amidship, helmsman and may I remind you captain that I am I am commander-in-chief of this fleet."

"And I, sir, am the captain of this ship."

The helmsman, now in a state of terrified, frozen, immobility, kept the helm amidships.

The admiral and captain then separated; the former going aft, and the latter going forward. In the course of a couple of minutes or so, each turned and again met nearly on the same spot, when Sir Charles quietly and coolly again addressed the chief.

"Please, admiral, I beg you again. Just break the line, Sir George, and the day is yours."

Rodney had cooled off somewhat by now. He hadn't slept in two nights, and he was feeling every one of his 63 years. The admiral then said in a quick and hurried way, "Oh, very well, do as you like," and immediately turned round, and walked into the after-cabin.

Douglas wasted no time. "Helm, hard to starboard!"

"Dash," he said waiving at the midshipman. "Go below and warn each gun deck officer that we will soon be engaging on the larboard side."

* * *

The word "chaos" doesn't begin to describe the pandemonium that reigned on the *Diadem*. She had just taken a pasting from the *Hercules* and the *Resolution*, and the worst was yet to come in the form of the *Duke*, the *Formidable* and the *Namur*. She had tremendous shot holes in her side, several below the waterline. The fore and mizzen masts were barely holding themselves upright because of snapped stays. The human carnage on the main and gun decks was unspeakable, and smoke filled the air making it nearly impossible to breathe, let alone see the enemy. This was *not* the time for the ship to loose steering.

Walker and Smith were slammed against the starboard bulkhead and fell on top of each other in a heap. The *Diadem* had violently swayed first one way than another, when they heard the screech of complaining wood and metal as the rudder slammed all the way over to the larboard stops. This threw the ship into a violent roll as the bow turned sharply to the left.

The two scrambled up the orlop and then the gun deck stairwells as best they could given the crazy angle of the ship. They emerged on deck just in time to hear the crack of sails snapping back against their respective masts. Anyone who hadn't been knocked off their feet by the sudden starboard roll was now on the deck due to the ship's sudden halt.

The helmsman was screaming, "The helm is not answering, sir! It's not answering. It's not me. The helm..." His voice was becoming higher pitched with each iteration of his defense.

The captain and several officers were trying to get men aloft to take in sails. A dozen commands were being screamed and, by the confused look of the men, not all were consistent with each other.

Suddenly, the captain stopped giving orders. He just stood there, open mouthed, looking aft. Walker and Smith followed his gaze; and it was like watching a slow motion train wreck.

The next ship in line behind the *Diadem* could do nothing. There was no force on heaven or earth that could have stopped her forward momentum. Slowly, almost gracefully, 25 feet of her bowsprit crashed through the windows of the captain's cabin and lanced upward through the aft end of the quarterdeck. This kicked the *Diadem's* stern around at the same time as the second ship's foremast came down, draping the *Diadem's* stern with heavy, but now useless, sails.

It was only a matter of minutes before the third ship piled into the second, and the fourth into the third. Four French ships of the line, in a massive wreck, all stuck together as if they were one ship, utterly unable to fight.

This was the target that presented itself to the *Formidable* as she altered course to position herself directly in front of the ruined ships.

* * *

Captain Douglas was looking aft, satisfied that the other ships in the column had taken his lead and followed him through the gap. When he heard his first lieutenant cry out: "Oh, NO," he spun around.

All firing had ceased. Indeed, all activity had ceased as officers and men stood in amazement. It was a sight none had ever seen before, and none would ever see again. Four massive ships of the line were slowly piling into each other; completely unable to avoid the catastrophe that was befalling them.

"Dashwood, go get the Admiral," he said quietly.

By the time Rodney had returned on deck the fourth ship was just sliding into the pile and Douglas was already giving orders.

He pulled a midshipman runner over to him. "Tell all the gun deck officers, I want the starboard side guns to rake the *Glorieux's* stern as we pass by. Then, I want all hands to shift over to man the larboard guns, load and await my commands." The midshipman disappeared.

"Signal officer! Where's my signal officer?

"I want you to signal the *Namur* to take station off our larboard quarter and be prepared to come to a stop. Then signal the *Duke*," he was looking over the signal officer's shoulder. "Never mind. Gardner's figured it out. He's already headed over there. Now, GO."

Douglas turned to Rodney who, by now, had taken it all in. "Is there anything else you think I should do, Admiral?"

Rodney stared over at the French ships, quiet for a moment, his hands behind his back, rocking on the balls of his feet.

"I take it we're going to be shooting some fish over in yon barrel?"

"Yes, sir, we are."

* * *

"Sidney, we've got to get out of here," Walker said as he looked out at the British ships. "Any minute they're going to..." But before he could complete his sentence the entire larboard side of the *Formidable* lit up, followed by the *Duke* and the *Namur*.

The three first-rates had formed a circle of death around the four disabled ships and were pouring in broadside after broadside. It was unbelievable carnage. Hideous. Ghastly. The British were so close that their gunners didn't even have to aim and every ball would strike home. Even if the French ships had been undamaged before, they were in mortal danger now.

Walker looked around him. A small French boy was standing next to a gun clutching his powder charge like a security blanket and shivering with fear. The gun was upended and the crew dead, but this was his post and he knew not what else to do or where else to go. It was like he was patiently awaiting his world to somehow return to normal.

He felt, more than heard, the sound of round shot slamming into the *Diadem's* hull. Two guns down; the ships side had been collapsed. Where there were once two neat gun ports, there was now one ragged hole.

A man sat next to the hole looking inquiringly at his left hand, which was no longer there. Toward amidships, another man had lost his right leg from the knee down. He held the limb, shoe still attached, as he dragged himself across the deck hoping somehow to get below so he could get some help. The path of blood across the deck ended just before the hatch where he died.

"Sidney! We've *got* to get out of here!"

"Not a problem, mate. You hold up your hands; that'll cease the gunfire. Then, we'll just walk across the water to one of our ships and we'll have a tot together while we enjoy the fireworks."

"I am serious, damn it. We've got to go over the side and take our chances."

Smith turned to him and snapped. "Lucas, how many times do I have to tell you, *I can't swim!*"

"You won't have to. Here." Walker went over to a large hatch cover that was secured to the deck. It was a six foot square piece of wood that was used to keep water from flooding below decks in rough weather. "Help me with this.

"It won't be much but it's big enough for the two of us and it'll float. We will toss it over the side and then go in after it."

"And then what? Walker, do you ever think about..." Smith continued to grouse, but he helped Walker to get the hatch cover on top of a rail and drop it down into the sea.

The two got up on the rail. "My God, do you see how far it is down?"

Walker said nothing. He grabbed Smith so he couldn't back out and jumped.

* * *

Bill Hanover was in a happy place. He was lying on something hard, but it was not uncomfortable. Lying beside him was one of the scullery maids. He wasn't even sure of her name, but she was soft and warm and clean. He rolled slightly to one side and started sliding his hand up along the inside of one leg. When it could move up no further he began ministrations with his fingers. He had experienced the dampness of a female before, but this girl was monumental in her lubrication, which bode well for future activity, he thought. Slowly the scene started to de-materialize and within moments he found himself on the planking of the gun deck. The body of a dead seaman was partially draped over him and his hand was almost inside the bloody stump where the man's right leg had once joined his hip.

A gurgled shriek escaped his lips as he violently pushed the dead man off him and shakily tried to get up.

"There yer are, Mister 'anover. We fought yer were dead." One of the older men was kneeling next to him and several others had gathered around.

"Thank God yor awright, sor. Mister DeWitt and Mister Padgett was taken in that last broadside along wiv 'alf the bloody gun crews. Yor the only officer left on this deck, is ta truth of it sor. Yer've got ter get up!! Wotcher want us ter do, sir? Wotcher want us ter *do*?"

Hanover's head was spinning and all of his senses had not returned as he struggled to sit up. He looked down at his blood soaked clothing and all he knew for sure was that he wanted to be away from this horror. But his parched lips and raw, gun-smoke ravaged throat would not allow him to do anything but make incoherent sounds.

One of the few remaining gun captains bent over the two. "Wossat 'e's sayin', Frankie? I can't 'ear 'im."

The old seaman leaned closer to Hanover's lips and ran the disjointed sounds through the only mental filter he had—30 years experience as a seaman.

The old man stood up, relieved that the responsibility of decision had been removed from all of them, for an officer had spoken. "Well, right then, have yer lubbers gone deaf, eh? Come on... load them guns and run 'em out, for God's sake. Didn't yer 'ear 'im? RUN EM OUT!!"

Hanover staggered to his feet and could see the men in various stages of clearing away wreckage and re-loading their guns. As they worked, to a man, they would periodically glance over to make sure he was still there. Their world had been rocked, but it had not been destroyed—not as long as he was there, not as long as *he* still functioned. The full meaning of combat leadership suddenly exploded in Hanover's brain, and right behind it he found a strange calm confidence that he was equal to its demands. Years of training now kicked in as he assessed what needed to be done.

"That's it! Let's go, you men! You there, help them get that wreckage cleared off that gun. That's it. You and you, go help them serve gun number 3, they're shorthanded. You over to gun 6. You and you over to 8. I WANT A BROADSIDE OUT OF THIS DECK IN THREE MINUTES. DO YA HEAR? THREE MINUTES!!"

Captain Saumarez knew his ship had been stung, but he didn't know how badly. One of the powder monkeys had emerged from the lower deck shrieking that everyone was dead, so Saumarez sent one of his junior lieutenants to investigate. He did know this much. The French were starting to untangle and unless he could get some shot into them quickly, they would soon have enough separation to possibly get away. Just then, he felt the deck tremble under his feet and heard the blast of a larboard broadside. It wasn't a full volley but it was enough to set the French back on their heels again. "I don't know who's in charge down there," he thought, "but when this is over I am personally offering him a toast."

It was hot, dirty, deadly work. Before the battle even started the men had stripped off their shirts and tied their bandanas around their heads. This not only kept the sweat out of their eyes but also, by wearing it low across their ears, muffled the worst of the thunder emanating from the guns.

Hanover could not do those things, of course. He was an officer. His face was blackened by gun smoke and his clothes were torn, bloody and disheveled, but he had to maintain his dignity. He wasn't a real officer yet, of course; he was only a midshipman. But that's almost an officer, and today he had certainly earned the right to consider himself such.

The one thing he wasn't was "Prince William." Somewhere in the crash of the guns, the smoke, the screams, the confusion and the carnage, he had learned to fight. He had learned to get men to put aside their fears and do things that no sane person would ever do. Sometimes it was with a curse, sometimes with a pat on the back; but it worked. He was leading men in battle and, in so doing; he had himself become a man.

* * *

To the shark, each day was like every other day and each night was like every other night. After all, his agenda was not a complicated one. He was swimming, constantly swimming, constantly looking for something to eat.

"There. Just there," his brain dimly thought. "Did you smell that? That little bit of copper in the water?" He started circling.

"Again, just there. There was some more." He headed off in that direction. As he swam, the odor of blood became stronger and he sped up.

The faster he swam the more intense became the odor until it reached proportions that obliterated what little rational thought he had in his tiny brain. He was being driven literally mad by the intensity of the odor. "Swim! Cut! Slash! Tear! Bite! Swim! Bite! Tear! Swim! Get there before the others! Faster!"

By the time he reached the source of the blood, he found a scene that was hard for him to comprehend. Food was *everywhere*! Strange creatures with four tentacles lay floating in the water, some inert, some still moving and almost all *bleeding*!

The final switch in his brain flipped closed and he became what 100 million years of evolution had trained him to be—a mindless, soulless, pitiless killer.

He picked out one of the creatures and decided to go for a tentacle. His powerful jaws bit through a soft part, met some resistance and snapped through it. He was dimly aware of a shrieking sound penetrating the water; but he had the middle third of a tentacle in his mouth and it was of no concern to him.

And, above the surface, the battle raged on.

CHAPTER ELEVEN

THE first shriek came from the starboard side and, at first, Susan had no idea what it was. She looked over the side and saw a man screaming and waving his arms. She then saw a bloody froth bubble up next to him, accompanied by a sharply angled fin. She knew now that to go into the water for any reason meant death. The sharks were here.

The reality of her situation finally struck home and she found herself falling back on the innate strength that seemed to always be there when times got tough. It was not something she had learned. It was not even something she desired. It simply had always been there and it told her now what she had to do. She could not be aboard ship to tend to the wounded, but she could do something that the ship couldn't. She could do something about the men who were in the water.

Next to her, neatly coiled, was the rope and buoy device that she had planned to use with Walker and Smith. Slinging the buoy around by the attached rope she flung it out to the closest man she could see. He was brown haired and clinging to a broken spar, that's all she knew. She didn't know which ship he was from or, for that matter, which country. It didn't matter.

At first, the man was too startled to act. He knew he was a dead man. It was only a matter of time before the fleet sailed on without him; and, after that, only a matter of time before he could no longer hold on to the spar. It was with a sense of unreality that, out of nowhere, a buoy and a line appeared and dropped only a few yards away. He followed the line back with his eyes and saw a woman in a boat, being towed by a warship, frantically waving for him to grab on.

"Imagine that. A tart in a boat's callin' me over ter her. So, that's the way of it, is it? That's wot yer spot just afore ya die? Strange, though. She don't 'ave a look like me Chris, and I would 'ave thought it's yor own luvd ones yer'd spot before ya go out."

Susan called again and waved. There was something in her voice that decided it for him. "Aright then. If this were the way ter the next world, I spect I can go brave as any man." With that thought, he slipped off the spar and thrashed his way over to the buoy. Susan pulled with all her might and slowly dragged him over to the gunnel. Pulling himself on board, he flopped onto the bottom of the boat and stared up at his rescuer.

"Who are you?" the vision asked.

"I am," he started. "Well, I was Cecil Durbin, able seaman 'board the *Marlborough*."

The apparition said nothing as she looked for the next person to whom to throw a line.

" Beggin' yor Grace's pardon, but..." He was at a loss for the right words. "I mean, I know ah'm dead; but woss gonna 'appen ter me now?"

Susan spun around, not quite believing what she heard. "To begin with you are *not* dead; and, second, you're going to get your carcass up, go to the bow and start throwing the damn line to people as I am doing."

* * *

Rodney felt the crushing apprehension of the past few weeks, lifting from him like a morning fog. It was going well, better than he could possibly have hoped.

The *Formidable* had broken the French line, his middle squadron had followed him and they were demolishing French ships in all directions. Adding to this was a freak occurrence further back in the line.

The wind had made a sudden shift, which opened up a second gap just after the French ships *Caesar* and *Hector*. Captain Affleck of the *Bedford* saw the gap; saw what Rodney had done a few minutes earlier and plunged his ship through. Behind the *Bedford* came the entire rear squadron under Admiral Hood who frantically signaled to all ships to follow *Bedford's* lead.

The French were now in serious trouble. In effect, their fleet was split into three disjointed segments, each incapable of acting in concert with the other two. Almost as bad, many of the British ships now had the weather gage and could dictate the terms of the battle.

On the other side of the battle line, Rodney knew he now had his middle and rear squadrons engaged. It only remained for his van, which had continued sailing on, to double back and join the fray. Rodney knew he could recall them, but recall them to attack where? He could throw his van at any one of the three French segments, but which one?

He glanced around and saw Admiral De Grasse's flag still flying from the mainmast of his ship and that settled it. This man had humbled them at the Capes and rampaged through the West Indies. He represented four years of reverse after reverse for the proud British Navy and it was going to end here and now.

First, he sent a signal to recall the van. The second signal came a few minutes later. It consisted of four flags and simply read: VAN. ATTACK. FLAGSHIP. IMMEDIATELY.

Captain Saumarez aboard the *Russell* did not need his communications officer to read the signal. He knew what it was because he had been expecting it.

The *Russell* was the last ship in the British van; but Saumarez was not about to play follow-the-leader while his squadron made a huge, ponderous, u-turn. He snapped a new set of sail orders, disengaged the *Russell* from the van, and headed straight for where the *Diadem* and the four-ship pile-up had occurred.

* * *

Susan's boat was never meant to hold more than a few people. There were already 12 men on board: seven British, three French and two who were unknown. The latter two didn't speak; they just kept staring blankly ahead, so no one knew what country they were from. Several of the men were hurt seriously and it was these Susan was tending while the healthier men continued rescue operations.

"Durbin," she called out.

"Aye?"

"We're running out of room here. I want you to take... You, what's your name."

"Pulley, mam. Isaac Pulley offn the *Princessa*." He knuckled his forehead in a rough salute.

"All right. You go with Durbin. I want you two to use the rudder to angle this boat over to one of the others that's being towed, transfer over and start pulling people in."

She no sooner said this then she was jerked off her feet. The *Russell* went into a sharp turn, snapping the towline taut, and headed directly at the French line.

"Durbin. Pulley. GO!!" She fired off the command like a bosun and nobody was about to challenge her. She looked a lot more confident than she was, however, for now she was mystified. Why on earth was Saumarez attacking the French head on? Her question was answered a few minutes later when the *Russell* pulled up behind the *Ville de Paris'* stern and backed sails.

The *Canada* had been there for some time. In an act of unbelievable courage, or unbelievable stupidity, Captain Cornwallis had decided to take on the *Ville de Paris* broadside to broadside. The *Canada* was no garbage scow. She was a 74-gun third-rate with a ship's company of over 600 men. But the *Ville de Paris* was a 120-gun masterpiece—the largest ship in either nation's Navy. Yet, the *Canada* was giving as good as she got.

As soon as the *Russell* slowed to a stop, the starboard side guns ran out and raked the huge three-decker. Susan gasped.

Being raked was the worst thing that could happen to a ship. It involves one ship crossing another and pouring gunfire through the bow or the stern and down the length of the ship. Susan knew exactly what was happening on the French vessel.

Round shot would be streaking down the entire length of the *Ville de Paris'* gun decks. Some of the balls would be passing through groups of men as they served their guns. Some would be striking gun carriages upending them. And some would be striking the gun barrels themselves, ricocheting in God-only-knew which direction.

To make matters worse, the *Duke* had followed the *Russell* over and, from a distance was already trying to get in its licks. The *Duke* was firing balls over the top of Susan's tiny boat. The crash

of her guns followed by the "wiss" of a ball overhead caused everyone to involuntarily duck.

For the first time, genuine fear entered Susan's consciousness.
All it would take would be one gun with a bad powder charge, or a
mistake in elevation by a gunner, or a shot fired on the down-roll
instead of the up-roll, or a change of munitions from the solid ball
to grapeshot. If any of those things occurred then she, and everyone else in the boat, would be so much ground meat.

She was not alone. She looked around and saw that several of
the rescued men were entertaining the same fears.

And the battle waged on.

* * *

Admiral De Grasse was many things, but incompetent was not
among them. He was as shrewd a tactician as ever sailed and no
one who knew him doubted his courage for an instant. He knew
his line had been cut. He knew the British were devastating several
of his ships. His own ship was being hammered. But, he was not
without hope for he had one more card he could play.

"Mr. D'Ethy," he called. A young lieutenant came running over,
covered with soot, his hat gone, his coat torn and a slightly wild
look in his eyes. He was the signal officer and he still clutched his
precious slate, chalk and code book in his hands.

"Sir!"

"Take down these signals. To Admiral Vaudreuil: REAR.
CLOSE. ON ME. Then send a second signal to Admiral Bougainville: VAN. RETURN. ATTACK. FROM WINDWARD."

The lieutenant ran off to the signal halyards while De Grasse
paced the quarterdeck trying to calm himself. He looked aft and
saw the *Glorieux* was in dreadful shape. He had no idea how she
stayed afloat yet; there she was, still getting off sporadic rounds of
gunfire. Off his starboard bow, he could see the *Caesar* and *Hector*
under attack from four British ships but still fighting.

"It is not lost yet," he told himself. "It is NOT... lost... yet..."

What he had just done was to bring his badly torn rear squadron up to join his center in a defensive position. He would create
what amounted to a floating fortress consisting of his two squadrons massed together so they could protect each other.

The British could encircle this cluster and eventually destroy them, but that's where he had played his ace. His van was almost unscathed. They could come back and attack the British even as the British were attacking them. He would have them caught in a pincer between his "fortress" and the ships of his free ranging van.

"It will work," he thought. "It all depends on the van, but it will work."

The signal lieutenant returned. "The signals have been sent and acknowledged, sir."

"Very well, Mr. D'Ethy. Stay near me in case I have more signals to send."

Several minutes passed. The remnants of the rear squadron were swinging around the four entangled ships and coming up to join the French center. But, the van was another question entirely.

"Mr. D'Ethy, are you certain Admiral Bougainville acknowledged your last signal?"

"Yes, sir. I am positive."

"Damn it. Send it again and this time fire a signal rocket. That should get their attention."

De Grasse continued pacing, feeling the hits his own ship was taking through his feet as he walked. He was determined not to show fear to the men. His pace was measured and steady, like he was taking a Sunday stroll.

He glanced over the side at the *Canada* just a pistol shot away. Secretly he admired the amazing rate of fire the ship was keeping up; but that was not a feeling he wanted to portray. Instead, he screwed his face up into a look of utter contempt and turned away.

D'Ethy returned. "Sir, I sent it again and they acknowledged it again. But, sir, except for the *Ardent*, they are not coming back. They're running, sir. They're running!"

* * *

"This is a hell of a time for the Froggies to be putting on a fireworks display," Walker said, nodding skyward.

"Trust me they aren't. It looks like someone's not paying attention to signals," Smith replied.

The two were bouncing around on their improvised hatch cover raft. They had each recovered a piece of broken wood and were paddling in the direction of the British line.

"Oh, Jesus God," Smith exclaimed. Walker looked over, saw he had stopped paddling and was staring at the water.

"What? What is it?"

"Look over there," Smith said, pointing. And, as if on cue, a shark fin broke the surface, leisurely making its way toward the raft.

"Oh, Jesus God," Walker echoed.

"Lucas, if he comes for us, what are we going to do?"

"All right, look, don't panic. I read once that if you bang a shark on the snout, he'll leave you alone."

"Are you sure?"

"Yes, positive. Sharks have bad eyes but great noses. Bang'em a good one and they'll turn tail. It's their most sensitive part."

The shark had to be at least eight feet long. Not at all large by Great White standards, but enough to scare the wits out of anyone who is in close proximity. He slid down one side of the raft, turned and cruised down the other, eyeing the occupants on each pass. Suddenly, he seemed to make a decision and swam toward the raft head on to see if there was anything he could snatch.

The shark had gotten his head over the edge of the raft and opened his huge mouth displaying several rows of serrated teeth. Smith scuttled backwards almost knocking Walker into the water.

"Hit him, Sidney! Use your piece of wood. Hit him on the nose."

Smith quickly got to his knees, reared back and cracked the shark, hard, right across the point of his snout. The shark slid back into the water."

"Atta'boy. Way to go, Sidney! That's giving it to him. That's the last we'll see of him!"

The shark retreated about thirty yards away, turned and headed straight back at the raft—800 pounds of thoroughly enraged carnivore. The shark plowed into the frail raft at full speed, smashing it to pieces. Walker and Smith spun into the water, right where the shark wanted them.

* * *

With the French van disappearing, ship-by-ship, over the horizon, De Grasse knew it was all over. His fleet—well, most of it anyway—had fought well; but it was now just a matter of time before they would all have to surrender. If it hadn't been for the betrayal of Bougainville... If it hadn't been for the cowardice of...

"Damn it," he suddenly yelled. "Will that poxy ship never stop raking us from the stern?"

The first ship to surrender was the *Glorieux*. Indeed, there were so few people left alive on her that she almost didn't surrender at all for lack of anyone to take down the flag. Her decks were littered with dead men, whose collective blood was flowing in torrents out the scuppers, creating numerous graceful red swashes along the side of the ship. Finally, the ship's only remaining officer staggered to the pole upon which the tattered French flag was nailed and tore it down. Her battle was mercifully over.

The next to go was the *Caesar*. The *Caesar* too had fought well, but she had been trapped by the second British breakthrough and was simply out-gunned. What happened to her, however, should not have happened to any ship, let alone one as brave as this.

The *Caesar* surrendered between one and two in the afternoon. When the British prize crew came over, the Frenchmen were so out of control that the British had to herd them quickly below decks and seal-up the hatchways so they could get the ship straightened up and underway. With no officers and no discipline, the men quickly got into the spirit room and spent the rest of the afternoon getting drunk and fighting among themselves.

Tragedy finally struck when a drunken seaman, carrying a lantern, bumped into a liquor cask whose top had been stove in. The flames quickly spread from one deck to another, trapping men by the dozens. The British prize crew, amid the demented shrieks of those caught below decks in the fire, worked furiously to put the fire out; but it was to no avail.

As the ship burned to the waterline, the prize crew threw open the hatches to let the Frenchmen out. The French seamen sized up the hopeless condition of the ship and, almost to a man, jumped over the side. What they hadn't figured on were the sharks.

All day the sharks had been feeding on men thrown or knocked overboard in the battle; but, still, they were not satisfied. With fresh meat in the water, they renewed their efforts. Men were grabbed, released, and grabbed again. Men, who a few hours earlier had been masters of the sea, were now being torn from retched scraps of debris to have huge chunks of their body ripped away.

Each of the British ships sent boats to help in the rescue, but little could be done.

About five o'clock, the *Hector* surrendered. She was trapped along with the *Caesar* in the second British breakthrough, but did not fight nearly as well.

When the British broke the line, the *Hector* faced the prospect of an entire squadron unloading into her as they passed by. It was more than the men could take and a near mutiny ensued. Men threw down their weapons and ran for the safer reaches of the lower decks. Their captain, however, was having none of it. He ran among the fleeing men, beating them with the flat of his sword, until order was restored. Unfortunately, a short time later, a British ball tore off the captain's leg at the hip and the last of shipboard discipline went with it.

The next to go was the *Ardent*, and this was the most poetic surrender of the day. To begin with, the *Ardent* was the only ship in the French van to return when ordered by De Grasse. Second, until 1779, the *Ardent* had been a British ship. The French had captured her in the Channel a few years earlier. It was as if her REcapture now symbolized Britain's return as a naval power.

* * *

Durbin and Pulley had made it over to a good-sized launch that was also being towed; and they began work immediately throwing lines to other men in the water. Their boat could hold 25 men comfortably and it was already starting to fill up.

Susan looked over at the launch, caught Pulley's eye and waved. Pulley smiled and waved back. As he did, however, something caught Susan's attention.

Over on the far side of the *Russell*, between the *Russell* and the *Formidable*, she thought she saw two men on a raft. The smoke would reveal them one moment and hide them the next. But, there was something about them.

"There. Just there. Was that not... yes, there were two people, one in uniform, one in civilian clothes." She put her hand up to shield her eyes from the sun. "Could it possibly be?" she speculated.

She finally decided she had to know for sure. "You, up forward. Cut the towline. The rest of you get out the oars, we're going to row over to where I think I see some men."

She had given an order, but no one moved.

At first, she couldn't believe it. Then the reality struck home that she was a woman in a boatful of men, seamen at that. They were used to taking orders automatically, which is probably why she had gotten as far as she had. But they were NOT used to taking orders from a woman.

She tried again. "Men, cut the towline and rouse out the oars. There are some people over there I mean to rescue."

A voice from amidships answered, "Bint, ain't nobody gonna cut that line. That's us only connection ter the ship. Wot 'appens if we cut it and the chuffin' ship, hell the 'oole damn fleet, gets under way, eh? We gonna row afta them?"

Susan found herself pleading. "You don't understand. There are two men over there. They are..." Susan stopped short, thinking how to describe them. "They're friends of mine. Very good friends. And I just can't leave them there!"

"No, 'mam. Th't line stays. And I ain't takin' no more orders from a bitch."

It was a standoff. The thin, nervous, man was as adamant in his position as Susan was in hers. The issue was finally decided in a very straightforward way.

Sitting in the back of the boat near the tiller was a huge seaman by the name of Raymond Hayes. Susan was to later find out he was Hugh Hayes brother. He sighed once, got to his knees, then stood up—all 6'5" of him—and started to slowly walk forward. When he got to the protesting man, he reached down, grabbed him by the neck and literally lifted him off the deck.

" Yer know, cully, 20 minutes ago I didn't 'ear yer callin' the lady a 'bitch' wen she were 'aulin' yor worffless 'ide out of the bloomin' drink, did I?"

The man tried to gurgle a response.

"No, I didn't fink so. Now, she says she 'as some mates over yonder 'oo need some 'elp. And if she 'as some mates in trouble, we're gonna 'elp 'er 'elp them, right, ain't we?"

The man gurgled again.

With that as an apparent assent, Hayes released his grip and the man crumpled to the deck.

He continued forward, took out his knife and slashed at the towline. When the line finally parted, he turned around.

"Right, yer useless lubbers, get them oars out. We got places ter go."

* * *

For the next half-hour after the *Ardent* struck her colors, De Grasse moved like he was in a bad dream. It was the kind of dream where you knew something bad was going to happen to you at any moment, but there was absolutely nothing you could do to prevent it.

The *Canada*, off his starboard beam, had surgically removed every stick of timber from his main deck. In a spectacular display of gunnery, there wasn't a single mast left standing taller than a man's height. The *Russell*, on his stern, had blown away his rudder and was streaking shot after shot down the length of his decks, mangling and mutilating men and material as they went.

In a daze, he looked at his feet and wondered when he had put a pair of red shoes on. He didn't remember even owning a pair of red shoes. He saw also that he was standing in a pool of blood, but he was not able to connect that with his shoes. The pool of blood was, in turn, connected to Lieutenant D'Ethy who in death was still clutching his slate and codebook. D'Ethy's body didn't register with De Grasse either.

Dimly, he knew he had to surrender soon, but to whom?

He looked over the side and saw yet another British ship coming up. Squinting against both the smoke and the setting sun, he could see a long, thin, blue pennant streaming from the newcomers foremast.

"NO!" He screamed. "No, I will not! Not to HIM!"

De Grasse rushed to a 12-pound gun that its crew had just loaded and run out. He shoved the gun captain away, took up the slow match and, just as the *Barfleur* came into his sights, touched off the gun. When it had finished its recoil, he climbed up on the rail to shake his fist and scream at his old nemesis, Admiral Hood.

To a 90-gun warship, being hit by a 12-pound ball was more puzzling than dangerous. "No matter," Admiral Hood thought. "If the *Ville de Paris* sill wanted to fight, that was fine by him."

Hood gave a series of rudder commands that placed him in-between the *Canada* and the *Ville de Paris*. Once he had pulled even, he gave the order for a broadside.

Even if the *Ville de Paris* had been a healthy ship, catching 45 balls, ranging from 12 to 32 pounds each, at point-blank range, would have been a serious matter. But the *Ville de Paris* was not healthy. She was, in fact, on her last legs.

The force of the broadside crashing into his ship's side knocked De Grasse off the rail and into an untidy pile at the foot of the catwalk. Suddenly, the daze he had been in for the past hour lifted. Suddenly, his head was clear. Suddenly, he knew what had to be done.

Doing his best to maintain his composure, he walked to the temporary flagpole the men had erected and, with shaking hands, took down the French flag. The shrewd and cunning victor at the Capes, had finally surrendered to the equally shrewd and cunning victor at Frigate Bay.

And, one of the bloodiest battles ever fought at sea was finally over.

* * *

Susan was at the tiller. "Come on, men. Pull. Get some way on. We're almost there!" The boat cut through the final cloud of smoke just in time to see Walker and Smith's raft being demolished by the huge shark.

"Oh my God," she screamed. "Pull, you men. Standby forward. Get ready to throw them a line." But they were still not close enough for the line to be thrown.

* * *

Smith had settled down somewhat from his initial thrashing in the water. "Just relax, Sidney, I've got you," Walker said as he held Smith around his chest from behind.

"But, the shark. Where's the shark?"

"I don't see him. I think he's gone." Walker said it, but he didn't really believe it.

As they bobbed around in soul-shattering terror waiting for the next shark attack, Walker realized he was hearing things. Strange, but he thought he could hear Susan calling to him. Then he heard her again, and again.

He finally turned around in the water far enough to see the boat heading straight for them.

"Sidney, look. There. It's a boat. It's Susan!" With that, he loosed one hand from the grip he had around Smith and started frantically waving.

Within a minute, a line with a loop tied on the end came snaking out toward them. Walker slid the loop around Smith's body, under his arms. "You go first, Sidney. You can't swim." Before Smith could object, strong arms were pulling him toward the boat and, soon after; even stronger arms were pulling him on board.

Susan was by his side as he struggled to his feet. There was no time for greetings, however. "Get that line out again. Quickly," she ordered. The line was tossed and it landed not more than five yards from Walker, but he never got the chance to get hold of it.

Walker saw the line coming toward him and, at the same time, felt a tug on his right leg. The sensation returned a moment later only, this time, it was not a tug.

He screamed. He couldn't help it. His calf felt like burning coals had been wrapped around it. He screamed again and thrashed his arms, but the shark had him in a solid grip. This was HIS domain. HE ruled here, not these silly creatures.

Walker managed to get in a breath of air before the shark pulled him under.

Susan and Sidney looked on in horror as Walker disappeared beneath the water. Within a few seconds, nothing remained on the surface to indicate that their friend had ever existed. Not a bubble. Not a ripple. They continued to stare at the spot.

* * *

Walker felt himself being pulled downward, ever downward; and he knew he was dead. In a few moments he would have to take a breath, only instead of breathing air, his lungs would fill with seawater. He would, of course, choke, gag, and try to breathe again, but nothing would do any good. Slowly he would black out and the shark would have his meal.

He opened his eyes to see nothing but blackness. The sting of the saltwater on his eyes was nothing compared to the burning that was starting to form in his lungs. As he went deeper, the water got noticeably colder and the pressure on his ears and chest was becoming intolerable.

At this point, two things happened that he didn't expect. First, a feeling of enormous peace came over him. He felt as though everything was just as it should be and he was looking forward to—no, he was longing for—the eternal sweet blackness that was coming. The second thing was even more surprising than the first. The shark let go.

He didn't know whether the shark had become distracted by something else or just chose to go on to something more interesting. But *he let go*! Walker could kick his legs again; and he instinctively fought for the surface. The race was no longer to meet the sweet blackness. It was a race for survival.

Walker kicked and swam vigorously, but this was a mixed blessing. Every kick of his legs, every stroke of his arms, consumed oxygen. His muscles were sending demands to his brain for more oxygen to feed his starved cells. His brain then relayed two simultaneous commands to his lungs: "BREATHE!" and "DON'T YOU DARE!"

He could feel the water getting warmer and brighter. He looked up and thought he could see the surface high above. The primitive side of his brain was screaming to breathe. The rational side was fiercely fighting for dominance, for enough control to override the demand for air.

"Just a little longer," he thought. Please God, let me hold on just a little longer." He forced himself to focus with an iron will on the surface above him; he could clearly see it now. Yet, even as he did so, a little voice was echoing through the pain that was now radiating out of his chest and into his arms. "Lucas," it said. "You *can* take a little breath, you know. Just a little one. A little seawater won't hurt you, not if it's just a small breath. You *know* how good that would feel, don't you? You *know* how sweet it would be."

* * *

Susan was the first to give up. She could no longer watch the empty spot where her friend went down. It was over, and he was dead.

For the first time since this whole thing started, she lost her self-control. Turning to Smith, she leaned against him and broke into shattering, soul wrenching, sobs. "It's so unfair, Sidney. It's so unfair," she kept saying over and over.

Sidney Smith was in tears himself. He was holding Susan and blankly looking out at the water, not knowing what to say... when Walker broke the surface.

* * *

To Walker's surprise, taking that first breath was almost as painful as holding it in. He gasped great lungfuls of air, again and again. The pain in his lungs began to ease, but he was a long way from having his mental faculties back. His brain was still oxygen starved and not thinking clearly. He flopped around in the water as helpless to decide what to do next as a newborn baby. Fortunately, he had no decisions to make.

Within seconds, the boat had reached him and he was dimly aware of being pulled aboard. He thought he saw someone who looked strangely like Sidney Smith being jerked out of the way by someone who looked like Susan Whitney. "How extraordinary," he thought. "What are they doing here?"

He looked up into the face of Susan who was peering down at him, asking some question or another. He neither knew nor cared what the question was, he was utterly fascinated by Susan's face. Her hair was a tangle of brown with unruly wiry shoots going off in all directions. Her face was covered with smoke soot except for the tear rivulets running down her cheeks. Her brown eyes looked at him with a mixture of fear, concern, and something else. Was that love he was seeing?

Just as he had decided that Susan possessed the most beautiful, most perfect, face ever seen on a human female, it disappeared from view. The next thing he felt was Susan tearing back his pant leg. "Oh, this is even better. Susan is trying to take off my pants," he thought and he felt a giggle start to form.

The giggle stopped abruptly, however, when Susan touched the shark bite. A shaft of pain flashed up his leg. He yelped and sat up on his arms so he could see. He was sobering quickly.

Around his calf were two semi-circles of vicious puncture wounds. The shark had sunk his teeth in, true enough, but for some reason did not take the bite. He looked on as Susan began tearing off parts of her dress to serve as bandages, when he noticed something strange. Something white was sticking out of one of the wounds. He reached down and pulled out a large shark's tooth— one of hundreds that sharks routinely loose each year.

He looked at it. Then he looked at the terrified concern on Sidney Smith's face. He looked at Susan Whitney furiously tearing strips of cloth, tears still in her eyes. He looked again at the tooth, and he knew.

"I belong here," he thought. "I belong here, to this place and to these people." And he quietly put the tooth in his pocket.

* * *

"I will exalt you, O Lord, for you lifted me out of the depths and did not let my enemies gloat over me.

O Lord my God, I called to you for help and you healed me.

O Lord, you brought me up from the grave; you spared me from going down in the pit."

Shivers ran down Walker's spine as the chaplain intoned the opening words of Psalm 30.

Preservation of bodies for later burial on land was simply not practical in the Royal Navy and everyone knew it. The ship was helpless to preserve food let alone bodies. This meant that those bodies not tossed overboard during the heat of battle had to be disposed of as soon as possible, but they needed to be disposed of with respect and dignity. The men would have it no other way.

Just after sunrise the following day, the *Formidable* laid her sails aback and came to a complete halt. The topgallant yards were set crooked to signify a death and a burial. The list lines were moved out of trim to signal the physical ship's grief at losing one or more of her own. The entry port on the starboard gangway was opened.

Next to the entry port were two lines of bodies. Each had been sewn up in their own canvas hammock, with two round shot placed at their feet to insure sinking. The last stitch in sewing the bags closed was always made through the person's nose—just to make sure he was dead.

The full ship's company was called to attention as the captain and chaplain approached. The captain was in his best uniform and the chaplain was in full clerical regalia.

"Ship's company... Off HATS," the bosun boomed, and, with that, the simple but elegant service began.

After reading Psalm 30, the chaplain continued: *"But Christ has indeed been raised from the dead, the first fruits of those who*

*have fallen asleep. For since death came through a man, the res-
urrection of the dead comes through a man."*

He then walked over to where the bodies were laid out, raised
his hand and said: *"We therefore commit these bodies to the deep,
to be turned into corruption, looking for the resurrection of the
body when the sea shall give up her dead, and the life of the
world to come, through our Lord Jesus Christ; who at his coming
shall change our vile body, that it may be like his glorious body,
according to the mighty working, whereby he is able to subdue
all things to himself."*

Each body had two men assigned to it, both messmates of the
fallen man. One by one, each body was put on a mess table placed
by the open entry port, and the body was covered with the British
flag. After a moment of silence, the messmates tipped up the table,
retaining the flag, and sending their shipmate into the water.

After all the men had been consigned to the deep, the chaplain
looked out over the sea, raised his hands, and said.

*"In the sure and certain hope of the resurrection to eternal life
through our Lord Jesus Christ, we commend to Almighty God our
shipmates as we commit their bodies to the depths.*

*"Ashes to ashes, dust to dust. The Lord bless them and keep
them. The Lord make his face to shine upon them and be gracious
unto them. The Lord lift up his countenance upon them, and give
them peace. Amen."*

Walker was standing next to Susan with the medical division.
They looked at each other and, briefly, he held her hand.

*"Lord, have mercy upon us. Christ, have mercy upon us. Lord,
have mercy upon us.*

The chaplain turned away from the entry port and stood once
again in front of the men.

*"Almighty God, with whom do live the spirits of them that de-
part hence in the Lord, and with whom the souls of the faithful,
after they are delivered from the burden of the flesh, are in joy
and felicity. We give thee hearty thanks, for that it hath pleased
thee to deliver these our brothers out of the miseries of this sinful
world; beseeching thee, that it may please thee, of thy gracious
goodness, shortly to accomplish the number of thine elect, and to
hasten thy kingdom; that we, with all those that are departed in
the true faith of thy holy Name, may have our perfect consumma-
tion and bliss, both in body and soul, in thy eternal and everlast-
ing glory; through Jesus Christ our Lord. Amen."*

Walker looked over at Smith standing with the officers and Bill Hanover standing with the midshipmen, and briefly caught their eyes. Nothing needed to be said.

"Merciful God, the Father of our Lord Jesus Christ, who is the resurrection and the life; in whom whosoever believeth shall live, though he die; and whosoever liveth, and believeth in him, shall not die eternally; who also hath taught us, by his holy Apostle Saint Paul, not to be sorry, as men without hope, for them that sleep in him: We meekly beseech thee, O Father, to raise us from the death of sin unto the life of righteousness; that, when we shall depart this life, we may rest in him, as our hope is this our brother doth; and that, at the general Resurrection in the last day, we may be found acceptable in thy sight; and receive that blessing, which thy well-beloved Son shall then pronounce to all that love and fear thee, saying, Come, ye blessed children of my Father, receive the kingdom prepared for you from the beginning of the world: Grant this, we beseech thee, O merciful Father, through Jesus Christ, our Mediator and Redeemer. Amen."

For the final time, the chaplain raised his hands and, facing the men, said: *"The grace of our Lord Jesus Christ, and the love of God and the fellowship of the Holy Ghost, be with us all evermore. Amen."*

With these closing words, the captain and the chaplain made their way aft and the bosun stepped forward.

"Ships company! Dismissed. HATS!"

The men quietly slipped away, some to continue their watch duties, some to continue repairs on the ship, some to just think about their good fortune at still being alive.

Walker thought about the shark's tooth that now hung around his neck, spontaneously took Susan in his arms and hugged her. Smith came up, Walker extended his arm to him, and he joined in the embrace. Hanover soon followed and the embrace became four-way. Each of them would forever be bound to the others by the experiences they had shared.

And Walker had found a home.

EPILOGUE

WALKER got up to put another log on the dwindling fire. He didn't mind cold weather; but this constant chill was something else entirely. He put the log in, stoked it, and returned to the only comfortable chair in his meager apartment in London's east end.

The *Russell* had been paid off for the French ships that had been captured at what was now called the "Battle of the Saints" and his share had come to a reasonable sum. All told the British had captured ten ships: the *Glorieux*, the *Hector*, the *Ardent*, the *Cato*, the *Jason*, the *Armille*, the *Ceres*, the *Caesar*, the *Diadem* and, above all, the *Ville de Paris*. This latter ship was a huge achievement for two reasons. First, she was the first three-decker in any war ever to be taken. And second, she was the paymaster for the French fleet. In her hold was found thirty-six strong boxes, containing over 25,000 pounds in gold that was added to the prize money. True, the prize money would be shared among every ship and every man who was in the battle; but, still, his share came to a tidy sum. He knew he could afford to live a bit better, but there was no telling how long that money would have to last. "Better to pinch pennies," he thought, "than to have no pennies to pinch."

The battle was being hailed as a major triumph by all the London newspapers. The French had over 8,000 killed or wounded. On the *Ville de Paris* alone over 300 men had died, which was 40 more than had died in all the British ships combined. But perhaps the greatest irony of the battle occurred when they pulled into Jamaica.

The Jamaicans went wild with delight over the British victory. In fact, their zeal was so excessive that Admiral Rodney preferred to remain aboard the *Formidable* rather than be literally killed by kindness ashore. Three days later a mail packet, the *Jupiter*, arrived from England with an urgent dispatch for the admiral. It seems the government of Lord Sandwich had fallen and the new government had no confidence in his abilities. He was ordered to strike his flag and come home. He was being fired. Apparently, the ship carrying the message of no confidence crossed paths somewhere in the mid-Atlantic with the ship carrying news of his crushing victory.

Rodney set forth in the *Montague* to return home. The *Russell* and several frigates were selected to escort him. On a bleak November day, they landed in Bristol and Walker will never forget the week that followed.

The fair citizens of Bristol were beside themselves and literally swept Admiral Rodney off his feet. Not content with offering him the keys to the city, they planned a massive parade in his honor. "What a sight *that* was," Walker thought.

First came a wagon with "Britannia" on board, strewn with flowers. Next came javelin-men, some trumpeters, a boat with fife and drums, more trumpets, flags, more flags, a boat called "The Rodney" manned by eight gentlemen dressed as common seamen, the city sheriff, floats of "Mars" and "Minerva," a banner with the words: "The gallant and illustrious Lord Rodney, savior of the country, protector of its islands, and scourge of his perfidious foes," and finally, bringing up the rear, Lord Rodney himself.

The people had forgiven the government for firing him and bringing him home because, well, they had brought him home. Any town that was anywhere, anyone who was anyone, wanted to honor him. His wife and daughters could not even attend a concert or a play without receiving a standing ovation, not only when they came in but also at odd intervals during the evening, which quite unhinged the performers.

"Oh, that was a time," Walker smiled in reminiscence. But it was also a sad period. A few days after they landed at Bristol, a platoon of Cold Steam Guards showed up to take Bill Hanover back to London in royal exile from the navy. Then Sidney Smith left to see if he could get a new assignment from the Admiralty;

and a day later Susan Whitney caught a carriage to Portsmouth, anxious to see if her mother was alright or, for that matter, even still alive. He would miss them. He really and truly would.

He heard a polite tapping at the door and his landlady came in bearing a letter.

"A messenger just came for you, sir, in a naval uniform. Such a handsome young man, too."

"Thank you, Mrs. Wilson."

He broke the red fouled-anchor seal on the back and opened it up.

Sir,

Your presence is requested and required at Admiralty House, this Thursday December 12th, instant, at 2:00 PM. A carriage will be sent for you at your lodgings at 1:30 PM sharp.

I am...

Your most obedient servant,

Lord Walter Howell

"Thursday? That's tomorrow."

* * *

As promised, a stately coach and four pulled up to his doorstep at precisely 1:30. It was big, black and quite out of place in his neighborhood. A very stiff and formal footman opened the door and Walker stepped in to see that both Sidney Smith and Susan Whitney were already inside.

They greeted each other as only old friends can, quickly getting caught up on the events of the past few weeks. Smith had been unsuccessful at getting another ship, but he still had hope. Susan's mother was visibly older looking than she remembered but in good health. Her mother couldn't believe the prize money that Susan took out of her purse and started crying. In her poverty, that small purse represented over two years living expenses—more if husbanded carefully.

"So why are we here? Walker asked. "Why are we going to Admiralty House?"

No one could think of an answer. Susan just commented on the stir it made in her neighborhood when the Admiralty messenger arrived to deliver her letter.

They entered through the ornate double oak doors of Admiralty House and were greeted by a reception clerk. They showed him their letters.

"Of course, Lord Howell is waiting for you. Follow me, please."

They were led up a flight of beautifully ornate wooden stairs, down a darkened hallway lined with portraits of famous captains and admirals, and escorted into a large conference room. At one end, seated behind a table was a gentleman preoccupied with the papers in front of him.

As they approached, he stood up and came around the table. He introduced himself as Lord Walter Howell and shook hands all around. He already knew the names of the three people standing before him.

"Thank you for coming. Please, be seated," he began. "I know you are all very busy people so I'll not keep you any longer than I must."

Walker thought, "Right. None of us is what you would exactly call 'busy' right now," but let it go.

Howell pulled together several sheets that were before him on the desk, adjusted his spectacles, and consulted the papers.

"I have recently come from St. James Palace. It seems His Majesty is most grateful for your efforts in rescuing his son, Prince William. The prince has told us all about the... ah... various adventures you had. The Queen Mother, after recovering several times from the vapors, told the king that he simply must do something for 'those young people,' and the King quite agreed. That's why I am here.

"More specifically..." and here he consulted his papers again.

"Lieutenant Smith." Sidney straightened up in his chair. "You are to be given command of the 18 gun sloop of war, *Fury*. The Admiralty Board has also received a 'strongest suggestion' from His Highness that this is to be viewed as a temporary command and that, as soon as you have acquired the requisite experience, you are to be promoted to post-captain and given command of a frigate of not less than 32 guns."

Sidney could hardly believe what he so clearly heard. He was to be made Post-Captain years ahead of his time; and, better yet, given the one thing that all naval officers desire most in life... command of a ship—his *own* ship.

"Miss Whitney. As a member of the fairer sex, His Majesty thanks you in particular for your heroism. As a small token of his esteem, he would be most pleased if you would accept Thistledown, a 500 acre estate, with manor house, in Kent and a stipend of 1000 pounds a year.

The color began to drain from Susan's face.

"Oh yes, one other thing. At the absolute insistence of the prince—and I know this for a fact as I was in the room at the time—you are to be appointed a 'Maiden-in-Waiting to the Court of St. James.' As a result of that appointment, you will henceforth be known as: 'Lady Susan Whitney.'"

The color now reversed itself, bringing a blush to her face as she thought about her mother and the discussion she once had with Bill... with the prince... so long ago.

"And, finally, Mr. Walker. The king thanks you as well for your heroic efforts and also awards you a stipend of 1000 pounds a year. In addition, and I am not quite sure I understand this, but... the prince insisted the Admiralty be given the king's 'strongest suggestion' to confirm your permanent, active-duty, warrant as a Ship's Surgeon and Natural Philosopher in His Majesty's Royal Navy—effective immediately."

Lord Howell looked up, smiling, only to see Walker's eyes open in horror. Walker's head whipped to the left and saw Sidney Smith convulsed with laughter. He knew. Smith *knew* this was going to happen. Hell, he probably arranged it.

"SMITH!!!" Walker screamed.

HISTORICAL POSTSCRIPT

In many ways historical fiction is, I believe, the easiest kind to write. The reason is because the things that actually happened usually outstrip anything the author could have imagined, or anything the reader would otherwise readily believe. Very little needs to be made up. You simply create the main characters, then get out of their way and let them bring the actual events to life. That's what happened here, and what will be happening throughout the Sir Sidney Smith series.

Be that as it may, most readers of historical fiction still have a question constantly running in the back of their minds. "Did that *really* happen, or did the author make that up?" "Did they *really* say that?" "Did they *really* do that?"

I can understand the question and, at risk of revealing how unfertile my imagination really is, I've written this postscript to separate fact from fiction in the novel you just read.

To wit:

CHAPTER ONE

The HMS *Richmond* was a real frigate in the British Navy and participated in the "Battle of the Capes." Captain Charles Hudson was her commander at the time. John Rooney is a fictional character, as is Susan Whitney and Lucas Walker.

William Sidney Smith, however, was very real and was, in fact, a young lieutenant serving on the HMS *Alcide* at the battle. I merely moved him to the *Richmond* to make the acquaintance of Walker and Whitney. Smith, later Admiral Sir William Sidney Smith, went on to a brilliant and daring career that rivaled that of the British national hero, Horatio Nelson—whom Smith detested. The remainder of the books in this series, will involve Walker, Whitney and Smith in some of Smith's actual, and most extraordinary, exploits.

The ship's various routines, including the flogging (which was not routine but certainly did happen) are, throughout the book, as accurate as I could make it.

CHAPTER TWO

Smith's personal history, as well as that of his father, is all true. Included in that, in case you're wondering, is the incident with the girl and the washtub boat. It happened exactly as described. Smith's description of advancement in the Royal Navy is accurate, along with the Army's policy of selling commissions.

The description of 18th Century shipboard medicine is as accurate as I could make it, along with the ease with which one could become a physician or surgeon in those days.

The British fleet that was on its way to Yorktown is accurate down to the ships names, respective sizes and commanding officers.

CHAPTER THREE

The Battle of the Capes took place exactly as described including the ship names on both sides, their formations, the times, places, signals, actions, reactions, tactical quandaries and mistakes. Admiral Graves and Admiral Hood literally spent the rest of their days blaming each other for the defeat in books, articles, and public appearances.

If the scenes of human carnage aboard the *Shrewbury* seem quite realistic, it's because they are. I worked from 18th Century eyewitness accounts of casualties in other naval battles of the period, condensed them, and placed our hero in the middle. If it seems too gory and cruel to believe, it's because it *was* too gory and cruel to believe. I did not make up any of it. It was the way things were.

Finally, Prince William Henry was indeed King George III's third son. He was indeed a midshipman of some promise, and he was in New York on a morale tour during this time period. I moved him down to Yorktown to thicken the plot, as it were.

Prince William eventually became King William IV. If there had been no William the IV, there probably would have been no Queen Victoria, his successor, and 19th Century British and world history would, I believe, have been quite different.

CHAPTER FOUR

The Town of York was as described in 1781. Indeed, Nelson House, the Swan Tavern and Moore House not only existed, but still exist and can be toured as part of the Yorktown National Battlefield. I highly recommend you visit it if you are in the area (and my thanks to the caretaker who let me in to see Moore House, even though it was past hours).

The *Richmond* and the *Iris* were, in fact, dispatched back to Yorktown to destroy the French anchorage. They were both trapped by the returning French fleet and captured.

William Sidney Smith did indeed have two brothers named Charles and John; but his sister with the fancy name, Victoria Alexandrina, is fiction. I contrived it as a device to get Queen Victoria's name into the story (and to show off that I knew her real name).

CHAPTER FIVE

The breakout along the beach is fictional, although the terrain, including the cove and sentry position, is correct. Our hero's inability to swim the cove is not exceptional. Almost no one in the 18th Century British Navy could swim and they could not for the reasons given in the story. If your ship went down, to where would you swim? Rescue helicopters were in remarkably short supply back then.

The presence of profiteers during the War of Independence was certainly a fact and many of them did trail the Army to sell the army back its own goods. The term "blagger" is an old British slang word for a "con man."

Susan's home neighborhood of Portsmouth Common is historical along with the school she attended, Portsmouth Grammar School on Penny Street. Portsmouth Grammar was considered radical in its day for providing free education to the poor and working class.

The descriptions of the woods and the fields of daffodils in the vicinity of Gloucester are accurate. It seems that area of Virginia is the perfect environment for daffodils to flourish. Early settlers brought the bulbs with them from England where they got passed around and planted in all sorts of locations. One variety in particular, the Trumpet Major, seemed to thrive on neglect. In the 1930's Gloucester was named the "Daffodil Capital of America" and, to this day, they hold a festival every spring to commemorate its history.

The description of Gloucestertown is historically correct including my descriptions of the Courthouse Tavern and the Debtor's Prison. The "Tavern at the Gloucester Courthouse" was described in an advertisement in a 1774 edition of the Virginia Gazette. Amazingly, it really did have a billiard table. Both buildings still stand. The fishing village, however, is fictional even though there is a "Drum Point" and there is a road called "Bailey's Wharf" in the vicinity.

Letters of Introduction were common requirements for travel in Colonial days and convicted criminals really were branded on the palms of their right hands. That is the origin of "raising your right hand" before giving testimony on a courtroom. The court is simply checking out your rap sheet.

The burley Hugh Hayes is a fictional character. Any resemblance between him and a certain All-State left tackle that played next to me on our high school football team is purely coincidental.

CHAPTER SIX

The Debtor's Prison is as described and can still be seen in the town of Gloucester, where the barred rear windows do indeed face the street as described.

Captain Finch is fictional but "Washington's Wolfpack" is not. They were the U.S. Navy before there was a U.S. Navy. Unfortunately, few modern readers have ever heard of them (H-m-m-m, might be the grist for a book there).

Hayes' description of the lot of a pressed man was accurate. They were literally picked up off the streets and involuntarily whisked away to a waiting ship. Each was asked if they were willing to join rather than be pressed. The only difference was that if you joined you received a shilling (known as "Taking the King's Coin") and the word "Vol" was put after your name in the ships muster book. Either way, you were going.

The press might sound like a cruel and capricious institution and, in many ways, it was. But, it would be a mistake to judge it from the standpoint of our modern, social safety netted, society. In 18th Century England, being "poor" did not mean you were unable to afford a color television—it meant you were unable to *eat*—and there was no shortage of poor people.

Yes, people were involuntarily swept up. But they were also guaranteed three meals a day, clothing, a sheltered place to sleep, a tot of rum per day, and medical care—all of which was unheard of in the slums of London. And yes, being in His Majesty's Navy was hard, dangerous, work where you could easily be killed or maimed. But that was equally true of working in the mines, mills and, later, the factories of the era. The very concept of OSHA would have been laughable in the 18th Century.

True, the Navy did not pay well, but you also had no immediate expenses and there was a possibility of growing relatively "wealthy" via the prize money you could earn.

Hayes' description of his torn loyalties between living under the Crown and living in a free society were representative of thousands of people in the colonies. His statement: "We just want to be left alone. Is that too much to ask?" pretty much sums up most people's attitude toward the whole war.

The first experimental military rockets were indeed developed by General Thomas Desaguliers (1683-1744) at the Royal Laboratory in Woolwich; but they proved to be too uncontrollable for practical use. After the time period of this book, however, Thomas Congreve, Jr. perfected several versions that were more workable. Indeed, when we sing our national anthem and relive "the rockets red glare, the bombs bursting in air" over Fort McHenry—those were Congreve Rockets. The stabilizing system that Congreve used was a long pole trailing after the rocket, sort of like the "bottle rockets" kids (young and old) will set off today on the Fourth of July. It wasn't until the fin was developed that rockets became stable enough for truly practical use, however.

CHAPTER SEVEN

The *Tisiphone* was a real ship, which, under Captain James Saumarez, distinguished itself at the Bay of Biscay and was selected to deliver the news to Admiral Hood in the West Indies.

Captain, later Admiral, Saumarez was to become one of the greatest fighting captains in the British Navy, some would say second only to the great Nelson (or Thomas Cochrane, or Sidney Smith—this topic will draw an argument every time among historians of the period). He distinguished himself in numerous major battles including being Nelson's second-in-command at the Battle of the Nile.

Cornwallis' surrender occurred as detailed including the alleged playing of the song: "The World Turned Upside Down." Modern scholars, however, now doubt that particular piece of musical tradition because: a) it is not mentioned in any of the eyewitness accounts of the surrender, and b) as Saumarez points out—Cornwallis had no band in his army. But it is true that Admiral Hood set forth to rescue Cornwallis on the very day he surrendered.

The Battle of Biscay (also known as the Second Battle of Ushant) occurred as described and dealt a crippling blow to France's attempts to reinforce and re-supply DeGrasse.

Hiram Boult is a fictional character along with his approach to medicine. Any resemblance between him and a former colleague of mine from my medical school teaching days is purely coincidental—even if Chad would have loved to serve on one of those ships.

The governor of Antigua was indeed Sir Thomas Shirley and the port of English Harbor was as described. Fort Shirley was in fact being built during this period.

The attitude of Saumarez to slavery was not un-typical of his day; and the points he makes are all historically accurate.

CHAPTER EIGHT

There was indeed a mail packet ship called the *Badger* and it was indeed commanded by a Lieutenant Cornwallis (no relation to the famous family). There was also, historically, an action between the British ships *Torbay* and *London* versus the French *Diadem* and *Sibylle,* which the *Badger* witnessed. The skirmish proceeded as described. The only variance with historical fact was that the *Badger* was not captured in this battle. But, it was time to get my characters into trouble again so the *Badger* had to go.

Sir Charles Douglas was an important character in 18th Century British naval history. He personally introduced every one of the gunnery improvements mentioned in the chapter and he was captain of the *Formidable* at he Battle of the Saints described in chapters 10 and 11. All descriptions of gunnery procedures and equipment are accurate.

The *Diadem* was a real French ship and played a pivotal role in the Battle of the Saints. I think Captain De Monteclerc might have been her captain, but I cannot absolutely confirm that.

"Parole" was something offered captured officers on both sides. It simply meant you would not try to escape, nor would you fight again until you were exchanged. The wording of Cornwallis's parole on behalf of himself and Walker/Smith is critical: "...until and unless this ship comes into armed conflict with one of our own." This caveat was what allowed Smith and Walker to later take up arms again, with honor, while they were still prisoners.

CHAPTER NINE

The Battle of Frigate Bay occurred as described, including the laughter at the end of it and the timed escape the next morning. Although most people have never heard of it, the battle was an important event. It not only served notice that De Grasse could be beaten; but it allowed Hood to justify his actions at the Battle of the Capes. At Frigate Bay, Hood employed almost exactly the same tactics that he urged on Admiral Graves at Yorktown, but was rejected.

Admiral Sir George Rodney was an historical character as depicted. Captain James Saumarez actually received command of the *Russell*, also as depicted, when, as he was leaving the *Formidable* with orders to go home, he literally bumped into a captain who was coming aboard to apply for leave.

CHAPTER TEN

The jockeying of the fleets prior to the Battle of the Saints was exactly as described.

The trigger for the battle was indeed the *Zele* colliding with the *Jason* and then later with the *Ville de Paris*—collisions number three and four in her sorry history. Unfortunately, I was not able to find out her actual captain's name.

The details of the battle are exactly as they occurred including: the "drag race" to see who would get to windward, Captain George Savage's verbal abuse of the enemy, and the bantam-cock on the rail of the *Formidable*. The *Diadem* did indeed cause a four-ship pile-up and a hole in the French line, although it was caused by a sudden freak shift in the wind, not because her rudder cable was cut. (Hey, I had to give our heroes *something* to do!)

The argument between Admiral Rodney and Captain Douglas over whether to exploit the break in the French line took place almost word-for-word as described. Midshipman Dashwood, who really did stir the Admiral's drink with his knife, later became Sir Charles Dashwood and left a letter describing the scene. It is one of those ironies of history that the thing for which Admiral Rodney is most known, "Rodney's Maneuver" the breaking of the French line at the Saints, occurred because he *lost* an argument with his flag captain. Talk about backing into history.

Sidney Smith, the real one, was also at the Battle of the Saints although not in the capacity described here. He was a lieutenant aboard the *Alcide* (74) and saw a great deal of action. As mentioned above, all future books will be based on the life of this unbelievable character.

CHAPTER ELEVEN

Admiral De Grasse was indeed undone when his van, under Admiral De Bougainville, fled the battle. Some historians have argued that De Bougainville did the smart thing. He tried to preserve his ships from a fight he knew was lost. Others have argued that, in fact, he left it up to each of his captains whether to go back or not and only one did. Most people, however, simply view it as an act of cowardice.

The *Glorieux*, the *Caesar*, the *Hector*, the *Ardent* and the *Ville de Paris* all surrendered as described. The fire aboard the *Caesar* and the shark feast that followed actually happened and was one of the more horrible incidents of the war.

The Burial at Sea service is, word for word, the way it was actually done.

EPILOGUE

Most of the epilogue is fictional, of course. I wanted to let you know what became of our heroes upon their return and (of course) set you up for the next book.

Walker's reminiscences, however, are all accurate. The battle casualty rates were as described and the *Ville de Paris* really did contain 36 strong boxes of gold.

Unbelievably, Rodney was in fact relieved of command *prior* to the battle, but word didn't get to him until after it was over and he had won.

And that bizarre parade in Bristol? It actually happened, folks, just as I described.

As with the rest of the book, I couldn't make this stuff up if I tried.

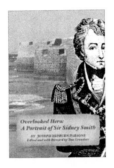

OVERLOOKED HERO:
A Portrait of Sir Sidney Smith
by Joseph Hepburn Parsons
Edited and with Forward by
Tom Grundner

Lost for almost 100 years
An engaging portrait of the man who is arguably the greatest Admiral of the Napoleonic Wars
Sir Sidney Smith

Everyone knows the two greatest heroes and the two greatest battles of the Napoleonic Wars. They were Admiral Horatio Nelson's victory at Trafalgar, and Field Marshall Arthur Wellesley's victory at Waterloo. However, it's entirely possible that there would have never been a Trafalgar or a Waterloo if it had not been for one man—Sir Sidney Smith.

Sir Sidney who?

Yes, exactly. That's the point of this book.

Joseph Parson paints an unforgettable portrait of a truly overlooked hero. It is not a history or a biography, as it makes no pretense at being exhaustive. Rather, in a short, easy to read, volume, he paints a vivid portrait of this man, and why he was so important.

"There is no way you can understand the Napoleonic Wars without understanding the contributions of Sir Sidney Smith—and this book is a great place to start."

Printed in the United States
152521LV00003BA/21/P

9 781934 757000